The Little Runaways

Cathy Sharp is happily married and lives with her husband in a small Cambridgeshire village. They like visiting Spain together and enjoy the benefits of sunshine and pleasant walks, while at home they love their garden and visiting the Norfolk seaside.

Cathy loves writing because it gives pleasure to others. She finds writing an extension of herself and it gives her great satisfaction. Cathy says, 'There is nothing like seeing your book in print, because so much loving care has been given to bringing that book into being.'

Also by Cathy Sharp

The Orphans of Halfpenny Street

The Little Runaways

CATHY SHARP

HARPER

Harper
An imprint of HarperCollins*Publishers*
The News Building,
1 London Bridge Street,
London SE1 9GF

A Paperback Original 2016

2

www.harpercollins.co.uk

A catalogue record for this book
is available from the British Library

ISBN: 978-0-00-811847-1

Set in Sabon LT Std by Palimpsest Book Production Limited,
Falkirk, Stirlingshire

Printed and bound in Great Britain by
Clays Ltd, St Ives plc

MIX
Paper from
responsible sources

FSC
www.fsc.org **FSC™ C007454**

ONE

Nancy stared out of the kitchen window at the piles of rubble across the street, where six houses had once stood. The space was due to be developed soon, and weeds grew between the cracks in the concrete, giving it a desolate air that echoed the feeling in her young heart. Every one of those terraced houses had been bombed during the terrible Blitz that had decimated the area round her home. Poplar and Bethnal Green had caught it as much as anywhere, because of their close proximity to the Docks. Other people said it was a miracle that the houses this side of the street had escaped the bombs, but Nancy wished that hers had been demolished that same night. Perhaps then she wouldn't be here, living in fear and misery, waiting for Pa to return from his job in the machinery works down by the Docks.

It was the 23rd of December 1947. Soon it would be the special, holy day that families looked forward to spending together – not that it would make any difference in this house. Nancy knew she would receive no presents from her parents and the only small gift her brother had was the colouring book and crayons she'd bought with what she'd taken from the house-keeping pot. Nancy felt no guilt for spending the few pennies on a gift and some sweets. If she hadn't walked all over the market to save money buying their Christmas dinner of scrag end of lamb, which she'd make into a tasty casserole with carrots, onions and potatoes, there would have been nothing left – and if she hadn't spent it on Terry, her mother would have taken it for drink.

Tears stung her eyes but she rubbed them away with the backs of her hands, which were red and stung from the soda she'd put in the water to soak Terry's sheets. He'd wet the bed again and if Pa came home and smelled stale urine he'd belt Terry, Ma and her – no, he'd reserve a different kind of punishment for her; one that turned her stomach sour and made her burn with resentment. What Pa did to her wasn't right, for all he claimed it was his due for feeding and housing them all.

'Any other man would put that useless slut out on the street and her brats with her. Think yourself lucky that I let you stay, and that idiot brother of yours,' Pa had sneered when Nancy protested at his behaviour the previous night.

'Terry isn't an idiot.' Nancy defended her brother fiercely. 'He might be a bit odd sometimes, but he can't help that . . .'

Pa leaned in close so that she caught the stink of beer on his breath. 'You listen to me, and listen good, girl. Breathe a word of what goes on to anyone outside this house and I'll have him put away somewhere he'll never see the light of day again.'

His threats terrified Nancy, because she knew he didn't

care for any of them, not even his wife. She glanced across the kitchen to where her mother sat nursing a bottle of beer, clutching it to her as if it was her very existence, her lifeless hair hanging about her face in greasy strands and her eyes dead as they stared into nothingness. She'd been like this since the night of that terrible raid when the Blitz was at its height during December 1940 – the night they'd lost all their family and friends.

Nancy shivered as she recalled how they'd hurried through the dark streets, the sound of the sirens already loud, fleeing for the shelter. The drone of the planes heading up the river was terrifyingly near. Ma was carrying Terry, who was not yet four, and Nancy was running to keep up with her, Bear clutched to her chest and a bag with a flask and sandwiches over her shoulder.

'Hurry up, Nance. If they start droppin' them bloody bombs we'll be caught like rats in a trap.'

Nancy had run and run until her chest hurt, hurtling into the shelter after all the other frightened people, and almost tumbling down the last of the steep stone steps. She and Ma had huddled together as the raid went on for what seemed like hours, Terry whimpering and grizzling, even though she'd remembered to bring Bear, the much-loved teddy that had once been hers. She'd given him a drop of sweet tea in his bottle and he'd quietened, holding his chubby arms out to her.

'Nance cuddle,' he'd said, and she'd taken him in her arms, crooning a nursery rhyme softly against his ear as she waited for the all clear.

It had been morning before they were finally allowed to go home . . . and when they did everything had changed. The sound of fire engines and ambulances screaming through the streets assaulted their ears, and the sky was red, flames still shooting skyward. When they approached their home, where two rows of terraced houses had stood facing each other across a narrow lane, only one row still remained intact. All the others had been damaged in some way or other, and the three opposite that had housed Gran and Grandda, Auntie Freda and Uncle Jim and their two young sons, and Auntie Molly were gone, nothing left but a pile of rubble. Smoke was still drifting from the blackened heap into the sky, though the firemen had put out the flames.

Ma had run at one of the men pulling at bits of wood and bricks in a fruitless attempt to discover anyone under the rubble, hitting at him in her terror, her eyes wild with fear and grief.

'Where are they? Where did they take them? I begged them to come to the shelter but they wouldn't listen . . .'

He shook his head sadly. 'If they were in the house when the bomb dropped they've had it, love. No one could survive under this lot. They took a couple of direct hits – the bloody Boche bastards! Why can't they drop 'em on the Docks or the factories and leave the poor bloody people alone for a while?'

Ma had staggered away, her face ashen. She stood staring at the piles of rubble that had housed her parents, her sister's family and her best friend, Molly, as if she couldn't take it in. Feeling cold and wanting her breakfast, Nancy pulled at her mother's arm.

'Come away in, Ma. If they find them they will tell us . . .'

'Get in yourself and look after your brother . . .' Ma said furiously. 'Leave me be, can't you?'

Nancy had never known her mother like this before. She'd always been cheerful, out in the street as soon as her chores were done, chatting to her friends with her hair in wire curlers and a headscarf. Now she looked like a wild creature, blonde hair flying in the breeze, her children forgotten as she mourned all those she'd lost. It was to be the first of many changes.

'Ma, hadn't you better get the tea on?' Nancy said now, trying to rouse her mother from her brown study. It didn't do to dwell on the past, even though she missed her gran and her aunts, particularly Aunt Molly, who hadn't truly been an aunt. If Molly Briggs had been alive Nancy could have talked to her about what was happening. She would have given Ma a good shake and told her to pull herself together.

'You've still got your children and a home, Sheila Johnson, so think yerself lucky!' Nancy could hear Molly's voice challenging her mother but it was only in her head, because Molly had died in the rubble of her home.

Ma was still sitting there, just nursing what was probably an empty beer bottle. Nancy took the wet sheets out to the yard at the back and threw them over the line. She just hoped her father wouldn't notice when he came back for his tea.

When Nancy got back to the kitchen she discovered that Terry was home from school, or wherever he'd been – more likely down the Docks, helping out with casual jobs. He'd cut a doorstep of bread himself and was getting dripping all over his chin and down his jacket, which was second-hand off the market but the best Nancy could get for the money her mother gave her from her meagre housekeeping.

'Ma!' Nancy shook her shoulder. 'You need to get Pa's supper on or he'll be angry when he gets back. I've got all this ironing to do and the bedrooms need a turn-out.'

Ma lifted hopeless eyes to hers. 'You can do the bedrooms tomorrow, Nance. Get your pa's tea like a good girl. The chops are in the pantry and there's some cabbage and cold taties you can fry together. I don't feel well . . . I think I'll go up and lie down.'

'I've got lots to do tomorrow,' Nancy said as her mother left the room but Ma didn't answer.

What about me? Nancy wanted to shout and scream after her. Every day she had to look after her brother, get the shopping, go to school and clean the house and her mother did nothing but sit around all day in a daze. Pa would be furious if the house looked dirty or if his tea wasn't to his liking, and the thought of her father in a temper made Nancy shake with fear. Terry would get a thrashing, and Ma would get a black eye . . . and she would be made to suffer his hateful touch again and again. Even the thought of it made her want to vomit.

It had started when Pa came back from the war with a wound to his leg that left him with a limp and in a permanent state of anger. Before that he'd been a bit rough sometimes, but he had never hit any of them that Nancy could recall. When he returned and found the way Ma had changed he started to lose his temper with her and then with Terry. He'd not taken much notice of Nancy at first, but then, when she was nearly eleven, just a couple of days before her birthday, he'd entered her bedroom and found her standing there with nothing on in front of the mirror.

Nancy had wanted to see if she had breasts yet. Her friend Janice was only three months older and she'd started to have breasts, but Nancy could see only a slight rounding and she was staring at herself in disappointment when Pa walked in.

'What are you doing, girl?'

'I was just going to have a wash.' Nancy grabbed a towel and covered herself, not liking the way Pa was staring at her. 'Go away and let me get dressed, Pa.'

'No need for silliness, girlie,' he said, a little smile curving his mouth. 'I hadn't realised what a big girl you're getting . . . almost a little lady, aren't you?' He'd moved closer to her, reaching out to pat her bottom as she scampered to the bed to grab her underclothes and pull them on. 'You don't have to be shy with me, Nance. I'm your father. It's all right for me to look at you like this . . . and to touch you, see. It wouldn't be right for you to let a stranger see you naked, but I'm your dear old pa and you know I wouldn't hurt you . . . not you . . .'

'Go away, Pa!'

'All right, I'll go, but I shall come back soon. You're nearly old enough to know what it's all about. I'll teach you things, sweet, secret things – and if you're good I'll buy you something nice. What would you like? Sweets or some ribbons for your hair?'

'I don't want anything.'

Nancy had known instinctively that it wasn't right

for Pa to look at her when she had no clothes on, and she didn't like what he was saying or that funny way his mouth went loose and wet. It made her shudder inside. She'd been innocent then; she hadn't realised what a beast he really was.

At first Pa had pleaded with her to let him touch her in places that made her recoil in horror, but when she was resolute in refusing he began to threaten, first Ma and then Terry. It didn't take him long to realise that Terry was her weak spot. When he'd started to hit Terry for no reason she'd known she had to let Pa touch her, even though she hated it – but it hadn't stopped at touching . . .

Nancy felt the acrid taste of vomit in her throat as she remembered what he'd done to her the previous night. She'd screamed and cried out, begging him to stop because he was hurting her, but he'd just gone on and on until she couldn't fight any more. It was the first time he'd done that, but she knew it wouldn't be the last and she wanted to run away and crawl into a big hole.

Why hadn't Ma interfered ever? She must have known what was going on. Pa hadn't bothered to hide it from her. He often touched Nancy's bottom or slid a hand over her breast when Ma was in the kitchen; Nancy had small breasts now that she was nearly fourteen. How could Ma just sit there and let him do these things to her own daughter? How could he do them?

'Nance . . .' Terry came to her, his bread and dripping finished, the only evidence the grease on his chin. 'What was Pa doin' to you last night? I heard you call out and I wanted to come and stop him, but your door was locked.'

'Nothing, Terry, love. You mustn't come even if I scream out, all right? If you interfere Pa will thrash you – and I don't want you to be hurt. Please promise me you won't do anything silly.'

Terry looked at her strangely, and for a moment his eyes seemed to glaze over. He put out his hand to touch hers.

'I hate Pa,' he said. 'He hurts Ma and me – but if he's doin' bad things to you I'll hurt him. I won't let him make you cry any more, Nance. You're the only person in the world I love – except Ma, but she don't know I'm here much.'

'Ma doesn't know anything much,' Nancy said, and bent down to hug him, inhaling the boyish scent of him, soap from where she'd washed him that morning, and his own special scent; a clean decent smell, not like Pa's . . . not like that salty sweet stench that she could always smell after he'd been doing things to her.

She wished she could take Terry and run away, somewhere they would be safe and Pa would never find them – but how would they live? She hated her father, wished that he would have an accident at work and never come home. Why hadn't he been killed in the war like so many soldiers? Why did he have to come home and make all their lives a misery? It would have been better if one of the V2 bombs had fallen on the house and killed them all than to live this way.

If there was only some way she could make them all safe . . .

'I'm not goin' to let him hurt you no more,' Terry said, and Nancy smiled. He was a good boy and she loved him. He'd never wet the bed until Pa started knocking him around. If it was just her and Terry she could be happy for the rest of their lives.

A cold shiver started at her nape as outside the kitchen door she heard the sound of brutish laughter and coarse voices, and she knew that Pa had started his celebrations early. By the sound of it he was drunk already.

TWO

Angela yawned, coming slowly awake to a feeling of luxury and excitement. She stretched in the comfort of the soft bed and then realised that she was home in her own room. It was Christmas and Mark Adderbury was coming to spend the day with them. A smile touched her lips, because she was aware of a sense of peace. Christmas Eve at St Saviour's had been so lovely, with the staff and children singing carols and Mark playing Father Christmas to the excited orphans of Halfpenny Street. It had been a very special time at the children's home in London's East End and Angela felt warmed because she knew that much of that happiness had been brought about by her efforts as the Administrator – and Mark's too, of course. In fact all the staff had played their parts in giving the children something they would always remember with pleasure, but for Angela it had been uplifting. She really believed that she had begun to come out of that dark place to which she'd been driven by the death of her beloved husband, John Morton.

John's death in the terrible war that was still fresh

in everyone's minds had sent Angela into a spiral of despair. Outwardly, she'd carried on at her job in the military hospital, but inwardly she'd felt the bleakness of an emotional desert. When she'd given up the job and returned home some months after the end of the war because her mother had been unwell and asking for her, Angela had felt as if she had little left to live for. Mrs Hendry had soon recovered from her chill and become her usual self and Angela felt trapped in the senseless round of entertaining and mindless chatter from her mother's social acquaintances. She'd wanted something to do, something worthwhile that would make her feel it was worth living again – and she'd asked Mark for help. He'd suggested the post at St Saviour's and she'd taken it instantly, and it had turned out so much better than she would have believed.

The children had touched her heart, especially one little girl called Mary Ellen and her friend, the rebellious Billy Baggins, but they all needed love and care, and Angela had discovered that she had a great deal within her still to give. Her heart might grieve for John but it was not dead. She could love the children, therefore perhaps she could find love for a man once more – know the happiness that had been hers so briefly before the cruel war had taken John from her.

For a long time she'd thought it would never happen, but recently she'd become more aware of Mark, of his strength and his generosity of spirit. In his work as a psychiatrist Mark helped his patients to recover and although Angela had never been his patient, she had learned to trust him and respect his judgement. She'd turned to him for help after John died and he'd always been there for her, as a friend; it was only recently, since she'd started work at St Saviour's, that she'd begun to feel there might be something more than friendship between them. A certain look in the eyes, a smile or the touch of his hand – but Angela had not been certain, either of Mark's feelings or her own. Perhaps it was still too soon – but she was happy to know that he was coming to lunch and would be with them until late afternoon, when he had to leave to visit some cousins.

She still didn't quite hit it off with Sister Beatrice, the nun who was Warden of St Saviour's, though they had somehow weathered the storm and were beginning to know each other a little better. Sister Beatrice acknowledged that Angela had her uses, particularly in the matter of overseeing the new wing, which would provide much needed extra space. Perhaps one day she would realise that what Angela really wanted was to help her and the children.

Hearing a crash from downstairs in the kitchen, Angela glanced at her watch and realised it was just after seven. Surely it was too early to start cooking the turkey for dinner? They would not eat their special lunch before two and it was the custom for them to get up at about eight, have a leisurely breakfast of warm muffins and jam or poached eggs on toasted muffins, when fresh eggs were freely available, and then start to prepare the turkey. So why was her mother up so early?

Dressing quickly in trousers and an old jumper, Angela went down to investigate. Slim and lithe, she had dark ash-blonde hair and eyes that someone had once said were azure. Perhaps not the perfect beauty she'd been in her twenties, at thirty-four she was still attractive enough to turn heads when she walked into a room. She discovered her mother in a kitchen that looked oddly disorganised. As a rule everything was set out neatly, but pans were everywhere, including the one on the floor that had recently been dropped.

'You're up early,' Angela said brightly. Her mother had her back turned to her and seemed to be intent on whatever she was doing. 'I'm going to help with the cooking, Mum. You don't need to start on the dinner yet.'

'What do you know of cooking?' Her mother turned round, staring at her in what Angela thought a strange, almost truculent, manner. 'I cook dinner almost every day of the year. Why should I need your help today?'

'Because Christmas is special. We always do it together – and you used to have help in the kitchen and with the cooking sometimes.'

'Mrs Downs decided not to come in any more,' Mrs Hendry said. 'If she hadn't I would have sacked her. She was rude and lazy – and I don't need her help. I don't need anyone's help.'

Angela was puzzled. Her mother seemed angry, resentful, and she couldn't think why. 'Are you upset about something? Have I made you cross?'

'Have I made you cross, she says . . .' Her mother's eyes seemed to glaze over for a moment, then she blinked and said, 'You know very well what you did, Angela. I begged you not to go away, but you had no consideration for me. Oh no, my wishes did not even enter into the equation. I am not cross but your obvious lack of interest in my opinion hurt me.'

'If I hurt you I am very sorry,' Angela said. 'It was

simply that I couldn't bear the emptiness of my life. You have such a good life, Mum, with your friends, your entertaining and your committees for the Church. You couldn't know how bored and empty I felt with nothing worthwhile to do.' She moved towards her mother and kissed her cheek. She seemed to smell very heavily of some expensive scent, and since she was wearing a very old dress covered by a pink and white spotted apron it seemed a little odd that she'd splashed herself so liberally with French perfume. 'Sit down and let me make you a lovely cup of coffee. I'll toast the muffins and then we can have some of that lovely jam we made in the summer.'

'If you insist. I'll have the Victoria plum jam – and a drop of cream and brandy in my coffee.'

'Do we have cream?' Angela investigated the contents of the large pantry. It made her shiver, because it was as cold as any refrigerator and kept even cream and butter really well. She found two glass jars of thick cream, which came from a local dairy farm and would be delicious with puddings and mince pies, also a jug of thinner cream, which she brought to table. 'Are you sure you want brandy this early?' she joked. 'We don't want to end up stuffing the turkey with the pudding instead of—'

'Please credit me with some sense,' her mother said sharply. She got up and fetched a brandy bottle from the dresser, and when Angela placed the beautiful French earthenware coffee bowl in front of her, she poured a liberal measure into hers and offered the bottle to Angela.

'No, thank you,' Angela said, smiling as she shook

her head. 'Not this early. I want to enjoy my dinner. I've been looking forward to this – I can hardly believe we've actually got a turkey this year. It seems ages since we could find one.'

'Suit yourself,' her mother said, and left the bottle on the table in front of her. 'How long are you staying?'

'Just until tomorrow after lunch.'

'Hardly worth the bother coming down,' her mother muttered. She tasted her coffee and then drank it all, but she didn't touch the lovely golden muffin that Angela placed in front of her, even though it sizzled with fresh farm butter and there was a dish of plum jam set before her. 'You eat it. I'm not hungry.'

'Why don't you sit and relax in the other room for a while?' Angela looked at her mother, noticing that her cheeks were flushed and her eyes a little red. 'Are you feeling a bit feverish, Mum?'

'I'm perfectly all right, but I'll go upstairs and get changed – if you insist on taking over.'

'I'll do the vegetables and various bits,' Angela offered, but her mother wasn't listening.

She frowned as she put an apron over her clothes. Going back into the pantry she saw that everything had been bought in preparation for this day, but although she noticed some sausages and jars of mincemeat, none of the usual Christmas fare had been prepared. It looked as if she was going to have to make a few things for after lunch herself. First she would get the vegetables done and make the stuffing for the turkey, which they had received as a gift from a grateful farmer her father had helped with a legal problem. At least there were plenty of ingredients and the turkey looked lovely.

16

She set to with a will and peeled, chopped and sorted the vegetables; then she made the stuffing and prepared the turkey for cooking. She had everything well underway when her father entered the kitchen. He looked apprehensive but his frown cleared as he saw that Angela was in charge.

'Your mother not down yet?'

'She had coffee but went back to her room to get changed.'

'Have you everything you need? I did the shopping this year, because Phyllis didn't have time. Have I forgotten anything?'

'I don't think so. I wondered why Mum hadn't made any mince pies or sausage rolls – though I see there is a trifle on the shelves.'

'Yes, a friend of mine made that for me as a gift,' her father said. 'Your mother was annoyed when I brought it home yesterday, but I said it would save her work – it is a sherry trifle and I know it will be delicious.'

'It does look lovely,' Angela said. 'Do you know if Mother made any Christmas puddings this year?'

'I believe she said she couldn't get the ingredients.'

'Then we shall have the trifle after dinner instead of a pudding. No one ever wants any tea anyway, just a few mince pies.' She put down her knife. 'Would you like some breakfast, Dad?'

'I'll have one of those muffins, but I can toast it myself; I often make my own breakfast these days. Shall I make us a cup of tea?' he asked, and then frowned as he saw the brandy bottle on the table. 'You didn't use this best brandy in the mince pies, I hope?'

'No, of course not. Mother had some in her coffee.'

He nodded, seemed about to say something and changed his mind. 'Well, it is Christmas. I'll make a cup of tea while you finish what you're doing . . .'

Angela went back to making pastry. She watched him, a little surprised at how easily he seemed to toast his own muffin and make a cup of tea. In the past her mother had always done everything, except when they had a housekeeper.

'Why did Mrs Downs stop coming in? I remember her as being a pleasant woman.'

'She was – is,' he said, looking up from spreading butter on his muffin. 'She and Phyllis had words, I'm afraid, and Mrs Downs wouldn't stay.'

'Oh, I see.' Angela wondered why it had come to that. 'Unfortunate. You need to get someone else, Dad. I think the housework is too much for Mother with all the other things she does.'

'Yes . . .' Once again he hesitated, seeming as if he wanted to say more, but then he just shook his head. 'Is there anything I can do to help – what about the washing up?'

'Yes, all right, if you like,' Angela said. 'I want to prepare these ready for cooking. I see we have some nice dripping for the potatoes – did you get that too?'

'Oh, a friend of mine got it for me from her butcher,' her father said, rising to gather the various pots and tins she'd been using in her cooking. 'I'm lucky in this village; there are a lot of people I count my friends.'

'Yes, I know. You've helped many of them with small legal problems without charging them huge amounts of money.' Angela had worked as a secretary for her father before the war, until she'd started her job at the military hospital, and she knew he made less money than he might have. His practice was successful, but he worked long hours and wasn't the kind of man who wanted or set out to make a fortune.

'It's what life is all about,' her father said. 'Doing what you can for your friends – and I've been lucky. I've done well enough. We have a decent life, I think, don't you?'

'Yes, of course,' she replied, wondering at the look in his eyes. 'I never wanted more. I didn't marry John for money. I had no idea his family were wealthy when he asked me.'

'Comparatively wealthy,' her father said with a wry smile. 'Your mother hoped you would marry into the aristocracy and be really rich, Angela.'

'I would only ever marry for love. I'm sorry if I let Mother down.'

'You didn't let me down. I only want you to be happy, my love.'

'Yes, I know.' Angela sighed with pleasure as she saw the tins filled with mince pies and sausage rolls ready for cooking. 'All done, I can stop now and go up and change. Mark will be here in a few hours.'

'Yes, you go, Angela. I'll pop in and see how your mother is. She may have one of her headaches.'

Angela came downstairs after she'd changed to discover that her mother was in the kitchen and seemed more like her old self. She was just about to put the turkey into the oven.

'Do you think it needs to go in yet?' Angela asked. 'It's not nine o'clock yet and the turkey isn't that big,

Mum. Mark won't be here until just before one and we want time for a few drinks first.'

'Allow me to know my own cooking methods,' her mother said, giving her an annoyed glance. 'Where have you put the brandy bottle? I usually put a little in my mince pies.'

'I've made them and put them in the pantry to keep cool until I cook them last thing,' Angela said. 'Dad thought perhaps you might have a headache? I think he took the brandy.'

Her mother made a rude sound that might have been laughter or derision. 'What your father thinks and what he says is not always the same, believe me.'

'What do you mean?'

'Never mind. I dare say he hid the brandy. He's rather greedy with it and won't let me use it in the cooking. We'll have a sherry instead.' She crossed to the dresser and picked up the sweet sherry, pouring two large glasses, which she brought back to the table.

'Happy Christmas, Angela. I am glad you could spare the time to visit – even though you seem to feel others need you more.'

'Oh, Mum,' Angela said, and took a tiny sip of her sherry. She noticed the strong smell of French perfume again. 'That's a new scent, isn't it? Not your usual . . .'

'It was expensive, too expensive for me as a rule. I was lucky to get it . . .'

'On offer?' Angela pulled a face. 'You were lucky. There is so little decent stuff in the shops yet – those that do have any charge the earth for it. If it wasn't a luxury in the first place the Government would fine them for profiteering.'

'You can afford it; John left you well off, didn't he?'

'Yes, but I've invested my money for the future – or Daddy did for me.'

Her mother sniffed. 'You could quite easily marry again, Angela. Your in-laws would gladly introduce you to their friends, if you would give up this foolish job of yours and go to stay with them.'

'I love my job – and I have no wish to live with John's parents. I am not sure I shall marry again, but if I do it will be because I can love again, not for position or money.'

'Well, if you're looking after the dinner I shall go down the road and have drinks with some friends of mine. Your father doesn't want to come – but there's nothing to stop me.'

Angela watched as her mother left. She wasn't sure anyone would want visitors at this hour of the morning, because even her mother's friends had dinner to cook, and excited grandchildren who would be opening their presents.

Angela noticed that her mother had drunk the large glass of sherry, but she wasn't interested in hers. Placing it on the windowsill out of the way, she made a pot of coffee and took it through to the sitting room. Her father was reading a magazine but put it down as she entered. They sat in comfortable silence enjoying their coffee until she returned to the kitchen.

Angela was busy looking after the dinner most of the morning and hardly noticed that her mother was absent. Peeking in the oven at a quarter to one, she saw the turkey looked beautiful, golden brown but not burned; the pastries she'd made were cooked and ready and she was just putting the vegetables on when Mark arrived. He came into the kitchen, bearing gifts and a bottle of champagne, which he placed on the dresser.

'Your father said you were busy cooking so I thought I would offer my services, Angela.'

He looked so handsome, dressed casually in light slacks, shirt and a V-neck sweater that her heart caught with pleasure when he smiled. She'd begun to like Mark more and more and it was good to have him here on this special day, not just as a formal guest, but as one of her family. He had a glass of sherry in his hand, which he sipped before placing it on the table. It was almost as if they lived together. Rather than having to leave everything to take formal drinks in the parlour, he was here offering to help – just as if he was her husband.

'Well, I should like someone to lift the turkey out in about twenty minutes and set it to rest on the board. I've put the plates to warm and I've made some little starters of salmon mousse with cucumber salad. I had to use some of the tinned salmon you gave me to bring home. It wasn't possible to buy fresh, but they taste nice just the same.'

'Your father said you've had a lot to do, Angela. Apparently, your mother hasn't been too well – a headache perhaps?'

Mark looked at her oddly. Angela wondered about that expression, because it made her feel that he was keeping something back; like the similar look in her father's eyes earlier it aroused her suspicions, but she was too busy getting the food ready to pursue it. Her father came into the kitchen and was given the task of carrying the starters through to the dining room.

'I hope Mum is ready for her dinner,' she said. 'If you'll bring the turkey through when we've eaten the first course, Dad, I'll fetch the rest.'

'Your mother isn't down,' her father said, and sighed. 'I'm sorry, Angela. She promised me it wouldn't happen today but . . .'

'What do you mean?' Angela asked. 'Is she lying on the bed?'

'Yes . . .'

'Another headache? Poor Mum. Is she coming down at all?'

'I don't think so. We'll see later. We'll eat our starter and then I'll check if she wants to come down – or I can take her a tray up.'

'I'll do that. Mark, I'll take Mum her starter up first and then we'll eat . . .'

'No, Angela,' her father said, and touched her arm. 'Leave it for now.'

'Why . . .' Angela looked from one to the other. 'What do you know that I don't? Please, tell me. I have to know.'

Her father glanced at Mark, then, 'She's right. I wanted to tell you before – oh, months ago, when it first started, but she begged me not to. It wasn't so bad then, but recently it has got so much worse.'

'Her headaches? Has she seen a doctor?'

'Phyllis refuses all help. She will not admit there is a problem.'

'What kind of problem? This is ridiculous. I'm not a child – I want to know what is going on. Please tell me.'

'Mark thought you were too wrapped up in your

23

grief and we shouldn't worry you. And she seemed better for a while after you came home from Portsmouth . . .'

'Angela . . .' Mark looked at her uncomfortably. 'You were so unhappy. I thought it might be more than you could bear . . .'

Angela was about to ask him what he meant when the door of the kitchen opened and her mother walked in. As she saw the lipstick smeared over her mother's face, her hair all over the place and her crumpled dress, she started forward, hands outstretched.

'Mum, what's the matter?'

'Who sh-haid anything whass the matter?' her mother demanded in a belligerent tone. 'Whass going on here? Let me through, I've got to dish-h up the dinner . . .' She took a step forward, crashed into the table and then crumpled to the floor in a heap.

Angela stared at her father and then at Mark. The looks on their faces were identical: guilty but not surprised. 'She's drunk. How long has this been going on – and why haven't I been told about it?'

'You were still grieving,' Mark said. 'I didn't want to put more pressure on you, Angela.'

'Your mother didn't want you to know, love,' her father said. 'It has been happening for some months, but she controlled it in between bouts of drinking, and I didn't guess how bad it was until a few weeks ago, when things suddenly got much worse.'

'Why did no one tell me?' Angela felt anger mixed with sympathy for him and a kind of anguish that she couldn't name for herself. Why did Mark think she was so fragile that she couldn't face the truth? 'If I'd been here perhaps I could have helped her.'

'She wouldn't let you. Besides, you have your own life, Angela. This is my problem. She's my wife and I'll cope with it.'

'Mark – surely you could have given me a hint?' Angela looked at him in reproach as her mother stirred and promptly vomited on the floor.

'I'll clear that up,' she said. 'Perhaps you could get Mother to bed between you – and then we shall have dinner. I'll put some aside for her if she feels like it later.'

For a moment they both stared at her, and then Mark bent and lifted Phyllis in his arms. 'I'll carry her up and then you can look after her, Edward. I'm sorry, Angela. If I'd thought this would happen I would've warned you . . .'

'Forgive me,' her father said after Mark had left them. 'There's a lot more to tell you and to show you – but it will keep until Mark has gone. You shouldn't blame him, Angela. She talked to him about it and I suppose he didn't want to betray a confidence, though she isn't his patient.'

'Yes, I understand that,' she said, but, left to herself to repair the damage and sort out the dinner she'd prepared so carefully before it ruined, Angela knew that she understood too well. Mark had been more concerned for her mental state than worried about giving her a hint of her mother's failings. She had been close to despair at times during the years since her husband's death – but surely Mark could see that she was much stronger now?

If he couldn't see her for the woman she was, how could he respect her? She wasn't some fragile flower that would bend in the wind, she was a strong woman who had known devastating grief and come through it.

Angela would rather have known the truth. She might not be able to do anything, but the last thing she wanted was to be treated as someone who couldn't face reality. John's death had devastated her, but the fact that her mother was an alcoholic was another matter – one that she was strong enough to accept.

THREE

It was early on Boxing Day but already Alice could hear the bitter quarrelling going on in her parents' room. Did they never stop this relentless bickering? She sighed, glad that she was going to her friend Michelle's home that day. Like her, Michelle worked at St Saviour's, though she was a staff nurse while Alice was merely one of the carers. She didn't think she could have stood being here all day if her mother was going to nag them the whole time. She stretched and yawned as Mavis slept on in the bed next to her. Mavis was also going out later to spend the day with her boyfriend, because she had several days off from her job at the factory.

Alice had opted to work on Christmas Day, because it was better than being at home with her mother, who made life miserable for her family on every day of the year and saw no reason to be any different at this special time. So Alice preferred her duty to being at home with her brothers, Joseph and Saul, her sister, Mavis, her father, who would probably get drunk by lunchtime, and her nagging mother. Besides, she didn't particularly want to sit down to a meal and be watched by Mrs

Cobb's sharp and knowing eyes. One of these days her mother was going to ask questions Alice didn't want to answer.

She'd missed a couple of periods and because of that she was sure that she was carrying Jack Shaw's baby. Alice felt a shiver of fear run through her as she thought about the future. Had Jack died in the fierce fire at the boot factory, or had he somehow escaped? Billy Baggins had been there and he'd told the police that it was Arthur Baggins, his elder brother, and Jack Shaw that had broken in and blown up the safe. Someone else had set the factory on fire while they were inside, and the newspapers seemed to think it was someone with a grudge against Arthur and Jack, or the factory owners. Most people believed it must have been Jack who had died, although something inside Alice wasn't ready to believe that.

How could he be dead? Surely she would know if he'd died; she would feel it inside – wouldn't she? The last time Alice had seen him, he'd dumped her outside St Saviour's and gone racing off in his car after telling her the Lee gang was going to kill him. All she knew for certain was that he hadn't tried to contact her since, and she couldn't help thinking that if he'd been alive he would surely have come back for her or at least sent her a letter. Jack had known Alice believed she was having his baby.

How could she know what he'd felt about that? Jack had pursued her, never leaving her alone, throwing off all her attempts to rebuff him, until she gave him what he wanted. Had she been a terrible fool to let him make love to her? Alice had thought she was in love with

28

him, rejecting the offers to go out with Bob Manning, a soldier she'd met at a dance with her cousin Eric. Bob was a nice steady bloke with a good job in the Army, but he didn't excite Alice the way Jack had – and so she'd been stupid and given herself to the wrong man. Now she was frightened, scared of what her mother would do when she discovered her daughter was pregnant.

What could she do if her mother threw her out? Their home was only three rooms in a shared house; it smelled awful when the toilet in the yard stank and it was cramped and often damp and cold, but it was still her home. Where would she go – and how could she manage with a job and a baby? That's if she still had a job when Sister Beatrice discovered the truth. It was unlikely the strict nun would keep her on once her condition became noticeable.

Alice thought about the previous day at work. After all the excitement prior to Christmas Eve and the fun of carols, Father Christmas giving presents to all the children – not forgetting their carers – and the party afterwards, Sister had decreed that the day itself would be spent quietly in order to reflect on the true meaning of Christ's birthday.

Alice had been happy just to be in the peaceful atmosphere at the home. The children all seemed satisfied to attend church or chapel in the morning and to spend their time eating a special dinner and reading or playing one of the new board games they'd been given. She herself had been asked to do Sally the carer's job after breakfast was over and gather the smaller children together in the playroom, where she'd read one of Mr

Markham's lovely books to them for a while, and given the others puzzles to keep them happy. It was as she was getting the children ready for tea that Nan came up to her.

'Some of the older children are going for a walk before supper. Jean will be going with them to make sure they don't get into any trouble. I want you to keep the little ones amused until it is time for their beds.'

'Yes, of course,' Alice said. She liked the head carer and often wished her mother was a bit more like Nan. 'They've been good all day.'

'Well, that takes care of the little ones.' Nan hesitated, then, 'Is something bothering you, Alice? You know you can come to me for anything – don't you?'

'Yes, thank you, Nan,' Alice said, but there was no way she could tell Nan what was really bothering her. 'I'll find some sort of game they can play quietly, because I know Sister doesn't want them running around today.'

'Off you go then, Alice – but don't forget I'm always here if you need me.'

Alice walked away, feeling a little easier in her mind. If the worst came to the worst and Jack didn't come back for her, perhaps she would talk to Nan about her problem . . . that's if she really was having his baby. Yet why was she kidding herself? She couldn't ignore the signs and they were all telling her she must have fallen for a baby either in late October or early November and she would have to accept her fate and find a way of coping with it.

If she worked extra hours she could perhaps stay out of her mother's way, and earn a little extra money for when she needed it, because she knew her mother would be furious when she found out that Alice was pregnant. She would probably throw her out on the street and the thought terrified her.

Lying in her bed beside her sleeping sister that Boxing Day morning, Alice turned the problem over and over in her mind. Silent tears trickled down her face in the faint light of early morning. She felt so alone, so miserable. What was she going to do when her condition began to show?

Even though Nan had been so kind, Alice respected her and it would shame her to confess what she'd done. Michelle wouldn't scold her but she couldn't help her to find a home for herself and the child – and Sister Beatrice would give her the sack. Alice couldn't think of anyone who would help her to find a place to live and have the child.

Alice had heard of those homes where girls like her went to have their illegitimate child. She had a vague idea that they weren't very nice, and they made you give up your baby. Alice didn't know how, but she wanted to keep hers. Even if it was possible to get rid of it – a shudder went through her, because she knew of a girl who had died of blood poisoning after visiting one of those backstreet butchers who got rid of unwanted children – she would never do that. She didn't want to die – and she wasn't going to kill her child. There must be someone she could turn to for advice – someone who would know what to do . . . perhaps Angela Morton.

Alice didn't know their Administrator well, but she admired her for standing up to Sister Beatrice when Mary Ellen had been banned from going to the pantomime.

Alice had never been to one as a child, and she knew how much it would mean to a kid from a poor home like her. It was rotten to take the best treat away from the girl and Alice had been on Angela's side when she took Mary Ellen to the pictures when the other kids were at the pantomime. Alice didn't know, of course, but she'd bet Sister Beatrice had had a few words to say about that!

Angela smiled and spoke whenever they met and she knew she was very friendly with Sally – but would she be sympathetic if Alice told her what a mess she was in? Angela could have no idea of the sort of family Alice came from so perhaps she would be like Sister Beatrice and take the moral ground. After all, she probably had a perfect family life at home and would think Alice a stupid girl who was no better than she ought to be.

Angela stared at her father in disbelief as he showed her the things he'd taken from her mother's wardrobe. Besides a lot of empty gin bottles, there was an assortment of dresses, handbags, perfume, soaps, scarves and hats – and many of them were stolen, according to her father.

'But why?' she asked. 'Why would Mother take things like this? The clothes wouldn't fit her or me – it doesn't make sense.'

'I asked Mark about it and he said that she's ill, Angela. Sometimes when she's had a few drinks she goes out and takes things from shops: local shops, where we have an account. That's how I found out about it. One of the managers telephoned me from his office in private; he didn't want to go to the police and asked me to discover whether she still had the things she'd stolen. Of course when I found all this – I didn't dare to ask if it all belonged to him. I simply arranged to pay for the items he'd lost, and then he asked if I would care to settle the account.'

'Was it very bad?' Angela asked, noticing the new lines about his eyes. No wonder he'd been looking worried the last few times she'd seen him. 'I can help with money, of course.'

'I'm all right for the moment,' he said. 'I've cancelled the accounts in her name and closed the joint account at the bank. I didn't want to humiliate your mother, Angela – but I couldn't let it continue.'

'So the drinking isn't the worst of it, then.' Angela reached across the kitchen table to squeeze his hand. 'I'm truly sorry – but what can we do? She needs help . . .'

'Mark says there is a very good clinic in Switzerland that would help with all her problems – the only trouble is your mother will not hear of it. She insists that nothing is wrong with her and said she hadn't realised she'd run up large bills and promised not to do it again.'

'What about the stolen stuff?'

'She absolutely refuses to acknowledge that she took anything.'

'It makes things so difficult for you, Dad. What are you going to do?'

'I can't force her to go away. She is my wife and I must try to protect her as best I can. I've told her she can't use the car in future and the bus only goes into town twice a week. I'll try to make sure she doesn't catch it unless I can go with her – what more can I do?'

'I don't know,' Angela said. He'd closed his eyes, as if he found the worry almost unbearable. 'What about you? Are you all right?'

'Just a little tired,' he said, but she had the feeling that he wasn't telling her everything. 'I've seen my doctor and he advises cutting down on work.'

'You must try not to worry. If you need me I could come down at a couple of hours' notice. You know I would stay if you thought it would help.'

'I don't think she would take any notice even of you, Angela. I had hoped that she would make an effort for Christmas – as she did for the dance she organised for your charity.' He sighed deeply. 'She used to have good days and I kept hoping – but her drinking is getting worse. She would only drink sherry or wine once, but now she will drink whatever she can get.'

'I wish I could do more.'

'Just being able to tell you has helped a lot,' he said and smiled. 'Mark has offered to advise her but so far she just refuses to listen.'

'I see . . .'

Angela turned away to pour more coffee, distressed by the news of her mother's illness. Mrs Phyllis Hendry was the last person to drink to excess or steal from shops – at least she always had been. Angela couldn't imagine what had happened to change the rather snobbish, intelligent woman she loved but couldn't quite like, into this person who drank too much and stole things. Yet Mark's attitude had distressed her more – or perhaps hurt was a more apt word. Yes, she was hurt that he'd decided he couldn't tell Angela in case it made her break down. Had he thought she would turn to drinking like her mother?

She felt a little diminished, too. She'd turned to Mark in her grief over John's terrible death, sobbing out her pain on the shoulder he offered – but now she felt patronised. When he'd suggested the job at St Saviour's she'd thought he trusted and respected her – but if he felt anything for Angela, he would not have hidden her mother's secret from her. There was little Angela could do here, it seemed, but at least she could offer her father support.

'If you need me – anything, you have only to call, Dad.'

'Yes, I know,' he said. 'Now go up and talk to your mother. She's feeling a little fragile – and ashamed. Try to make peace with her before you leave, my love.'

'Yes, of course,' Angela said and kissed his cheek. 'I do love you, Daddy.'

'I love you,' he replied. 'You're the light of my life and always will be. Please don't worry. I'll manage somehow. Perhaps in time she will agree to go somewhere they can help her . . .'

FOUR

'I'm cold, Nance, and 'ungry,' Terry sniffed, and wiped his dripping nose on his coat sleeve. 'When are we goin' 'ome?'

'We can't go home, love,' Nancy said, and put her arm round his thin shoulders, pulling him close in an effort to inject some warmth into them both.

'Why not?' He tugged at her arm. 'I want me ma . . .'

'Don't you remember what happened?' she asked him. Terry shook his head and Nancy bit her lip, because he surely couldn't have forgotten the terrifying events that had led them to flee the house as it was burning. Nancy had such terrible pictures in her head of the door of their parents' room. It had been blazing by the time she'd reached the landing and saw her brother staring wide-eyed at the door. She'd known immediately that it was impossible to reach them, and as Terry started to scream, Nancy had seized him and pulled him down the stairs, grabbing coats and a hunk of bread that had been left on the table earlier. There just hadn't been time to bring anything else; besides, there was never much food in the house.

'We shan't talk about it then, Terry.' What was she going to do? Nancy hadn't thought past their escape from the fire, but now after several days hiding in a disused shed on the Docks, and eating only the scraps of food that she could beg from a night watchman, she was beginning to realise they couldn't stay here for much longer.

'Nance, me stomach hurts . . .' Terry whined, and rubbed grubby fingers at his face. 'I want ter go 'ome . . .'

'Shush . . . someone is coming,' Nance hissed at him. She clutched hold of her brother's arm as the door was opened and a large man in working clothes entered. She'd thought no one came near this place, and that they were safe from discovery because the Dock workers were still having their Christmas break. 'Let me do the talking, Terry. Don't say anything but agree with whatever I say.'

'What 'ave we got 'ere then?' the man said, and frowned as Nancy pushed her brother behind her.

'We're not doing any harm, mister,' she said defensively. 'We've got nowhere to go . . .'

'Why aren't you at 'ome?' he asked, and then his frown cleared. 'I reckon you're them kids the coppers 'ave been lookin' for . . . the ones whose folks got burned in the fire.'

'What's 'e mean, Nance?' Terry pulled at her arm and she saw a flicker of fear in his eyes. 'Where's Ma? What's 'e mean they got burned?'

'My brother doesn't remember anything, mister,' Nancy said, though she remembered all too well. 'We didn't know what to do when we ran away . . . it all happened so fast. We had to leave quick and I couldn't help them . . .' A choking cry broke from her. 'I had to get Terry out . . .'

'Yes, o' course yer did,' he said soothingly.

'I didn't know where to go . . .' Nancy was poised ready to flee, though she knew there was nowhere she could go, because they were both filthy, cold and near to starving.

'Well, I reckon the coppers will know what to do,' he said gruffly and kneeled down beside them. 'You can't stay here or you'll freeze – tell me, 'ave yer had anythin' ter eat today?' Nancy shook her head. 'You come along of me then, and I'll sort yer out . . . no need to be frightened, nipper. I ain't goin' ter 'urt yer.' He reached out towards the boy.

Terry pulled back from the man, looking wildly from side to side, as if he wanted to escape, but Nancy took a firm hold on his arm. 'Come on, love,' she said. 'We haven't got a choice. You'll be all right, I promise.'

'Constable Sallis won't 'urt yer,' the man said. 'I reckon as he'll be right glad ter find yer . . .'

'Well, here you are then, Sister, our little runaways,' Constable Sallis said. 'I told you the other day that we feared the pair of them might be dead in the fire, but they'd run away because they were frightened and they were found down at the Docks, hiding in one of the sheds. One of the Dockers discovered them late yesterday afternoon on his way home and brought them to the station. We've kept them there overnight.'

'What are their names?' Sister asked, glancing towards the children, who were at that moment being cared for by Nan, St Saviour's head carer.

'Terry and Nancy Johnson,' he replied. 'Amazingly, neither of them was burned or had any ill effects . . . well, not physical. The boy seems terrified and screamed when I tried to touch him earlier, but that is natural enough. The girl is older and she says she was in the kitchen when she smelled smoke. She rushed upstairs to find her brother and dragged him out of bed and downstairs, and finally out of the house through the back yard – that's why he's in his pyjamas and his mother's coat . . .'

'We'll soon sort them some clothes out,' Sister Beatrice said. 'How long were they missing?'

'Well, the fire must have started some time on New Year's Eve – and here we are 9th of January. I think one of the night watchmen gave them some food. They weren't lost long enough for them to become really ill or to pick up lice anyway.'

'I dare say they need a nice bath and some good food,' Sister said. 'You did right to bring them straight here, Constable. We'll look after them now.'

'I'll get off then,' he said. 'It's bad news about their parents – the fire started in a locked bedroom and neither of them got out, I'm afraid. Terrible time of year to find themselves orphans and homeless, isn't it?'

'I doubt it matters what time of year something like that happens,' Sister said wryly, and he shook his head as he went off.

Sister Beatrice went over to Nan. 'I'll just take a look at them and then you can pop them in the bath . . . the boy first . . .' Nan turned to try to help Terry get undressed, but he kicked out at her and backed away, his eyes rolling wildly.

'Don't yer touch me . . .'

'You have to be examined and then have a bath,' Sister told them. 'It's just routine, Terry.'

'Nance, don't let them 'urt me,' he cried, and clung to his sister.

'It's all right, love,' his sister said. 'We've got to do what they say for now, Terry – and they won't hurt you.' She turned to Nan with a look of appeal in her eyes as she removed the coat and pyjama top. 'Please, let me help him. He's used to me.'

'If you wish,' Nan said, 'but Sister needs to make sure he doesn't have . . .'

Her words were left unfinished as she saw the marks on the child's torso where he had obviously been beaten recently.

'Who did that to him?' Sister asked, shocked by the sight of his thin body and bruised flesh. She'd seen children in this condition often enough, but this was a particularly severe beating by the looks of it.

'No one,' Nancy said quickly. 'He fell over and hurt himself – at the dockyard, after we ran away because of the fire.' Nancy looked at Terry urgently. 'That night I sent Terry to bed with a hot drink and then I went down and cleaned the kitchen . . . and then I smelled the smoke . . .' She caught her breath and put her arms protectively around her brother. 'Everything was blazing upstairs. I just grabbed him and we ran away . . .'

'Yes, so Constable Sallis told me,' Sister said. 'Well, that was a brave thing to do, to go upstairs to rescue your brother when the fire must have been very strong – so I suppose you can be left to bath him. Just let me look at you, child. I promise I shan't hurt you.'

40

'You're quite safe here,' Nan told him, and looked kindly at Terry as he reluctantly submitted to Sister's brief examination.

'Caught you!' Sally Rush gave a little scream and turned swiftly as she felt the hands on her waist. She was looking into the face of the man she loved but had not seen since Christmas Eve. He'd gone out of London for the festivities but she'd expected him back several days ago and been disappointed that he hadn't kept his word to take her somewhere nice when he returned. 'I've missed you, Sally,' Andrew Markham said, and snatched a quick kiss on the mouth. 'Any chance you missed me?'

A pretty girl with reddish brown hair cut short to form little flicks about her face, and melting chocolate eyes, Sally couldn't help a smile peep out at him. She'd been feeling annoyed because he hadn't contacted her in the New Year as he'd promised, but he was so attractive with his light brown hair and gentle smile, so the slight feeling of hurt melted away in her pleasure at seeing him.

'Oh, Andrew, you know I did. I thought you would be back in London days ago . . .'

'I intended to be,' he said, and his smile dimmed. 'Forgive me, darling Sally. My aunt had a bit of a turn and I had to take her into the hospital. She is over the worst, thank God, but she will need to stay in a nursing home for a few weeks.'

'Oh, I am so sorry,' Sally said. 'I hope she isn't really ill?'

'Her heart isn't strong,' he said. 'The specialists say she may have a few years yet. I must hope so. Aunt

Janet brought me up after my parents died and I'm fond of her. I have to look after her now – as she did me.'

'Yes, of course you must,' Sally said, giving him a loving smile. 'It was just that I missed you.'

'Had you been on the telephone I would've called, but telegrams only ever carry bad news and I didn't want to scare you, hence the surprise.'

'You certainly did that,' she said, her cheeks warm because Nan had just entered the playroom. 'Did you want me, Nan?'

'I need you to help me with a couple of new arrivals,' Nan said.

'Yes, of course,' Sally said, and turned to Andrew. 'Shall I see you later?'

'I'll call for you at home at half past seven.'

Sally nodded and turned to Nan as they went into the hall together. 'Who have they brought in for us today?'

'It's a brother and sister. Their names are Nancy and Terry Johnson. They both seem nervous – the boy is terrified, I think. The police have been looking for them, as they were missing after their home caught fire, and found them hiding down the dockyard. Unfortunately, the parents were killed but the children got out somehow and ran off in fright . . . I suppose that is natural enough. It must have been terrible.'

'It's a miracle they got out, isn't it?'

'Constable Sallis thinks the girl pulled her brother out of bed and they fled, not knowing what else to do.'

'Poor little things,' Sally said. 'How old are they?'

'I think Nancy must be nearly fourteen and her brother . . .' Nan frowned. 'I'm not sure, because he looks as if he might be ten or so but seems backward for his age. I left him with Michelle. She was giving them a little check over when I left . . .' Nan's words were cut off by the sound of screaming from the bathroom. They looked at each other and Sally broke into a run, arriving just in time to see the boy sink his teeth into Michelle's hand.

'No, stop that, child!' Nan cried as she followed her into the room. 'You mustn't bite. It isn't nice . . .'

'Has he drawn blood?' Sally asked the staff nurse. 'Shall I put some disinfectant on for you?'

'The skin isn't broken,' Michelle said with a wry look. 'Terry objected to my trying to take his pyjama bottoms off – didn't you, Terry?'

'Don't like you,' the boy muttered sullenly. Sally could see what Nan meant because he was nearly as tall as his sister, thin and wiry, and he looked quite strong, but his attitude was that of a small child. 'Shan't be washed. Nancy washes me – don't yer, Nance?'

'Yes, Terry, love, I look after you.' Nancy came forward and placed herself between Michelle and the boy. Her eyes were filled with a silent appeal as she said, 'Terry relies on me. I'll give him a wash if you let us alone for a while.'

'Staff Nurse Michelle wants to help you,' Nan said. The children often resented the implication that they might have nits, but many of them were crawling with lice when they first arrived, and these two had been living rough, although if Constable Sallis was right, only for a few days. 'No one is going to hurt either of you, Nancy, but you must have a bath – you may wash him if that is what you both wish.'

Nancy stared at her defiantly for a moment, and then inclined her head. 'I'll take your things off, Terry. Nurse has to look at us both but she won't hurt you. I'm here to protect you.'

His sullen expression didn't alter but he allowed Nancy to take everything off. Nancy turned him round so that they could see his thin body and Sally caught her breath as she saw the bruises all over his back, arms and legs.

'Who beat you, Terry?' Nan asked, but he just stared at her. She looked at Nancy, who hung her head but then mumbled something. 'Speak up, my dear. We want to know who did this to your brother. It wasn't just a fall, was it?'

'It was a tramp where we were hiding,' Nancy said, contradicting her earlier statement. 'He was drunk. I pushed him over and we ran off and hid somewhere else – didn't we, Terry?'

The boy nodded his head, seeming almost dazed as if he wasn't sure what was going on. Sally suspected Nancy was lying to them, but if she didn't want to tell them the truth there wasn't much anyone could do.

'I'll leave you two to get on,' Nan said, and went out.

'Shall I show you how to run the water?' Sally asked, leading the way to the old-fashioned bath at the other end of the large room. 'Have you ever used a bath like this, Nancy?'

'No, miss,' Nancy said, staring at it. 'We brought in a tin bath from outside when we had a bath – but we mostly just had a wash in the bowl in the kitchen, miss.' She stared at Sally and then back at Michelle. 'Are you all nurses?'

'I'm a carer and my name is Sally. Nan is the head carer and she looks after us all. She is very kind, Nancy. You can trust her – and all of us. You've been brought here so that we can look after you. Once you've had a wash you'll go into the isolation ward for a while, and then Sister Beatrice will decide which dormitories to put you in.'

'What are they – dormitories?'

'It's another name for bedrooms. The girls go one side and the boys another.'

'No!' Nancy was startled, a frightened look in her eyes. 'Terry can't be separated from me in a strange place. We have to be together . . . please, you must let us. He won't sleep and he'll be terrified. Please, Sally, help us to stay together.'

'I'll talk to Nan about it,' Sally said, 'but I'm not sure what I can do – we've always separated the boys from the girls.'

'Don't tell Terry yet. Ask first, because he'll get upset,' Nancy begged.

'Yes, well, you'll be together for a while anyway. So I'll see what Nan says. Now, I'm going to stand just here to make sure you can manage everything. If you need help, you only have to ask . . .'

Angela heard someone call her name as she walked towards the main staircase of St Saviour's later that morning and paused, smiling as she saw it was Sally. She liked Sally very much because she was the first person to make her feel welcome at St Saviour's when she'd arrived, feeling very new and uncertain just a few months earlier. Her friend looked happy and cheerful, even though her rubber apron was a bit wet and she'd obviously just come from bathing one of the children.

'New arrivals?' she asked, with a lift of her fine brows.

'Yes, brother and sister,' Sally said and sighed. 'They were in a fire. I understand their parents died of smoke inhalation before the fire service got there.'

'Oh, how tragic,' Angela said. 'Only a short time after Christmas and already we have another tragedy.'

'Terry seems to be in a traumatised state. We couldn't do anything with him but, fortunately, he does whatever his sister tells him so we're getting by, so far.' Sally frowned. 'The boy has a lot of bruises. He looks as if he's been beaten pretty severely recently. His sister said he'd had a fall and then a tramp had attacked him, but I think she was lying.'

'At least he is safe now. He won't be beaten here.'

'No.' Sally beamed at her. 'It's good to know he is safe with us . . .' She hesitated, then, 'Have you moved into your apartment?'

'I got the keys two days ago and much of the stuff my father is sending up is coming later today. I have to meet the removers at around two o'clock so I'd better get going – I have a lot of work to do first.'

'Perhaps I'll see you tomorrow?'

'I'll be here later this evening. I've arranged to help out with the night shift.'

'I'll have finished my shift by then. Andrew is taking me out soon. We're going somewhere special.'

'Andrew Markham?'

'Yes . . .' Sally's cheeks were flushed. 'We've been going out since before Christmas, but just casually. It's going to be different now, I think.' She paused. 'You did once say I might borrow a dress sometimes, if you remember?'

'Yes, of course, Sally. Pop round tomorrow evening – say about eight? I'll can show off my new home and you can choose something.'

'I wouldn't ask, but Andrew mentioned taking me to the theatre and I don't have anything suitable. Mostly, I can wear my own things, but . . .' She stopped and blushed, embarrassed at having to borrow Angela's clothes.

'Sally, I'd happily lend you anything of mine. I should have remembered my promise before this, but I haven't stopped since we came back after the holidays.'

'I don't think any of us have had a spare moment,' Sally said. She looked shyly at Angela. 'I don't want to let him down, you see.'

'You couldn't do that,' Angela assured her. 'You'll look wonderful whatever you're wearing.' She glanced at her watch. 'I must fly or I shall never get there.'

'Go on, you don't want to be late,' Sally called after her but Angela didn't stop to look back.

FIVE

Angela looked around the spacious sitting room with satisfaction. She'd been lucky to find an apartment of this size so close to her work at St Saviour's, and after hours of moving furniture about and hanging curtains, she was finally happy with the effect. From outside, the building looked almost shabby, in keeping with its situation near the river and the old warehouse it had been some years before the war. During the bitter war that had wreaked so much havoc on the East End of London, it had sustained some fire damage but remained structurally sound. The building had since been restored to become a block of flats, some of which were quite small and others, like Angela's, large with rooms big enough to hold her beloved piano and her gramophone, both of which had now been brought up from her father's house in the country. Besides the large, comfortable sofa and chairs, and a selection of small tables, there was also a pretty mahogany desk and an elbow chair set near the picture window Above her head, a wintry sunshine poured in through the skylights. Angela had fallen in love with it as soon as she walked in even though it had cost her more than she'd intended to spend on her new home. Her mother would think it an extravagance if she'd asked her, but her father had told her to go ahead and buy with confidence when she'd asked his advice.

For a moment Angela's eyes filled with tears, because the thought of her mother's behaviour at Christmas still made her want to weep. She hadn't come to terms with what her father had told her concerning her mother's mental breakdown – because, of course, that was what it was. Mrs Hendry had always been a highly strung woman but something had changed her. In her right mind, her mother would never have stolen things from shops or drunk so much or run up a huge debt for her husband to pay.

When she saw him alone after returning to London, Angela had asked Mark if he knew why her mother was ill but if he did he hadn't told Angela.

'People sometimes become overwhelmed by life,' was all he would say. 'Something was triggered in your mother's mind and . . .' He shook his head. 'If I understood why these things happened I would be able to do more for my patients. I believe it was a slow, gradual illness, made worse by the war and then . . .' Mark had refused to elaborate. 'I'm sorry, Angela, but I cannot reveal confidences.'

'But she isn't actually your patient.'

'No, but your father is trying to persuade her to consult me – and she has talked to me in confidence.'

'And you feel you can't talk about it?' Mark nodded and Angela felt annoyed with him. 'I wish you'd let me know sooner that she was drinking too much. Perhaps I could have helped her.'

'I doubt it,' Mark said. 'Even had you been living at home it would still have happened – it was already happening before you took the job at St Saviour's. You'd had enough to bear with John's death. I just wanted to spare you the pain of knowing for as long as I could. We hoped that she would conquer the habit. Instead, it has become very much worse. I thought she was much better at the dance she organised – but perhaps that was because you'd trusted her to do it. She is very proud of you, Angela.'

'She never shows it.' Angela shrugged the suggestion off. The fact that Mark had kept her mother's addiction from her rankled more than she liked and she wasn't ready to forgive him yet. She'd believed they might be getting closer to one another – but a man who truly cared for her would have known she was strong enough to face up to the challenge.

She put the thought from her mind, glancing round her apartment once more. She would have a house-warming party soon, Angela thought, going through to the modern and very new kitchen to boil a kettle. Yes, something simple would do; with a buffet if she could find anything nice in the shops.

'I'm glad you're here, Angela,' Sister Beatrice greeted her as she walked into the sick bay that Sunday evening. 'Nurse Paula has gone down with flu and rang to say she would be off work for the rest of the week.'

'Oh, poor Paula,' Angela said. 'It is as well we've taken on Staff Nurse Carole.'

'Yes, she has excellent references. We were lucky to get her – and that's down to you, I suppose.'

50

'Why down to me?' Angela was surprised at the praise, faint though it was.

'Yes, because of the extra funds you raised before Christmas, we've been allowed to employ another nurse with the necessary level of experience.'

'Oh . . . well, yes, I suppose that did help but once the new building is finished we shall need more . . .' Angela's words were lost as they heard blood-curdling screams from the isolation ward next door. 'What on earth was that?'

'I think it must be Terry Johnson,' Sister Beatrice said, 'and that is why I'm glad you're here this evening. We tried to separate him and his big sister, Nancy, into different dormitories earlier this morning, because they been here a couple of days and are obviously not carrying an infection, but the boy became violent and bit Staff Nurse Carole when she tried to part them. His sister intervened and he quietened, but he is going to need watching. We were forced to give him a mild sedative and leave them both in the isolation ward – but it sounds as though it has worn off.' She hesitated, then, 'I think Nurse will need help in there this evening.'

'I'd better go and see whether he needs anything,' Angela said, though the first screams had not been repeated.

'I imagine his sister is calming him down, but they can't be ignored. Go and talk to them, Angela, see what the matter is if you can. He won't speak to me, I'm afraid. Usually, I can get children to talk, but not this boy. He just stared vacantly at me, though I'm sure he understood every word I said.'

'Yes, Sister, I'll see what I can do,' Angela promised.

She left the sick bay and went through to the isolation ward. The dormitories were almost full in any case, because since Christmas six new children had been brought to the home and it was just about at bursting point. Angela knew that Sister Beatrice was impatient for the new wing to be ready, but although the builders had promised to be out by the end of this month, it looked as if they might not be finished for weeks yet. Angela would have to do what she could to hurry them up.

Entering the ward quietly, Angela saw a girl of slight build, perhaps thirteen or fourteen years of age, sitting on the edge of one of the beds. She had fine fair hair and was talking softly to the boy in the bed, stroking his much darker hair, her voice gentle and comforting.

'Was it 'cos the door was locked, Nance?' he asked, his eyes wide and scared. 'I can't remember . . . was it my fault . . . did I do something bad . . .?'

'No, of course not, love,' she murmured. 'Pa was a brute – what he did to us both . . . He made it happen – it wasn't your fault—' Suddenly, she broke off and turned her head to look at Angela, a look of fear in her soft grey eyes. 'Who are you?'

'I'm Angela Morton. I work here, in the office, and sometimes help out with our children. I've been asked to see that you and your brother are safe and have all you need . . .'

'Thank you,' the girl said, and the fear in her eyes lessened, though Angela sensed hesitation in her. 'Terry was having a bad dream – about our ma and pa . . .'

'You're Nancy, aren't you?'

'Yes, miss,' she said, her eyes never leaving Angela's face, almost as if she were trying to assess her, to see if she could be trusted. 'I'm the eldest, almost fourteen. Terry is only ten; eleven in September. He's usually as good as gold but . . .'

'Yes, of course. We do understand what you've been through, Nancy. I hear you were a very brave girl. You should be proud of yourself for saving your brother's life. It must have been terrifying to go back upstairs when the fire was raging.'

'I had to, miss. It wasn't his fault that the fire started – Pa was drunk. He must have knocked over the lamp and not noticed what he'd done. He was always getting drunk, miss, and Ma wasn't much better. They locked Terry in his room and went out drinking together that night. Terry didn't have any supper and he was crying but Pa had the key in his jacket pocket, and after they came back drunk, I unlocked the door and gave Terry a drop of tea and a crust of bread and jam . . . I was still in the kitchen clearing up the mess they'd made when the fire started. I heard Terry scream and went up and dragged him down the stairs. He just stood there staring . . .'

Nancy's voice had risen, and she seemed on the verge of hysteria herself. 'Terry shouted to Ma but their door was locked to keep us out and they either didn't hear or they were too drunk . . . I couldn't get them out, because the door was blazing – it was too late.' Her voice broke on a sob of despair. 'Too late . . .'

Angela could see that the girl was suffering from delayed shock herself. 'It was a terrible tragedy, Nancy. No one blames you or your brother for what happened. You got your brother out, and you tried to save your parents too.'

Nancy's gaze veered away, seeming to look into the distance. 'Yes, miss, that's what the policeman said. The firemen tried to get in but they couldn't reach them; the stairs were all afire by then and no one could get to the bedrooms that way. When they got in through the window, they were dead from the smoke. We ran away because we didn't know what to do – and Terry said Ma was screamin' but I didn't hear her. I think it's just in his head, 'cos he loved Ma. It wasn't our fault . . .'

Nancy was so intense. Angela reached for her hand and pressed it reassuringly. 'I am quite certain it was not, Nancy. As you said, your father probably knocked his oil lamp over and didn't notice because he was drunk. Fire spreads so quickly in old houses and by the time the fire service came it was too late. I am so sorry for all you and your brother have suffered.'

'Yes, miss, thank you, miss,' Nancy said and rubbed at her eyes. 'I don't want to lose Terry, miss. He's all I've got now – and it's always been the two of us . . .'

'I'm sure you love him. He will be quite safe with us, I promise you. In time he will stop being so afraid and then he will realise that we are here to help children who have lost their homes. Do you have any other relatives?'

'No, miss, not that I know of. They mostly died in the Blitz. Me ma once spoke of her cousin in the country, but she never come to see us . . .' Tears welled in Nancy's eyes. 'Ma didn't deserve to die. She did what she could for us until she got bad. Pa spent all he earned on drink and she gave us most of her food. I wanted to save her, miss. Truly I did, but the flames were so hot I couldn't get near the door . . .'

Angela handed her a clean white handkerchief. 'Wipe

your eyes and blow your nose, Nancy. I am quite sure you did what you could for your mother and your father. It isn't your fault. They were the adults; it was their job to keep you safe in your own home – no one will blame either of you.'

'Will that Sister Beatrice let us stay here if Terry keeps screaming and being wild? She was very cross when he fought the nurses who tried to give him a bath. The only person he trusts near him is me.'

'Why is that, Nancy?' Angela asked, but the girl just shook her head. Clearly she didn't want to talk about it, and it was too soon to press for details, although Angela suspected that the bruises on Terry's body might have been inflicted by his father and not a tramp. No doubt Nancy would tell them the truth when she was ready.

'I've always cared for him.'

'The nurses have to make sure you don't have anything infectious when you come – but perhaps Sister will let you stay here in this ward until he is more himself.'

'Will you ask her if we can stay here together, miss? Sometimes, he wets the bed, and he walks in his sleep. If I'm not there to take him back to bed he might . . . hurt himself.'

'Yes, I can see that,' Angela said. She thought privately that Terry was a very disturbed child and might benefit from Mark Adderbury's attention. Mark specialised in helping mistreated children in his spare time from his busy practice. Sister Beatrice relied on the help and advice he gave freely. 'I'm sure you can stay in here for a while, just until we can sort something out . . .'

'Thanks, miss. You're kind.' Nancy sniffed into the handkerchief and then offered it back.

'You keep it for a while; you must have lost everything in the fire. I know St Saviour's provides new clothes, but is there anything I can get for you that you need?'

'Terry had a teddy bear he used to take to bed, but it was left behind when we escaped. It might have helped him to sleep . . .'

'I can't give him back the one he lost, but I do have my own very old and much-loved bear, if you think he would like that?'

'You'd really let us have it?'

'Yes,' Angela said. 'I'll bring it tomorrow – and I've got a few pretty things you might like, Nancy. A case to put hankies in, and a brush and comb for your hair – and some satin ribbon to tie it up. You've got nice fair hair and it curls naturally.'

Nancy blushed, the tears glistening on her lashes, but she didn't cry. Terry had been lying in the bed, just staring up at her, but now his eyes closed and Nancy smiled.

'I think he will sleep now, miss. Shall we see you tomorrow?'

'Yes. I shall be in and out this evening, just to make sure you're both all right. I can get you a mug of cocoa to help you get off to sleep if you like?'

'No, miss, I'm all right. I'm going to get into bed with Terry so that if he wakes again he won't start screaming and wake everyone.'

'Well, make sure you get out before the morning staff come on duty – they might not approve of you sleeping in his bed.'

Nancy looked at her sadly, reflecting more knowledge than ought to be in the eyes of a girl of her age. 'I know, miss, but our Terry wouldn't hurt me: he isn't like Pa . . .'

'Nancy.' Angela caught her breath in shock. 'Your father didn't . . .?'

Nancy's eyes filled with suffering but she didn't say anything. Angela couldn't bring herself to ask the questions that hovered at the back of her mind. If her suspicions were correct, Nancy had been interfered with by her own father and she was less than fourteen years old. What kind of a man would subject his own daughter to something so vile? He had more than likely beaten his son as well. She couldn't help thinking that neither Nancy nor her brother would mourn him, though both seemed to be upset over their mother.

Angela left the children to sleep, but she couldn't put the look in Nancy's eyes out of her mind. Perhaps it was an act of fate that had caused the fire and set them free – and yet Angela had an uncomfortable feeling that there was much more that Nancy could have told her had she wished.

The problem was, what ought she to do about it? She supposed she should report what Nancy had let slip to Sister Beatrice, who would no doubt inform the police – but what was the point of that? Nancy hadn't really told her anything and it could lead to lots of questions for the girl, and she'd already been through so much. She'd trusted Angela enough to open up a little and it would be a betrayal of that trust to tell. For the moment Angela would keep her suspicions to herself. What harm could that do?

SIX

Carole looked at herself in the rather mottled mirror on the wall of her room at the Nurses' Home and patted her natural blonde and very short hair with satisfaction. It was important to keep hair clean and neat for work, and her new fashionable boyish crop suited her. She was pleased with herself for finding this job. After completing her training at the London Hospital, in Whitechapel, she'd wanted a change, somewhere that she could influence her own life.

The Sister in charge of her ward at the teaching hospital had disliked her almost from the start and Carole was fed up with being picked on the whole time. She was an excellent nurse and had passed all her exams easily, and yet Sister Brighton seemed to hate her. That was probably because Dr Jim Henderson had taken an interest in the younger nurse, and everyone knew that Brighton was mad about him. Unfortunately, he hadn't looked at her and it had turned her sour – at least, that was what all the nurses under her supervision thought.

For a while Carole had believed that Jim Henderson was the right man for her. Yes, she had imagined being a doctor's wife and all of the perks that it would have brought. But he had been too dedicated to his job for Carole's liking, neglecting her to work all hours and talking endlessly of going overseas for a few years to work in a mission hospital and taking her with him to do his charitable works. That was the last thing she'd wanted. Besides, she wasn't in love with him; there had been a man once, but he had died on the beach at Dunkirk . . . Carole had hardened her heart after that and now she kept her distance. If she did marry it would be because it fitted in with her plans for a good life – and that didn't include being a missionary's wife in some godforsaken backwater. Once the romance was over, she'd given in her notice and taken this job. She was glad to see the back of Henderson and Sister Brighton; they were welcome to each other as far as she was concerned.

At least here she didn't have to share a room any more. One day she'd have her own little flat, but this would do for now – besides, if you had your own place men tended to ask if they could come back for a drink when what they really wanted was something more. Carole wasn't a complete innocent, and she would have gone to bed with Jim if he'd shown more interest in her sexually . . . but he was too intent on his good works. Next time, she would choose a man who was more worldly . . .

St Saviour's had exactly what she was looking for. The atmosphere was more relaxed than at the hospital, though Sister Beatrice was a bit of an old dragon. She breathed fire and brimstone whenever she considered someone had done something wrong, but Carole knew her standards were excellent and the nun would be unlikely to find fault with her work. If she'd guessed what was in Carole's mind, well, it was doubtful that she would ever have taken her on.

Men were unreliable and selfish, and apart from using them to further her ambitions, Carole was opting to focus her efforts on building her career – in her own way. Sister Beatrice was getting on a bit and old-fashioned. An intelligent nurse such as herself could work hard and find a way to make herself indispensable so that when the old harridan retired in a few years she would be the natural successor.

Carole fixed her cap at the precise angle, smoothed her uniform and left her room, locking the door behind her.

It was chilly as she walked to the children's home through the connecting gardens. St Saviour's was almost unique in having more than a back yard in this area of London, but it was a relic from the past, when the house had been an impressive early Georgian mansion – and then later a hospital for contagious illness. Similar buildings had grown up all round as the area was peopled with silk merchants, and then the Jewish immigrants who had taken over the streets around St Saviour's when the rich merchants had moved up West. The house had been used as the old fever hospital until it was closed in the early 1930s, but since then many of the Jewish synagogues and shops in the area had been replaced and there was a mixture of cultures and peoples working and living in the narrow dirty streets. St Saviour's had become a home for children in need during the war, and the house the nurses occupied was what had once been a rather grand home for the Warden of the fever hospital.

Carole was surprised that the buildings here had survived the bombing in the war. The surrounding streets were filled with large empty spaces overgrown with weeds and neglected, awaiting renovation. In Bethnal Green several bomb sites had been turned into gardens and small allotments for the local residents; here the ruins were just left to decay while local children made a playground from the ruins of their former homes. The Government was going to build houses and shops to replace those lost in the war, but because of the shortage of building materials they were instead putting up prefabricated bungalows and they were dotted here and there amongst the decay and destruction; some had been built further out from the centre, where the air was fresher. Londoners were starting to drift out to the suburbs with the promise of new homes and a better life. From the outside St Saviour's looked grubby like the rest of the buildings in the area, though inside it was as clean as Sister Beatrice could persuade her staff to keep it.

Most of the girls here were all right. She quite liked Staff Nurse Michelle, though she hadn't seen much of her, but she was an East End girl and didn't seem a threat to Carole's ambition. Angela Morton was a different matter; she wasn't sure whether she liked Mrs Morton or not, because although she was always friendly there was something about her – something that made Carole sense a rival.

Carole hadn't yet worked out what Angela's role was here. She talked of herself as being the odd-job lady, but she carried authority, speaking with a confident smile and amusement in her eyes. Everyone seemed to like her – at least Nan spoke very highly of her and Sally Rush seemed to think she was wonderful. Nan was a surrogate mother to the children, helping with everything, from washing them to giving them hot drinks in the night, taking them to the toilet if they couldn't manage, or out on school trips. She was the lynchpin of the home and she seemed to be in Sister Beatrice's confidence. But Nan wasn't an ambitious person and wouldn't think of herself in the position of Warden – though Angela Morton might.

Yes, *she* would bear watching, Carole thought as she let herself in through the back door and went along the rather dark corridor to the dining room, where breakfast was still being served. Helping herself to coffee and a piece of toast with a scraping of what looked suspiciously like margarine and a spoonful of marmalade, she sat down at the table reserved for nursing staff.

Most of the children had already eaten and were leaving the tables in an orderly fashion, under the eye of some of the senior children: new monitors that Angela had appointed since Christmas, so Carole had been told. Sally Rush was gathering the smaller ones, preparing to take them to wash their hands and jam-smeared faces. She saw Carole and nodded to her in a friendly way. Sally was all right; Carole had already marked her down as harmless.

Carole glanced at the little silver watch pinned to her uniform. She had another fifteen minutes before she was due on duty, but she might as well go up to the wards and look in on the new arrivals. Being early for work was always a good way to impress and she wanted Sister

Beatrice to think well of her, because she knew she was still on probation as far as the crusty old nun was concerned. She was wed to her order and her religion and had probably never had a man in her life; at least that was Carole's guess. Her whole life revolved around St Saviour's and the children. Carole would never be like that; even if she did stay on to become Warden, she would never let her job become her whole life. No, she wanted it all and she intended to get whatever she could out of her present position.

Patting her mouth with the napkin, she stood up and straightened her uniform and then walked briskly from the dining room, almost colliding with a young red-haired boy who was running as if his life depended on it. She grabbed hold of his arm to steady him as he almost fell over in his efforts to avoid knocking into her.

'Sorry, Nurse,' he said. 'I was in a hurry to catch up with Mary Ellen – you won't tell on me, will you?'

'You must be Billy Baggins,' Carole said with a frown. 'I've heard about you. You're the little rebel. You really should start looking where you are going, but no, I shan't tell on you – this time; just don't do it again.'

'Thanks, Nurse.' Billy grinned cockily and walked nonchalantly away.

Carole guessed he would run as soon as he was out of view, but why should she care? She smiled, because she was a bit of a rebel herself and always had been. Perhaps it came from being the youngest of a clever brood and always the last to know what was going on in the family home. Not that she had much family now: the war had seen to that, taking her father and two elder brothers and leaving her with just her sister, Marjorie, and her mother.

Just as she reached the top of the stairs she saw a man come from Sister Beatrice's office. He walked towards her, stopping to smile as they came face to face outside the sick bay, and then he offered his hand. Carole noticed at once that his hand was strong and assured as he clasped hers firmly; on the little finger of his right hand he wore a solid gold signet ring.

'I'm Mark Adderbury,' he said. 'You must be Carole Clarke, the new staff nurse. Sister Beatrice told me about you. I'm glad to meet you, Carole.'

'Yes, I've heard a bit about you too.' Carole gave him the special smile she reserved for men who passed the test, and he did with flying colours. Good-looking, mature, rich and intelligent, he had all the necessary qualities – but what was he like as a man? 'You visit the disturbed children, I think?'

'Yes, that's my job, but I'm interested in everything that goes on here and all the children. St Saviour's gives hope to children who had none when they were brought here, Carole. I think helping a place like this to exist is the best job in the world.'

'Yes, of course,' Carole said, groaning inwardly. Not another man bent on a mission! She didn't want to dedicate her life to good causes, unless there was something in it for her. Yet Mark's smile was rather enticing and she decided to let the jury stay out for a while on this one. She wouldn't mind getting to know him better before she wrote him off. 'I do enjoy working with children; they are much easier than adults, I think. Elderly patients complain all the time and the younger men never do as you tell them.' She gave a soft laugh to show that she was teasing and saw the flicker of appreciation in his eyes.

'Yes, I imagine so, though I work with all ages. This is my pleasure in a way, though I wouldn't want you to imagine that I have no other interests – good music, the theatre, dancing, books . . .'

Carole raised her eyes to his, seeing the sparkle there. Just the sort of things in life she liked herself – but was he taken?

'I expect you and Mrs Adderbury have a wonderful social life . . .'

'We had one, but my wife died some years ago.'

'I'm sorry to hear that,' she said, though she felt quite the opposite at the news he was a widower.

'Thank you, but I have a pleasant life and lots of friends,' he murmured.

Carole felt a spurt of annoyance. Did he mean women friends? Men usually fell at her feet, but Mark Adderbury showed no sign of following the herd and that aroused her hunting instincts – better to keep him keen.

'Gracious, look at the time,' she said, though she was still early. 'It was nice meeting you, Mr Adderbury, but I must fly.'

'Oh, Mark, surely,' he said, calmly. 'But I mustn't keep you waiting and I too have to hurry . . .'

Carole could feel her heart racing as she went into the sick ward. She rather liked him, even if he did look at her as if she were a charming child rather than the exciting woman most men seemed to think her . . .

'Oh, you're early,' Nurse Paula said as she entered. 'Good, I can tell you the latest and then get off.'

Carole nodded and smiled. 'I just met Mr Adderbury. He seems very nice?'

'Yes, I suppose he is. I've hardly spoken to him, other than about the children. He and Angela Morton are good friends, I think – not that there's anything in it. Sally says she still loves her husband: he was killed in the war . . .'

'Lots of us lost loved ones in the war, my fiancé, father and brothers were all killed,' Carole said without blinking. 'But some of us choose not to wallow.'

'What rotten luck, to lose so many men in your family. I can't imagine how that feels,' Paula said, looking sympathetic. 'When I'm not on nights we might go to a film together sometime?'

'What about your boyfriend?'

'I don't see Fred all the time,' Paula sighed. 'I used to go out with Sally sometimes, but she doesn't have time these days.'

'Oh, that's a shame,' Carole said. It was always best to make allies but she'd no need to commit herself at this point. Something better might come up – she thought again about Mark Adderbury. 'Now, shall we look at what's been happening? What about the new arrivals?'

'Medically, they seem all right now; they were not much affected by the smoke, because Nancy got her brother out quickly – but the boy is difficult; he just stares vacantly, though I'm sure he knows what I say.'

'Still in shock, I suppose, though he can talk when he likes. Has Mr Adderbury visited them?'

'Yes, a little while ago. He said the girl was the best judge of her brother's behaviour and very good at handling him; he advised me to just leave him for now and hope that he comes out of it – but he never tells us nurses more than he thinks we need to know.'

'Well, all we can do is to keep an eye on Terry,' Carole said. 'If he is calmer now we shall not need to sedate him. We must just let his sister look after him and wait until he recovers. It was a terrible thing – to lose both parents in that awful fire.'

'Yes, horrid,' Paula agreed but frowned. 'I don't know why but that boy gives me the shivers. I wish they could be moved into one of the dorms.'

'Don't be foolish, Nurse,' Carole said briskly. 'Terry is just a child and he's been through an ordeal. You must learn to make allowances.'

SEVEN

Nan walked through to the hall of her small prefabricated bungalow and picked up the envelope the postman had just delivered. She'd been fortunate to get this place, having been bombed out twice during the war: the first time she'd lost almost everything, recovering only a few precious photographs and papers that were saved from the fire because she'd kept them in a biscuit tin, which miraculously survived under the rubble. The second time she'd merely had a room in a terraced house, sharing with three other families, and she'd been lucky, because it was the house next door that took the direct hit and she'd had time to pack a few things before the wardens came and moved everyone out as the fire spread. The powers that be had rehoused her here after the end of the war and she was gradually turning her little bungalow into a home.

She took the letter into the warm kitchen. These prefabs were not popular with everyone, because outside they looked a bit soulless, but the fortunate tenants loved them. The kitchens had modern electric fittings and hers had a nice closed-in stove that she could cook on and kept a steady temperature; the rooms were also warmed by coal fires and a copper boiler heated the water and provided a bath whenever she needed one. Nan thought she'd landed in heaven the first day she moved in. God knew, her life had never been easy, but at least here she was warm and comfortable and she only had herself to worry about . . . Well, that wasn't strictly true, of course. She worried about Maisie in that place – but she was a fool to let herself think about things that distressed her. It was her daughter's choice and Nan had to accept it, as Beatrice had told her when it all happened.

'The girl has a right to her own life, Nan,' her friend had said as they talked over a cup of tea. 'We've both suffered tragedy, and you know as well as I do that we just have to get over it. You have a home and you have a decent job – and if Maisie is happy where she is . . .'

'I know it has to be her decision after what happened to her,' Nan agreed. 'I don't want to force anything on her, but I wish she would talk to me – she won't even see me, Beatrice. She blames me for what he did . . .'

'She's wrong to blame you, Nan. It wasn't your fault. After you lost your Sam and the boy – you had no choice but to take in lodgers.'

Nan felt a choking sensation in her throat. She'd been lost in her grief after her husband and her son, Archie, had both died of the typhoid fever. Maisie had been just a child of twelve then, and perhaps she'd neglected her – she must have done something wrong or Maisie wouldn't have turned against her, because Nan couldn't have known what that filthy brute had on his mind.

If she'd known she would have taken the meat cleaver to him!

Tears stung her eyes as she looked at the writing on the envelope. She didn't recognise it, although it had come from that village down there in Cornwall. It hadn't been written by her daughter, she knew that much.

Tearing the envelope open, she saw that her last letter to Maisie had once again been returned unopened. Slumping down at the kitchen table, Nan bent her head and wept. How could Maisie do this to her time and again? She was supposed to have devoted her life to God and was bent on becoming a nun and yet she didn't care about the pain she inflicted on her own mother.

There was a brief note of regret from the Mother Superior and that was all. Sister Mary, as she was called these days, did not wish to receive letters from her mother just yet, but she would be informed if there should be a change . . .

Angry with her daughter and with herself for caring, Nan threw the letters into the fire. She looked at the precious photos in the frames she'd bought as and when she could afford them; they took up a whole shelf of the old oak dresser she'd purchased when she came to live here. There was only one of Maisie – after it all happened, looking pale and withdrawn, so different from the happy, pretty child she'd been when her father and adored brother were still alive.

Maisie had been Archie's twin, and the change in her had started after he died, because she'd kept asking why she was alive and her twin was dead of the typhoid. Nan hadn't been able to answer that, any more than she could explain what had happened between them

– why she'd drifted away from her daughter, why she hadn't seen what was happening, hadn't realised what that filthy beast had on his mind.

No, she wasn't going to let her thoughts drift in that direction. It was madness to dwell on whether she'd been at fault, as Maisie had claimed that day when she'd told her mother she was retiring to a convent to give her life to God.

'You must have known what he was,' Maisie had said calmly in a voice of ice. 'How could you not have seen what was happening – the way he looked at me . . .?'

'I was too busy, too tired.' Nan had tried to explain that she had thought her lodger wanted to get her into bed rather than her twelve-year-old daughter. Yet she knew that however many times she apologised, however many times she begged Maisie to forgive her, she could never take away the horror of her daughter's suffering at the hands of that beast.

Maisie had run away and it had taken months of searching before Nan found her living rough. She'd never known what had happened in those intervening days and weeks, because her daughter refused to speak for years. All the doctors she'd taken her to had been baffled, expounding all kinds of theories, but they'd all been wrong. Maisie had simply refused to speak until she was ready – until she'd made up her mind to leave her home for good.

It was all Nan's fault, because she hadn't looked after the girl; she hadn't noticed what was happening under her nose, and for that she was to be punished for the rest of her life, it seemed.

Nan's throat swelled with emotion, choking her, but she fought down the anger and the self-pity, refusing to give way.

She couldn't let the past haunt her because Maisie had returned her letter again, and she wouldn't, Nan decided. She'd been so happy while Sam lived but these past seven years had been nothing but grief – or they would have been had it not been for the friendship she'd formed with Beatrice.

Beatrice had suffered enough herself, though she never spoke of it to anyone, as far as Nan knew. Her secret remained locked inside her, and she had never revealed the whole of it even to Nan. Their friendship was strong and they'd grown closer over the years, especially since Beatrice had joined the staff at St Saviour's. They'd met when Beatrice was ill in the Infirmary years before and Nan had been one of the cleaners on the ward. That was before Beatrice had decided to become a nun and take up nursing. Nan remembered taking her cups of tea and sitting on the edge of her bed talking to her until one of the nurses asked her what she was doing. Even then she hadn't talked about what had made her so ill or why she'd decided to enter a convent, though Nan knew it was a personal tragedy that had brought her so low.

Sighing, Nan took out a clean handkerchief and wiped her eyes and then blew her nose. This wouldn't buy the baby a new coat! The old saying made her smile, reminding her of her grandmother and happier times. They'd been really poor in those days, but everyone seemed more content, at least that was the way she remembered things. It was ridiculous to feel sorry for herself when there were so many worse off than she was; so many war widows and orphans. Nan was lucky to have this new home, a job at St Saviour's that she loved and several good friends – a reluctant smile touched her lips as she thought of one of her newer friends. She liked Angela a great deal, and she had something to ask her . . .

Getting up, Nan pulled on her rather shabby grey coat, set a little blue felt cloche on her head and picked up her gloves and handbag. She must be getting back to St Saviour's, because she knew that two of the kitchen staff were down with sore throats again, and Cook would be shorthanded. Besides her own work with the children, she would have to lend a hand with the fetching and carrying. Not that she minded what she did, and she had a scheme that might give her something to think about and stop her fretting about Maisie.

Going out into the morning air, she discovered it was colder again, a light dusting of snow on the ground, and she pulled her coat collar up around her throat. The weather had been bitter ever since the turn of the year, the coldest winter Nan could recall, and the snow had caused endless problems in many parts of the country. It was never quite as bad in London, because the traffic soon cleared much of the slush and ice away, but they'd had another power cut the previous evening. Nan was fortunate to have the stove, which kept her warm. She'd bought in a good store of coke and coal before Christmas, but she knew that some people were running short, especially those who could only afford to buy in small amounts. The last thing Nan wanted was to get ill again. She'd had a touch of flu late last year and she didn't want another chill just yet.

Her bus was drawing up as she reached the stop and the conductor gave her a cheery smile as she climbed on board and found her seat. He was usually on the run to her stop just outside St Saviour's and it was like meeting a friend every morning.

'Usual fare, love?' he asked, churning his machine without waiting for her answer and handing her the ticket. 'Bit nippy out, ain't it?'

'Yes, very cold,' Nan said, smiling at the understatement. 'How is your wife getting on, Ned? Still got that nasty cough?'

'She's about the same, but she won't go to the doctor's,' he said and winked. 'Says a drop of brandy will set her straight and mebbe she's right.'

He moved off down the bus as it drew into the next stop and a man in a grey coat and black trilby got on. He was carrying a newspaper, some worn leather gloves, and a brown paper parcel tied up with string; he dropped the parcel as he reached the seat where Nan was sitting. The conductor retrieved it for him and he struggled to tip his hat to Nan, dropping his paper on the seat in the process. She moved along to give him room.

'All right if I sit here, ma'am?' She thought his accent sounded a bit northern but wasn't sure, because it wasn't pronounced.

'Yes, of course. I've got four stops to go yet.'

The man sat down and handed his fare to the conductor, then hunted for his newspaper. Nan wriggled it out from beneath him and he chuckled, his eyes sparkling with merriment. He must be in his early sixties, Nan thought, but attractive with it and clearly good-natured.

'I should lose my head if it wasn't stuck on,' he confessed. 'I always start off with half a dozen things and end up with most of them left on the bus or train.'

'That must be awkward?'

'They know me well at lost property,' he said cheerfully. 'I usually get everything back, though the newspaper doesn't get handed in very often.'

'I expect people think it has been abandoned and take it home.'

'Very likely. I hope I haven't forgotten anything important today. I'm delivering this parcel and I'd hate to lose it. It's part of the job I started last week, see. Work is hard enough to come by for a man like me.'

'Yes, that would be awkward,' Nan said, and laughed. 'My name is Nan. I work at St Saviour's – it's a home for children in need . . .'

'Yes, I've heard of it,' he said, and offered his gloved hand. 'I believe it's run by Sister Beatrice – a friend of mine says she's a marvel.'

'Yes, Beatrice is wonderful with children. She is strict, because she has to be, but underneath she loves them all, as I do.'

'What do you do there? Are you a nurse too?'

'No, I've never had any training, but I had a family – and I help to look after the children. I suppose I'm the head carer. I just pick up the pieces and look after anything that needs doing, for the children, but also for everyone else. I do whatever I can to help, you see – and sometimes that is just a matter of a little tea and sympathy.'

'Ah yes, I'm a great believer in tea and sympathy,' he said. 'Army life depends on it, you know. I was with the medics during the first war, just an orderly, running around fetching stuff for the doctors, and sorting out the men's problems in me spare time. This time round I helped out at a care home; a biscuit and little drink of tea in my room helped to break down their reserve sometimes. Poor young devils; they'll suffer for that damned war for the rest of their lives.'

'Are you still in the Army?'

'No, they threw me out after the Armistice; too old, they tell me,' he said, and his eyes twinkled again. 'I am lucky enough to have found myself a little job delivering books to the college. I've been taken on by a professor at the University. Nice chap, doesn't ask much. I fetch his shopping, mostly cakes for the teas he gives his students. Like I said, a cup of tea makes the world go round and I enjoy meeting the lads. Decent bunch but a little mad at times.'

Nan laughed, because he was an old soldier, a bit like her Sam had been; he made her feel comfortable and she knew he must get on well with his employer and the students. He seemed an amiable, fatherly sort of man whom everyone could trust and rely on.

'I expect they are just grateful that they didn't have to fight that awful war.'

'The lost generation,' he said, and the smile left his eyes. 'So many friends were killed in the Great War, though I came through it almost unscathed, but this time it was my friends' sons . . . they deserted their education and their jobs to fight for King and Country and too many didn't come back.'

'Yes, it is so sad, but wars always are,' Nan said. 'Well, it was nice talking to you, but the next stop is mine.'

'Ah, then I must let you escape.' He got up, his parcel sliding to the floor. Nan squeezed out into the aisle and then picked up his parcel, handing it to him as he sat down. 'Goodbye, Nan. I enjoyed our chat.'

Nan smiled. He hadn't told her his name but he probably didn't realise that.

'So did I,' she said. 'I hope you don't lose anything . . .'

He murmured something but Nan was moving down the bus ready to get off at the next stop. Something made her look back before she stepped down, and he lifted his hat to her.

Nan smiled inwardly as she started the short walk to St Saviour's. It was funny how often you met pleasant people on a bus and fell into conversation, yet you probably never saw them again. She wouldn't mind travelling with the old soldier more often, but doubted if it would happen.

One thing, he'd cheered her up. She no longer felt so distressed by that letter. After all, Maisie was old enough to know her own mind and she would have to decide for herself if the future she'd chosen was what she truly wanted.

EIGHT

'Are you sure you can part with them?' Sally asked that Monday evening as she tried on the beautiful gown in Angela's apartment. It was a delicious powder-blue satin with thin straps and a low back, and then there were two gorgeous fine wool dresses that were simple in design and suitable for an informal evening out or lunch at a nice hotel. This was the second time she'd tried on Angela's clothes; she'd borrowed a smart grey dress when Andrew took her to the theatre the previous week. Sally had returned it nicely sponged and pressed, but now Angela had offered to give her these. 'I've never worn anything like this, Angela. The material is wonderful and the styling – I only meant to borrow something now and then and I ought not to take them . . .' She looked a little embarrassed.

'I'm happy to know they will be useful to you,' Angela said. 'Honestly, Sally. I shall never wear them and I would much rather you had them than give them to the jumble sale.'

'You're so kind,' Sally said, and slipped out of the gown, pulling on her own tweed skirt and pink and grey striped hand-knitted jumper. 'If there's ever anything I can do for you, you must let me know.'

'I shall,' Angela laughed, and poured more coffee for them both. 'I'm arranging some fundraising events soon at the church and I'd like to enlist your help if you're free.'

'Of course. What are you thinking of doing next?'

'Well, I'm considering putting on a concert of some sort. Some little sketches, a few songs, that sort of thing. We could involve the children and the staff and hold it at the church hall, sell tickets for a raffle and refreshments.'

'I'd love to help. I could do a bit of sewing for the costumes or painting scenery,' Sally offered. 'I don't think I'd be any good on the stage though.'

Angela shook her head. 'Some of the staff at St Saviour's have lovely singing voices. I noticed it at the carol service. Father Joe helped with that, but I don't suppose he would want to help with a concert . . .'

'Not unless it was a religious one for Easter.'

'I was thinking of a simple theme with some of the popular songs. I could play the piano for them myself.'

'You're so talented, Angela,' Sally said. 'I often wish I had some kind of talent.'

'But you do.' Angela contradicted her instantly. 'You're so good with children, Sally. Even the naughty ones do as you tell them, and the little ones love you. I've seen the way they cluster about you when you read to them. Sometimes I think you should have been a teacher.'

'I've never thought of that as a talent.'

'We shall all miss you if you leave to become a nurse.'

'It won't be just yet. I have to take one more exam and pass my scholarship to the college before I can get taken on at the hospital. I'm not sure if I can afford to take it up even if I do pass. It depends on whether my father gets this new job.'

'Has he applied for one?'

'Yes. A builder got in contact with him and asked if he was interested in taking on the job of helping to restore some war-damaged buildings. It was such a surprise, because although Dad had put his name down all over the place he didn't think anything would come of it . . . but this looks like it might lead to something, if Dad fits the bill and has got the right skills.'

'Well, that is encouraging,' Angela said, and turned away to look at some sheet music, because she didn't want Sally to guess that she'd had a hand in getting Mr Rush a chance of this work. She'd spoken to the builder who had renovated her flat. He'd been talking about the lack of skilled men, because of all the casualties during the war, and she'd mentioned Sally's father. He'd promised to give it some thought, and it seemed as if her suggestion might have borne fruit, but Angela had no intention of telling anyone that she'd mentioned Mr Rush's name. It would only embarrass Sally.

'Dad says it will mean giving up his job on the Docks, but his firm have been cutting his hours for months, because the work just isn't there now since the war ended. The returning soldiers took all the jobs there were going and Dad lost out. There are all sorts of schemes for the future, but nothing certain. Mum says he's a fool if he turns this offer down.'

'He wouldn't do that, would he?'

'He said that you couldn't teach an old dog new tricks, but Mum has talked him round, and I'm sure he'll go if he gets the chance.'

'Let's hope he does,' Angela said, and looked at her thoughtfully.

She'd been wondering whether she should voice her suspicions about Nancy. Had the girl really been implying that her father had abused her or had Angela imagined that look? That kind of thing was too horrible to contemplate. Angela couldn't be certain, yet she'd sensed it that night when Nancy looked at her so oddly. If she spoke to Sister Beatrice or Father Joe, she knew that they would both want to investigate immediately – and Angela felt that Nancy needed a little time to recover from the trauma she'd experienced.

'What do you think of Nancy and Terry?' she asked casually. 'They ought to be in the dorms with the other children, but he screams if anyone tries to take him away from his sister.'

'I haven't seen much of them,' Sally said. 'I've been on normal duties recently. Michelle asks for me to work with her when she needs a carer, but Staff Nurse Carole, she sort of ignores me. Oh, she says hello if we meet in the staff room, but she never says about going out or talks about her life – not that I've seen her much.'

'We've just sort of smiled in passing.' Angela raised her fine brows. 'I expect most of your evenings are taken up now?'

'With Andrew? We've been out three times since he got back after the New Year. He takes me to lovely places – what about you and Mark?'

'Mark and I are just friends, Sally.' Angela frowned slightly, knowing she sounded defensive.

'Oh yes, I know that,' Sally was quick to reassure her friend, 'but sometimes he takes you out, doesn't he?'

Angela felt a slight hesitation. She knew that she was still smarting over the business with her mother. She had been avoiding him at St Saviour's and the thought of it made her unhappy, so she quickly changed the subject.

'We've both been busy,' Angela said. 'Let's see, this is Monday and I'm actually dining out with another friend of mine this week, Nick Hadden, but I'm free on Thursday evening. I think *Forever Amber* is on at the Regal; it came out last year but is still doing the rounds. I'd like to see it – if you would?'

'I'd love to, but you mustn't feel you have to.' Sally looked shy.

'Oh, I wouldn't, believe me.' Angela and Sally both laughed. 'Like you, I haven't made much headway with Carole Clarke yet. I like Michelle and I'm hoping she will come to my house-warming, but as yet I don't have many friends here in London.'

'Perhaps Carole is just slow to make friends,' Sally said. 'I must try to get to know her.'

'Yes, me too. I'll ask her to come to my house-warming. You're right, Sally. We mustn't misjudge her.'

'Well, I ought to go now,' Sally said. 'I can't thank you enough for what you've given me, Angela, and remember I owe you a favour.'

'Forget the clothes. I should never wear them because of the memories they arouse. Now don't say another word about them, and if you need to borrow shoes or anything for a special date just tell me . . .'

Sally laughed. 'You're a real friend, Angela. I'm glad you came to St Saviour's.'

'So am I; it's given me a new life,' Angela said, and pecked at her cheek. 'Are you all right walking or can you get a bus? I imagine it is a bit slippery out, because I think there was some more snow – just a sprinkling, thank goodness, but it can be treacherous to walk on.'

'Don't worry, I'll go carefully. I'll walk over the bridge and then take a bus,' Sally said, picking up the bag of clothes. 'Goodnight, Angela. I think your apartment is lovely . . . different and smart.'

Angela accompanied Sally to the door and waved her hand until she was in the lift going down. Then she locked her door, collected the dirty dishes and took them into the small kitchen. As she did so she thought again about Mark and realised that she hadn't seen him since Christmas. He'd been in and out of St Saviour's over the last week or so but she had deliberately avoided him and he hadn't rung to ask her out. She knew that her feelings of anger at him were silly and unfair. She'd missed his company and yet was somehow reluctant to repair the breach between them; Mark was at fault, he should come to her.

Sighing, and feeling annoyed with herself, Angela ran a bath and slipped into the water scented with Yardley's English Lavender. She knew she ought to talk to Mark about Nancy, because she had a feeling something was wrong with those children – something that wasn't visible on the surface. Angela didn't know why she felt so uneasy about them. St Saviour's took in a lot of mistreated or damaged children, but there was something different about these two – something hidden.

Perhaps, she should invite Mark over for a drink one evening and ask what he thought of the children. Angela trusted his judgement and if he thought all was well, she would keep her suspicions to herself.

It was perhaps fate that Angela should bump into Mark a couple of days later when she went into the isolation ward. She'd made some lemon barley and was bringing a jug of it to the ward, and felt pleased when she saw that Mark was standing close to the boy's bed with Staff Nurse Carole, checking the records. He turned as Angela entered and smiled, his eyes holding hers for just a moment.

'Good morning, Angela. This young man was just saying he was thirsty.'

'Yes, I came earlier to bring him something . . .' Angela's words died away as she saw her own teddy bear that she'd given to Terry. It was lying on the floor and its head had been torn off the body. The sight of her much-loved toy mutilated like that made Angela go cold all over. This was the teddy she given him to replace the one that Nancy said he'd lost in the fire. *Why had he destroyed it?*

Glancing at Terry, she saw a gleam in his eyes and knew that he was waiting for her to say something. He looked expectant, wary but excited, as though he had deliberately done it to make her angry. Carefully keeping her expression blank, she poured two glasses of lemon barley and took one to Terry and then one to Nancy, standing them by the sides of the beds.

'I'm sorry, miss.' Nancy spoke in hushed tones, glancing anxiously at the nurse and Mark, who were talking and looking at her brother. 'I know you meant it kindly, but it upset him. He didn't mean to do it, but when he gets upset he sometimes does silly things.'

'It is all right, Nancy,' Angela managed, though she was upset. 'It was only an old thing. I just thought he might like it.'

'He will like it after I've mended it,' Nancy said. 'If I could have some sewing stuff – I've always looked after him, sewing buttons on and things . . .'

Angela saw the frightened look in the girl's eyes and reached down to touch her hand sympathetically. 'Is that what you would like – some sewing things? I have some spare bits and bobs you could have if you like, and I could get you some material to make yourself a pretty dress you can wear for best.'

'Sister Beatrice came earlier and told us I should join the others for meals and other things. I've been given two skirts and two blouses; they're nice, better than my own clothes. She says I ought to go to school next week – but Terry isn't well yet, miss. I can't leave him or he'll start screaming and breaking things; it was after she said that we should soon have to move to the dormitories that he did that . . .' Nancy's eyes flicked to the mutilated teddy bear. 'Terry cried after he did it, miss. He wants me to mend it.'

Angela looked at Terry, but his eyes were flashing and it wasn't remorse that she saw there. She looked back at his sister reassuringly. 'All right, Nancy. I'll fetch the sewing things in my lunch hour and bring them for you.' It was very unusual for the brother and sister still to be in the isolation ward almost two weeks after they were admitted; but because Terry still woke screaming sometimes, Sister Beatrice had thought it might be for the best until they could decide what to do with them, otherwise they might wake the other children in the dorms. 'Why don't you sit over there by the window and look at the garden as you work? It would be better than being in bed when you don't have to be.'

'I pretended to have a headache so Sister wouldn't make me get up and leave him . . .' Nancy shut up abruptly as Mark approached them, looking thoughtful.

'Hello,' he said, bending down to pick up the mutilated bear. 'What happened to this?'

'We had a fight over it,' Nancy lied. 'I'm going to mend it.'

'Well, poor teddy,' Mark said, and put the bear down on a chair. 'You seem well recovered, Nancy. Sister says you can get up but don't want to – would you tell me why, please?'

'I can't leave Terry. He's frightened on his own and he'll start screaming.'

'Yes, I thought that might be it,' Mark said. 'Well, I'll have a word with Sister Beatrice for you and see if we can sort something out.' He looked at Nancy a moment longer and then turned to Angela. 'If you're going to your office, I'll walk with you.'

'I wanted to talk to you,' Angela said hesitantly. She glanced towards Staff Nurse Carole at that moment and was surprised to see the annoyed expression on the attractive girl's face. Her pale blue eyes glinted with ice, and Angela received the distinct impression that the girl had taken a dislike to her, though she had no idea why.

She nodded her head at Carole and walked to the

door. Mark opened it and held it for her, closing it quietly behind them.

'That was your bear, wasn't it?' he asked. 'I've seen it before – when we brought some of your stuff to London just before Christmas?'

'Yes, it was mine; fancy you remembering. I think it was getting very fragile, but Terry lost his in the fire.'

'So you gave it to him and he destroyed it.' Mark frowned. 'It was a shame after you'd had it all those years.'

'It didn't matter. I expect he is just upset. It may have reminded him of things he doesn't want to remember.'

'Very shrewd,' Mark agreed. 'Yes, Terry is extremely disturbed and at the moment refusing to accept what has happened. He doesn't want to remember anything. I'm not sure why – though of course the fire was terrible and they've lost their parents, but . . .' He shook his head. 'It's all rather troubling. I'm sorry, I shouldn't be burdening you with my musings, Angela. It's just that I wondered about the bear.'

'I'm not upset, Mark. Perhaps he did it to see what I would do. Sort of testing me, so I thought it best not to mention it to him. Nancy apologised.'

'Yes, well, I shall have to see how things go,' Mark said, and then smiled at her. 'You wanted to talk to me?'

'Yes. Actually, it's about Nancy.' Angela hesitated, she felt a sudden urge to make things right between them and it seemed silly to be avoiding him. Her father was right: Mark always did things for the best of reasons, even if she didn't like the outcome. 'Perhaps not now, Mark . . . I wondered if you would like to come to the apartment for a drink one evening? Not this evening because I'm going out with Sally to the pictures – but perhaps tomorrow, before you go down to the country?'

'I can't manage it this weekend unfortunately,' he said. 'Friday next week would be perfect. I was going to ask you for dinner one day soon but I never seem to have time these days.'

'Yes, lovely. We'll talk about it on Friday week – about eight?'

'Just right,' he said as they arrived at her office. 'Well, I need to speak to Sister Beatrice about those two. Do you think you could find them a small room to themselves somewhere? Have a think about it and tell Sister if you can work out where we could put them together.'

'Yes, all right, I will,' Angela said. 'I'll look forward to Friday then . . .'

She went into the office and closed the door. It was only as she sat down at the desk that she recalled the way Carole looked at her.

NINE

Carole glared as the door closed behind Angela and Mark Adderbury. She'd been getting on so well with the psychiatrist until Angela Morton turned up, breezing in on a cloud of fresh perfume – very expensive by the smell of it, her dress simple but well-cut and elegant, her shoes low-heeled patent leather. She looked confident and sure of herself – and of Mark Adderbury, smiling up at him in that guileless way of hers: the supercilious cat! Carole had decided she didn't like the other woman, because she was too damned sure of herself and always looked as if she'd stepped out of a glossy magazine.

Carole felt a frump in her regulation uniform. Mark had been on the point of asking her to dinner, she was sure of it, before Angela Morton wafted in. Then there were all the questions concerning those two peculiar children. Neither of them was truly ill in Carole's opinion. Nancy was putting on her headaches to get her own way, and the boy was just sullen. What they both needed was a good shake. Sister should put her foot down and make them separate into their various dorms. If she were in charge she wouldn't take any nonsense.

Oh, well, it wasn't part of her job to decide what happened to the children at St Saviour's. All she was employed to do was to look after the sick ones.

Carole popped next door to the sick ward. Her patients were being served hot drinks by Jean Painter.

'I've got some girls with sore throats to visit, Jean,' she said to the young carer. 'You can stay until I get back, can't you? I don't like to leave my patients alone – and the boy next door may start screaming. If he does just leave him to his sister. She can cope.'

'Oh – if you're sure,' Jean said, and looked a bit nervous. 'I haven't been on sick ward duty alone before. Sally asked me to bring these drinks, because she was busy. It's all right, isn't it?'

'Yes, fine,' Carole said impatiently. The young carer was inexperienced and clearly unsure of herself, but she could manage for a while. 'I don't suppose I'll be long.' She picked up a bag containing various bits and pieces she might need and took it with her. Nan had said it was the second room along the girl's corridor. She was new here herself and it took time to find your way about, because the building was old-fashioned with unexpected staircases that led to different parts of the house. Completely unsuitable for its purpose in Carole's opinion.

She took the lift up to the next floor and counted the rooms, but the sound of coughing from one of them would have told her where the girls were. She entered and saw they were all huddled in their beds, looking sorry for themselves.

'Have you had anything for your sore throats?' she asked, and got nothing but moans and complaints about aching limbs and feeling hot.

A brief examination of the girls told Carole that they had all gone down with a nasty bout of flu. Immediately, her training kicked in and she became the efficient and capable nurse she was when a patient was truly ill. These girls ought to be in the isolation ward so that she could keep an eye on them. It was so ridiculous that the brother and sister from the fire should be taking up much-needed beds.

'How are they?' Nan's voice asked from behind her, and Carole turned with a frown.

'They're suffering from flu as you suspected. I can't keep running up and down stairs. I must speak to Sister Beatrice about getting Terry and Nancy moved into the dorms.'

'Let me speak to her. I quite agree that these children should be in the isolation ward – either that or we need another nurse on duty . . .'

'Yes. It may come to that if more of the children go down with it.'

'I'll speak to Sister Beatrice now, but I know we don't have much room.'

Nan went out and Carole checked the girl called Sarah's temperature again. It was a little lower but she was still very flushed and moaned when Carole took her pulse, crying a little. She was certainly worse than the other two. Carole felt a little anxious about her, but she ought to go back and see how Jean was coping.

She was returning to the ward when she saw Sally Rush coming towards her and stopped her. 'It's Sally, isn't it?'

'Yes, Sally Rush. Can I help you with anything?'

'Are you very busy this morning?'

'No more than usual,' Sally said. 'I'm just about to take my lunch break – but that doesn't matter if I can help?'

'Thanks.' Carole felt relieved. 'I know you've been here longer than most of the carers and I've got rather a lot to do. Could you give me a hand this afternoon?'

Sally hesitated. 'I should be taking the little ones to the park, but Jean could swap duties with me.'

Carole felt the relief flood over her. 'Thank you. I should feel easier in my mind if I knew you were around. I am quite anxious about one of my girls. Sarah is very feverish.'

'Sarah Morgan?' Sally looked concerned. 'Yes, with good reason. She has a history of respiratory trouble. When she came to us she was recovering from pneumonia in the children's hospital and she was in the sick ward for months before she was able to join her friends in the dorm and at school.'

'Nan never said a word about her needing special care. I ought to have been told,' Carole snapped.

'Nan probably thought you knew,' Sally said. 'Sorry, you haven't been here long. You couldn't know about Sarah's weak chest but of course it was a long time ago.'

'At least I know now. Thank you, Sally. This makes it even more important that Terry and Nancy should be moved.'

'Are you too busy?' Nan asked, poking her head round the door of Sister's office. 'It is quite important.'

'Come in, Nan. Mark has been telling me that Nancy and Terry must not be parted, but we need the isolation

92

ward free. I can't let them stay there indefinitely – but I don't have anywhere they can be put together . . .'

'Have you asked Angela?' Mark said, and received a glare for his pains.

'She brought me an up-to-date list of available beds this morning. It's impossible – until the new wing comes on stream.'

'This is why I came to see you. The children can have my sitting room,' Nan said. 'It's big enough for two single beds and I can use the staff room when I need a rest. It would be a temporary thing, until they can be split up – besides, we'll have the new wing in a few weeks.'

'Nan! You need a room where you can be private sometimes,' Beatrice said, but the relief was in her eyes. 'I suppose it would be useful for the time being . . . It means inconvenience for you, though.'

'Oh, I don't mind. Excuse me now; I am supposed to be taking the younger children out. We're going to Itchy Park, as it used to be called – Christ Church Gardens, as you probably know it.'

'I won't ask why it was called Itchy Park, I can probably guess – because of all the down and outs that congregated there?' Mark followed her from the room. 'You get on,' he said, and watched her walk off down the hall.

Mark's thoughts turned from St Saviour's problems as he remembered the look in the attractive young nurse's eyes. Staff Nurse Carole had been giving him sweet smiles and discreet hints ever since they met. She was very young, of course, but there was something about her that he was drawn to. He liked her and if it wasn't for Angela . . .

Not that he knew where he stood with the woman who had become so important to him. Angela had grown since she came to St Saviour's. If he'd helped her achieve peace of mind and a new confidence he was glad – but he still had no idea whether she thought of him as any more than a friend. At times he'd thought he was making headway but then, after Christmas, when she'd discovered her mother's illness, she'd seemed to withdraw – even to blame him; though how he could have told her what was going on when both her parents had asked him not to, he had no idea.

Angela had embraced this new life with enthusiasm and it had given her the purpose she needed to live and be happy. He thought she was happy, though he could never be quite sure what lay behind the quiet eyes – as blue-green as a mountain pool. She was a deep character and he found her captivating, but Angela never gave him reason to think that she felt more than friendship.

What was it he wanted from his own life, he wondered. Was he content to continue as he had for years, living as a bachelor without a wife or family? He wasn't too old to start a family, surely? For years he'd felt that he didn't deserve a second chance, because after he and his wife, Edine, had lost their son, they had drifted apart and she'd died a pointless, lonely death.

Yet of late Mark had begun to think of a time when his working life was over. Did he really want to dwindle into some crusty old man living alone, too old for a social life and no family to care what happened to him? Mark laughed at himself for brooding. He would advise his patients not to dwell on negative things . . .

If he was to marry again, he would need to be sure

it was to the right woman; that they had the rest of their lives together to look forward to. Was there anything wrong with asking a pretty girl out, even if she was too young? If he did, it might even make Angela notice him as a man rather than a friend.

He found he had a spring in his step as he went down the stairs and out of the home into the cool air. He loved this old city, with so much history in its ancient buildings – a good brisk walk as far as the London Hospital would clear his mind – and he ought to be thinking about his patients' problems, not his own love life, or lack of it.

TEN

Alice came in from the yard, shivering from the bitter chill and still wiping the remains of vomit from her lips. Her soft fair was lank because it needed washing and her pretty face was pasty. Always a little plumper than she'd have liked, she'd been putting on weight recently and her clothes had begun to feel tight around the waist. She'd already been sick twice that morning; once into the chamber pot in the chair commode both she and Mavis used in their bedroom, managing to empty that into the outside toilet without letting her mother see, but then she'd felt ill when she saw her brother eating bread and dripping and she'd had to make a dash for the yard to be sick again.

'And what have you been up to, miss?' Alice's mother greeted her with a scowl. 'What did you go dashing off like that for?'

'I felt sick,' Alice admitted, because she couldn't get out of it. 'I think there's a bug going round at work. I must have got a touch of it.'

'Yeah, several girls at the factory are off sick too,' Mavis said, swiftly coming to Alice's aid. 'I felt a bit sick myself this morning . . .'

'Well, I hope you don't give it to me,' their mother said unsympathetically. 'I've got meself a little job scrubbing floors at the offices down the Docks. I can't rely on your father bringing in money so I'm off to earn a wage meself. It means yer'll 'ave to see to yerselves and yer brothers for breakfast from now on.'

Alice and Mavis looked at each other in relief as she left the kitchen. 'I'll do the washing up,' Mavis offered. 'You have to get to work before me, Alice – if you're home early you can tidy up or get the vegetables done.'

'Thanks, Mave,' Alice said. 'Are you goin' out this evening with your fella?'

'Might be,' Mavis said and grinned at her. She turned on Saul as he grabbed another slice of toast and spread the rich fatty dripping on it. 'Oi, take it easy with that, you greedy monkey, or you'll be sick too.'

'I'll blame it on Alice if I am,' he quipped. 'If I was sick I wouldn't have to go to school. I could go down the Docks wiv me mates and find meself a job.'

'No, you couldn't,' Alice said sharply. 'You have to work hard at school so that you can get a good job when you leave. Do you want to stand in line like Dad all the time and hope for a few hours' work?'

'That's his fault,' Saul said. 'If he weren't drunk and late all the time he'd get more work. They won't take him because he's unreliable.'

Alice didn't answer as she took her coat from behind the door and went out into the street. Her young brother was right, of course, but her father drank because it was the only way he could bear his life – and that was Alice's mother's fault. Her tongue was like a razor and

97

she never gave her poor husband a minute's peace, even when he wasn't drunk.

Pulling her coat collar up around her neck to keep out the icy wind, Alice walked quickly. It had been a close thing this morning. If Mavis hadn't intervened about girls at the factory going sick, their mother might have suspected that Alice was pregnant. She wasn't sure how much longer she could keep her mother at bay, and she was terrified of the row that would erupt once her secret was out. Her mother would raise hell and then she'd throw Alice into the street. She didn't know what she would do if that happened and she was close to despair. Oh, why had she ever let Jack get her into this mess?

So far she didn't show very much so she should be able to keep her job for a while but what was she going to do when it became obvious? Her mind felt numb with fear and she couldn't think past the day when her mother found out.

Smothering her sigh, she nodded and began to walk as fast as she dare; it had frozen again last night and the pavements were icy. During the worst of the weather, shops and factories had closed, because the electric kept going off and even the schools had shut their doors some days because they were too cold for the children. Alice thought it seemed a little better this morning and she didn't want to spend money on a tram while she could manage the walk, because she would need all her money once her condition left her homeless and without a job.

'Alice,' Nan called to her as she entered the home, still hurrying; it had taken her longer to walk to work, because of the slippery pavements. 'I wanted a word with you, please.'

'Yes, Nan?' Alice paused, the breath catching in her throat because she was always aware that she was here on probation. One false move and Sister Beatrice would send her packing. 'Do you need me to do something?'

'One of the children in room five was sick all over her bed this morning. I think there must be a bug going round. I've been busy since I got here and I haven't had time to clear it up. Can you change all the sheets and covers and take them to the dirty laundry room, please?'

'Yes, of course,' Alice said, relieved that it was just a straightforward request to clean up a bed. 'I'll be glad to.'

'Make sure to wash your hands afterwards. We don't want you to go down with the sickness, Alice. I've enough trouble with the kitchen staff. Muriel was complaining of feeling a bit under the weather first thing. If she goes off sick I'll be left with all the cooking.'

'I don't mind working a bit longer today,' Alice volunteered. 'I don't need a lunch break, just a cup of tea.'

'You need to keep your strength up,' Nan said, looking at her with concern. 'You've been a bit pasty recently, Alice. You're not sickening for anything yourself?'

'No, I'm all right, thanks,' Alice replied more cheerfully than she felt. 'If you need me to stay on, just ask.'

'You're a good girl, Alice.' Nan hesitated, then, 'It was a pity about what happened to your boyfriend, Alice – though perhaps you're better off without his sort.'

Alice didn't answer. Any girl in her position wanted to be married and respectable. Alice knew that once her condition became known people would turn their backs on her and whisper about her. Girls who went with men before marriage were not considered decent where she came from. You might be poor and you might have to mend your stockings and the holes in your clothes, but you kept yourself decent if you wanted to hold your head up high. Alice had broken the code when she'd let Jack make love to her and she was going to have to pay for it soon enough.

As she turned away, Nan touched her arm. 'If you're ever in trouble, Alice, come to me. I'm sure I can find a way to help . . .'

Alice stared after her. How could Nan know that she was in trouble? Of course she couldn't – surely there was no way anyone could guess her secret yet?

ELEVEN

The old house was silent apart from the whispering of the wind in the eaves and the occasional soft tread of a carer's footstep as she passed their room. Someone had looked in about ten minutes earlier, which was what had woken Nancy, and then she'd heard her brother whimpering in his sleep and the words he muttered sent chills down her spine. No one else must ever hear what he was saying or they would both be in terrible trouble.

'Listen to me, Terry,' Nancy said, leaning down to whisper close to his ear. 'You've got to behave, because if you don't they might try to separate us again. You'll be taken somewhere they put bad boys – no, you're not bad, but they'll think you are if you say things like that – and they might lock us away in prison. You don't want that, do you? You mustn't ask who locked the door . . . if you do they might put us both in prison.'

Terry clutched at her hand, his dark eyes wide and fearful as he gazed up at her. 'I don't want to say, Nance, but the dreams keep coming. I'm frightened that he'll come after me again. Next time he'll kill me . . .'

'Pa won't hurt you no more,' Nancy said, reaching out to smooth his dark curly hair back from his forehead. He felt damp to her touch, because he'd been sweating. The nightmares kept on returning and then he woke screaming, his body drenched. 'I told you, he died in that fire. Him and Ma . . .'

'I didn't want Ma to die.' Terry's eyes spilled their tears. 'What happened, Nance? I can't remember when I'm awake but – I dream terrible things, hear them screaming but the door is on fire and it's locked. I can't get to Ma in my dream – I can't get her out . . .'

'Hush, now,' Nancy said, and stroked his face gently. He was so terrified of his father's cruelty; it was better if he didn't remember what had happened. 'It was Pa's fault. He was drunk when they came back that night and so was Ma. He left his jacket on the chair and I took the keys and unlocked your door. I gave you some bread and dripping and a drink of tea and then – I left you to go back to sleep while I cleared up the kitchen. They had made such a mess . . . Pa was sick all over the floor. He shouldn't have drunk so much and then it might not have happened.'

'Pa beat me again, didn't he?' Terry clung to his sister's hand. 'He was bad, Nance – what he done to you. He deserved it but Ma didn't deserve to die – why didn't she come out?'

'Stop thinking about it,' Nancy ordered. The door had been blazing and she'd known it was too late when she saw how fierce the fire was and him standing there staring at it. 'You have to forget it, Terry. Ma should have left him and taken us with her years ago.'

'Are you angry?' Terry asked, looking at her strangely.

102

'You're not angry with me? I was just standing there in the hall and then you grabbed me and pulled me down the stairs and we ran away . . .'

'You didn't do anything wrong.' Nancy gave him a little shake. 'Listen to me, Terry; this is important. You were in your room until I came and got you out of bed. What happened wasn't your fault. Remember that if the police ask questions.'

Terry was shaking all over. 'Why should they ask questions, Nance? We didn't do nothing wrong, did we? Did I do something bad, Nance?'

'No, you didn't,' Nancy said, her fingers digging into his shoulders as she shook him again. 'Just remember, you were asleep until I grabbed you out of bed and shoved you down the stairs. Your dreams are just nightmares – you stopped on the landing and looked at the door. It was a sheet of flames and you just stared at it and then you screamed for Ma, but there was nothing we could do. Pa locked us out. It was his fault, that's all you have to remember.'

'I didn't do anything bad?'

'No, love,' Nancy said, and held him in her arms, kissing the top of his head. He smelled clean and decent and she loved him. He didn't carry the foul stink of a man that clung to Pa: sweat and beer and other things that made her shudder.

'Nance, you won't ever leave me? You won't ever go away? I'm afraid of the dreams – afraid of what I see; afraid they might be true next time.'

'It's only because of the shock,' Nancy said. 'That doctor with the funny name said you were traumatised. I think that means you don't know what's happening – all those things you think happened are just bad dreams. Pa used to hit us, but that's all.' She smiled at him. 'I'm your own Nance, ain't I? And I'm never going to leave you. I shall always look after you – just as you looked after me.'

'Did I look after you, Nance? What did I do?'

'You stopped Pa hurting me,' she said. 'You kicked and punched him and that's why he went mad and beat you with his belt. He sent you to bed with no supper and said he'd deal with you in the morning.'

'What was he doing to you, Nance? I heard you crying lots of nights – but I can't remember what he did . . .'

'That's because it wasn't important. He just hit me, the way he hit you and Ma – there was nothing else. You forget about it. We're all right here for the moment, but you have to be good. Sally, she's the nice one who came and brought us some sandwiches and talked to us today – and Miss Angela. They're friends, Terry. You mustn't pull the head off that teddy bear again or they will think something is wrong.'

'All right. I'm sorry, Nance. I was just angry because my bear was lost in the fire and I couldn't remember what happened . . .'

'I should've brought Bear but there was no time. I'm sorry, love – but you must try, please, for both our sakes. I want to stay here, 'cos some places they might send us are terrible – worse than being at home with Pa.'

'I'll do what you say, Nance – as long as they don't part us. I can't be alone at night or the dreams will come true, I know they will.'

'No, they won't, because they can't; it's all over now,' she soothed. 'Now, I'm going to go down to the kitchen and ask for a hot drink for us both. Nan said that was what I should do if we woke in the night. She said some-one would be about, because there are nurses and carers on duty all night – but you mustn't be frightened. You mustn't scream or call out. I shall come back. I promise I'll always come back for you, Terry. They can't part us for ever.'

Unless the police thought they'd planned it together and then they might put Terry in a mental institution and Nancy in prison.

'All right,' Terry said. 'Go on then; I'm awake now. It's only when I'm asleep that the dreams come.'

'I know, but they will fade in time,' Nancy said. 'I miss Ma too – but Pa was bad. He deserved what he got – you're not to blame, love.' Their parents wouldn't have known anything about what was going on, because the smoke would've killed them long before the fire touched them. Nancy couldn't be certain how it had started, though she had a terrible suspicion that her brother might have had something to do with it. No, she wouldn't let herself think it; her father had been drunk and he must have knocked the oil lamp over, mustn't he? It had all been so quick and nothing was clear in her mind.

'Just forget it, my love. We mustn't think about it any more.'

Terry nodded; his eyes were wide and frightened even now. Nancy squeezed his hand and then left him to look for the hot drink she'd promised. He wasn't the only one to have bad dreams; it was just that hers were with her all the time, waking and sleeping, but she could control them, could stop herself crying out things, and he couldn't.

Nancy knew that she had to be careful. It was easy to make a mistake and say too much. She'd let her guard down with Miss Angela and she thought the woman might have guessed her secret – a part of her secret, but not the dangerous bit. Their lives depended on people believing her story. If they knew what Pa had done to her they might suspect she'd intended him to die and then . . . no, she had to keep it all inside.

It *was* Pa's fault that he and Ma had died in the fire, though Nancy's guilt over her mother was sometimes unbearable – but Pa was evil. He'd abused and ill-treated them all. He deserved to be dead and Nancy was never going to cry for him. She'd cried for Ma at first, but now she cared only about her brother. It was her duty to protect him from – whatever came along. Her eyes were burning with the need to weep, but she forced herself to keep the pain, the grief and the shame inside herself. She could never tell anyone the real truth as long as she lived . . .

TWELVE

'You must promise to have tea with me every day, at least until you get your room back,' Beatrice said when Nan came to visit her the next morning. 'I told you that you would have your own sitting room when I took over here – and I feel guilty about turning you out for that pair.'

'Don't make a fuss, Beatrice.' Nan smiled comfortably. 'We have a perfectly adequate staff room I can share and I like chatting to the younger ones. I've known you too many years to make a fuss over something like this – besides, what else could you have done?'

'I should have insisted on splitting them up, as they ought to be. It isn't natural for a girl of that age to be sleeping in the same room as her brother.'

'I dare say there are thousands of them sleeping top to toe all over the country. Most families cannot afford the luxury of separate beds for the children, let alone separate rooms. My mother had five children and two bedrooms; we kids had to crowd into one room, but at least we were all girls. Two of my sisters died of scarlet fever when they were eleven and ten, and my eldest sister caught diphtheria when she worked at the Infirmary and died of it when she was seventeen. There's only Geraldine and me left now and she lives down in Dorset. Apart from a Christmas card, I haven't heard from her in years – but I don't think our upbringing did us any harm.'

'I know you're right. In a perfect world – but I doubt we shall ever have that, Nan.'

'Perhaps one day things will change. They will build lots of lovely houses with electric, modern bathrooms and enough bedrooms for a family . . .'

'And if they do a lot of the tenants won't be able to afford the rent, unless the Government pays out money to keep them.' Beatrice smiled wryly. 'How are you anyway? Have you heard anything positive from Maisie?'

'No,' Nan sighed. 'We don't have much luck, you and I, do we?'

'Not with our private lives. You should go down there – insist on talking to her. She's your child, Nan, and you have a right to at least talk to her.'

'I tried that last year and the Abbess told me I was wasting my time. She was very kind and understanding, but said Maisie needed privacy to recover and heal – but she didn't call her by her name, of course. She's known as Mary there.'

'You've never known why she suddenly took it into her head to go off and enter a convent?'

'She didn't speak to me for years after I found her living rough with those tramps under the arches, but on her eighteenth birthday she told me that she had to find peace, and that she had to be away from me. I've never understood why she blamed me for what that brute did to her.' Nan closed her eyes in remembered grief. 'I can't believe I was such a fool – but he was kind to us and I was missing Sam.'

'You shouldn't take all the blame, Nan. Why didn't Maisie tell you when it began? She knew it was wrong, but she didn't give you a chance to help her.'

'Perhaps she tried and I didn't listen. I remember being tired and feeling unwell a lot back then. I suppose I was lost in my grief over Sam and Archie.' Nan shook her head. 'I shouldn't talk about it, it only upsets me.'

'My fault. I know how you feel – but if I had a chance to make amends . . . It is too late for me, Nan, but not for you. Don't ever give up. Maisie is alive and one day she might need you again. I needed the protection of the convent when I made my vows and I dare say Maisie did too, but she is very young. You should let her know that she can return to her home if she needs to. Not every nun remains a nun for the rest of her life. There is a chance that Maisie will change her mind one day.'

'I only wish I could believe that,' Nan said, 'but I don't think she will ever leave that place now.'

'I'm sorry. I know how it feels to lose those you love, but perhaps there is still hope. You are still young enough to find happiness again, Nan.'

Nan shrugged and then smiled a little sadly. 'I travelled with that old soldier again this morning. He invited me to have tea with him one day.'

'Shall you go?' Beatrice asked. 'He sounds rather pleasant?'

'Yes, he is in his way. Very polite, always carrying too much and dropping things, but he asked me to meet him for tea now and then and I just might. It's nice to have a few friends.'

'Yes.' Beatrice placed her hands together in a steeple position. 'Your friendship means a lot to me, Nan – of course I have my sisters at the convent, but it is not quite the same.'

'No, I imagine not,' Nan said for she had never understood why Beatrice had chosen to become a nun, although she did know something terrible had happened to her friend before they met.

After Nan left, Beatrice took a look at the two new cases of flu that had been brought to the isolation ward the previous evening. Five of them in one ward was a bit of a squeeze and she would be glad when the new wing was ready. The builders had promised it would be finished by January, but the last time she'd looked inside there still looked to be a lot to do and they were nearly into February.

'How is Sarah this morning?' she asked as Carole returned to the desk. 'I can't see her notes.'

'I left them on the end of her bed. I'm taking her temperature every hour or so and recording it, because she's still very unwell. The other two that went down at the same time are much better, but because of her history of a weak chest she can't shrug it off as quickly as they others.'

'I'll have a look at her,' Beatrice said, and went to the sick girl's bed. She was right at the end of the ward.

Going inside the drawn curtains, Beatrice saw the girl was lying with her eyes closed and looking very pale and still. She moved closer and took her pulse, frowning as she discovered it was very weak. According to the chart at the bottom of the bed, Staff Nurse Carole, and Michelle during the night, had monitored her and done all they could to lower her temperature, but her hair was damp and Beatrice felt very worried. Perhaps the girl should be in hospital.

After speaking to Sarah and receiving no answer, Beatrice decided the time had come for another opinion. She left the bedside, intending to telephone from her office, but as she emerged from the ward she almost bumped into Mr Markham. He was an eminent surgeon, and also wrote remedial books for backward or abused children. He volunteered frequently at the home. Strictly speaking, he wasn't their GP, but she needed a doctor's advice immediately.

'Mr Markham, I wonder if you would take a look at Sarah Morgan? I'm a bit anxious and I was about to send for Dr Price, but as you're here . . .'

'Yes, of course. How long has she been like this?'

'Ten days or so . . . but it isn't the flu, it's just congestion.'

Beatrice led him back inside the ward, indicating the curtains. Mr Markham entered the enclosed area and looked at the young girl's flushed face. He took her pulse and then opened his case and pulled out his stethoscope, which he blew on to warm before placing it against the girl's chest beneath the neck of her night-gown. Sarah moaned and opened her eyes.

'Feeling pretty groggy, are we, Sarah?' he asked, and she nodded. 'Can I just have a listen at the back now?' He leaned her gently on her side and placed the instrument on her back.

111

After a moment or two he withdrew it and Beatrice made the girl comfortable again, looking at him anxiously.

'Well, Sarah, I'm going to recommend a very nasty medicine for you, young lady, and you must drink it all down – we don't want that big giant coming to carry you off to his dungeon, do we?'

His little joke raised a smile, because all the children knew his gruesome stories about giants and the big hairy spider.

'Will you come and rescue me?' Sarah asked weakly.

'I'm sure Sister will be a match for the giant if he comes.' Mr Markham winked at her. 'Well, Sister, I'm going to write you a prescription, which may be a little stronger than you would normally use – but I think it will help.'

He left the curtained area and smiled at Beatrice. 'She is still weak from the illness, and her chest is a bit congested. Her heart is strong enough, but sluggish, the beat slow; I think this will help her to feel better.' He took a pad from his case and scribbled something just about legible, handing it to Beatrice. 'I don't believe she needs hospital treatment; however, you were right to ask.'

'Thank you. I was in two minds but didn't want to send her into hospital if it wasn't necessary. It's nice to have a doctor's opinion sometimes, though in general I trust my nurses.'

'And so you should. I've seen many hospital wards that could learn something from you and your staff, Sister. Now, I'll just have a word with the others and then I'll be off.'

Beatrice thanked him, feeling surprised. It wasn't often that a man in his position handed out such praise and she was feeling lighter of spirit when she returned to her office. She had just decided to make herself a cup of tea when someone knocked at the door.

'Come in,' she said. 'Oh, Angela, good, I'm glad you've come. I was going to ask you if you will take this to the chemist straight away. Mr Markham wrote this up for Sarah Morgan.'

'Yes, of course. I'll go now – after I've shown you this . . . I'm afraid we've gone into the red again last month.'

'Yes. Part of it was the new locks on the cellar and the windows – and there always seems to be something we have to replace. It was sheets this time, I think.'

'I see.' Angela frowned. 'Yes, it's never ending. I'll make a note. I dare say we can take the extra from the money raised before Christmas.'

'That money is for the children's treats but we had to have that security work done after Arthur Baggins broke in and threatened to set the place on fire. At least the paraffin is no longer stored here – or only one can in the garden shed.'

'I'm sure we're safe enough now,' Angela said. 'No one else would dream of trying to burn the home down, Sister.'

'I hope you're right. It's a nuisance that we've gone over budget again but the money never seems quite enough.'

'Because we're always taking more children, and they all need clothes, shoes and food,' Angela said practically. 'I'll make a note of the rising prices in the monthly

113

report. The Board should grant you what is needed, not expect you to manage on the same money when we are forever taking in more children.'

'I dare say they do as much as they can. We have to remember that the charity set this up as a response to the increasing number of children left homeless because of the war, and they have limited funds.'

'It isn't just the casualties from the war these days; there are always going to be children from the slums and families who are down on their luck. Illness, accident and poverty are the three main enemies and they don't go away just because the war is over. Besides, we are not entirely a charity now; we do have some Government funding.'

'Yes, I know that, but a grant of five hundred pounds a year doesn't go far amongst so many children.'

Beatrice didn't need a lecture from Angela. She was well aware of how vital St Saviour's was, and that they now had Government funding for the new wing – but where was the extra money coming from for the next influx of children?

'I'll make it plain we need at least another hundred pounds a month,' Angela said. 'We can't do miracles, Sister, and you shouldn't be worried about it.'

'Yes, but that will not make the Bishop happy . . .'

'Happy or not, the money has to be found. I shall have to have another jumble sale.'

THIRTEEN

Angela poured more wine into Mark's glass; he'd finished his first drink, though she'd hardly touched her own. She smiled as she saw that he'd chosen the most comfortable of her armchairs and was stretched out with his feet up on a little stool, his eyes closed. He looked tired and, noticing a sprinkling of silver at his temples, she felt a surge of affection, because he was such a good friend. She knew he worked all hours, giving so much of his valuable time free to good causes.

Angela was aware he took his work seriously and he was regarded as a very dedicated and brilliant man, who more often than not got results. She knew how good he was with the damaged children they had at St Saviour's and now and then she was able to see an improvement in the behaviour or attitude of the individual child.

Her anger with him for not telling her of her mother's illness had faded now and she felt something flicker inside her, a need to touch him and to be close to him that made her draw her breath and wonder. She'd been aware of a growing need for physical contact for a while now, and yet guilt held her back. How could she think of caring for another man after the way John had died fighting for his country, to keep people like Angela safe?

Mark opened his eyes as she placed the glass of wine on the small occasional table beside him and smiled at her apologetically.

'It was a long day,' he explained. 'I was called into the hospital to see a child who was behaving violently at three this morning.' He sipped his wine. 'Did you see the paper today? There are riots in India, because of the assassination of Mahatma Gandhi . . .

'Yes, it was a terrible thing to happen,' Angela agreed. 'I expect his people will feel his loss . . . Oh, don't let's talk about it. I had hoped things would settle down once the war ended, but it seems as if there's always trouble somewhere; Palestine is in turmoil and now India.'

'Yes, I'm afraid that's the way of things,' Mark said heavily. 'This country has been through hell. I'm glad to see some signs of rebuilding now, anyway. It's going to take years to get London back to what it was before the bombing.'

'Yes,' Angela agreed, 'it still gives me the shivers to walk past the piles of rubble and remember that people once lived there.

'Man's inhumanity to man is sometimes impossible to understand,' Mark said. 'I think we just have to be glad we survived and lick our wounds.'

'Hitler's bombs cleared away some of the worst of the slums in London,' Angela said, 'so perhaps some good will come out of it. We have to hope that the rebuilding is better than what came down. I visited Nan at her prefab last week; she loves it, but it wouldn't suit me. I wonder what the city will be like in twenty or thirty years.'

'I doubt we shall know it,' Mark said, raising his thick dark brows. 'You told me you were worried about Nancy when we spoke last week – are you still as worried?'

'Yes, I am worried, Mark. Nancy said something to me soon after she was admitted. I think it was a slip of the tongue, and it wasn't much, more the look on her face. I didn't know who to tell. Sister Beatrice would probably call in the police and then I think Nancy would just close up and refuse to speak . . .'

'What did she say that worried you?'

'Terry had been screaming and she was going to get in bed with him to comfort him. I suggested she shouldn't let the day staff see her in case they thought it wasn't right for her to sleep with her brother and she said: "Terry isn't like Pa. He won't hurt me." Or something to that effect. It wasn't the words, but the look in her eyes . . . I think her father interfered with her.'

'Yes, not much to go on. It *is* a look in the eyes that often gives them away.' Mark sipped his wine again, seeming thoughtful. 'I think I agree with you, Angela. You shouldn't tell Sister Beatrice yet, because she would think it her duty to inform the police. The last thing those children need is a constable probing into their lives. Nancy seems in control on the outside, but I noticed she is wary of saying too much, and is probably hiding something. Terry is too traumatised to know what really happened. He's frightened, I know that much. Getting to the bottom of it will be a long process.'

117

'Her father is dead, but does she need help, Mark? If she has had to suffer in such a way, perhaps on a regular basis, she'll be very damaged. Is there anything we can do?'

'Well, a lot of abused children do keep it inside for years. Sometimes it comes out when they're older and they repeat the same behaviour with their own children . . . it's like a sickness in some of them, but of course others manage to overcome it and go on to lead fairly normal lives. It's better if they are helped to understand that they didn't do anything wrong and are believed and listened to. A lot of victims are told they are liars or believe that it was their fault . . . they've been told they're wicked and that they brought their punishment on themselves.'

'They ought to hang the people who do this,' Angela said, rage making her want to strike out. 'I feel as if I want to scream when things like this happen, Mark, but I know I can't do anything. In this particular case it seems as if their father has been punished for what he did.'

'Yes, perhaps.' A dark look clouded his features. 'Though I'm not sure it is the result of divine justice in this case.'

Angela felt a chill creep up her spine. 'What do you mean, Mark? Are you thinking what I'm thinking?'

'It depends on what you're thinking,' he said grimly.

'I sensed something not quite right with her story about the fire . . .'

'Do you want to tell me?'

'Well, the police version was that she got her brother out of bed – but she said he was standing staring at the bedroom door, which was on fire . . .'

'Yes, I see. Nancy has had time to get her story straight now. Now she says that she got her brother out of his bedroom and then down the stairs. He stopped to stare at their parents' room, but because the fire was too hot they couldn't get near and she had to drag him away – and she says her father always locked the door to keep them out.'

'That makes sense. Terry might be shocked and call out to his mother but . . .' She shook her head. 'I had the feeling she hated her father – and if she's been abused that is only natural.'

'Enough to burn both parents in their beds?' Mark mused thoughtfully. 'A child would have to be very disturbed to do that, I think.' He sighed. 'All of this is speculation, Angela. Unless Nancy confides in one of us, or Terry blurts the truth out, we may never know. It's the shame factor, you see. Too often the victim is made to carry the shame, rather than the perpetrator. I'm not sure we would like the truth if we did know it all. The details are sometimes hard to take, even for me.'

'But for their sakes, shouldn't we try to discover what really happened? Nancy – Terry too – has been damaged by a violent father . . .'

'What I do for the children is not a precise science, Angela. They are not adults. We cannot expect them to think like adults, and both of them are frightened. It could well be simply the fire and the trauma of losing their parents – but we now both have a sense of something simmering beneath the surface, and it worries me. Just be careful of Terry and of the girl. They may be even more disturbed than we think.'

Angela felt cold all over, thinking about her teddy

119

bear and Nancy's secretive nature. 'They aren't dangerous, are they? We have to think of the other children, Mark.'

'There aren't many suitable places for mentally unstable children, Angela. To incarcerate one or both in a mental institution would be a terrible undertaking. However, you may rest assured that if I think either of them is dangerous, I *shall* have them moved. For now, it is best that they are kept together.' Mark gave her a straight look. 'Don't try to talk to Nancy about the fire – or her father's abuse. She might become violent to protect herself and her brother. If she wants to talk, let her, but don't force anything – for now they need to feel safe and to be given time, but just tread carefully, Angela.'

'This is awful, Mark.' Angela felt shocked. 'Until I went to St Saviour's I had no idea that things like this happened on a regular basis.'

Mark looked regretful. 'Did I do you a bad turn by getting you the job, Angela?'

'No, of course not. It has given me something to live for, Mark. I love my work – but cruelty and abuse make me so angry. I wish I could do more – stamp out this wickedness.'

'I know; it's enough to make grown men cry.' He gave Angela a bleak smile and finished his wine. 'We all wish we could sweep such evil out of the door for good, Angela, love, but all we can do is to try and pick up the pieces. Just now and then, if we can prove abuse, the guilty are punished.'

'Oh, Mark.' Angela's eyes stung with tears. 'You're such a wonderful man. You just get on and do your job and none of us knows . . . it must affect you too?'

'Yes, at times,' he agreed. 'It's not always easy. Like

I said, tread carefully, Angela. If you notice anything don't hesitate to telephone me, but don't try to handle it yourself. I may be completely wrong, of course, and they will get over the fire and be normal happy kids. I'm hoping it won't be necessary to mention it to Sister Beatrice just yet.'

'Let's hope so,' Angela said. 'Would you like some more wine? Or something to eat? I have a couple of steaks and salad in the refrigerator. I suddenly feel starving!'

'Wonderful! Why don't we prepare supper together?' he asked. 'I've had enough of work for one evening. I'd just like to enjoy your company.'

'I didn't know you could cook, Mark?' she teased.

'Living alone it is a matter of survival – but I'm better at salads so I'll leave the steak to you. Make mine a medium rare.'

'Yes, I know,' she said. 'I've not been blind when we've been out, Mark.' Angela went through to the kitchen, followed by Mark and they set about preparing their supper, chatting about lighter things.

'I called round on Wednesday night as a matter of fact; you were out.'

'Yes, I went to dinner with Nick Hadden; we go out most weeks.' Mention of Nick made Angela a little uncomfortable. Nick was just a friend, but she still felt the need to explain. 'He's a lawyer, as you know. I get on quite well with him; he's a friend of my father's . . .'

'Anything serious?' Mark asked as he rummaged around in the refrigerator for the salad vegetables.

'Oh, no. I'm not looking for romance in my life – just friendship. For the moment I'm more interested in the children and what I can do for them.'

Even as she spoke the words Angela knew that she was not sure they were completely true.

'I'm glad you've found something that makes you happy,' Mark said as he took the items from the fridge. 'You won't forget me when you do start looking around, will you, Angela?'

Their eyes met briefly, but Angela looked quickly away. 'No, of course not,' she said, but felt a tingle at the nape of her neck. She felt that Mark wanted something more from her than friendship and support but she wasn't being fair to him if she could never really love another man again – it would be wrong to encourage him. 'But I'm not sure I ever will . . .'

'The future is a long time,' Mark said, with one of his winning smiles and Angela found it impossible not to return it. 'I'm looking forward to this.' He turned away and began to chop the salad. 'It's not often you manage to find a decent steak these days.'

FOURTEEN

'Well, what do you think of Angela's idea?'

Father Joe blinked at Sister Beatrice, aware that he'd been guilty of not listening. 'I'm sorry, Sister – what were you saying? I had something on my mind . . . just a Church matter, nothing important.'

'This musical show she is thinking of putting on at the church hall to raise funds. I was asking if you would be prepared to help. You were so good at Christmas with the carol service and I should like you to keep an eye on things,' Sister Beatrice said. 'She means well, but . . . I'm not sure that this show is a good idea. Some of the songs today can be vulgar, don't you think?'

Father Joe kept his amusement to himself. He knew exactly what the Sister was thinking, but he had no fears that Angela would include anything faintly immoral or even racy in her show. However, the idea of the show appealed to him, because of that soft spot he had inside for the beautiful young widow.

'I wouldn't mind helping out with the songs,' he said. 'You know I'm always willing to lend a hand. Now, what about those children you're concerned for? Are they Catholic?'

'I don't know. I shouldn't think so, but I should like you to have a talk to them just in case. The girl seems fine, except that she is over-protective of her brother – but the boy is difficult. He has nightmares and has wet the bed a few times, which many of them do, but we know that bed-wetting often hides something more serious. Mark Adderbury says Terry is very disturbed by the fire and the death of his parents, but I'm not sure it isn't just wilfulness on the girl's part – because she doesn't want to give up responsibility for her brother. If you just went in to visit sometimes . . . keep an eye on him.'

'Of course. I'm always willing to do that, Sister. Adderbury is a good man. I should trust his instincts if I were you.'

'I do, of course I do – but you have so much experience dealing with troublesome children. You've devoted your life to them.'

'I'll visit them this morning. If the boy trusts me he might tell me what is troubling him, but I can't promise anything.' He patted her hand.

He smiled to himself as he saw Sister's slight frown at his familiarity. Joe was well aware that he was taking a liberty, but he understood Sister's calm, practical and slightly stern manner covered up a great deal of tenderness and pity, and her feelings for the children ran deep.

'You think they may have been treated extremely badly, don't you?'

Her eyes met his frankly. 'I fear it, yes. The boy had obvious signs of a beating, but the girl . . . there's something very defensive about her. She closes up whenever

124

I speak to her, but my gut feeling is that she has been sorely mistreated.'

'And if they have, what then?'

'In most cases it would be up to the police, but this time . . . well, I would rather avoid that for the moment. I want to help them, not cause them more harm. I have to be alert to a problem, because the safety and care of all my children might depend on it. If Billy Baggins' brother had set this place on fire . . .' A shudder ran through her. 'Well, it doesn't bear thinking about. I misjudged Billy, thought he was a troublemaker and I was wrong. This time I have to be sure. I thought he might trust you . . .'

'I have the knack with some of them,' Joe said. 'I'll not do anything that would harm him.'

'I've always known that,' she said, and smiled. 'You're a good friend, Joe, and a good man.'

'I'll be away and see what young Terry has to say for himself,' he said, and smiled as he rose to his feet.

FIFTEEN

Alice came in from the yard that morning, still tasting the bitterness of the vomit in her mouth. She went to the sink and ran the tap, filling her glass and sipping it to take away the awful taste. Her mother was standing behind her when she turned, red work-worn hands on hips as she glared at Alice.

'What's the matter with you, girl?' she demanded. 'Don't tell me it's a bug you picked up at work, because I'll not believe it. I want the truth – you're up the duff, ain't yer?'

Alice knew there was no point in lying. She was putting on weight and in a few weeks her clothes would be too tight and need the seams letting out. Her mother would notice then even if she hadn't already.

'Yes, I am,' she admitted, feeling the hot tide of shame wash into her cheeks. 'I shan't lie to you, Ma – he promised to marry me but then he cleared off and I haven't heard from him.'

Her mother's hand snaked out, hitting her three times in succession across her face, the first blow cutting her bottom lip. 'Yer filthy little slut,' she cried. 'What kind of a girl are yer? Bringing shame home to yer family like this – how could yer!'

'It wasn't supposed to be this way,' Alice said, crying as the blows rained down on her. She took them without fighting back because she was ashamed and thought her mother had a right to punish her. 'Jack was going to take me away and we were to have married but he had to leave town in a hurry and I think he might have died in that factory fire . . .'

'Don't make excuses, girl. You knew what yer were doin'.' Her mother looked at her in disgust. 'Well, you go out of this house this mornin' and you'll not come back while I'm breathin'. You can pack yer things and think yerself lucky I let yer take anythin' . . .'

'Ma . . .' Alice caught her breath, staring at her mother in dismay. 'Please, don't throw me out yet. At least let me stay until I find somewhere to live – please.'

'Yer don't deserve I should let yer take yer clothes, let alone give yer a bed for another night. You're a filthy slut, Alice Cobb, and I want yer out now – before yer father realises what a viper he's harboured in his house.'

'Ma . . .' Alice's eyes stung with tears. She turned away from the harsh look on her mother's face and went through to the next room. She pulled a battered old case from beneath the bed and placed it on top before proceeding to empty her possessions from the chest of drawers she'd shared with Mavis. Her sister came in as she was trying to cram everything she owned into the case.

'What are you doin', Alice?'

'Ma knows,' Alice said, and sniffed. 'She's thrown me

127

out and I've got to take all I can because she won't have me back.'

'She can't do that. What will happen to you, Alice?' She flung her arms about her. 'I don't want yer to leave, love.'

'She won't let me stay,' Alice said, unable to stop the tears and be brave for her sister's sake. 'I can't take all my things. You have them, Mave. Don't let her sell them . . .'

'I'll bring them to you,' her sister promised. 'Let me know as soon as you're settled and I'll bring them round to you.'

'She won't let you if she knows. She'll forbid you to visit me.'

'She can say what she likes,' Mavis said stubbornly. 'I shall visit when I like and I'll help as much as I can.' She caught a sob in her throat. 'I'm goin' ter ask Dad tonight if I can get married. I shan't stay here now she's thrown you out. If he won't sign for me to wed my lad I'll run away . . .'

Alice hugged her tightly. 'You mustn't be silly, Mave,' she said. 'I want to see you, you know I do – but don't cut yourself off from everyone for my sake. She'll calm down in the end, but you must be careful. Wait for a while before you speak to Dad; he's goin' to be angry too when he finds out who it was . . .'

'I know.' Mavis looked at her sadly. 'Anyone but Jack – and Dad would've made him marry you.'

'If it had been Bob's child he wouldn't have needed to be forced into it,' Alice said. 'Jack told me he loved me. He promised me he would come back for me but it's been ages now and I haven't heard a word.'

'Surely you know he died in the fire?' Mavis said, looking at her sadly. 'You can't keep hanging on, fooling yourself that he's still alive, Alice . . .'

'I know, but I can't stop hoping . . .'

Alice broke off as the door opened and their mother entered. She glared at them both and then grabbed Mavis by the arm and thrust her out of the room, even though she struggled and protested.

'I don't want yer contaminatin' yer sister wiv yer filth,' she hissed, her hand connecting with Alice's cheek again. 'You've got enough stuff. Get out and never darken me door again or I'll take a stick to your backside.'

'Don't worry, I'll be glad to go,' Alice said, driven now to retaliation. 'You've made this house a hell on earth, Ma. You've ruined my dad's life and you'll do the same to us all unless . . .'

Alice got no further because her mother flew at her in a rage and started hitting her. She might have killed her had her brother, Saul, not come in at that moment and grabbed at her skirt, pulling her back.

'Leave our Alice alone, Ma,' he said, and screamed as she turned on him. He kicked out at her and she gave a cry that might have been pain or rage. Saul dodged out of the way. 'You go, Alice. The old devil won't hit me again 'cos if she does I'll tell Dad what she's been up to wiv that bloke down the Docks . . .'

As she left the house, Alice heard her mother's yell of rage as she turned on Saul. She could hear the raised voices of Saul and Joseph behind her and then Mavis joined in. For a moment she almost turned back to defend her brothers and sister, but what could she have done? It would only make a bad situation worse for all of them, too. No, there was no going back now. Mavis had a chance of getting out, but Saul and Joe would have to fend for themselves – the boys were stuck for years.

Tears trickled down Alice's cheeks as she walked to the bus stop. She rubbed at her eyes to stop them. The gossips would only have a field day if they saw her. Somehow she had to find a place to live but she didn't even know where to start looking. Alice was terrified, because even though it was hell at home, the alternative was worse – and what would happen when she lost her job, which she was bound to when Sister Beatrice found out? She had a few pounds saved and when that had gone she would either starve or end up in the work-house . . . No, not the workhouse these days; it would be one of those mother and baby homes. They would make her go there if she was destitute and then they'd take her child away from her. Alice felt sick as she contemplated the future, because whichever way she looked it was bleak.

Michelle saw Alice arrive at the home with her case. It was obvious that her friend had been crying and her face had red patches from where she'd been hit hard. She ran to her in concern.

'What's wrong, Alice, love?'

'Ma threw me out,' Alice said, catching back a sob of despair. 'She wouldn't even let me stay until I could find somewhere to live.'

'She knows about the baby?' Michelle whispered in a low voice and saw the answer in Alice's face. 'She hit you?'

Alice nodded, wiping her cheeks with the back of her hand. 'Yes. I had to tell her the truth.'

'What are you going to do?'

'I've no idea,' Alice said, and caught back a sob. 'Do I look awful?'

'Yes, a bit. You'll need to wash your face but the bruises are going to show whatever you do. Someone is bound to notice.'

'I can't tell anyone what happened,' Alice said. 'If Sister knew she'd sack me and I've got to work for as long as I can.'

'Of course,' Michelle agreed. 'Look, I'm going home now as my shift's finished. I'll ask Mum if you can stay for a while. I'll tell her you quarrelled with your mother. She knows what your mum's like, Alice. You can share a room with me but it won't be for very long. My mum is as strict as yours. She wouldn't have you if she thought you'd got into that kind of trouble.'

'Oh, Michelle, I'll only cause trouble for you . . .'

'I'm your friend, Alice. I'll help as much as I can, but Mum mustn't know the truth or she won't have you to stay.'

'I'll think of an excuse,' Alice promised. 'It will only be for a day or so until I find a room somewhere.'

'Have you got any money?'

'I've got a bit saved,' Alice said, and forced herself to smile. 'Jack was generous; he gave me some money to buy things and I didn't spend it all.'

'That's something,' Michelle said, and gave Alice an encouraging smile though she knew the future didn't look good for her friend. 'Look, we'll find a room for you, Alice. I'll do my best – and Bob would help if he knew . . .'

'No, you mustn't tell him or Eric,' Alice said. Alice couldn't ask Bob for help, because it wouldn't be right. She'd had her chance with Bob and ignored it in favour of Jack and now she would just have to put up with the consequences. 'I'll manage, Michelle. It was just the shock of Ma finding out and the way she attacked me.' Alice straightened herself up. She'd got herself into this and she'd just have to face up to it. She returned Michelle's smile with more confidence that she felt. 'I'll be all right, as long as Sister doesn't discover the truth and sack me.'

SIXTEEN

Angela looked at the surprising letter that had just been brought up to her. It seemed that a substantial bequest had been left to St Saviour's by an elderly lady. Apparently, she'd once been nursed by Sister Beatrice at the Infirmary, and because of her kindness the lady had decided to leave all she had to the children's home. The letter had been sent on to Angela from the Bishop for her to deal with in her capacity as the Administrator.

She smiled at the terms of the Bishop's letter, because he'd said that he was confident she would know how to use it to the best advantage of St Saviour's and she felt pleased because it meant that her past efforts had been noted and approved.

She decided to take the letter to Sister Beatrice and tell her about it. The bequest was a generous one. Sister remembered clearly and told her about the elderly lady who had been brought into the Infirmary suffering from pneumonia and had not been expected to live.

'She was stronger than the doctors thought and she fought it off,' Sister Beatrice had told Angela. 'Before she left she thanked me for caring for her and said she would never forget my kindness, though all I did was listen. She was a widow, you see, and both her sons were killed in the first weeks of the war – it was not long before I came here to St Saviour's . . .'

'And she obviously never did forget you,' Angela said. 'Because of what you did, our children will benefit from this wonderful bequest.'

She asked the Warden if she wished to accompany her. However, Sister Beatrice shook her head.

'I have no wish to become involved matters of money, in fact my order forbids it, Angela. I am quite sure we can leave it safely in your hands and I will write to the Bishop and tell him so.'

The Bishop had enclosed the solicitor's letter in his correspondence, which gave the address of the house in South London. A little to her surprise, Angela discovered it was a substantial semi-detached house of red brick with bay windows. Inside, she'd been excited to discover that though most of the furniture was heavy Victorian stuff, and some things worth only a few shillings, there were many small pretty things that she knew would fetch several pounds.

On her return to St Saviour's she'd given the news to Sister Beatrice, who looked pleased.

'You do not think it a waste of your valuable time to undertake the clearance and sale of this property?'

'Not at all,' Angela assured her. 'I shall be able to raise quite a substantial sum from the contents alone. However, I think the house is worth more than the one thousand pounds the solicitor suggested and I shall seek other offers for it.'

Sister Beatrice frowned, then, 'Every penny you can raise is needed, Angela. Please do as you think fit.'

'The terms of the will said the money was for St Saviour's,' Angela replied. 'We might be able to do some of the work you would like done here . . .'

'Indeed, the Lord has provided for us and now the matter is in your hands. You must do as you consider right and just, Angela.'

'I shall arrange for it to be cleared and the property sold as quickly as possible.'

There was no point in wasting time and so she decided to clear the house immediately, and then put it up for sale.

Angela found the man who offered his services and his van for five shillings an hour through a card in the newsagent's window, and discovered that apart from a slight limp caused by an injury he'd received during the war, he was young, strong and very willing. She'd packed all the bits and pieces she thought were worth saving, including some wonderful pre-war linen tablecloths, sheets and table runners she'd found in the drawers upstairs; a little yellow now, but nothing that a good soak in bluebag wouldn't help. There was also a set of silver cutlery that had never been used, some old lace and a few more pieces of jewellery, as well as some very old silk underwear. Downstairs, she'd taken an oak gate-leg table, a couple of Windsor chairs, the pretty needle-work box and lots of small bits and pieces as well as a nursing chair, various boxes, brass and copper items.

First of all she asked Ned to help her load all the things she wanted to keep and then cart them up to her apartment, then she telephoned a dealer in second-hand furniture and asked him to meet her at the house. Ned took her back in the van and she made him a cup of tea while they waited for the dealer to call. When he arrived, twenty minutes late, he was a shifty-eyed man with a thin nose and broken teeth. Angela instinctively felt uneasy and was glad that Ned was with her. The dealer looked in all the rooms and offered ten pounds for the lot.

'Do yer think we're daft, mate?' Ned asked before Angela could answer. 'I know someone who will give us a decent price for this lot. We weren't born yesterday, yer know.'

'I couldn't pay more than twenty at most.'

'Don't choke yerself, mate,' Ned said. 'We want thirty quid cash now or we'll take it to the sale room – I reckon we could get more than double there.'

'Is he selling this stuff or are you?' the irate dealer demanded of Angela. She smiled and nodded at Ned.

'My friend here seems to know what he's doing so I'll let him make the decision.'

'All right, I'll give you thirty, but I want help with loading the stuff on me van now.'

'Keep yer hair on, mate. I'll give yer a hand.' Ned winked at Angela, forcing her to turn away to hide her smile. She'd taken anything she thought of any value, leaving what had looked like pure junk to her, but Ned was certainly worth his five bob an hour, and she told him so after the rather sullen dealer had driven off with his van filled with the kind of old-fashioned furniture that most people would think only fit for the bonfire these days.

Just as they were about to leave, a ring at the front door heralded the estate agent. Angela invited the man in, apologising for the way the house looked.

'I haven't had time to clean it up, I'm afraid.'

'It's all right. I like to see it this way – warts and all.' He grinned at her. 'May I walk round on my own?'

'You're not selling the house too, are you? Only, I know someone who buys properties,' Ned said as the agent wandered away, making notes on his pad.

Angela laughed. 'You know a lot of people, Ned?'

'Well, I clear houses for him, see. Yer get to know people in my business.'

She did a little tidying while the estate agent was making notes. He looked pleased when he returned.

'I think we could market this at twelve to fifteen hundred pounds,' he said. 'Would you like us to put it on our books?'

'I'll think about it and let you know,' Angela said, and showed him out.

'I wouldn't let them sell it for that,' Ned remarked as the door closed behind the man.

'I had a similar estimate from the solicitor. He said a thousand pounds . . . but added that we might have to take a bit less if the structure wasn't sound.'

'Looks sound enough to me,' Ned said. 'My contact bought one of these houses a couple of months ago and he paid eighteen hundred for it. He was chuffed to bits over it, thought he'd got it cheap. Do you want me to telephone him and ask him to take a look?'

'There isn't a phone here . . .' Angela glanced at her watch. 'I have to get back by six. As I said, it isn't my property and I shall be busy all day tomorrow . . .'

'If you give me the key I'll meet him and ask what he thinks about the price.'

Angela hesitated, because it wasn't her house; it

belonged to the charity. Did she know Ned well enough to trust him with the key? She hesitated for a moment and then decided to go with her instinct.

'If you're sure you want the bother?'

'No trouble at all, Mrs Morton. I'll bring the key back to your apartment on Saturday and if you're not there I'll put it through the letterbox. You just leave it to Ned, he'll see you right.'

Sister Beatrice was in the sick ward when Angela took in a tray of drinks for the late-night staff. She told her the good news.

'I cleared all the good things out and I'm going to book the church hall and auction it all for St Saviour's – and for the heavy old stuff I managed to get thirty pounds, at least Ned did. He'd been helping me and he bartered with the dealer, who only wanted to give me ten pounds.'

'The Board will be pleased with thirty pounds, especially at this time of year. As you said, the donations tend to slow up for a while after Christmas.'

'Yes . . . is there anything else I can do tonight?'

'You could bring some more drinks up for the isolation ward, if you will – you know the procedure. Just leave the trolley outside and knock. There's no need for you to go in and perhaps catch it yourself.'

'Yes, I know,' Angela said. It seemed that whatever she did to help, she would never persuade the Sister that she was both sensible and capable.

SEVENTEEN

'Alice.' Nan stopped her as she was on her way to the sick ward with a tray of drinks and biscuits for the children. 'Will you come to the staff room when you've taken that up, please? I wanted a word with you.'

'Yes, of course.'

Alice felt a tingle at her nape. Nan had looked very serious and she wondered if she'd heard rumours. Mavis had brought a bag of clothes and small bits she'd left behind to St Saviour's and Nan had seen her carrying it when she left after work that evening. It was only a matter of time before either Nan or Sister Beatrice noticed that Alice was putting on weight and put two and two together.

She took the drinks to the sick room and knocked at the door. It was opened by Staff Nurse Carole, who glared at her.

'Oh, it's you,' she said. 'Why on earth have you taken so long? Hurry up and put the drinks on the trolley, over there.'

Alice was so flabbergasted that she couldn't think of a retort. There was no pleasing some people, and this nurse turned her nose up at most of the carers, treating them as if they were a bit of dirt on her shoe. Michelle didn't like her and Alice thought she was a snooty bitch, but she daren't say a word. Sister Beatrice would take the word of a nurse over hers every time and besides, she could do without bringing attention to herself right now. Carrying the tray inside, she smiled at the children but kept her mouth shut.

Walking back down to the staff room, Alice's heart was racing. Why did Nan want to speak to her? It was useless to lie if she'd guessed the truth; in a few weeks she would be showing anyway.

Nan had boiled the kettle and turned with a smile as Alice entered.

'Ah, there you are, Alice. I'm making a drink – would you like a tea or coffee?'

'I don't mind, whatever you're having,' Alice said, and sat down nervously. 'Is something wrong, Nan?'

'Possibly, Alice. You haven't looked at all well recently; too pale and tired. Are you going to tell me what's the matter, dear?'

Alice hesitated, then she knew she couldn't hold it back. 'You saw my sister bring me some things yesterday, didn't you? My mother threw me out and I'm staying with Michelle for a little while, until I find a place to live . . .'

'I thought that might be the case. I saw the bruising on your face but we were busy and I didn't get a chance to talk to you. Why did your mother do such an unkind thing, Alice?'

'Because she's ashamed of me . . .' Alice's cheeks flamed, and she couldn't stop herself blurting out the truth. 'I'm pregnant – I'm sorry, Nan.

Nan frowned as she handed Alice a cup of tea. 'Oh, Alice, love. How did you end up in such a pretty pickle?'

'I got involved with a fella, he said he wanted to marry me, but he's gone now and . . . I hope you won't ask me to leave just yet, please. I don't know what I'd do. I know I can't stay on for ever, but just for a while longer.'

'That won't be easy.' Nan's face was etched with concern as she watched Alice sip her tea and saw the bruises blooming on her cheeks; no doubt from her mother's hand. 'Do you feel well enough to carry on?'

'Yes, it's just the sickness in the mornings – but once that is over I'll be all right.'

'Well, I'm very sorry for your trouble, Alice,' Nan said. 'But there's no way around telling Sister Beatrice.'

'Do you really have to tell her?' Alice asked, her throat catching with sudden tears. 'She'll sack me, I know she will.'

'You shouldn't assume that,' Nan said gently. 'I know Sister better than anyone here and I believe she will be more sympathetic than you imagine. The time will come when you will be asked to leave, but perhaps not just yet.'

Alice choked back her emotion. 'I know it was wrong, Nan; I know I've disgraced myself – but if Sister sacks me I shan't have enough money to last me through the birth.'

'We won't desert you in your time of need,' Nan told her earnestly. 'I can promise you that whatever happens both Sister and I will have your best interests at heart. Now dry your eyes, drink your tea and then go and clean Nancy and Terry's room. For some reason, the cleaner just refuses to go in there – she says the boy gives her the creeps.'

'I'll do it for you,' Alice said, determined to grin and bear it. If she made herself invaluable to Nan perhaps Sister would let her stay on until she began to show too much, and maybe by then she would have a plan for the future, though at the moment she was still terrified at the prospect of being a single mother. Everyone would whisper behind her back and call her names, and no respectable landlady would take her in . . .

Terry stared at her as she knocked and then entered the room. He was alone and she guessed that Nancy had left him while she fetched something or visited the bathroom. His eyes narrowed, staring at her oddly, and she understood why Kelly said he gave her the willies, but Alice was made of sterner stuff.

'Hello, Terry,' she said. 'I'm Alice and I've come to change your sheets and clean the room for you – make it smell lovely of lavender polish.'

'We don't want you here,' he muttered sullenly. 'If you don't go away I'll scream.'

'You'll have to scream then,' Alice told him cheerfully. 'I've been given the job of changin' your bed and I'm goin' to do it – why don't you go and sit by the window and look at the garden? There are lots of birds out there to see.'

'I hate birds. Nasty fluttery things – I'd like to kill them all.'

His words sent a chill up her spine. Her brothers were rough, tough little monsters at times but she'd seen Saul pick up a half-dead robin that had been caught by a stray cat and nurse it carefully until it died. Surely Terry didn't mean what he was saying? He was just a scared little boy who was hurting inside and wanted to hit out at everyone in sight.

'I've got some fruit drops in my pocket,' she said. 'Would you like one?'

Terry nodded but didn't answer. Alice took the packet from her pocket and offered it to him. He hesitated, then grabbed the bag and ran from the room, slamming the door behind him.

'What an evil little devil,' Alice said to the door. For two pins she'd have gone after him and given him a clip round the ear, but then she remembered. She was already in trouble and she'd better be careful or she would find herself in the street. 'Good riddance,' she muttered to herself and began to strip the bed.

As soon as she stripped the sheets from Terry's bed she understood why he didn't want anyone to change it. It stank of urine and he'd ripped a hole in the bottom one. Alice sighed as she gathered them up, ready to take to the laundry.

She had just finished cleaning the room when Nancy returned with a tray and two cups of cocoa. She looked for her brother and frowned as she saw he was missing.

'Where did Terry go?'

Alice shrugged. 'I think he didn't want to be here while I cleaned so he just ran off. He'll come back soon enough, I dare say.'

'He's ashamed because he wet the bed again,' Nancy said and looked sad. 'I expect he was rude to you. I'm sorry.'

'Not your fault or his,' Alice said. 'Lots of kids wet

143

the bed. We're used to it, love. Don't you worry. He'll get used to us in time.'

'I hope so,' Nancy said but she still looked sad.

Alice was thoughtful as she left with her arms filled with dirty sheets. So many of the children had terrible lives before they came here and the memory of it haunted them for years. She wasn't the only one with troubles and maybe hers weren't so bad after all. Alice was strong and able to work; even if she got the sack she'd find another job somewhere. She loved her job with the children, but there were plenty of factories and not all of them would bother because she wasn't married; maybe she could get herself a cheap ring and pretend to be a widow. The idea made her feel less frightened. She gritted her teeth as she headed down to the laundry. Yes, she'd get by somehow.

EIGHTEEN

Ned didn't return the key on Saturday as promised, but Angela hardly noticed. She was busy all day preparing food for her guests at her house-warming. Her spare bedroom was filled with the bits and pieces for the auction and she had decided to keep the door firmly shut, because it was rather untidy now.

Once the evening started, her guests began to enjoy themselves and Angela found that she was laughing far more than she had for a long, long time. She'd decided to invite all of her new friends from the home as well as some other new acquaintances. Sally was accompanied by Mr Markham. Mark had come alone, but Carole arrived a few minutes after he did, and Angela couldn't help but notice she seemed glued to his side. Michelle popped in for half an hour on her way to St Saviour's, where she was on duty that evening; Jean brought a rather shy, sandy-haired young man with her, introducing him as her brother, because she'd been told she could bring a friend, and Alice arrived alone at half past eight, having been on the early-evening shift. Nan had declined, because she was working, but Nick

145

Hadden arrived at a quarter to nine, bearing a bottle of sweet white wine and some chocolates.

'I'm sorry to be so late,' he apologised. 'I had an appointment and was kept much longer than I expected.'

'It doesn't matter,' Angela said. 'Lovely wine, Nick. I shall forgive you if you open this and pour me a glass.'

'Your wish is my command,' he said, bowing to her, his eyes sparkling with mischief. 'You know I am your slave, Angela.'

'I know nothing of the sort,' she retorted, but felt the laughter bubbling up inside her. It was a good turnout, with friends from St Saviour's taking up most of the seats. She'd also asked a young couple who had moved into the flat next door recently, Ken Middleton and his wife, Susan. He'd been an officer in the RAF and was now something in the City. Susan didn't work and was expecting her first child, not that it showed. Susan had popped round to invite her for coffee soon after they moved in and told her.

'I'm glad to know you've taken this apartment,' she'd confided in Angela as she sipped her coffee. 'It's nice to have one of your own sort living next door. One never knows these days and I'm a little nervous of being alone when Ken is out – now I know there's someone I can talk to . . .'

'I'm afraid I'm at work most of the time, and I don't always stay at night,' Angela admitted, and saw disapproval in the other woman's eyes. Susan didn't say anything, but it was obvious that she thought women of their class ought not to work.

'Doesn't your husband mind you going out to work? Ken practically forbade me to even think about it. Of course I did volunteer for stuff during the war, but we all did . . .'

'My husband was killed in the war,' Angela replied, managing to keep her voice steady, which was something she couldn't have done a few months ago. 'I needed a job to fill my time.'

Susan went red and hastily apologised, but Angela shook her head. 'You couldn't know, of course. It happened to a lot of us, I'm afraid. I'm not the only one having to make adjustments.'

'No – and it isn't always plain sailing if they do come back,' Susan had told her. 'Ken was a little quiet at first, but he's come out of it – not all of them do. A friend of mine said her husband had changed completely. He has become bad-tempered and dominant – he's moody and different, not like the man she'd married at all.'

Angela wondered if John would have changed if he'd come home at the end of the war. War did change men, and she knew that Susan's friend wasn't the only woman who was finding it hard to cope with the stranger that had returned.

Her gaze drifted across the room to Mark. He was laughing at something Carole was saying to him and seemed to be enjoying the young nurse's company. Angela felt a tightness in her throat, but she told herself that if she didn't want him as a husband herself, she shouldn't resent another woman making a play for him. Perhaps if he'd paid attention to one of the other girls instead . . . she wasn't sure Carole was right for her friend. Instinct told her that the girl was selfish and vain and she felt annoyed with him for falling for Carole's lures. Surely he had the sense to see through her – or was he like a lot of other men, a sucker for that come-on look? She'd thought better of him.

Feeling unaccountably upset, Angela turned and smiled at Nick, who had brought her another glass of her favourite wine.

'That is lovely, Nick. Even better now it has been chilled. I was so lucky to get a refrigerator with this flat. I don't know how the builder got hold of it; they seem like gold dust.'

'One day everyone will have refrigerators,' Nick assured her. 'When this country finally gets back on its feet, life is going to change for the better. Things are beginning to pick up, but we're not there yet by a long way.'

'No, I suppose not,' Angela sighed. 'It's hard to believe the war is over, isn't it? We all thought life would be perfect once it stopped – but we still have to queue for bananas and oranges, and some things are impossible to get hold of – simple things like soap.'

'We're still paying the yanks back for all their help to keep us going through the war. Rationing and short-ages won't get better for a while yet.'

'Oh, you're not droning on about the rations, are you?' Carole asked, coming to join them. 'I hate it when everyone starts complaining. It makes life so miserable – where on earth did all this food come from, Angela? Do you know someone who can get it for you under the counter?'

'No, I certainly do not.' Angela frowned at Carole in consternation, upset at the accusation that she'd got the evening's food on the black market. 'It's mostly game and that isn't on the ration – you just have to think a bit differently . . .'

'Clever girl, aren't you?' Carole's lips veered on a sneer. 'I don't like game – or I thought I didn't.' She sniffed at something on toast, which she had been eating quite happily until she knew what it was.

Nick winked at Angela behind her back. 'Doesn't know a good thing when it's handed to her,' he said as she walked off. 'I wouldn't have thought she was your sort, darling?' He let his hand trail down her bare arm, giving her a smile that seemed to say he thought she belonged to him.

When had he started calling her darling? Angela wasn't sure. She hoped he wouldn't assume that he had any hold over her, just because they had been out together a few times. She enjoyed his company but she certainly wasn't ready to begin a relationship with Nick, or with anybody. Angela cast a wistful look at Mark, because somehow the sight of him flirting with the young nurse made her feel jealous and a little angry – as if he belonged to her.

Of course he didn't and Angela had no right to think anything of the sort. Besides, Mark would want a proper relationship and she couldn't betray John's memory by loving another man – could she? Her mood didn't improve, especially when she saw Mark help Carole on with her coat at the end of the evening, his eyes sparkling as she said something that clearly amused him. He kissed Angela chastely on the cheek as they said their goodnights, and Angela felt sure she saw a look of triumph in Carole's eyes as she left with Mark. Surely Mark wouldn't take her home – what if she invited him in for a nightcap?

Her thoughts were tangled and didn't get any better

when she lay in her bed that night. Just why was she feeling like this? She thumped her pillow and turned over, torn between the hurt he'd inflicted even if it was without realising it, but also jealousy that he could look at Carole in that teasing way. She'd thought that look was just for her. Even the idea that he was looking at someone else that way . . . Angela wasn't sure why but the thought made her want to weep.

'Have you placed the house with an agent yet?' Sister Beatrice enquired when they met on Monday. 'The Bishop is very pleased with it all – and I've been thinking of some jobs that really do need to be done in the cloakrooms.'

'Not yet. I let someone have the key. He's going to show it to his friend and we should get a good deal . . .'

'You've given the key to someone else? I hope you know what you're doing, Angela. That property doesn't belong to you; it is for St Saviour's and I should not like to think you had put it at risk.'

'No, I'm sure Ned will look after it for me,' Angela said, but she couldn't help worrying about it a bit, because Sister was right. It wasn't her property. She would have to call at Ned's home and ask why he hadn't put it through her door as he'd promised.

Ned wasn't there when she went to his house. His mother told her he'd gone out on a job, and she didn't know anything about a key but would send him round as soon as he got home.

Feeling remorseful and disappointed, Angela caught the bus that took her home. She unlocked her door and

150

went in, flicking on the electric light. Immediately, she saw the large brown envelope lying on the floor just inside. It had been slipped underneath the door and shot across the polished wooden boards to come to rest at the edge of a bright cotton rug. As soon as she picked it up, she felt the hardness of the key inside and a wave of relief went over her. She hadn't been taken for a fool after all.

Inside was a letter typed on white paper. It thanked her for showing him the house before putting it on the market, confirmed that he would like to make an offer and was signed, *Harry Brooks*. His offer caused Angela to gasp.

Two thousand three hundred pounds and all lawyer's fees paid!

It was more than twice what the solicitor had advised and Angela burst out laughing. It was such a relief, because she could imagine what Sister Beatrice might have said if she'd put the home's bequest at risk.

NINETEEN

Beatrice glanced up as someone knocked at the door of her office, smiling as Nan entered.

'Nan, did you come for a chat – or is it something important?'

'We've just had a little girl brought in, Beatrice. She has been released from hospital after being treated for appendicitis but has nowhere to go. Her father was killed in the war and her mother has disappeared. She just went off with a man while Betsy was in the hospital.'

'Oh, no, not again,' Beatrice said, her own problems forgotten. 'Don't they realise what it does to the children? Being told that your mother has run off and left you. How old is she?'

'About eight I should say. I haven't read the notes that came with her yet, and she doesn't have much to say.'

Beatrice shook her head. 'Where are we going to put her, Nan?'

'I suggest she takes Sarah Morgan's place in the dorm; Carole says her tonsillitis case is ready to return to her dorm, so that leaves a bed for Sarah in the sick room until she's fully fit again.'

Beatrice frowned, because it was the same old problem. 'Well, I dare say the new building will be ready shortly.'

'Angela's hoping things are coming together. She's going to order the new beds this week,' Nan said cheerfully.

'You seem to have more of a spring in your step recently?' Beatrice arched her brows in enquiry.

'Yes, it's my old soldier. His name is Edward Charles; he remembered to tell me over tea this week – with a little prompting.' Nan chuckled softly. 'He is such a nice man, Beatrice. I didn't think I would ever trust a man again after what happened to my daughter . . . but Eddie makes me remember what life used to be like years ago, so perhaps I'm softening. He's got that old-fashioned courtesy that seems to have got lost these days – and he's very kind. I've invited him to have dinner with me next Sunday.'

'Well, you've been out to tea with him several times now, haven't you?'

Nan smiled happily. 'Yes. We're becoming good friends.'

'I'm glad you've found a friend,' Beatrice said.

Nan nodded in agreement and then hesitated. 'There is something else, Beatrice. I'm afraid you will not like it, but I hope you will deal with the girl as gently as possible. She is one of my best girls and I don't think this was all her fault.'

Beatrice looked at her through narrowed eyes. 'Who are you talking about, Nan?'

'Alice Cobb.'

'What has she done now?' Beatrice sighed and pushed back her chair.

'She is pregnant.'

'That girl is nothing but trouble!' Beatrice shook her

head. 'I gave her one chance, Nan. This time she will have to go. I cannot have girls bringing shame on us . . .'

'I agree that she will have to leave once it begins to be noticeable, but need it be before then, Beatrice? She will have time enough to cope with her shame once her condition is apparent. Her family don't want anything to do with her. Her mother disowned her and she's staying with a friend until she finds a room of her own. We can't just abandon her. She is really a good girl in her way.'

'She has loose morals and I do not want her contaminating my other girls or the children.'

'Beatrice, think what you're saying, please. Alice made a mistake, but she isn't the first girl to get caught – we've seen enough of the result of peoples "mistakes" come through these doors, haven't we?'

The expression in Nan's eyes made Beatrice look away. Beatrice might have her morals, but she knew morals counted for little when young women got caught in the snares that men set for them. She was angry with Alice for being so foolish, but her friend was right to say that the girl wasn't the first to get caught in the age-old trap.

'Oh, Nan, don't look at me like that,' Beatrice said, smiling wryly. 'Of course I shan't abandon the girl. We'll help her – arrange for her to go into a Church home when her time comes to have the baby.'

'Those homes make the girls give the baby up,' Nan objected. 'I'm not sure that Alice will agree to do that.'

'But surely she has no choice?'

'It would be difficult to keep the baby,' Nan admitted, 'but it might be possible. I shall try to help her myself. All I am asking of you at the moment is that you allow her to stay here for a few weeks – until she can sort herself out. Once she has somewhere to stay she will be able to think of the future.'

'I suppose she could stay at work until she starts to show . . .' Beatrice sighed. 'You'd better ask her to come and see me. Don't worry, I shan't be unkind, but you know we couldn't keep her here once the pregnancy shows, don't you? People would condemn her and the Bishop and the other guardians would be outraged. It isn't up to me alone.'

'No, I understand that, but just for a while?'

Beatrice hesitated, but she felt obliged to grant her friend's request. 'I really ought to let her go but . . . very well, Nan. We shall help her to get settled. As you said, she isn't the first and she will not be the last.'

'I hope you think I did right in letting the girl stay for a while – just until she begins to show her condition. Alice is a good worker and in difficult circumstances, because her mother will not have her at home,' Sister Beatrice explained.

'Her shame is not uncommon these days,' Father Joe said, looking grave. 'I would not have you cast the girl out too soon, but we cannot condone her behaviour, Sister. It would set a bad example to others – and the young girls in our care. Once she begins to show she must be sent to one of our homes. I shall make arrangements for her perhaps six weeks from now?'

'I must consult Alice about her wishes, Father. She must decide what to do. Her mother may take her back after she has considered fully.'

'The girl has shamed herself and her family. It is wrong

that she should be allowed to bring up a child, Sister. It will result in neglect and poverty, because she will not find a decent job and in the end may turn to an immoral life to support both the child and herself. We try to help such children here, but is it not better if it can be stopped before it starts?'

'Do you not think it a little harsh to impose our ideas on Alice?'

Father Joe frowned and Beatrice knew that it was one of those occasions when they came to loggerheads. Father Joe was a good and compassionate man, but he took Church doctrine seriously and didn't always see the subtleties in life. 'I am certain you will see that I am right,' he said sternly. 'We cannot be seen to condone immorality, Sister. You must know that it would offend the Bishop if it came to his ears?'

'You would not inform him, surely?'

'No . . .' The stern look faded from his eyes. 'I shall not – but I believe you must consider whether you feel it your duty to insist that Alice is properly cared for in her time of need.'

'You're right,' Beatrice said, 'but perhaps she may be persuaded . . . or her family may come to her aid before then.'

'Yes, perhaps,' he said, and smiled

Beatrice was relieved, because although her head told her that Father Joe was right to say that Alice must conform to the rules of society and the Church, she could not help feeling that it would be a shame to force the girl to give up her baby if she wished to keep it. Beatrice could imagine only too well the pain of losing a child.

TWENTY

'I won't go, Nance,' Terry said as Sister Beatrice left the room. She had come to tell them that both he and Nancy would soon have to start going to school, as the other children did. He kicked moodily at the wall near the window overlooking the garden. 'Don't let her send me to school. The other kids pick on me because I can't read or write or do sums – and you can't leave me here alone. I want to go home to Ma . . .' Tears welled in his eyes as he looked at her desperately. 'I want Ma . . . Nance, I want to go home . . .'

Nancy moved towards him, drawing his thin body close and holding him pressed against her, stroking his dark hair. She bent her fair head to his, kissing his hair. He smelled of the soap she'd washed him with earlier and she smiled, because she loved him with every fibre of her being. Terry was all she had now, all she'd ever had really, because Ma had stopped caring after that terrible night of the bombing, and Pa had never liked her. He'd got worse after he came back from the war; he'd never been violent before that, but he'd always more or less ignored Nancy. She thought he'd cared for Terry a bit, until a doctor told them Terry was backward and after that he'd ignored his son – but then, when he returned after the war, he'd been brutal and violent.

She wouldn't feel guilty or sad over the way her parents had died. It was their own faults, Pa for being so cruel to them – and Ma for not sticking up for her children. All she'd cared about was where the next drink was coming from – and now she was dead, like Pa.

Nancy had to protect Terry and make sure that Sister Beatrice didn't send him away somewhere. She'd been kind enough in her way, asking them both if they were settling in and if they had all they wanted to eat – but she didn't understand. How could she? No one could know that Terry was haunted by his nightmares. He'd often had bad dreams in the past, and it was always Nancy who comforted him. It was because he'd wanted to get into bed with her after he had bad dreams that he'd discovered what Pa was doing to her – and he'd gone wild.

Nancy had never seen her nervous little brother fall into a rage like that before. He'd gone for Pa with his hands, fists and teeth, biting his bare legs when Pa knocked him down, biting so hard that he'd drawn blood and made Pa yell in pain. It was then that Pa had grabbed him, hitting him over and over again until Nancy flung herself at his back and clung on, almost strangling him in an effort to stop him from killing his son.

'He's hurt, Pa,' she'd said as he towered over her. 'If you hit him again you'll kill him – and then they'll lock you up.'

Pa had calmed down then, glaring at her as he recovered his breath. 'If he ever comes in here again when I'm here I shall kill the runt,' he muttered. 'Tell him to stay away, girl. I'm warning you – and I'll have him locked up as soon as I can find somewhere to take him. Where your ma got that idiot from I've no idea, but he's not my son. She always was a damned whore.'

What did he mean, that Ma was a whore? Nancy knew what that word meant and her mother had never been that sort of woman. It was just Pa being mean and nasty, and she'd hated him then, hated him so much that she could taste the bitterness in her mouth.

She was glad he was dead, but she wished Ma was still alive and that they could go on living at home, just the three of them. Tears stung Nancy's eyes but she blinked them away as she saw what was happening to Terry. He'd gone rigid, his body starting to shake as he stared at something only he could see – just as he had on the night of the fire when she'd dragged him away from that burning door.

Now, Terry had his hands over his ears. 'They're screaming,' he cried. 'Stop them, Nance, stop them screaming. I can hear Ma crying . . .'

'No, Terry, no,' Nancy said, holding him as the shaking increased and he seemed on the verge of having a fit. 'They died in their sleep from the smoke – they didn't scream; they didn't feel anything, because they were dead before the flames touched them. The police told us it would be like that when they found us in the warehouse.'

Terry had tensed again and opened his mouth. Nancy slapped his face, cutting off the scream. She saw the stiffness go and he collapsed into her arms, sobbing against her chest as he mumbled something incoherent.

'I didn't mean Ma to die . . .'

'Hush, love.' Nancy bent to kiss the top of his head.

'It's all right, Terry. You didn't do anything, I promise you. It wasn't your fault . . .'

'Yes, it was, Nance.' Terry raised his head and looked at her, and something she saw in his eyes then sent chills down her spine. 'I did it to punish Pa. I wanted him to be hurt, but I didn't mean Ma to die. I wanted to wake her but the door was locked and – then I couldn't get near it for the flames, because it was so quick.'

'Don't say such things,' Nancy said, her heart beating so fast she thought she would suffocate. He couldn't mean it! He was all muddled up in his head; he'd imagined this because of the nightmares. 'It was an accident; you know it was, Terry. Pa must have knocked the lamp over and was too drunk to know what he'd done. You've made this up in your head – like some of those other things you think you did . . .' Terry couldn't have done it deliberately; Nancy wouldn't believe that her little brother could have knowingly done such a thing. No, it was just his nightmares. Their father had started the fire in a drunken stupor. The police had told them it must have happened that way . . .

Terry's gaze narrowed, frightening her. 'I know what I did, Nance – and if that horrible woman thinks she's going to send me away I'll make her sorry.'

'No, Terry, you mustn't think like that,' Nancy said, cold all over. 'Please, promise me you won't be silly. I have to go to school for another year so that I can find a good job and make a home for us, and perhaps we can find somewhere for you to go while I'm at school . . . but you must promise me to be good. You mustn't say wild things or we might be in trouble – and they would lock us both away somewhere.'

'I wouldn't ever hurt you, Nance,' Terry said, and smiled, the shadows suddenly gone from his face. 'Perhaps Father Joe will come and see us today. I like him.'

'Yes, I know.' Relief flooded through her. Surely she'd imagined that look in Terry's eyes. He couldn't have set fire to the door of their parents' bedroom; it was just his imagination playing tricks. 'Perhaps he will help you, Terry. We'll ask him next time he comes, shall we?'

'Yes.' Terry was all smiles now. He kneeled down on the floor and started to play with the wooden train that Father Joe had brought in for him, his temper tantrum forgotten. 'I like him, Nance. He's my friend . . .'

Nancy watched him and smiled. He was such a darling when he was good, but there was no doubting that he had a temper and she would never forget the way he'd gone for Pa that time – but Pa had deserved it and poor little Terry had come off worst.

Nancy knew that there was a violent streak in Terry, just as there had been in Pa, but he wouldn't hurt anyone when he was happy and felt safe; it was only when he was threatened or when anyone hurt Nancy that he went wild. She would just have to look out for him and make sure he didn't say or do foolish things.

Yet she couldn't quite forget that look. For a moment he'd stared at her as if he didn't know her, as if she were a stranger, and the malice in his eyes had chilled her. Just for a brief instant she'd been frightened – but that was stupid. Terry was her darling brother; he would never hurt her. He'd hated Pa but he loved Nancy and she would make him understand that they were safe here . . . once he'd got over his fear of the fire he would be her loving little brother again.

TWENTY-ONE

'I've managed to get two tickets for this evening – and I thought supper somewhere special afterwards?' Mark said. Angela was looking even lovelier, her ash-blonde hair freshly washed and gently waved on her collar. 'Any chance of your company?'

'Oh, Mark, I'm so sorry,' she said, and felt a guilty sensation as she told him of her plans. 'If you'd asked sooner I should have loved to come to the theatre with you, but I've arranged to have dinner with Nick Hadden this evening.'

Mark's face looked momentarily crestfallen, but he regained his composure. 'I wasn't sure I'd get tickets for this particular play. They are a bit like gold dust these days . . . Perhaps another time?'

'Yes, of course. I should have liked to see *Blithe Spirit* again. I think it is the best of Noel Coward's plays.' She glanced at her watch. 'I'm sorry, I have to go. I've arranged to see the vicar about hiring the church hall for a charity auction.'

'I shan't keep you.' Mark stood aside, watching her walk swiftly along the hall and down the stairs. He'd assumed that Angela would be free most evenings, but she was clearly more involved with Nick Hadden than he'd known. He felt wounded by the idea that her happiness came from being with another man, but tried to put it out of his mind as he knocked at the door of Sister Beatrice's office.

'Come in.'

Entering, he saw that the Warden was sitting at her desk, several papers spread out in front of her. She was frowning, as if she'd been concentrating and was annoyed by the interruption.

'You asked me to call. I hope you're not too busy?'

'Not at all,' she said, and shuffled the papers together. 'I was just looking at some accounts for this month. Angela has some rather adventurous ideas for fund raising . . .'

'Oh? Something rankles?' Mark arched his brows.

'No, I'm very grateful to her.' There was an oddly defensive air about her. 'I wanted you to take another look at Terry for me. Nancy ought to start school again – but the boy still refuses to be parted from her. He's been here some weeks now and I'm a bit anxious about him, because of the way he clings to his sister – though he gets on well with Father Joe.'

'I'll call in and speak to them both, but my advice is to give them both enough time to recover. Nancy could perhaps do some school work here? I doubt if she will want to take her higher exams but you never know. See what she has to say about her future before you decide.'

'Yes, perhaps we could arrange something with the school. I've done it for my patients who were not well enough to attend, but Nancy should be mixing with girls of her age and having fun. I'm not sure about the brother – my instincts tell me he could be difficult.'

'Yes, I'm certain he could if pressed. I had hoped he might get back to normality here, but if you feel you cannot keep him then it might be best if I had him transferred to a more specialised home for damaged children.' Mark had been turning the matter over in his mind, unwilling to act precipitously but aware that he might have to move the child at short notice. 'There is one I think suitable, but they do not often have space, and a mental institution is rather drastic – unless he has shown signs of violence?'

'No, apart from kicking the nurses a few times when he was first admitted. It was just something in the way he looked at me when I spoke to them yesterday. I tried to be gentle, to explain that Nancy needed to go to school and that he should go too when he's ready but he just kept shaking his head and I felt he resented me.'

'I'm sure he did,' Mark said. 'He has escaped from a dominant father who beat him and now finds that he is being told what he must do by a stranger. I shall advise you to go very slowly. If he becomes violent I need to know at once.'

'You will visit him?'

'Yes, of course. I'm always happy to look at any of the children.'

'Thank you.' Sister Beatrice smiled her relief. 'I do not want to do him an injustice but I must protect the others.'

Mark smiled and left her. He walked back down the hall and then took the lift up to the next floor. His own feelings about the brother and sister were as yet uncertain. Nancy was definitely hiding something and both of them were nervous; the girl was frightened every time he spoke to her brother. He thought back to his conversation with Angela. What did she think Terry might tell him?

Approaching the room that had been Nan's sitting room, he saw Nancy disappearing down the stairs at the other end of the hall. He hesitated for a moment outside the door and then entered. Terry was standing with his back to him, close to the window; he seemed intent on something – catching something. Mark saw the butterfly fluttering desperately against the glass just as Terry cupped it with his hands. It must have been brought out by an unusually warm day for February, because the wintry sunshine was hot through the glass, but a butterfly could not survive in this weather. He was just about to say he would open the window so that the poor thing could be let out and take its chance when he saw Terry quite deliberately pull first one wing and then the other from the struggling creature. The wingless insect floundered on the windowsill as Terry dropped it and turned to face Mark.

'It should be dead,' he said in a flat tone. 'It was the sun what brought it out from its dark corner – but it would die outside.'

'The poor creature is suffering,' Mark grunted. He picked up one of Nancy's shoes from the floor and delivered a sharp blow, putting the mutilated butterfly out of its misery. 'That was cruel, Terry. What made you hurt it?'

'It was a prisoner. It's better to be dead than locked up. I would've killed it if you hadn't come.'

'You should have let the poor creature take its chance outside.'

Tears welled in Terry's eyes. 'I didn't mean to do it, sir. Honest. I just thought it was pretty and I wanted to catch it for Nancy – and the wings just pulled off. You won't tell her, will yer?'

'I shan't tell her, but you must never do anything like that again, Terry.' Mark opened the window and brushed the evidence outside so that it fell to the ground. 'Do you think Nancy would say it was all right?'

'Nancy would cry,' Terry said. 'She's gone down to have her dinner with the others and she says she'll bring me a sandwich back. She was cross because I wouldn't go, but I want to go home to Ma. I want my ma . . .'

'Are you very unhappy here, Terry?'

'It's all right – but that old witch wants to send me away. Nance says I have to be good or they might lock us up in prison. She would be cross if she knew what I'd done. Nance mustn't be cross . . .'

Mark had never heard Terry speak more than two words when his sister was in the room. He tried to analyse the situation clinically, shutting out all personal feelings. Was Nancy the dominant one – did Terry take his lead from her? Was he afraid of his sister?

'She won't be cross because I shan't tell her.'

'It can be our secret. Nance says I have to keep secrets – all our secrets. If I'm good Ma will come and take me home . . . won't she?'

'Your mother can't come for you, Terry. You know she can't.' Mark saw him flinch, saw the pain in his face. He was perfectly capable of understanding when forced to it, but he was trying to block it all out – why?

What was he hiding – what were they both afraid of revealing? 'One day Nancy will make another home for you, but she has to go to school and learn things so that she can get a good job – you know that, don't you? You ought to go to school, too, Terry. Wouldn't you like that – to be with boys of your own age?'

'I can't learn things. The teacher says I'm backward and the other kids hate me. Pa says I'm an idiot. I heard him tell her that if she didn't do what he wanted he would send me away somewhere they would lock me up in a dark room with bars on the windows and never let me out, and that made Nance cry . . .' Terry blinked and rubbed at his eyes. 'She will be cross with me for telling you. I want Ma . . .'

'Yes, I'm sure you do,' Mark said, looking at him sadly. 'Father Joe might be able to find you a place at a special school he helps to run. You learn different things there, Terry – not sums and writing, but working with your hands; perhaps pottery or wood carving. Would you go there sometimes if Nancy went to her school?'

'I might – if Nance told me to. I have to do what she says or she'll be cross.'

'Well, we'll see,' Mark said. 'Aren't you hungry? Wouldn't you like to go downstairs and have something to eat?'

'I don't know where to go . . .'

'Supposing I take you and show you?'

'All right. I'm hungry.' Terry's eyes were very bright as he looked at Mark. 'You will keep our secret?' He gave a little high-pitched nervous giggle.

'Yes,' Mark assured him gently. 'Let's go and find Nancy now, shall we?'

167

'All right, if you say so.'

Mark guided him from the room, feeling the ache of sympathy start inside. The boy was more damaged than he'd imagined at the start. If he was right, this boy wasn't insane, but on the edge of a mental breakdown, his natural backwardness having been pushed into something dark and unpleasant. Sister Beatrice was right to have asked for Mark's advice. It was just luck that he'd found Terry alone, because if Nancy had been present the boy wouldn't have shown that hidden side of him – the part that might become violent if pushed too far.

It was going to take a while to place Terry where he could live in a safe environment and receive the treatment he desperately needed. Mark didn't consider it necessary to have him sectioned, but there were special places that could help very disturbed children: unfortunately, there were not many of them and it was difficult to find an opening in a good place, because Terry needed special treatment, not just a school for backward boys. He must warn Sister Beatrice to use caution. Terry wasn't dangerous, but there was something unpleasant simmering deep down inside – it had shown itself briefly in the way he'd mutilated the butterfly.

Mark couldn't be certain, but he was pretty sure it was a case of two diametrically opposed personalities: one of them was the shy, nervous boy who relied on his sister for everything and the other – Mark could hardly contemplate the other, because it could mean that Terry might never be allowed his freedom again and the thought of what that would do to the child was desperately sad. To put Terry away in one of those soulless places, where he would be incarcerated in a ward, probably with children or even adults, who were truly mad, would be an unforgivable thing. No, Mark must trust his instincts and find a place where Terry had a chance of a decent life, but he must do it as swiftly as he could. Yet in his heart he could feel nothing but sympathy both for the boy and his sister when they learned of the inevitable parting.

After leaving Terry with his sister in the dining room, Mark went back upstairs to the first floor. He ought to have another word with Sister Beatrice before he left, but finding her office empty, he walked along to the sick ward, knocked and entered. Staff Nurse Carole was alone with her patients, one of whom was Sarah Morgan, who was looking much better and sitting up eating a dish of rice pudding with strawberry jam.

'Sister not here?' Mark asked.

Carole turned and gave him a dazzling smile, walking towards the desk where he stood. 'No, she came to look at our star patient – Sarah is getting on famously now – but she's gone downstairs to talk to Nan.'

'I'll try and see her before I go,' Mark said. 'But I have to get back to the hospital; I have patients in an hour.' About to turn away, he remembered, with some irritation, the theatre tickets and Angela's date with Nick Hadden. 'I suppose you wouldn't like to come to the theatre with me – and supper afterwards?' Mark marvelled at himself for asking her. It hadn't occurred to him before he'd seen her, but she was looking at him in a way that was hard to resist.

'When?'

'This evening? I know it's short notice, but I only managed to get them this morning on my way here.'

'I should love to,' Carole said. 'Where shall we meet?'

Mark laughed, surprised by her quick reply. She hadn't even asked what was on, which meant it was his company that she was interested in. He was pleased and flattered, because she was very attractive, younger of course, but he wasn't old, in his prime really. Occasionally, when dealing with children like Terry, he felt like living dangerously. Tonight, of all nights, he could do with leaving all thoughts of work behind. The company of a pretty and vivacious woman was just what he needed. And if not Angela, then why not Carole?

'I'll call for you here and we'll take a taxi,' he said. 'At seven, then?'

'Lovely. That gives me time to get out of this uniform, into something more suitable.' Carole threw him a flirtatious look. 'You know, I thought you would never ask . . .'

Mark couldn't ignore the suggestion in Carole's words and in her eyes. She wasn't Angela, but she was sexy, good-looking, and he thought she would be fun to be with – and there was no harm in a date with a pretty girl. After all, Angela was meeting Nick Hadden; so why would she complain if he took Carole out? It might even make her a little jealous.

TWENTY-TWO

Mary Ellen went to sit next to the new children at breakfast on Saturday morning. Betsy was sitting with Nancy and Terry and looking miserable, because they were ignoring her. She pulled out a spare chair and sat down, looking at each of the new arrivals in turn. Betsy was about her own age, but pale and thin with lank mousy hair that straggled on her neck and fell into her eyes. One of the carers ought to have washed it for her, thought Mary Ellen.

'You haven't eaten much,' she observed, looking at the toast and marmalade on Betsy's plate. 'Aren't you hungry?'

'I don't like marmalade,' Betsy snivelled, and wiped her nose on the back of her hand. 'Ma always gave me dripping in the mornings.'

'Marmalade is lovely,' Mary Ellen said. 'There were some boiled eggs yesterday, but none today. The chickens aren't laying and Cook says there's no fresh eggs in the shop this week. The scrambled egg is made from that powdered stuff. It's all right but I like jam best, especially strawberry.'

'I like strawberry,' Betsy said, and looked more cheerful. 'But I didn't see any.'

171

'Have mine, and I'll have your marmalade.' Mary Ellen held out her plate. 'Go on, take it. I haven't touched it – and I'll take the bit you haven't bitten.' The exchange was done and Betsy munched away, looking happier. Mary Ellen turned her attention to the boy sitting across the table from her. 'I'm Mary Ellen O'Hanran – you're Terry, aren't you?'

He stared at her and then looked at his sister. 'I'm going back to the room, Nance. I don't like it here . . .'

'Terry, don't be rude,' Nancy said disapprovingly. 'Mary Ellen is just being friendly.' But Terry glared at her and ran off and Nancy smiled apologetically at the other girls. 'I'm sorry about my brother. He's still upset about what happened to our parents. I'm pleased to meet you both. Have you been here long?'

'A few months,' Mary Ellen said. 'I came in to stay while my mother went to hospital. I was going to live with her when she got better but she died – and Rose, my sister, is training to be a nurse.' Nancy was surprised by the matter-of-fact way that Mary Ellen told her story. 'She's coming to visit me this morning, which is why I'm late to breakfast. Sally washed my hair – she would do yours if you asked her, Betsy.'

Betsy blushed and got up suddenly, and then ran off. She looked close to tears and Nancy stared after her in surprise.

'What is the matter with her?'

'She hasn't been here long, and new kids are often like that,' Mary Ellen said. 'I've heard her mother went off and left her while she was in the hospital – her mother probably used to wash her hair for her. I upset her.'

'You didn't mean to,' Nancy said. 'Her hair needs washing or she'll pick up nits. I used to wash Terry's hair when we were at home, lots of kids in the street had nits, but we didn't.'

'Didn't your mother do it for him?'

'She was ill,' Nancy said, and quickly changed the subject. 'Do you like being here? What are the carers like? I've only seen a few of them, because Terry won't let them wash him. I take him to the bathroom myself, though he can wash himself if he wants to – but you know what boys are.'

Mary Ellen laughed. Nancy was nice, better than her brother and Betsy. Yet Marion and Billy were her best friends; Billy had gone to football practice and Marion was helping Sally with the little ones, as Mary Ellen usually did on a Saturday, but today was special, because Rose was coming to take her out.

She finished her toast and her milk, then scraped back her chair. 'I have to go now and get ready. I hope you'll be happy here, Nancy – and your brother. I'm sorry if I upset him.'

'It's not your fault.'

Mary Ellen nodded and left Nancy, who had started to clear the dirty plates onto a metal tray. It looked as if she meant to carry them to the kitchen. That was the kitchen girls' job but it wasn't up to Mary Ellen to tell her not to if she wanted to help. No one knew better than Mary Ellen how difficult it was to find your place in the first few days and weeks. Nancy had obviously been used to helping her mother at home and she must feel a bit lost here with little to do.

*   *   *

'You look well.' Rose looked down at Mary Ellen and smiled. 'I think you're happier than you were, aren't you?'

'I'm all right, but it isn't like being at home,' Mary Ellen said, and took hold of her hand. Rose had had her dark hair cut and was as pretty and smart as ever. 'Billy is staying here now for good, and I really like him, and Marion – and I like Sarah Morgan too and Nancy too.'

'As long as you have friends, and it won't be for ever, you just have to make do for now,' Rose said. 'I thought we'd go shopping and then have something to eat at the Lyons' Corner House. I've got some good news for you, love. I've passed my first exams with flying colours and I'm officially called Nurse now. I'm still a junior but I'll be taken on the staff in another year and then I'll start to get paid more than a pittance.'

'Will you fetch me away then?'

'No, not until I'm fully qualified,' Rose told her firmly. 'I have to live in the Nurses' Home until then – and even after I've passed all my exams I shall have to get permission to live out. When I'm a senior staff nurse, then perhaps I could manage to find us a place.'

'Could Billy come too? In a few years he will be able to work and then he could pay towards his keep.'

Rose frowned slightly. 'I know you think a lot of him, Mary Ellen, but you shouldn't get your hopes up too high. What sort of future has he got? Ma and Pa wouldn't have wanted you to get involved with a ruffian – or worse . . .'

'Ma and Pa aren't here, are they?' she answered defiantly, though the thought of her mother and of having to stay in the home for longer than she could imagine tore at her insides. 'Billy isn't a thief like his brother,

174

Arthur,' Mary Ellen said, indignantly defending her friend and determined not to succumb to tears, knowing it would only annoy Rose. 'He is going to study hard and learn to be a train driver.'

'In that case he will be studying for a lot of years yet,' Rose said. 'Come on, let's forget about Billy for the moment. I've come to take you shopping for some nice new shoes for best.'

Mary Ellen looked sideways at her, but she knew better than to labour her point. Rose could be sharp when she wanted to and they mustn't spoil the day out. Billy was her special friend, and even if she went to live with Rose and he didn't, Mary Ellen would never lose touch with him.

'All right,' she agreed. 'It's a long way off and things may be different by then . . .' Rose didn't know Billy the way she did. If she gave him half a chance, she'd soon see that he was worth far more than the rest of his family ever were. 'I'm looking forward to my new shoes.'

Billy took his football boots off in the garden. He'd rushed back to the home after football practice and hadn't had time to change back into his school shoes. He would walk upstairs in his socks, because the football studs scraped the polished floor and he'd be in trouble if he got caught sneaking in and making the floors muddy.

He was just straightening up after removing the boots when he caught sight of someone sitting on the wooden seat, staring moodily ahead of him. The boy was of a similar age, and Billy grinned at him, pointing to his boots.

'Been to football practice,' he said. 'Sister Beatrice

will have my guts for garters if I wear 'em in the house. I'm Billy Baggins. Do you like playing football, mate?'

The boy stared at him moodily for a moment and then shook his head. 'I ain't never played, 'cept with Pa in the lane when he was in a good mood.'

'Don't know what you're missin',' Billy told him cheerfully. 'We play a lot of matches at our school. You'll be comin' there now – and they'll teach you how to play if you want. Mr Harrison is all right for a teacher and great at training.'

'I don't go to school. I ain't no good at learnin'.'

'Nor was I once,' Billy said. 'I thought lessons were a waste of time – but that was before I caught on. It's them what don't bother that waste their time. I want to get on and be better than my pa – and my brother. Pa used to drink too much and Arfur was a bad one, but I don't have to be the same, do I? I'm going to learn to be a train driver. What do you wanna do?'

Terry shrugged. 'I ain't never thought about it.'

'Well, you should. If you don't try you won't learn and then you'll end up with being pushed around by some so-and-so in a rotten job and be stuck with it for the rest of your life.'

'What could I do?'

'You could drive a bus or a tram, or be a foreman at the factory, if you've learned your letters and numbers,' Billy suggested. 'Depends what you like doing, mate.'

'I could be a soldier and kill people,' Terry suggested, and brought his arm up, making a shooting motion. 'Bang, yer dead – you've got no head left . . .' He giggled and looked at Billy expectantly. Billy made a groaning

176

sound and tottered around as if he were dying and Terry's laughter rang out. 'Yer all right, mate,' he said, copying Billy. 'I thought they were all rotten 'ere, 'cept for Father Joe – but you're all right.'

'Most of us are all right,' Billy said. 'Come on in now. I've got to change my things and then it will be time for tea. We've got proper fish and chips today with squashy peas and brown sauce. Do you like fish and chips?'

'Only 'ad it once,' Terry said, and grinned at him. 'I like yer, Billy. I'll sit with yer at table and I'll go to school and be a soldier if yer want me to?'

'That's it, mate,' Billy said. 'Come on now and you can meet me other friends, Mary Ellen and Marion.'

Terry hesitated. 'I don't like other children much – they make fun of me and throw things.'

'Not my friends,' Billy said. 'If anyone did that when I was around I'd bash 'em for you.'

'I'll shoot their heads off,' Terry said, and giggled. 'All right, I'll come with yer. I'm hungry.'

'What did you bring that Terry to our table for?' Mary Ellen asked Billy after tea that evening. 'I'm not sure I like him – or the way he tried to shut Marion and me out. He wanted you to himself – and he was horrible to Betsy when she sat next to him. I think he pinched her and made her cry.'

'She told him he was rude because he talks with his mouth full,' Billy said. 'I don't like her much either, but it was you what made her welcome. I'd rather have Terry at our table than her.'

'Betsy is lonely and doesn't have any friends. Terry

has his sister – he wants to be with her most of the time anyway.'

'Well, he's going to come to school with me soon,' Billy said. 'He's all right underneath, Mary Ellen. I reckon he just needs a bit of looking after. I think he's had a rough time at home. He didn't say much but it's there in his eyes, you can tell them kids when they come in 'ere. He needs help as much as Betsy.'

'Well, I'll help her and you help him,' Mary Ellen said, and looked at him uncertainly. 'You're not going to let him take you away from me, are you, Billy?'

Billy stared at her and then burst out laughing. 'You're jealous,' he said, and looked delighted.

'No, I'm not.' Mary Ellen stalked off, refusing to look back even though he called after her.

'I'm sorry,' Billy called. 'Of course I shan't, Mary Ellen – you're my best mate, you know that.'

She kept on walking and wouldn't look round. Billy wanted to go after her, but something kept him from giving in. Whether it was his pride or a feeling that he liked her being jealous, Billy wasn't sure – but he'd make up with her next time they met. Besides, he couldn't just dump Terry. Billy's instincts told him that the other boy was desperately in need of a friend and he couldn't let him down now. Mary Ellen would get over her sulks and they would all be friends again. Yeah, he rather liked her being a bit jealous over him; it showed she cared and Billy thought it was a nice feeling.

TWENTY-THREE

Carole was busy on the wards, but she wanted time to think about the evening she'd gone out with Mark the previous week, when he'd taken her to the theatre and then to an intimate supper in a nightclub.

She'd danced with him twice, and the nearness of his body was thrilling; there was something special about the way he held her, strongly but with care. Most of the men she'd been out with recently had used the dance floor as an opportunity for a grope and it usually ended up with sharp words, but Mark was the perfect gentleman. Yet she'd sensed that he enjoyed being close to her as much as she had being close to him. She thought he would be an exciting lover, because his hands looked so sensitive and the fingers were long, his nails short and clean; she imagined his hands caressing her body . . . Mark smelled of soap and a fresh cologne and she'd found it intoxicating.

Love didn't enter her mind, but lust certainly did. Carole didn't particularly want to fall in love with anyone; it got in the way. No, what she wanted was a strong, caring man she could rely on if she needed him, and one who wouldn't be bothered about having children – there were enough spoiled brats in the world, or little guttersnipes like the children at the home. She wanted a man who was rich enough to give her the kind of life she craved.

One day she might like to be a kept woman . . . with a wedding ring and security thrown in, of course. Her dreams of travelling had been put on hold during the war, but now it was beginning to be possible again. Mark might be the right sort of man – the kind of man who could give her what she wanted from life.

Carole's thoughts were rudely interrupted as Angela Morton entered the ward carrying a tray of drinks and food for the patients. She was looking particularly elegant that morning in a dark green skirt with a fine paler green sweater with short sleeves, puffed at the shoulders.

'Could you not knock before you enter?' Carole snapped. 'I might have been bathing one of the patients and we do need some privacy, you know.'

'Sorry,' Angela apologised. 'It's not easy to knock carrying a heavy tray and Michelle always says not to bother.'

'Well, I'm in charge here at the moment and I'd prefer you to knock.'

'Very well, I shall try to remember.' Carole noticed a flush creep up Angela Morton's cheek, but she used a conciliatory tone. 'I didn't mean to intrude. I knew you were busy so I thought I would save you having to come down. We're short of kitchen staff again.'

Carole checked herself because she knew that Angela didn't have to help out the way she did; it wasn't her job to run up and down stairs with loaded trays.

'Sorry to be snappy. We're a bit stretched here, too.' Carole forced herself to be nice. She knew that knocking at doors had nothing to do with it; it was Angela's friendship with Mark that was eating away at her. 'Just a bit tired, I was out until the early hours the other night – theatre, supper and a nightclub. Haven't got over it yet . . .'

'Goodness, lucky you. Did you have a good night?' Angela said. 'A heavy date with the boyfriend?'

'Well, perhaps you could call him that.' Carole looked at her boldly. 'Mark Adderbury took me out, in fact.'

Carole was trying to goad her, but frustratingly, Angela's voice was steady. 'Well, I'm sure it was a lovely evening.'

Carole had expected to provoke a reaction but she was disappointed. Angela's tone was even and devoid of emotion. Angela even smiled at her as she left the ward, leaving Carole smarting with resentment. She'd love to wipe that smug smile of her face.

Well, she probably thought she had Mark Adderbury twisted round her little finger but Carole was determined to prove her wrong. She was pretty certain that Mark had wanted her that night. While they were dancing Carole had pressed herself close to him, closer than she normally dared and she'd felt his body respond; his hand caressing the arch of her back as he drew her even closer. Now she was going to turn that to her advantage. She would make him fall for her and then, if once she'd decided that he was up to the job, she'd make him marry her.

A smile touched Carole's mouth. Mrs Toffee-Nose Morton would wake up one day and discover that Mark Adderbury had been snapped up by the better woman. And that wasn't the limit of her ambitions either. Sister Beatrice was efficient, but she was too trusting. It had occurred to Carole that rather than waiting for the Warden to get too old, she might find a way of making it appear that the caring Sister was becoming careless . . . Yes, this haughty St Saviour's lot had it coming to them, all right . . .

Mark saw Angela walking ahead of him along the hall and stepped into the lift rather than taking the stairs as he normally did. He wasn't sure why he didn't want to speak to her that morning, perhaps it was something to do with getting a bit carried away the night he took Carole out.

Whatever had made him suggest going on to that nightclub he could not imagine, but he'd been a little intoxicated by Carole's company and with the gin cocktails; flattered, he supposed, because she was beautiful, young and altogether too alluring. He'd noticed the envious looks he was getting all night. Carole had worn a skimpy black evening dress, the skirt short and flared so that it flirted about her swaying hips as she walked. The top of the dress had narrow straps and a tight-fitting bodice, which dipped to a daring V at the back – the sight was intoxicating.

He brought himself back to the present as he left the lift and tapped at Sister Beatrice's door. He'd been thinking a lot about Terry and, without alarming her too much, he felt he must warn her not to endanger her own safety by pushing Terry too far.

'Come in,' Sister called, and Mark entered. He discovered that Angela was in the office with Sister Beatrice, she was bending over the desk, a sheaf of papers in her hand having beaten the lift by running upstairs.

'Ah, Mark,' Sister said, glancing up. 'Did you need to speak to me?'

'I can come back later if you'd rather?'

'Don't worry, I'm on my way out.' Angela gave Mark a brief impersonal glance and said, 'I'll leave the list with you, Sister. You can tell me if you need changes later.' She nodded briefly at him but without her usual smile. Sensing a new coolness, Mark knew deep down that it had something to do with taking Carole to the theatre. He found the realisation made him uneasy.

'I'm sorry to interrupt.' He smiled apologetically at Sister Beatrice.

'Well. I imagine what you have to say is important or you wouldn't be here.'

'You asked me to take another look at Terry the other day, and I have. For the first time I was able to speak to him without Nancy being there.'

'Yes, go on?' Beatrice looked at him intently.

'Although I wouldn't class him as insane, he is unstable. One minute he's a nervous, frightened little boy, who cries for his mother and can't remember that she died in the fire and the next he's – well, a different and more violent personality altogether.'

'Is he a danger to my children?'

'I don't believe so, providing neither he nor his sister is threatened. I don't want the lad sectioned and put away in an asylum, because that could be disastrous for him and send him over the edge – but he ought to be transferred to a more suitable place where he can be monitored and treated. I wanted to warn you to be careful personally.'

'Why me personally?'

'Terry has taken a dislike to you, and if he thinks you're threatening his security, which is represented by Nancy, he could turn nasty.'

'It sounds to me as though the sooner he is moved the better.'

'I'm inclined to agree with you,' Mark told her. 'But it would be hugely damaging to separate him from his sister and put him away unless it is necessary.' He met her doubtful look with a lift of his brows. 'Will you allow me the time to find him somewhere suitable? I don't feel there is any immediate danger to anyone.'

Sister Beatrice hesitated, then inclined her head. 'I have always trusted your judgement, Mark, and if you feel we have time then I'll comply. I'll be careful when dealing with the boy now that you've warned me.'

'I hope that I can find a good place for him. There are still some terrible institutions out there but things are changing, especially where young children are concerned, and very few respected experts in the field of mental illness feel that locking someone up and throwing away the key is the right answer any more; not for seriously troubled children, anyway. It might even be possible for his sister to be relocated close to his placement so that she can visit – but it will take a few weeks.'

'Yes, I understand,' Sister Beatrice said. 'But if you see any signs that he is deteriorating – well, I do have all the other children to think of, and much as I would regret it, I cannot have one child being a danger to the others. Or indeed to my staff.'

'Yes, of course I see that. If I thought he was really dangerous I would take him away immediately. It is still hard to be completely sure it isn't simply the trauma of the fire. I'm sorry to be so inconclusive, but it is often like that in my work. We have to hunt for the key that unlocks the patient's mind so that we can be sure, and sometimes it takes many hours of talking and analysing.'

'I understand that your work isn't a precise science but a matter of observation and judgement; it's a bit like that in nursing too.' Sister gave him a fleeting smile. 'We'll leave it there for the moment, shall we?'

Mark smiled and took his leave. He'd bought himself some more time to think things over. Terry had pulled the wings from that butterfly but other children sometimes did similar cruel things without thinking. The lad had been terrorised by a brutal father and then lost both his parents in that fatal blaze. If the police had some idea of how the fire had started it might be a help. Had it been an accident – or was there a more sinister cause?

Had one of the children deliberately set fire to the door of their parents' bedroom? If so, which one was more likely to have planned it? Mark frowned as he wondered. Once or twice he'd thought Terry almost afraid to make his sister angry. Could it be possible that she was the dangerous one and the boy just a backward lad who hadn't understood what he was doing when he mutilated that poor insect?

A cold shiver ran down his spine; he hoped he had what it took to get to the bottom of it, and he'd need his wits about him when dealing with the brother and sister.

TWENTY-FOUR

Angela realised that she'd been staring at her typewriter for ages without typing a word. Somehow, she hadn't been able to get the expression in Carole's eyes out of her head all day – and then there was the way Mark had avoided looking at her, as if he were guilty of something, which was ridiculous. Even if he were seriously dating the pretty nurse he had no reason to feel guilty, because he didn't owe Angela an explanation. They were just good friends. It was true that she'd come to rely on his friendship, to feel that he was always there for her if she needed him – but surely she was over all that now? She no longer needed Mark to prop her up. Yet she was conscious of a deep and painful hurt inside her chest. Somehow, she'd begun to think of Mark as hers . . . and the triumphant look in Carole's eyes had told her that she was mistaken. But she'd kept Mark at arm's length for a long time now, even though before Christmas she'd been pretty sure he wanted to be more than a friend. Could she be surprised if he'd turned to a pretty nurse, who was several years younger than Angela?

No, she couldn't and it was ridiculous to feel as if he'd let her down. She'd enjoyed her evening with Nick Hadden, but even that bothered her a little, because she was afraid that Nick might be getting serious. She wasn't ready for anything more than friendship with anyone just yet.

Angela laughed. She was being foolish. There were far more important things to think about than her personal relationships. Including the auction of the bits and pieces she'd reserved from that bequest to St Saviour's; which, now that she'd finally got a date when the church hall was free, was set for the following week.

'Angela, may I come in?'

Sally popped her head round the door, looking rather like an expectant robin with her bright eyes and inquisitive expression; wearing her pink gingham uniform, her short reddish-brown hair curling about her face, she was a pretty girl. Angela smiled. 'Yes, of course you can.'

'We hadn't talked in the staff room recently, so I thought I would pop in. It's your auction for St Saviour's next week, isn't it?'

'On Tuesday. I thought I would do an evening auction so that more people could come.'

'Is there anything I can do to help? Stick tickets on things, make lists – whatever? Andrew is away at a conference for his work then and Tuesday isn't one of my class nights so I could come and help out if you like?'

'Yes, to both kind offers.' Angela beamed at her. 'I'm listing everything by numbers now and need some help attaching the tickets – you could come and help and we can drink coffee and moan about the world.'

'I should love to,' Sally said. 'And on the night?'

'I'm going to need people watching the stuff once it is set out. When the buyers pay I'll need someone there too, because I'm conducting the auction. I asked a professional but he wanted too much. I can do it myself, I'm sure.'

'As good as he can, I'll bet,' Sally assured her with a big grin. 'I'll come over this evening, how about half seven?'

'Lovely,' Angela agreed, and settled back to her work, pleased with life once more. If Carole resented her for some reason that was her affair. Angela had made friends here and she wasn't going to bother her head over the nurse's strange looks.

'Miss Angela,' Nancy called to her as she was leaving the dining room after tea that evening. 'I wanted to thank you for my sewing kit and the material you gave me. I made a new dress for Sunday outings. I'm allowed to wear it if I go to church, Sally says.'

'Yes, and for outings with family. Have you any family, Nancy? Anyone who lives away and could be written to, someone who might visit?'

'No, miss. Pa had no family I've heard of, and all Ma's family and her special friend, Auntie Molly, were killed in the war. Ma was devastated when they all got killed: it was the reason she started to drink so much.'

'I'm truly sorry, Nancy.' Angela was appalled by the girl's plight. That wretched war had done so much damage, ripping whole communities apart and destroying families. 'Would you like to come out with me one day – perhaps to the pictures or tea at Lyons' Corner House?'

'Could Terry come too, miss?'

'Of course, but we have to ask Sister for permission first. I'll see if I can arrange it soon. I take Mary Ellen and Billy Baggins out for a treat sometimes, so I see no reason why I shouldn't take you and Terry.'

'That would be something to look forward to, miss. Terry is so unhappy here. He wants to go home. He knows he can't really, but he gets muddled when he's upset and keeps asking for Ma.'

'It was a terrible thing to happen, Nancy. It must have upset you too.'

'Pa deserved what happened to him.' Nancy's eyes glittered with anger. 'But Ma didn't. I wish she was still here – but you can't bring someone back when they're dead, can you? You can't change things even if you want to.'

'No, you can't,' Angela agreed seriously. 'Take care of your brother, Nancy. Family is very important and I know how much you care for him.'

'He's all I've got, miss. I don't know what I'd do if anything happened to Terry.'

'I'm sure nothing will happen.' Angela felt a rush of sympathy for the girl. Her protective instincts came to the fore. Nancy needed a friend, someone to fight for her. 'I think I've seen Terry with Mary Ellen and Billy at tea, haven't I?'

'Yes, miss. He likes Billy, and says he's decided to be a soldier when he is old enough. I told him he should go to school and he says he will if he can go with Billy.'

'Well, that's an improvement.' Angela was pleased with the news. It must mean that Terry was getting over his trauma; if he was prepared to go to school with his

189

new friend and had decided to be a soldier when he grew up, he was feeling a little better. 'I'm so pleased, Nancy. I'll see if there's a war film on – not too violent, naturally, but there are some funny ones with soldiers in.'

'You're very kind,' Nancy said, 'but I shan't tell Terry until Sister gives permission, because I don't want him to be disappointed.'

'Let's keep our fingers crossed.' Angela smiled reassuringly and gave Nancy's hand a squeeze.

TWENTY-FIVE

'Guess what? Miss Angela is taking us out this Saturday,' Nancy told her brother excitedly when Angela gave her the news that Sister Beatrice had given permission. 'We're going to the pictures to see a film about soldiers or something – and then we shall have tea at Lyons.'

'So what?' Terry kicked at the ground moodily. It was wet and slushy, because the snow had melted during the day and there was no longer enough of it to build a snowman. They were in the small garden at the back of St Saviour's and he'd expected to see Billy but his new friend had gone to school and Terry had been told that he couldn't go with him until things were arranged. 'Can Billy come too?'

'It is just us this time.' Nancy felt annoyed because she was looking forward to it. 'She asked us special, Terry, and you should be pleased. You've never been to the pictures and nor have I since Auntie Molly died in the Blitz.'

'I ain't goin' if Billy can't come,' Terry said stubbornly. 'I ain't sure I want ter be a soldier no more. I might be a tram driver.'

'Oh, Terry . . .' Nancy caught back a sudden sob because his moodiness seemed too much on top of everything else. There seemed nothing she could do to please him. 'Please don't be like this, love. I really want to go.'

'I want Billy ter come,' he said angrily and glared at her. 'I hate bein' 'ere, Nance. I shan't go to them pictures unless Billy comes too.'

'I can't ask Miss Angela to take Billy too.'

'Then I ain't goin'. Yer can go without me. I want ter go home.'

'All right, I will go,' Nancy said, tears in her eyes. 'Why do you have to spoil everything? We can't go home, it's gone – burned to the ground. You know what happened, Terry.' She knew that this would upset him, but she couldn't help herself for once.

'I don't know. I can't remember,' Terry said, his eyes now dark and anguished. 'I don't want ter know. I want Ma . . .' His voice rose in a trembling whimper. 'I want me ma . . .'

'Stop going on about her all the time, and don't be a baby,' Nancy snapped, disappointment making her sharper with him than she intended to be. Terry let out an outraged cry and flew at her, kicking at her shins. Nancy grabbed him by the shoulders and shook him, and when he tried to bite her, she slapped his face. 'Just you stop that, Terry. I've let you get away with a lot but I won't stand for this – if you don't stop I'll never look after you again – I mean it this time.'

Terry stopped yelling and stared at her in shock. For a few seconds resentment and bitterness, even hatred, flashed in his eyes, but then almost as quickly the tears started. He rubbed at his eyes with dirty hands, leaving smears on his cheeks.

For a moment, the suspicion that Terry was turning on the waterworks popped briefly into her mind, but when she saw the pitiful look on his face, Nancy's remorse was instant. 'Here, have my hanky, love. I didn't mean to be cross, but you upset me. I was looking forward to Saturday.'

Terry stared, sullen and silent for a moment, then he sniffed and offered her crumpled hanky back. His eyes were dark with suspicion. Looking at him now, Nancy felt as if a shadow had passed over her and shivered as her neck grew icy. Terry had always trusted her implicitly before this, because she'd always been on his side against their father, but now she'd slapped him and threatened him, and she knew he was turning this new situation over in his mind. Nancy regretted the little surge of temper that had made her strike out at him.

'I know it's hard for you here, love, but I'm your sister and we've got to stick together, see. Billy is your friend, but I'll always be here for you, and friends come and go.'

Terry's voice was toneless when he answered her. 'All right, I'll go with yer, Nance. It's just that Billy's me friend and I ain't 'ad a friend before.'

She could only hope that their disagreement would be forgotten and he would go back to being her devoted shadow, and yet she had a feeling that her brother was drifting away from her somehow. Nancy didn't mind if he was getting pally with Billy Baggins, because it might mean she could do things on her own and with other

193

girls of her own age, go back to school perhaps – but she had a little flicker of unease.

'Come on, let's be friends again, Terry.' She put her arm around her little brother but he was stiff and unresponsive. Ice prickled at her nape. Terry could be the most devoted boy in the world, but if he took against someone . . . well, she just prayed that neither Billy, or indeed herself, got to see any more of his dark side.

'You're not really mad at me, are you?' Billy asked as he sat next to Mary Ellen at breakfast that morning. 'You know you're me best mate, don't you?'

'I'm your friend, Billy.' Mary Ellen looked at him with hurt in her eyes. 'But you've spent more time with Terry than me lately. I know I'm a girl and he's more of a mate for you, but I thought we were best friends . . .'

'You spend time with Marion and other girls, and that Betsy. I don't like her because she's always snivelling over something. 'Sides, Terry needs a mate. You're still me best friend, but I have to be with Terry sometimes; it's only fair – he ain't got any others.'

'Don't say any more; they're coming now, Nancy and Terry.'

Nancy sat down with them. 'We were a bit late. You don't mind if we sit here? Where's Marion and Betsy?'

'Marion has been moved to a new dorm so she's sitting with the girls from there,' Mary Ellen said. She wasn't going to tell Nancy that Marion had refused to sit with her if the brother and sister were going to keep joining them.

She looked about her at the rows of crowded tables, all covered with gingham-pattern oilcloths so that any spills could be easily wiped up. The sound of children's voices chattering made the room noisy. Nan was with some of the younger ones, helping them with their breakfast, and Sally was talking to a group of older girls and boys.

'I don't mind her, but I don't like him,' Marion had complained to Mary Ellen the previous evening after tea. 'He pinched Betsy and made her cry just now. She didn't say because she's afraid of him. She says he looks at her funny and she doesn't want to sit with him any more.'

'If you don't sit with me I'll be stuck with just them for company, because Billy likes him – even though I don't much. He should know what Terry did to Betsy to make her cry.'

'If you tell on Terry he may start on you,' Marion said. 'We'll still be friends, Mary Ellen, but I shan't sit with you and Billy if they're going to – and nor will Betsy.'

Mary Ellen felt a kick on her leg and looked at Terry. He had a malicious smile and his eyes dared her to say something. Well, he might have frightened Betsy but Mary Ellen wasn't afraid of him.

'Don't kick me, Terry,' she said. 'It isn't nice – and no one will want to sit with you if you do things like that. I know you pinched Betsy yesterday and that's what made her cry. She's frightened of you, but I'm not – if you do it again I'll tell Sister Beatrice.'

'You're a snitch,' Terry taunted. 'Good riddance to that little cry-baby Betsy. Who wants to sit with her anyway? Me and Billy don't need her or you – do we, Billy?'

Billy stared at him sternly. 'Don't talk to Mary Ellen like that, Terry. She's me friend too. I like yer, mate, but Mary Ellen and me are best friends.'

Terry stared at him for a moment, surprise turning to displeasure and then anger. He kicked out at Mary Ellen beneath the table again, more sharply this time, and she gave a cry of pain.

'You little beast! I shall tell on you.'

'I hate yer,' Terry cried, and suddenly threw his bowl of porridge all over her. 'I'll get yer fer what yer done . . .'

'Terry, stop that,' Nancy cried as he jumped to his feet. 'Come back here and apologise to Mary Ellen . . .'

Terry didn't listen as he rushed from the dining hall, not pausing to look back at her even though she called his name loudly. Her cheeks flushed bright red, because the children were all staring as Billy tried to help Mary Ellen wipe away the clumps of porridge that clung to her skirt and blouse. Nancy looked at Mary Ellen, tears sparkling in her eyes as she tried to explain.

'I'm so sorry. It's just that he's never had a friend before and he doesn't understand that you have to share friends . . .'

'He's rude and spiteful,' Mary Ellen said, feeling more angered than frightened by Terry's outburst. 'You're all right, Nancy, but no one likes Terry. I tried to be nice to him, but he doesn't want to make friends.'

'Terry's not all bad,' Billy said, feeling the need to come to Terry's defence, 'but he shouldn't have kicked you, Mary Ellen. I'm sorry he took against you. Shall I go after him?'

'No, please, I'll talk to him later,' Nancy said. 'I'm sorry . . . He never used to be like this, honestly. It's only started since the fire . . .' She choked back her tears. 'Perhaps I'd better go.'

At that moment, Sally approached their table, alerted to the fracas by the clattering of the thrown porridge bowl and the cutlery.

'What happened here?' she asked just before Nancy had a chance to go after her brother. 'Why did Terry throw porridge over you, Mary Ellen?'

'It was just a silly joke,' Mary Ellen said, and Nancy looked at her gratefully. 'I'm sorry we made a mess, Sally.'

'Well, you'll have to change your things before you go to school. I'll clear this up,' Sally said, and walked away to fetch a cloth.

'Thanks for not telling on him,' Nancy said. 'Perhaps I'll just leave him to calm down and then he might apologise to you.'

'You spoil him. If he doesn't behave himself, Sister will hear about it and then he'll be in trouble.'

'Yes,' Nancy agreed. 'That's what worries me – in case someone tells her.'

'Sally won't,' Mary Ellen assured her. 'And I won't, but you must tell him to stop being so naughty, Nancy.'

Nancy bit her lip, but didn't answer.

Nancy found Terry in their room, sitting staring at the wall, when she got back. She tried to speak to him but he wouldn't look at her and she could see that he'd been crying. Dropping a kiss on the top of his head, she stroked his hair.

'Mary Ellen won't tell on you, love. She's all right, but you mustn't kick her or pinch Betsy. You have to make friends here if you want to settle in and be happy.'

197

'I want ter go home ter Ma.'

'How many times do I have to tell you?' she said in anxiety and exasperation. 'Ma's dead – she died in the fire with Pa. You know that, Terry.' She felt a surge of emotions as she remembered that awful night, but what was the use? Nothing could change what had happened.

'No . . .' He looked at her in bewilderment. 'You pulled me away from the door . . . it was on fire and I wanted to get Ma out but you said it was too late – and you dragged me down the stairs and outside. If you'd let me open the door Ma could have come too . . .'

'We couldn't get near it for the flames, don't you remember? Besides, the door was locked. Pa always locked it so we couldn't go in when . . . when he and Ma were sleeping . . .' Nancy choked as the tears built inside her. 'Don't you think I wish it was different? Anything would have been better – even what Pa used to do to us . . .' Tears burst from her and suddenly she was crying as if her heart would break. It was all her fault and her secret weighed heavily on her – but she couldn't have known what would happen. 'I wish they were both still alive . . .'

'No, it's better that Pa is dead,' Terry said, and for a moment the look in his eyes chilled her, then his face puckered and he put his arms about her and pleaded, 'Don't cry, Nance. I won't kick her no more . . . I'll be good fer you, Nance. I promise. It don't matter about Billy comin' to the pictures. He ain't me friend, he's hers. It's just you and me, Nance – just you and me . . .'

Nancy had gone somewhere. Terry wasn't sure where. His mind was hazy most of the time now and things got so muddled up that he wasn't sure what had happened to them. Nancy would be back. She would never leave him, she was his Nance; she was always there, always ready to comfort him; it was the one thing he could rely on in this strange world in which nothing made sense any more.

He knew that he hated that girl, the one who had her long hair in plaits. Mary Ellen, Nancy called her. She was a snitch and she'd threatened to tell on him – but she mustn't. If she told they would lock Terry away . . . He shook his head, because she couldn't know his secret. Even Nancy didn't know everything – a little giggle left Terry's lips because he'd punished Pa for hurting him and doing those things to Nance what made her cry.

Terry stared into the darkness that seemed to take over his mind these days. He'd punished Pa and he could punish that girl; she'd taken Billy from him and he wouldn't forgive her for doing that – maybe he'd burn her too if he could get some paraffin, but even if he couldn't he'd find a way to punish her, and the other kids that laughed at him . . . Terry would make them sorry one way or another.

He couldn't think how for a minute, then he looked at the red scratch on his hand and smiled. Yes, that was clever. People thought he was stupid, but he knew more than they thought, and he could do things when he wanted to – and he knew just how to get his own back on that Mary Ellen and the rest of them. He would go to the pictures with that Miss Angela and his sister on Saturday, but that didn't mean he couldn't do what he wanted and get his own back on all the others . . . but

199

he'd be careful until then, because if they didn't go on the treat Nancy would be cross.

'Oh, Miss Angela, I did enjoy that,' Nancy said as they left the Regal cinema together that Saturday after seeing John Wayne in *A Lady Takes a Chance*. 'He was so handsome and she was such fun.' She glanced at her brother. 'Did you enjoy it, Terry?'

'The cowboy bit was good,' Terry said, 'but the girl was soppy. I'd like to be a cowboy and carry a gun like he did.' He went through the shooting motion, pointing an imaginary gun at Angela. 'Bang, you're dead!'

'That's not very nice, Terry, after Miss Angela took us to see the film,' Nancy said, but Angela laughed.

'Terry is just pretending. I'm sure he enjoyed it as much as we did, Nancy. Now who wants to go to Lyons and have some lemonade and cream cakes?'

'I do,' Terry said, and grinned at her. 'You're all right, really, miss. It were good. I've never seen nothin' like it – can we come again?'

'One day,' Angela said. 'Next Saturday I'm taking some children to the zoo – I expect you could come too, both of you, if you would like?'

'I don't like animals,' Terry said, his good humour disappearing. 'They bite and scratch.'

'Dogs and cats don't seem to like Terry,' Nancy said, and frowned. 'These animals are big ones, Terry, and they're shut up in cages.'

'Don't want to see them.' His scowl deepened. 'Don't like things locked up.'

'Well, you don't have to come,' Angela said. 'Forget about the zoo, Terry. Let's go and have our tea.'

Angela led the way to the Lyons' Corner House and they went inside. Most of the tables were occupied and the waitresses scurried about in their little black uniforms and white caps and aprons. The chattering was loud, but Angela made herself heard above the hubbub and they were led to a table in the corner, where they could look out of the window at the busy street. A tram was clanging in the distance and the road teemed with buses, trucks, cars, vans and bikes, but a dray cart pulled by big shire horses seemed to be clogging the traffic at one point so that the confusion was total as a policeman blew his whistle and made frantic signals until things started to move again.

Nancy was clearly excited, looking about her with interest as the girls rushed here and there with their trays piled with food, cups, saucers and teapots. One came up to them and Angela gave the order; tea for herself, ice cream and lemonade for Terry and Nancy and a plate of cakes to share.

'Do you think I could get a job working here?' Nancy asked as the girl went off.

'I think you have to be lucky to be taken on here,' Angela told her. 'There's a lot of competition for jobs at Lyons – I've heard they're very strict and it's hard work. One girl from St Saviour's did get taken on in the kitchens before Christmas, but you need to be eighteen before you can apply to be a waitress. You might get that kind of work elsewhere in a year or two, if you wished . . . but Lyons is more particular.'

'You don't want to work here, Nance,' Terry said. 'When I'm a tram driver you can live with me and I'll look after you.'

'I should like to work here,' Nancy said, ignoring her brother. 'One day I will – even if I have to work somewhere else first.'

'Well, that is a good dream to have,' Angela told her. 'Ah, here are our cakes and drinks. Now, Terry, which would you like, we've got battenburg, rock cakes and fruit cake? I only want one small piece of fruit cake; you two can share the others.' She couldn't resist smiling as Nancy and Terry dived in like starving animals. She knew there was no replacement for a real home and family, but little trips like this gave the children a lift – Mark was right when he said children from deprived areas needed to have their minds opened to what the world could be like – she was glad they'd come.

TWENTY-SIX

'Have you finished polishing the front room?' Sally's mother asked her that Sunday morning. 'If you have, you can set the table with your granny's best linen tablecloth – and make sure you rub the cutlery well. It might only be silver plate but it belonged to my great-grandmother and it still looks like new.'

'That's because it is new; we never use it,' Sally's father chimed in. 'I don't know why you're making all this fuss, love. Anyone would think it was royalty coming to lunch.'

'Well, he isn't far off, is he?' Mrs Rush snapped back. 'A surgeon and an author . . . he'll think he's landed in a foreign country if I entertain him at the kitchen table.'

'Mum,' Sally said, feeling all knotted up inside and uncomfortable. She almost wished she hadn't asked Andrew to lunch, but he'd wanted to get to know her parents and her father had insisted she invite him and her mother hadn't stopped fussing since. She hadn't been able to get hold of a piece of roasting beef, but she had managed to buy the ingredients for a steak and kidney pie. Knowing how light and delicious her mother's pastry was, Sally was sure that Andrew would enjoy his meal. There were just two courses, the meat pie and vegetables followed by spotted dick and custard. It was the kind of hearty meal they often had in the Rush household but Sally wondered if Andrew would be able to eat such heavy fare. 'Andrew isn't a bit stuck-up and I'm sure he wouldn't want you to go to a lot of trouble.'

'Well, he'll have a good tasty dinner in this house, but nothing fancy. He'll just have to make do like the rest of the country, though I don't doubt that the toffs all manage to eat better than we do.'

Sally knew that Andrew would have been happy with something simple, but she hadn't dared to object to her mother's menu. She knew that her mother had gone along with this invitation only because Sally's father had insisted on it, and there was no sense in provoking an argument for nothing.

Sally helped her mother in the kitchen as much as she could and then went upstairs to change into a pretty dress, but not one that Angela had given her. She kept those for the occasions when she and Andrew went somewhere special, though her mother frequently dis-approved of what she called 'showiness'.

'Why you need clothes like that I don't know,' she'd told Sally more than once. 'If your own aren't good enough for him, you should consider if he's the right person to be stepping out with, Sally.'

'We go to some posh places, Mum. I wear the clothes for myself, so that I feel comfortable – Andrew thinks I'm beautiful in my uniform at work.'

'Well, at least one of you has some sense.'

That didn't mean that her mother approved of Andrew.

She accepted that he was a decent, dedicated man, but that didn't make him right for her daughter. Sally knew that her mother was trying to safeguard her, but she didn't understand that they were in love.

'We love each other, Mum. I don't know why you're so against Andrew,' she said when told to keep an eye on the dinner while she changed into a clean dress.

'It's not that I have anything against him, Sally,' her mother replied. 'You haven't thought things through yet, love. You want to be a nurse. You've wanted it for ages – and you wouldn't be happy staying at home with a brood of children round your skirts. You deserve more from life than I've had.'

'Aren't you happy, Mum?'

'Yes, happy making do with little and scrubbing floors for a living to make ends meet, but we're not talking about me. This is your future – the future you've been planning for ages. What has all the saving and night school been about if you're just going to give up the idea and get married? Me and your dad want more for you than that.'

'I don't want to get married for a while,' Sally said, and saw a look of satisfaction in her mother's eyes. 'But I do love Andrew and when I marry . . . it will probably be him, if he asks me.'

'Hasn't he then?'

'Not really . . . just vague hints about where we'll live, things like that . . .'

'He'll want a nice house in the suburbs with a garden for the children and he'll want you to stay at home and give up your nursing.'

Sally didn't answer. She couldn't deny that assertion

because she knew it was exactly what Andrew had in mind. He'd mentioned it once or twice in passing, when they'd been kissing or just sitting together in his car somewhere secluded. He'd driven her out of the city a couple of times, for lunch at a nice pub by the river, and they'd gone for walks, holding hands. Sally sensed that Andrew was getting close to a proposal but hoped he would wait for a while.

At Christmas he'd given her a pretty gold locket on a chain, which she wore next to her skin under her uniform, and visibly when they went out together. She'd half-thought he might give her a ring then, but thankfully he hadn't – because her parents would never have agreed to an early marriage without even getting to know him. She guessed that Andrew was hoping this lunch would bring the day closer when he could speak to her father, but Sally had an awful feeling it might not help their cause – it might even make things worse.

Sally was certain in her own mind and heart that she loved him, but her mother was right in saying that she couldn't just throw her hard work away in order to get married and settle down. She was young yet and if she were honest, Sally wanted to experience the excitement of becoming a nurse – the training with other girls of her age, the exams and the pleasure of putting on her nurse's cap and knowing she'd earned the right. Surely Andrew wouldn't expect her to give that up before she'd even had a chance to prove what she could do . . .

'And where did you go for your holiday last summer?' Andrew asked Sally's mother politely as they all sat round the table eating the delicious pie she'd prepared. The pastry just crumbled in the mouth and Sally knew she'd done her best to make things nice for Andrew, even if she didn't approve.

'Holidays aren't something we've had much of recently. What with the war, then work being thin on the ground for Mr Rush and it's been tough round here for us ordinary folk.' She pursed her lips and gave Andrew Markham a pointed look.

Sally's father came to the rescue. 'Come on now, love, things aren't that bad. We had a week in Southend, didn't we?' Sally's mother frowned at her husband but nodded reluctantly.

'Of course, it's been a rough few years for many.' Andrew nodded in understanding. 'I see it all the time at the hospital. I'm not one for holidays myself, I only popped up to stay with my friend Henry Fitzhugh on his estate in the Highlands,' he added. 'They have acres of mountainous land, which is only fit for the deer and some Longhorn cattle. I enjoy a spot of salmon fishing when I can get it – and if you catch something you can eat it.' He looked enquiringly at Mr Rush. 'Do you fish, sir?'

'No, I've never had the time or the inclination,' Sally's father said, knotting his brow slightly. 'I dare say it's nice up there?'

'Yes, beautiful in the summer and autumn, but a bit chilly in the winter,' Andrew replied easily. 'You mustn't think I often indulge myself. Most of my time is given to work – and then there's my aunt. I visit her in the country when I can.'

'No doubt she has a big house?' Sally's mother said.

'Well, it has four bedrooms, but it isn't excessive, nothing like Henry's draughty old castle,' Andrew said and laughed. 'Don't imagine the Fitzhugh family are wealthy, Mrs Rush. Henry has to wring a living out of his land – and that castle is nowhere near as warm and comfortable as your home.' He looked around the dining room of the Rush family's new council house.

Sally saw her mother and father exchange a look at this.

'Well, we think we've been fortunate since the council condemned the slum we used to live in; we're one of the lucky families. Some folk are still waiting for new homes and are stuck in those flimsy prefabs.' She stood up. 'If everyone has finished, I'll clear this and bring in the pudding – it's spotted dick with custard, Mr Markham. The men in my family have always been big eaters – they work hard with their hands, you see. It's what we're used to.'

'Please, call me Andrew. I loved spotted dick and custard when I was at school,' he said politely, but Sally could tell that he couldn't face another heavy plateful of food after all that pie. 'Just a very small piece for me, please. I'm rather full after that delicious pie.'

Glancing at his plate, which her mother had piled high with pie, carrots, cabbage and boiled onions, she saw that Andrew had left some of the pastry and most of the cabbage. At once she knew that her mother had taken it as an affront, even though she'd given him more than she would normally serve her husband after a day spent working. No one else's plate had been piled quite as high and Sally was embarrassed. Perhaps the food hadn't been to his taste and he was probably used

208

to much smaller portions. As it was, he'd done the best he could.

'If you're not hungry just have tea,' she said, smiling at him. 'I'm going to – I couldn't possibly eat anything else just yet, Mum.'

'I'm not bothered myself, love,' Sally's father said, and received a glare from his wife. 'Why don't you save it for supper and we'll just have a cuppa?' He smiled at Sally. 'Help your mother clear the table and make the tea, Sally. I'll have a drop more of the excellent wine Mr Markham brought us – and I'd like to hear a bit more about this place in Scotland.'

Sally shot her father a look of pure gratitude. It wasn't the first time he'd intervened during the difficult time since Andrew arrived, bearing a bottle of good burgundy, a box of milk chocolates for her mother and flowers for Sally. Wine was something they'd never had at home before and chocolates were still like gold dust due to the continuing rationing of sugar. Her father was enjoying the wine, probably a bit too much for her mother's liking. It was something else for her to be resentful of and it seemed there was no pleasing her. Sally gathered up several plates and took them into the kitchen.

'Mum, don't be offended. The meal was lovely, but there was rather a lot. No one can manage a pudding . . .'

'Oh, I dare say he would have eaten a coffee mousse or a soufflé . . .'

'Please, don't be upset. Dad seems to like him.'

'Your father can be a soft fool, especially where you're concerned.'

'He's interested in hearing what Andrew has to say . . .'

209

'And I'm not?' Her mother glared at her. 'You're trying to mix oil and water, Sally, and no good will come of it – just be warned. I dare say it all seems glamorous now, but wait until you've been married for a while and the gloss wears off. You'll feel awkward with his friends and family – and you'll hate holidays in the wilds of Scotland fishing. You're a town girl, Sally, an East Ender – and you'll be miserable anywhere else. You should wait, just for a year or so, and see how you feel, that's all I'm saying.'

'Please, Mum, try to like him, for my sake?'

'I never said I didn't like him. He's good-looking, generous and polite – but he's not our sort and if you marry him you'll break the family apart.' Her mother's face was set and Sally could see there'd be no persuading her otherwise for now.

'I'm sorry about Mum,' Sally said when she and Andrew took a little walk after lunch. It was cold but they were both wrapped up warm and it was nice just strolling through streets that were much less busy than they were in the week. 'She's used to my father and brother . . .'

'You don't have to apologise for anything,' Andrew said, and smiled warmly at her. 'I've never tasted a better steak and kidney pie. I'm sorry I couldn't finish it all, but she did give me rather a lot.'

'Too much,' Sally said, hugging his arm. But of course the day-to-day vegetable dishes they normally used were chipped and Mrs Rush wouldn't put them on the table for a guest like Andrew. Her mother was guilty of snobbery, Sally thought, and laughed inwardly. If she really didn't care what he thought of them, she would have given him pot luck in the kitchen. 'I hope it hasn't put you off my family? Brenda will love you and I think you got on with Dad?'

'Your father was very pleasant to speak with,' Andrew assured her, and then he turned to look into her eyes. 'I don't want to marry your family, Sally. I hope we shall all get on well together and I want them to like me for your sake – but it's you I love, you I want to marry one day.'

'I'm not twenty-one yet,' Sally said. 'I think they might say we should wait.'

'Not for too long,' Andrew said, and leaned in to kiss her. 'Besides, you'll be old enough to choose for yourself in a few months – and then I hope you'll want a nice house away from the city where we can give our children the kind of family life I never had. I want several, Sally, and I want to spend my life with you, but we've got plenty of time to decide these things . . .' He put his arm about her. 'Your family is delightful, Sally – besides, when we're married we shan't live in their pockets, shall we?'

Sally ate a piece of cold spotted dick with hot custard for her supper. She'd stayed with Andrew by the river for most of the afternoon and had a lovely tea of tiny cucumber sandwiches and scones with jam in a nice hotel. She'd enjoyed herself and when Andrew kissed her goodnight on the step, her heart had leaped for joy. It was only when she came back home and saw her mother, father and sister sitting together drinking tea in the kitchen that she began to feel a little uneasy.

She loved Andrew and she enjoyed being with him

– and she did want to marry him one day – but it would be a wrench to leave the people and the places she knew so well. Living in the suburbs was all right, and she would probably find friends soon enough, but she wasn't sure she was ready to make the break yet. She liked the independence of working at St Saviour's, and if she ever managed to become a nurse she would like that even more. Sally had thought she might apply to work at the children's home once she had her nursing certificate. It would be near her home and her family; her sister and her brother would both settle in the East End, not far from their parents – and if Sally went off to the suburbs she wouldn't see much of them. She would probably have to work somewhere else . . . if Andrew even agreed that she could continue. He didn't seem keen on her working after they were married. Sally wasn't sure how she felt about that. Naturally, the children would need her while they were little, but why should she give it up completely? Things had changed over the course of the war and women wanted more choice now – wasn't that part of what they'd fought for?

If Andrew loved her as much as he said, he would surely understand that Sally was a modern girl. It was a new world out there, and she didn't want to be just a housewife for ever.

TWENTY-SEVEN

The auction was going well, hands shooting up all over the place, and the prices Angela was achieving were far in excess of what she'd hoped for when she'd decided to sell off the bequest St Saviour's had received. Nick Hadden had brought a party of wealthy friends with him, and they had purchased all the silver pieces between them.

'Well, here is my final item, ladies and gentlemen,' Angela said, holding up a pretty brush, which was part of a silver dressing-table set. It had been as black as ink but she and Sally had cleaned it and it looked beautiful. 'What will you bid me for this genuine silver set, please?'

'Ten pounds,' a voice said from the back of the room, and Angela saw that it was one of Nick's friends.

'Eleven pounds,' a new voice chimed in and Angela saw that Mark Adderbury had joined in the contest.

'Twelve.'

'Fourteen.'

'Twenty pounds,' another new voice said, and Angela

smiled as she saw that Mr Markham had taken up the fray.

'Twenty-five,' Mark offered, smiling broadly at his friend and colleague.

'Thirty.' Nick's friend returned to the bidding, minus the friendly smile.

Mark bowed his head. 'I leave the field to the victor,' he said, and everyone laughed and then applauded.

'Thank you so much, gentlemen,' Angela said, flushed with triumph. 'I would like to thank everyone who came this evening for their generosity. Every penny of the money from this auction will be going to St Saviour's, because every one of my helpers has given their time free and I am grateful to all of them.'

Another round of applause greeted her announcement, and then there was a general movement as people paid for their goods and collected them. Sally had been in charge of the money and was sitting at a desk, keeping count of everything. She looked up with a smile as Angela approached.

'The cash box is nearly full,' she said. 'I couldn't believe how much that dressing-table set sold for – and it looked like rubbish until we cleaned it.'

'I'd seen that old mark,' Angela said. 'The bowls were the best cut glass and not chipped at all, and the silver pieces were by a good maker. I know because they have the same hallmarks as on a mirror given me by John's mother – she said it was by Hester Bateman.'

'Is that why it fetched so much?' Sally said, and turned aside to take the thirty pounds from the gentleman who had bought it. 'I hope your wife will be pleased with the set, sir.'

'It is for my daughter's eighteenth birthday. I've been looking for something good for her for ages, but this was a bargain.'

'I'm so glad you're pleased,' Angela said.

The hall was emptying of people, except for Mark, Nick and Andrew Markham. Ned and Jeff said goodnight; Angela thanked them again for all their help, and then it was just the five of them. Andrew Markham walked up to Sally, smiling at her in approval. Angela saw the way the girl's eyes lit up and realised she was truly in love with the brilliant young surgeon. She noted the way Sally went to him and took his arm, her confident smile and the look in his eyes. Their happiness made Angela blink and she couldn't help wishing she had someone who felt that way about her.

'You've been busy,' he said. 'I think you deserve a nice meal before I drive you home, Sally.'

'Thank you. Is it all right if I go now, Angela?'

'Yes, of course. Thank you for all your help, Sally. I'll see you tomorrow at St Saviour's.'

'Yes, I'll be there bright and early.'

Sally went off with Andrew and Angela was left with Nick and Mark, who eyed each other warily for a moment.

'I think that was an excellent idea of Markham's,' Mark said. 'I suggest I take you for a meal, Angela.'

'I have already laid my claim earlier this evening,' Nick said smoothly. 'My car awaits you outside, Angela darling.' His eyes told her that he believed she was hers. Mark looked annoyed and for a moment the air seemed to crackle between them.

Angela was tempted to laugh, because they were like two terrier puppies about to fight over a bone. 'Thank you both for a lovely idea, which I will take you up on another evening, Mark. However, all I need is a lift home, because I want to put this money away safely and have it ready to bank in the morning. I'm a little tired and would prefer to go back and have a nice cup of cocoa and then retire to bed.'

'Your carriage awaits,' Nick purred, with a look of triumph. 'You're out of luck this evening, Adderbury.'

'So it would seem.' Mark accepted his dismissal with grace. 'I shall not intrude on your evening further, Angela,' he said softly. 'I only wished to congratulate you on yet another resounding success.'

'You're not intruding, Mark.' She gave him a warm smile to soften the awkwardness. 'Thank you for all your help – and I shall be happy to have dinner another evening.'

'Would you like me to lock up for you and return the key to the vicar?' Mark asked.

'Would you? That would be kind.' She picked up her warm coat, gave the locked cash box to Nick and nodded at him. 'Shall we go, Nick? I know I can trust you to guard this with your life.'

'Of course, my lady,' he said, dark eyes alight with amusement. 'I am always at your service. Goodnight, Adderbury.'

Angela walked from the hall, knowing that Mark's gaze was following her. She was conscious of feeling that she was at some sort of crossroads, of having arrived at the stage where she might have to choose between her friends. It wasn't something she wished to do, because

216

she liked both men, and would have preferred to keep things on the friendship level all round, but Nick had clearly laid down a marker by calling her darling.

Oh, she couldn't be bothered to think about it that evening. Everything had gone extremely well, but she'd found the auction hard work and wasn't in the mood for heavy romance for the time being. Venturing out into the evening air, she shivered in the sudden chill. There was only the shadow of a moon and the sky was cloudy and dark. She would be glad to be home in the warm, because it looked as if it might snow yet again. She couldn't wait for the warmer days of spring. Surely it couldn't be much longer now.

Angela locked the money from the auction in her desk after counting it twice. Sally's accounts tallied perfectly but she found it difficult to believe that they had raised over four hundred pounds in one evening. It was twice what Angela's mother had raised from her charity dance for St Saviour's and many times what she'd raised from her clothing sale. Had she employed people to help it would have reduced the takings by twenty or thirty per cent, but because everyone had given their services free she had a really useful sum to bank the next day.

Her smile lingered as she sipped her cocoa. Perhaps it was churlish not to invite Nick to come in for a while, but she was too tired for dinner though he'd tried hard to persuade her on their way home, but she'd been firm in refusing.

'I'm sorry, but I really am tired, and I have a bit of a headache,' she'd told him. 'I'll cook you dinner another evening. We can spend a little time together then, if that

217

will do? I'm not that much of a cook, but I can manage a steak . . .'

'Sounds just the job,' he said, and reached out to draw her into his arms before she had a chance to resist. 'I'm glad you can manage my favourite meal – but it's not as a cook that I want you, Angela, but as a wife.'

Angela was taken aback. He was taking too much for granted. He was very skilled at manoeuvring her into going out with him when sometimes she would rather not – he was good company and at times she felt rather alone. But this talk of marriage was unexpected.

'It's you I care about, Angela, the woman you are – caring and strong. I shan't mind you giving your spare time to St Saviour's or whatever else you choose to support when we're married – as long as you have time for me and the children.'

Nick leaned in to give her a lingering kiss on the lips. For a brief moment, the feel of his strong arms around her, the scent of his cologne and the warmth of a man's body so close to her own was a heady mixture. Their lips met, and briefly she was transported, but then an image of Mark Adderbury pushed itself into Angela's mind. She pulled away.

'Oh, Nick.' Angela struggled to find the right words. Marriage was something that she wasn't ready for, and even if she was . . . Nick was perfect husband material, but why didn't he feel right for her? 'I'm can't commit to marriage yet. I have told you . . .'

'Shush, my darling,' he said, and brushed his thumb over her full bottom lip. It was a sensual caress and she felt her insides jump with what could only be desire, but she fought it. Angela didn't want to be rushed or pushed into anything. She liked Nick, but she liked Mark too. She wasn't going to be swept along by Nick's strong personality.

'I know you need a little more time, but soon you will be ready . . . and I want you to know how much I adore you. I don't need a slave, just a warm, loving woman – a woman who knows her own mind and her own heart.'

'Nick, I like you very much and I'm flattered, but . . .' Nick hadn't allowed her to go on. He'd kissed her again. 'Please, Nick.' She pulled gently away. 'I'm awfully tired.'

'Yes, I can see that, darling.' He kissed the top of her head, then collected his coat and hat from the hallway. 'We'll talk again.' She could hear him whistling cheerfully as he headed out into the night.

Angela switched off the lights and wearily headed into her bedroom. She was too tired even to get into her silk nightie and instead slipped out of her clothes, climbing into bed in just her camisole and knickers. As her head sank into the pillow she thought about that evening. She knew Nick believed he was wearing her down, gradually defeating her resistance. Maybe she should be content to be married to him? He would be a caring husband, but also possessive and domineering. He would expect Angela to fall in with his plans, had already shown signs of riding roughshod over her wishes and imposing his own. His kisses stirred something inside that she'd thought dead, and Angela knew that she would enjoy the physical side of marriage. She'd discovered passion in John's arms, and it had been a revelation and a joy to her, and although she wasn't the kind of woman who gave herself easily she'd been tempted more than once when Nick kissed her. Yet she knew it would be wrong to give her body if she couldn't also give her heart and her mind. Deep down, Angela knew that she was avoiding thinking about the real reason she couldn't give herself fully to Nick and that reason was Mark Adderbury.

She sighed deeply, feeling confused. No, romance was too complicated. It was better to continue with her life the way it was, enjoying her work and helping the children at St Saviour's. She'd had love once, perhaps it was too much to expect it again, but as she fell into a slumber it was Mark, not John or Nick, who crept into her jumbled dreams.

TWENTY-EIGHT

Nan popped in to Beatrice's office around three in the afternoon for a cup of tea. The Warden had put her kettle on the little gas ring in readiness and greeted her with a sigh of relief.

'I'm glad you've come, Nan. We've had such a day! Two children were brought in first thing this morning, and we've had three more since then. At least they were healthy and we managed to squeeze them into the dorms, but the two girls were difficult. It seems they have a father, but he's been drunk ever since the mother died six months ago, and taken to beating them. They didn't want to tell us their names because they were afraid they would be sent home.'

'That won't happen, will it?'

'If I have my way the father will be prosecuted for maltreating his children,' Beatrice said angrily.

'And so he should be,' Nan agreed. She sighed as she sat down by the fire. 'I could do with a cuppa.'

'We both deserve this, I think,' Beatrice said. She took out a small tin of Scottish shortbread biscuits, which a grateful relation had brought in, and offered them to

Nan. 'Sometimes, I wonder if I'm getting too old for this job.'

'You wouldn't think of retiring?'

'No, not at all.' Beatrice shook her head. 'Take no notice of me, Nan. It has been one of those days.' She sipped her tea. 'How are you getting on with your bring-and-buy sales?'

'We raised five pounds at our first evening.'

'That is excellent,' Beatrice said. 'Have you seen your soldier friend recently?'

'Well . . .' Nan's cheeks were a little flushed. 'I've asked him to lunch again this Saturday. I've saved my meat coupons and we're going to have a beef and ale casserole with apple crumble and custard afterwards.'

'It sounds delicious,' Beatrice said, and for the first time in years she was aware of her own loneliness. 'I'm glad you've found a new friend, Nan.'

'I was wondering . . . I mean, there will be plenty for three,' Nan said. 'Would you come and meet Eddie, Bea? I'd love you to come . . . if you would?'

Beatrice hesitated. She was tempted but it wouldn't be fair to her friend. Stretching her rations to include another was difficult enough, and Nan would have enough to do looking after her old soldier.

'Perhaps another time,' she said. 'I'm on duty this Saturday, because both Mary and Carole are off – so I need to be here just in case.' She hesitated, then, 'I need to talk to you about Alice. We cannot keep her here for much longer, Nan. Father Joe thinks she should go to a Church home for unmarried mothers.'

'But they will force her to give up the child. I don't think Alice will do that, Beatrice. I think she might run away, go off somewhere and try to manage alone if we were to insist she have the child there. No, no, let me think about this a little more – I might have a solution. I'll try and speak to her later, ask her how she's getting on. I think she may have found lodgings but I'll see what she has to say before you make up your mind.'

'Very well, you must do as you think fit. You know her better than I do.'

Nan sipped her tea. 'I'm going to tell Eddie about Maisie. I want to ask his advice. She never answers my letters, as you know – but perhaps if I were to go down to see her . . .'

'Do you think that is wise? Why not ask the Mother Superior if she will talk to her? If you make that long journey alone and Maisie refuses to see you it will be so upsetting for you, Nan.'

'Yes,' Nan sighed. 'But I can't bear things the way they are, Bea. I need to see her just once, to talk to her again.'

'Well, I can't stop you, but I know how much it upset you the last time she refused to see you.'

'I'm going to see Maisie somehow. She's my daughter and I'll never give up.'

Later, as Nan left the staff room carrying a tray of used mugs, she saw Alice coming towards her. She had her coat on and it was obvious she was about to leave for the evening.

'Ah, Alice dear,' said Nan. 'I'm glad I've caught you. I wanted to talk to you for a few minutes.'

'Have I done something wrong, Nan?' Alice looked apprehensive and Nan felt sad, because she knew what she had to say would upset the girl.

'Your work is faultless, Alice,' she said gently, 'but you know that you will have to leave soon, don't you?'

'Yes – but need it be just yet?'

'I'm afraid that is up to others,' Nan said, still in that soft, caring tone. 'I've been asked to enquire if you've decided what to do when the time comes – are you planning to have the baby at your home?'

'Ma won't have me,' Alice said. 'Mavis says she won't even discuss it. As far as she's concerned she doesn't have a daughter called Alice.'

'Ah, I see.' Nan sighed. 'That means you will either be entirely on your own – or you might consider entering a mother and baby home.'

'You mean a home for fallen girls where they take your baby away even if you want it,' Alice said, and her head went up. 'I'm not going to get rid of my baby and I'm not going to let a stranger have it either. I loved Jack and I want my child.'

'But he's gone, dear.'

'I know,' Alice admitted. 'But it doesn't matter. I shan't give my baby up. I'll manage somehow, even if I have to scrub floors or work in a factory.'

'You haven't thought what will happen once the child is born. Not many landladies will let a room to an unmarried mother, Alice – and you'll have to pay someone to look after the child while you work. It will be so hard for you.'

'I know.' Tears trickled from the corners of her eyes. 'I'm frightened, Nan. I know that I'll have difficulty once it shows – but I'll get through somehow. I can't give my baby up. I won't.'

'Well, you've told me what I wanted to know,' Nan said. 'I'll talk to Sister again and hear what she says.'

'Do you think Angela might help? She might know of somewhere I could go – a place where they let me have the child and won't take it away from me.'

'Well, she might, I suppose,' Nan said. 'I'll have a word – don't worry, Alice. I'm on your side, and in her heart Sister Beatrice is too, but she can't do just as she thinks, because there are others involved. I'll see what I can come up with. Off you go now and try not to worry too much, my dear . . .'

Alice left St Saviour's late that night. It was the end of February and still bitterly cold and she pulled up her coat collar around her neck, feeling tired and dispirited as she contemplated her lonely little room at Mrs Brook's respectable lodging house. The room had a small gas fire, which she could light to warm herself for a while, and a ring that she could boil a kettle on to make a cup of tea, but she didn't use either of them much, because she had to feed shillings into the meter and it was frightening how quickly they ran out.

Although she still had her savings, Alice was reluctant to use them just yet. Once she was forced to leave work she would soon find that her small store of money was dwindling away.

It wasn't that she missed her mother's nagging or the crowded, smelly house she'd lived in, but she did miss seeing her father now and then and she missed her sister sleeping beside her at night. During the time she'd shared Michelle's bedroom she hadn't realised how much she would feel the separation from her sister, but since she'd moved into the lodging house she'd been very much aware of her loneliness at nights.

It was going to be so much worse when she left St Saviour's. Sister had called her in soon after Nan told her that Alice was determined to keep the baby. To her surprise the nun had been more sympathetic than angry and promised her that she could stay on until her condition could no longer be hidden.

'The trustees would not tolerate a girl in your position working here, Alice,' Sister had told her, 'so I can only give you a few more weeks. However, if you should change your mind, I imagine I can find a place for you in one of our homes.'

Alice had thanked her, though she'd made up her mind she wasn't going to have her baby in one of those places where they treated the mother as if she were a leper and took the baby away for adoption soon after it was born. She would like to stay on at Mrs Brook's house but doubted she would be welcome once the good woman knew the truth. She certainly wouldn't want a young baby in the house, because the child's crying might upset her other lodgers and the washing would get in the way.

Alice wasn't sure where she could go. Perhaps she ought to look elsewhere for a couple of rooms where she would be allowed to keep the child. It might be best to buy herself a cheap wedding ring and pass herself off as a widow. Even if she went out of town to have the child . . . her thoughts were abruptly suspended as someone came up to her out of the gloom and she jumped, thinking it was one of Butcher Lee's henchmen come to grab her again.

'Alice.' Her cousin Eric's voice calmed her. 'I saw you leave and I've been callin' to you but you didn't hear me.'

'Sorry, I was miles away,' she said. 'I didn't know you were home on leave?'

'Yes, just for a few days. I went round to see you, because Bob asked me to find out how you were – and your sister told me you were living here.' His eyes went over her. 'You're havin' a kid, aren't you?'

'Did Ma tell you that?'

'No, I guessed, because it's the only reason she would throw you out. It was that Jack Shaw, wasn't it? I'll not tell anyone else – but, Alice, what were you thinkin' of?'

'I loved him,' she said. 'I know I'm a fool, but I couldn't help myself. He just kept after me until I finally gave in and then I believed that he cared for me – that he would marry me but he just went off . . .'

'And you in the pudding club,' Eric said scornfully. 'How are you supposed to live once it's born?'

'I'll manage somehow,' Alice said. 'Don't look at me like that, Eric. There's nothing I can do about it now.'

'You could let Bob look after you,' Eric said, gazing at her intently. 'He really likes you, Alice. Why don't you ask him to come round and then tell him the truth? I'm sure he's in love with you.'

'I couldn't do that to him, Eric. It would be so unfair to Bob. Don't you see how mean that is – to take advantage of his good nature and who would want another man's child foisted on him?'

'A lot of girls wouldn't think twice of getting Bob's ring on their finger and worryin' about the fairness afterwards.'

'I'm not a lot of girls, Eric.' She smiled wryly. 'I like Bob – probably more than I thought at first, but it's too late. It just wouldn't be fair. No, I have to wait and work for as long as I can . . . but I need somewhere to live.'

'I'll see if I can find a place. I've got a few friends and some women are not as holier-than-thou as others.' He looked at her quizzically. 'I would ask you to marry me, Alice, love, if I could.'

She laughed and shook her head. 'I'm fond of you, Eric, but we're cousins and we don't think of each other in that way – besides, I think there's someone else you do care for a lot?'

'If you mean Michelle that's another lost cause,' Eric said gloomily. 'She lets me take her out occasionally, but only so that she can ask me to look after you. I don't think I have a hope in hell of getting her into bed with me!'

'I should think not either.' Alice was indignant.

'I would put a weddin' ring on her finger first if she'd have me,' he said, and laughed. 'Michelle wouldn't let me kiss her properly let alone anything else. I might as well wish for the moon as have hopes in that direction.'

'I think she's been badly hurt in the past,' Alice said thoughtfully. 'We're good friends but she's never told me about her past. But I think she likes you, Eric. You shouldn't give up. Perhaps one day she'll realise she can trust you.'

'That's what I tell Bob when he talks about you,' Eric said, and grinned ruefully. 'We're not a lucky pair, are we, Alice?'

'At least in the Army you've got a good job for life.'

228

'I'm not sure if I really want to stay on for the rest of my life,' Eric said. 'They've told me I could get overseas service. A lot of the chaps like being posted abroad but I should hate it – unless I could take Michelle with me . . .'

'Have you told her how you feel?'

'I don't think she would be interested,' he sighed. 'Anyway, I'll keep an eye out for that new place for you.' He stopped and looked at her. 'You've only got to go across the road, love. I'll be seein' you before long – and do what I said, let Bob come and see you and tell him. You'll have a decent chance of a good life with him, Alice.'

Alice shook her head but didn't answer. She thought too much of Bob to put him in an awkward position, just because of a mistaken sense of duty or just because he felt sorry for her. No, she'd have to go it alone . . .

TWENTY-NINE

Angela finished her work and covered the typewriter. For some reason her mind just wasn't on her work that afternoon. She kept thinking about Nick's reaction when he'd taken her home from the auction, and her own conflicting emotions. The truth was she didn't really know what she wanted. When John's death was first reported to Angela, she'd imagined that her life was over. Now she knew that if she had three lifetimes it would never be enough for all she wanted to do. If it were not for her mother's illness and the toll that had taken on her father, Angela thought she might have been content. She decided that she would ring her father that evening and talk to him, perhaps ask him up to dinner or just go down and stay for a couple of days. She ought to make the effort to visit and see for herself how her mother was getting on.

'Angela, may I take up a few minutes of your time?'

Angela smiled as Nan put her head round the door. She was carrying a tray with a pot of tea and two cups and had clearly come for a chat.

'Yes, of course,' Angela said. 'I always have time to talk to you. How can I help you?'

'Well, it's about one of our carers,' Nan said. 'Normally, I don't discuss their private affairs, but I have Alice's permission to talk to you about her problem.'

'Ah, Alice . . .' Angela nodded as she took the cup Nan offered. 'I think I might be able to guess – she's pregnant, isn't she?'

'Yes, and I think there's no hope of the father marrying her. She has told me she intends to keep the baby whatever happens, and I believe her. Father Joe thinks she should enter a mother and baby home, but they will force her to give up the child and Alice is set against it. Beatrice wants to help, but her hands are tied. Alice wondered if you might know of somewhere she could have the child – away from London. Without a husband we couldn't employ her here. Father Joe feels to keep the child would lead Alice to fall into a life of vice in her efforts to support it, and the Bishop would agree with him. Beatrice is in the middle. She knows I feel we should help Alice, but she cannot go against the Church in this matter.'

'Very difficult for her,' Angela agreed. 'I don't know of anywhere at the moment, Nan, but I'm sure something could be arranged. These things are always possible if one has the will – and the means. Alice is sure she wants to keep the child? People still look harshly at girls who have an illegitimate baby.'

'Yes, I'm sure she understands what she is facing. She will have to find lodgings with someone who will let her keep the child – and perhaps pay for it to be looked after. Without a husband she will have a terrible life alone.'

'We'll have to put our thinking caps on,' Angela said.

'We cannot allow Alice to sink into a life of poverty and depredation – and yet she is proud and an offer of financial help might easily be rejected. You say Sister Beatrice is sympathetic?'

'Yes, if she could help, she would.'

'Then we shall all think about it and see what we can do to help Alice.'

'I've arranged for us to stay with a friend of mine this weekend,' Nick said over the telephone the next morning. 'He has a fantastic place in the country and you'll love it, Angela – tennis courts and plenty of fresh air!'

'I'm sorry, Nick. I simply can't manage it,' Angela said. 'Tomorrow I'm taking some children to the zoo, then I'll be catching the late train back home to see my parents.'

'Cancel it, darling. Life is too short if you devote yourself to duty and work.'

'I want to see my parents, and I promised the children this trip – and I don't feel inclined to cancel.'

'I've made all the arrangements. Surely you won't let me down, darling? I'm relying on you to sweet-talk some business acquaintances of mine into a deal I have going. You're just the person I need . . .'

'Perhaps if you'd asked first, Nick, I might have managed to change things – but I simply can't put this trip off and my father wants to see me. I'm sorry. You'll have to go alone – or take one of your other friends with you.'

'You know you're the only one I want, Angela. Are you sure I can't persuade you – pretty please?'

'I'm sorry, Nick, but this time I mean no.'

Angela replaced the receiver, feeling annoyed. Nick was too fond of making arrangements without consulting her. He seemed to imagine she could drop everything for him at the last minute, but this time she wasn't willing to change her plans. The children were looking forward to their treat – and her father was worried about her mother. She was anxious too because he'd sounded very tired when she rang the previous evening . . .

THIRTY

Nan looked at her friend across the table in her kitchen. The long pine table had a spotless white cloth and a bowl of snowdrops stood on a blue crochet mat in the middle. They had eaten a comfortable meal together and then Eddie had helped her to clear the dishes and wash up at the deep sink, stacking the blue and white crockery on her dresser. It was an old one, bought from the second-hand shop after her home was lost in the Blitz, but she'd painted it white and gradually collected bits and pieces from the stalls in Portobello Road to give it a bright, cheerful look. She'd made a pot of tea, which they had lingered over as the afternoon seemed to speed away, and Nan was surprised when she heard the ancient American wall clock in the hall strike five o'clock.

'Goodness gracious,' she exclaimed. 'Where has the time gone today?'

'Time is the thief of pleasure,' Eddie said. 'We were enjoying ourselves, Nan – and I wish I might stay longer, take you for a drink this evening perhaps, but I fear I have some work on. When are you free next for tea?'

'I've promised to go to the zoo with the children tomorrow. Angela took some of them today and Sally and I are taking some others tomorrow. I may go down to visit my daughter next weekend,' Nan said hesitantly. 'I do not know what to do. Beatrice thinks I shall only be upset if Maisie refuses to see me again.'

'When will you go – on Saturday or Sunday?'

'Friday evening, I think. Sunday is always a day of prayer at the convent so I need to visit on Saturday.'

'Would you permit me to accompany you? It's a long journey alone, Nan. We can take rooms somewhere and travel back on the Sunday. If you think my company would help you?'

'Oh, would you, Eddie?' Nan was overcome with relief, because she'd dreaded the prospect of the long journey alone, especially if on the way back she was faced with having failed to see her daughter once more. 'It would mean so much to me to have you with me. We haven't known each other long, but I feel that you are a true friend to me.'

'I feel privileged to know you, my dear,' he said, a wistful expression in his faded blue eyes. 'I have spent most of my life in the chaotic world of the Army, and I was always a little afraid of the female sex.' His naughty smile twinkled out at her. 'My mother was very dominant and she led my father – and her children – a merry dance. I believe I have spent most of my life hiding from her kind of Amazonian woman. You have been a revelation to me, Nan. In you I see nothing but kindness and love for others, particularly for your children at St Saviour's – and, of course, your daughter.'

Nan felt her cheeks grow warm and knew that for

the first time in many years she was blushing. She did not recall being made to blush since she started courting her husband, Sam. Not that she imagined Eddie was courting her. He was merely offering her friendship and his old-fashioned courtesy, which Nan liked so much. In a world that was changing constantly, it was lovely to discover a true gentleman, not by birth but by nature. He might be an old soldier, but he was honest and a man of gentle ways.

She knew that he had only his small wage from the fetching and carrying he did for his professor at the University, and a tiny pension from his Army days, and he'd told her that he lived in modest lodgings.

'I shall probably drop in harness,' he'd confided to Nan. 'I'm content enough with my life – but it has brought me great pleasure to know you, my dear.'

'And I am happy to have a new friend,' she said simply. 'It was a lucky day for us both when you caught that bus for the first time . . .'

'Yes, fortunate indeed,' he agreed. 'That is settled then. We shall travel down to Cornwall on the train together. You may rely on me to book the tickets and the rooms.'

'You must tie a knot in your handkerchief,' Nan said, smiling at him affectionately, because he did tend to forget things sometimes.

'No, for then I should forget what it was for. I shall write it on my shirt cuff,' he said, and took out his battered old fountain pen, scribbling a note that only he could understand. 'Now you write off to the convent and tell them we are coming, and leave the rest to me.'

*   *   *

236

Angela frowned as she went down to the dining room on Monday morning, the conversation that she'd just had with Nan going through her mind.

'I was coming from the kitchen early this morning when I saw that young lad Terry running out of the dining room,' Nan had told her. 'He had a look on his face – well, it wasn't a nice look. I'm not sure but I think he'd been up to some mischief . . . what do you think, should I report it to Sister?'

'Terry is difficult to understand,' Angela said with a little frown. 'I can't make up my mind about him, though I do like Nancy. At first I thought she was hiding something, but now I suspect that she is just worried about her brother. I saw him kick the children's pet cat the other day and reprimanded him; he had scratches on his hand but that doesn't excuse what he did. He said he was sorry and then ran off.'

'No, it certainly doesn't excuse such behaviour. Unfortunately, some children do not see that it is cruel. If a cat scratches them they hit back – I suppose in retaliation.'

'Nancy would be upset if she'd seen him – he was vicious . . .'

'I imagine she's had to be a mother to the boy for years,' Nan said. 'Well, I must get on, but I wondered if someone ought to check – see if he's left any nasty surprises lying around.'

Nan was probably worrying for nothing, but she would have a look around, make sure nothing unpleasant was waiting for the unwary. Entering the dining room, Angela looked about her. The rows of tables were all as neat as ever, covered with the red gingham oilcloth

237

that was easy to keep clean. On a table at the end of the room a pile of clean plates, glasses, cups and saucers stood ready for the next meal. The knives, forks and spoons were in a wooden tray, and there were clean napkins in a neat pile, also several salt, pepper, vinegar and sauce bottles, and glass sugar castors for sprinkling into drinks or on fruit sometimes.

Angela walked past the tables, glancing at the chairs, and stopping at the table used by Mary Ellen and Billy, but everything was in order. She could see nothing different . . . nothing that need concern anyone. About to leave, her gaze returned to the table where the condiments stood. For a moment she wasn't sure what had caught her eye, and then she saw that the metal top of the sugar castor was on crooked.

She approached thoughtfully. Surely Terry wouldn't do something so foolish – why should he?

She picked up the castor and sprinkled some sugar on the palm of her hand, then licked a finger and tasted the white substance, pulling a face of disgust. Salt had been added to the contents, which would be horrible in drinks or on a fruit pudding.

'Oh Terry, why?' she sighed. She tried the next castor and found that was also salt, and when she tasted the salt from one of the shakers, discovered that it had pepper mixed in with it, and the pepper had sugar. From what she could see he had tampered with most of the pots on the table, which meant they must all be emptied and refilled – and that was both a waste of time and money.

Why had Terry done it? Who did he want to hurt? Any of the children could have been affected and it was a spiteful act intended to cause distress and upset, though it wouldn't actually harm anyone.

Angela could not imagine why the lad would want to strike out against the other children. Surely, he must know that he was lucky to have been given a place at St Saviour's?

Angela collected all the shakers and castors on a tray and carried it into the kitchen. Muriel the cook was busy mixing one of her fatless sponges in a pudding bowl. She looked surprised as Angela set the tray down and started to empty all the containers into the rubbish bowl.

'What is the matter?'

'Someone has put salt in the sugar, and sugar in the pepper, and pepper in the salt. I'm afraid it all has to be thrown away and the shakers washed and dried.'

'How foolish,' Muriel said, looking cross. She stopped beating her mixture and put her finger in to taste it. 'Whoever it was hasn't been at my sugar, thank goodness. Really, some of these children! Do you know who did it?'

'I'm not certain,' Angela said, because even though Nan thought Terry had been up to mischief they hadn't seen him do it.

'What made you suspect it?'

'It was just that the top of one of the castors was on crooked and I tasted it. I thought I'd best try several and most of them seem to be contaminated – so the only thing to do is to start again.'

'I'll bet it was that Terry,' Muriel said. 'You know, the boy whose parents died in a fire. I caught him in here the other morning. He was after one of my jam tarts but he's a sly one. I dare say he's the culprit . . . sulky child, to my mind.'

'We mustn't forget that he has lost both parents. It was a terrible experience for him.'

'Most of the children here have had bad experiences, but we've never had anything like this happen before.'

'Well, I discovered the foolish prank before any harm was done.'

'That isn't the point,' Muriel objected. 'Who knows what he might take it into his head to do next? It could have been rat poison . . .'

'No, surely not! Where would he get such a thing? It was merely a silly prank.'

'The caretaker has rat poison in the cellar. You mark my words, Angela. Now he's done this he won't stop there. You must tell Sister Beatrice. He has to be punished or next time he might do something really bad.'

'Perhaps.' Angela frowned as she worked at refilling the clean containers. She'd hoped she need not tell Sister, but if she didn't, Muriel probably would and then it would cause more trouble. 'Very well, I'll speak to her when I go upstairs.'

She picked up her tray to return to the dining room, but as she entered it, she saw the back of a child running through the door and knew immediately that Terry had been spying on them, listening to her conversation with Muriel.

THIRTY-ONE

'Mark . . .' Angela called to him as she saw him turn away from Sister's office. 'Have you seen Sister anywhere? She wasn't in her office a few minutes ago.'

'And isn't now,' Mark said. 'I need a word with her rather urgently, but I'll try the wards in a moment. How are you? We haven't seen much of each other recently.'

'No, I always seem to be busy and I dare say you are too.'

'Yes, but . . .'

He shook his head, experiencing a pang of regret as he met her clear eyes and felt that hunger for her that had been growing inside him for a long time now. Carole was pretty and available, and he'd enjoyed his evening out with her though he hadn't felt inclined to repeat it, but there was something about Angela that made him want to carry her off to his lair. He laughed inwardly as he recognised the caveman instinct and told himself not to be a fool.

'I imagine Sister is busy too, wherever she's got to. She will undoubtedly turn up soon.'

'Undoubtedly,' Angela laughed. The sound caught at

241

his stomach. She had such a wonderful laugh and it was good to hear it again. If Nick had made her happy he couldn't begrudge her that happiness. 'Was it very important? Can I give her a message?'

'No, I need to speak to her myself.' Mark lingered, wanting to keep her talking for a bit longer. 'How is everything? All your schemes on course?'

'Yes, I'm going home tomorrow to talk to my father. I popped down last Sunday. Mother was in bed with a headache and I thought he seemed very tired so I've decided to take a couple of days off this week to see how things really are at home.'

'If you'd told me sooner I could have driven you down, but I have appointments all day tomorrow.'

'Oh, Nick is going to drive me to the station, and then he'll come down again on Wednesday to pick me up – but thank you, Mark.' Angela averted her eyes from him at the mention of Nick. 'It was good of you to offer, because I know how busy you are. Your work is so important. I know Sister Beatrice relies on you for advice all the time.'

'Not too busy for you, if you need me,' he said wryly. 'Remember I'm always ready to help if you need me . . .'

'Yes, I know,' Angela said, and smiled. 'I think Dad is worrying about my mother – he didn't say, but I believe the drinking is worse. I think she needs to see someone and perhaps go to a clinic or something.'

'I might be able to help, Angela – and there is a place in Switzerland that would suit her. It is expensive of course . . .'

'I have money that John left me that I've hardly touched. We could manage that side of it – it's just getting Mum to acknowledge that she's ill. At the moment she won't talk about her problem.'

'I'm going down soon myself. Shall I call on her as a friend and suggest that she consults me professionally?'

Angela was silent for a moment, and then inclined her head. 'Yes, she might talk to you, Mark. She hardly speaks to my father and she just tells me that I'm making a fuss over nothing. It doesn't seem fair to involve you, because you have enough to worry about – but it would make me feel easier in my mind. Poor Daddy looks worried to death.'

Mark hesitated for a moment, he felt a desperate need to declare his feelings before it was too late, to let her know that he would do anything to win her love and trust – but her casual manner told him it would be useless and perhaps it was already too late. Perhaps she would never see him as a man with needs and desires, but only as her friend. Perhaps he should have spoken more plainly before this about his feelings, but he'd known she was emotionally fragile after her husband's death, and that she wasn't ready for a relationship. It would be his own fault if he'd missed his chance with her.

'I'll do what I can, speak to her myself,' he promised. 'And it's no trouble – you and your family are my friends, Angela.'

'Thank you, Mark. I'm so grateful.'

'No need.' He didn't want gratitude, he wanted love – sweet, lasting, passionate love, but he wasn't sure Angela would ever feel that way towards him.

He was frowning as he walked away, his thoughts turning to his work. It was a pity that Sister Beatrice had been out, because he'd wanted to tell her that he'd found a place for Terry in the country. The home was a secure clinic, pleasant and modern in its outlook, but, unfortunately, they couldn't take the boy for another month when their new building would be finished. Mark had provisionally booked the boy's place, but he would need to talk to Nancy first and try to explain that she could visit her brother often. His latest observation of Terry earlier that morning had convinced Mark that the lad was teetering on the edge, one minute a likeable boy and the next . . . malicious and sly. If he'd ever been in doubt that Terry was unstable he was no longer uncertain.

It had shocked him to see that Terry had completely ripped apart the teddy bear that Angela had given him. When he'd mentioned it, Terry had laughed and said it served her right.

'She's got Nance on her side, but I ain't fooled; I know she's the same as them others,' he'd said viciously.

'And what are all the others like, Terry?' Mark asked in a casual tone.

'They're against us, me and Nance,' he muttered. 'I hate it here. I want to go home to me ma. I want me ma . . .'

Always that same phrase, over and over again. It was as if Terry had erected a mental block in his mind, refusing to remember the fire or what had happened to his mother. In his confused thoughts he'd convinced himself that everything would be all right if he could go back to his mother. Mark was sure that he knew the truth, but didn't want to face it . . . perhaps because he was afraid of what he would see if he let the memory back in.

The police had not been able to give him conclusive proof of how the blaze had started; it was thought that the bedroom door had been the seat of the fire, and that perhaps an oil lamp had been dropped, but it was still mere speculation.

If there was somewhere else he could put Terry he thought he might do it today, and yet the only alternative to waiting for the special clinic was a secure mental institution and if Terry was teetering on the brink that would surely push him over the edge, because they were terrible places – especially for a young child.

As yet Terry's small acts of violence had done no real harm, but what would happen if he were ever really crossed? Mark needed to talk to the boy's sister, to make her understand that Terry needed special treatment for his own sake.

Mark believed that the situation was still stable, providing Terry was not pushed too far. As was his habit with such important matters, he had taken his time coming to a decision, but something in the boy's eyes had been different this morning and he was a little uneasy, his intuition being that Terry had taken a step towards the darkness. Yet still Terry had done nothing that made him a danger to anyone; it was just a gut feeling that he might if upset. Once Mark had the lad at the clinic he could bring in several colleagues and ask for their opinions, though his own was growing stronger all the time. He would have to write up a report to justify taking the boy into secure custody, because it wasn't something you could do on a whim or an instinct: you had to have clear, concise reasons for your actions.

Yet there were so many others needing his attention,

and Terry was not officially his patient, until the actual commitment papers were signed and he was taken into the clinic – something that would cause distress to the boy and his sister. It was a hard decision but he was rapidly coming to believe it was the only one.

He really needed to talk to Sister Beatrice about the boy, but she seemed to have gone missing – unless she was in the wards.

'I was looking for Sister Beatrice,' Mark said as he entered the sick ward and discovered Carole standing by the desk. 'She isn't in her office.'

'I think she went out to see someone,' Carole replied, looking at him expectantly. 'She came in to check everything was all right here and said she wouldn't be back until later this afternoon. She didn't say where she was going – but then she often goes off without telling us where she will be.'

'Really? I wouldn't have thought that of Sister. She always seems so reliable.'

'Yes, of course she is . . . only – no, I shouldn't tell tales . . .' Carole shook her head. 'It's just that she has seemed a bit forgetful recently.'

'In what way?'

Carole hesitated, then, 'I found the medicine cupboard open yesterday and Sister's keys were left in the door. She'd been checking it and her list . . . well, she appeared to have left it half done and gone off to do something else, leaving the cupboard unlocked.'

'I dare say she was called away and it slipped her mind.'

'I'm sure you're right,' Carole said. 'I wouldn't want

you to think I was finding fault, but . . . it isn't a good thing to leave the medicine cupboard open. The children could have taken something and swallowed it out of curiosity . . .'

'I imagine Sister thought it was safe enough. She trusts her staff to watch out for such eventualities.'

'Yes, but . . .' Carole bit her lip, seeming uncertain. 'No, I'm sure you're right. It was an emergency, I expect.'

'I imagine so.' Mark smiled at her. 'How are your patients today, Nurse?'

I think most of the children are quite well at the moment . . .' She paused, pouting at him a little and fluttering her long lashes flirtatiously. 'You haven't been to see me for ages.'

'A couple of weeks or so – hardly ages.' Mark raised his dark eyebrows. It had been a conscious decision not to see the pretty young woman, because he didn't want to get too involved, and yet it seemed that Angela saw him only as a colleague and a family friend. When it came to her free time, she preferred Nick Hadden's company. Mark would be a fool to ignore the signals Carole was giving him, when he clearly had no chance with Angela. He hesitated a moment longer, then, 'I suppose you wouldn't be free for dinner this evening?'

'I might be able to squeeze you in, if you're asking?'

He laughed because the message she gave out was blatant and he found himself responding to the invitation in those sparkling eyes. Every time he'd asked Angela out recently she'd refused him, either because she was too busy or she was already promised to someone else – mainly Nick Hadden. Mark thought it might be serious between them and that was hard to take. Suddenly, with all of the anxiety around Terry and his own hurt feelings because Angela preferred another man, Mark felt reckless.

'No theatre this time,' he said, 'but dinner . . . and then we could go dancing if you like?'

'Yes, please. I'll wear my best dress for you . . .'

Mark responded to the teasing in her voice. He liked Carole, enjoyed her company, and he'd been a fool not to follow up on that first evening. Angela didn't want him, why shouldn't he enjoy an evening out with a young woman who did? What harm could dinner and a few drinks do?

THIRTY-TWO

'I've brought these drinks up for you,' Sally said as she carried the tray into the sick room and placed it on the desk. 'I wondered if you wanted to take your break now. I could serve the drinks and watch over the patients until you return.'

'I will take my break at the proper time,' Carole said. 'I have a bed bath to do before I'm ready to leave the ward.'

'I could help you,' Sally offered. 'I'm free for a while, because Angela has gone down to read to the little ones. She was talking to Mr Adderbury earlier. I think she's going home for a couple of days tomorrow. He sometimes takes her down in his car, so they were probably arranging it. I think he's a bit sweet on her . . .'

'Thank you, but I'm perfectly capable of doing a bed bath on my own.' Carole glared at her. 'You can send Jean up to fetch the tray in half an hour or so and I'll take my break then.'

'Oh, all right.' Sally looked hurt. 'I was only offering to help.'

Carole knew she shouldn't have snapped at Sally who was one of the best, always willing to do what she could, but the thought of Mark talking to Angela, and of driving her down to her parents' house rankled with her. Of course they had homes in the same village and had been friends a long time, from what Carole could gather . . . but that didn't give Angela first call on his time.

She felt a surge of jealousy. Mark was hers now. If he was going to take her out, she wanted to be sure his mind was on her and not on Angela. Determination settled on her mouth as Sally left, and she made up her mind. She wanted Mark because he had influence and could help her ambition to become the Warden here one day – perhaps sooner than she'd thought when she first arrived. Finding Sister's keys in the door of the medicine cupboard had given Carole an idea. Mark had been right when he said Sister had been suddenly called away and she'd returned shortly afterwards and asked Carole for her keys. It was a minor lapse, but Carole intended to make the most of it. She'd planted a tiny seed of doubt and she would find a way to make that seed grow – before long she would have him and others thinking that Sister Beatrice was getting too old for her position. Carole could think of ways to put Sister in the wrong, but Angela was sharp-eyed and clever. It wouldn't suit Carole to see her elevated to the post over her head.

Tonight, she would do her best to end up in Mark's bed. She'd noticed he seemed a bit low and with a little persuasion he could be induced to drink rather too much. It wouldn't be Carole's fault if he took advantage of her good nature. She smiled to herself as her plans to better herself began to take shape in her mind. Carole wasn't going to be just a staff nurse for much longer. She might even get Mark to marry her. He was attractive and rich – and he could help her get what she wanted, which was a good job that would always stand her in good stead. Husbands didn't always work out, but as Warden of St Saviour's she would be in position of authority – and she'd be rid of Angela Morton the first chance she got, but she needed to make sure of Mark first . . .

'Thank you for reading to them while I took the trays round,' Sally said when she entered the schoolroom and found the little ones clustered about Angela, their faces entranced as they listened to the story. 'Nan asked me if I could carry the trays, because she was on laundry duty today, but Jean was busy too with cleaning the bathrooms and I didn't have time until you came.'

'I'm always happy to help, you know that.' Angela smiled at her. 'You never complain whatever you do, Sally, but really the kitchen staff ought to take trays up to the wards.'

Sally shrugged. 'We all help each other – or most of us do . . .'

Angela quirked an eyebrow. 'Who has upset you, Sally?'

'It's just Staff Nurse Carole's attitude. I've tried to be friendly, as we said we would, but she is always so abrupt – well, rude really. I can't help it, I don't like her.'

'She is a little spiky,' Angela admitted. 'There must be a reason, I suppose.'

'I offered to help her so that she could take her break and she snapped my head off.'

'Perhaps she is unhappy about something?'

'I think she is just – well, not very nice,' Sally said, 'I much prefer Michelle.'

'Michelle is popular with all of us,' Angela said, and then changed the subject. 'Have you been out with Andrew recently?'

'Yes, two days ago. I wore some new shoes I bought in Petticoat Lane – well, new to me. They had hardly been used, and they are real leather. I long for the day when the shops have lots of pretty things in again, don't you?'

'I think there's more material and clothes about now but shoes are still hard to find. I suppose the good leathers have to be imported.'

'Yes,' Sally agreed. 'How long will you be in the country?'

'Only a couple of days – why?'

'Andrew was asking if I would like to ask someone out for a meal in a nice hotel. Another couple, I think he means. I wondered if you would come – and perhaps Mr Adderbury?'

'Is it a special occasion?'

'Yes, it's my birthday.' Sally blushed rosily. 'I thought as Andrew and Mr Adderbury are colleagues and friends . . .'

'Yes, of course I'll come and I'll ask Mark – or perhaps Mr Markham should do that? When is your birthday?'

'Friday the 12th March . . .'

'Gosh, it's March already!' Angela said. 'We've got behind with the concert. I think I'm going to have to move it forward into April, but don't worry, Sally. I wouldn't dream of missing your birthday celebration.'

Sally was glad that she'd invited Angela, and Andrew would ask Mr Adderbury. Andrew had asked her if she would like a party for her twentieth birthday, but she'd told him she would prefer to invite a couple of friends to a nice restaurant for dinner.

'Who would you like to come?' He'd seemed pleased by her choice.

'Angela is the person I get on best with at work, and I think she and Mr Adderbury are friends . . .'

'That would be perfect,' Andrew said, 'but wouldn't you like to invite your sister and your family?'

'Not really.' Sally grew awkward as she felt his probing gaze on her. She couldn't explain to him that her family didn't approve of her going out with a man ten years older and from a different class, and her sister, Brenda, could be a blabbermouth. Her father hadn't said much more than that she should think carefully about what she wanted, but her mother never stopped nagging her.

'He's pleasant as a friend, love,' Mum had said to her in one of their arguments. 'But you must see that it is all wrong? You're out of your league and you'll be giving up your dreams, Sally. Please don't try to be something you aren't. It will end in heartbreak for you – and me, because you'll leave us behind. Once you're his wife we shan't be good enough for you.'

'Mum! I would never do that,' Sally cried. 'You've got Andrew all wrong. He isn't proud or stuffy – and he liked you and Dad. Why can't you try to like him . . . for my sake?'

'I've told you, it isn't that I dislike him – I just feel he will hurt you. Besides, he won't want his wife to be a nurse – he'll expect you to stay at home and wait on him and his children.'

Her mother's words had hurt Sally, even though they hadn't been unkindly meant. Her family saw Andrew as being from a class they had been taught to distrust if not actually dislike, and it would take time to win them away from their old-fashioned prejudices. They didn't understand that his smiles made her knees go weak and the very thought of giving him up would break her heart. Yes, she did want to be a nurse, but if she explained Andrew would understand – wouldn't he?

Besides, there was another reason that Sally would rather her family and work colleagues didn't meet again yet. Her father was just settling into his new position, and proud of the fact that he'd been recommended for the job. He believed the recommendation had come from one of the builders he'd worked for doing odd jobs. If he ever guessed that it came from Angela he would be angry and humiliated.

Sally had found out about it by chance. Her father had come home glowing with pride because he was going to work for this wonderful builder who was restoring fire-damaged property, old warehouses and factories that had been partially destroyed by the bombing but were structurally sound. Remembering all that Angela had told her about the man who had sold her the lease of the beautiful apartment she now lived in, Sally had swiftly put two and two together. Angela hadn't breathed a word about having told the builder that Mr Rush was looking for work; in fact she'd been strangely quiet when Sally had told her the exciting news, hardly commentating, and that wasn't like her.

Although she wouldn't dream of embarrassing Angela by thanking her, Sally was very grateful. Her dad's new job had made all the difference. He was bright and cheerful again, filled with hope for the future and her mother had stopped saying she was going to find a job. She'd told Sally that she didn't need the extra money she'd been giving her since her father was put on short time at the Docks, and so she'd been able to start saving and continue her night classes.

Sally would take her exams very soon. If she got the certificate – and her tutor at night school was sure she would – she could apply for a place at a teaching hospital. Yet now that the opportunity was fast approaching, Sally was feeling oddly reluctant. She didn't want to leave her friends at St Saviour's . . . and she wasn't sure how Andrew would react if she told him that she wouldn't be able to see him as often. The training would be hard and the rules were strict, much stricter than those Sister Beatrice imposed. Sally lived at home now, but she would have to live in the Nurses' Home when she entered the teaching hospital as a probationer.

If he proposed and she agreed to marry him, he wouldn't want her to go off and start training to be a nurse, and the hospital probably wouldn't want her because it would be a waste of a place if she started a family . . . Marriage or the career she'd always longed for? It was a choice Sally didn't want to have to make.

Sally wasn't certain of her own mind. She loved

looking after the children, and secretly believed that she might be happiest of all married to a man she cared for with a large family of her own. She couldn't marry until she was twenty-one unless she had her father's permission. Sally thought he might give it grudgingly if Andrew asked, but did she want to get married for a year or two?

Being in love was wonderful, and when Andrew kissed her, Sally could only think of him and the way he made her feel, but the divide was there and she couldn't quite forget it just yet. Her mother's doubts were like a dark shadow hovering at Sally's shoulder. Mum thought she should do her training as she'd planned and when she'd passed her exams and had a future career in prospect then it would be time enough to think of marriage and babies – but Andrew was older and he wanted to settle down and have a family quite soon.

Sally smothered a sigh as she went to collect the younger children and take them to the bathroom before lunch. There was no use in fretting about things until Andrew asked her. If he did the most likely person to help her would be Angela. She could talk to her far more easily than she could to her mother or sister these days.

THIRTY-THREE

'How are you really, Daddy?' Angela smiled lovingly at him. He was a handsome, distinguished man, kind and generous, and she adored him. 'Don't say you're fine, because I know you're not.'

Her father looked at her intently for a moment, sadness in his eyes. 'You've really grown up, haven't you, Angela? It started when you married John. I thought his death was the end for you . . . but this job at St Saviour's, well, it has been the making of you as a person. I'm very proud of you, my dear.'

'Thank you, dearest, but please don't change the subject. Is there anything the matter with you – or is it just worry?'

'A bit of both, I imagine,' he said in the calm, gentle manner that made her love him so much. 'I am very concerned about your mother – but after you spoke to her last night she agreed to see Mark when he comes down. We can only hope that he will persuade her to go away for treatment . . . if it isn't too expensive.'

'You're not to worry about that,' Angela said, relieved that here was a way she could help him. 'I'm earning a wage and I don't need the income from my investments for the moment so let me pay the fees. No, don't refuse. I want to do it – for both of you.'

'Thank you, I may need help with the fees,' he acknowledged. 'As far as my health is concerned I've spoken to my doctor – and he says there's nothing to worry about. It's just a little warning to slow up a bit and not do so much.'

'Is it your heart?'

'No, not really, just a little murmur,' he assured her. 'Forget it, my love. Once we get this business of your mother's settled I shall be fine.'

Angela accepted his word, because she knew he wasn't going to tell her even if his doctor had given him bad news. 'Well, do as Dr Horne said and take care of yourself.'

'Oh, I shall,' he said. 'Now, I have to visit my office. What are you going to do with yourself?'

'I'll walk down to the church with some flowers and bits of greenery,' Angela said. 'Mum asked me to give Mrs Jenkins a hand with them, because it should have been her turn and she doesn't feel up to it.'

'Off you go then,' her father said. 'I'll be back in time for tea and your mother is having a nice little sleep.'

The church was very ancient and very beautiful, and it was here that she'd married John, the man she'd believed that she would love for the rest of her life. Angela knew that a part of her would always remain his, but she needed to move on. Life was exciting and she wanted to live it to the full again – but whether that included making Nick Hadden a permanent part of her future she wasn't sure, and Mark had given no sign that he was interested in anything but friendship. Standing in the beautiful church she found her memories flooding back and she wondered if she was truly ready to love again. John was too strong here, his presence almost tangible – yet life had so much to offer and she refused to look back in regret.

'Well, those lilies look magnificent.' The vicar stopped to admire her work. 'Your mother has always supported us, Mrs Morton. I do hope she is recovering from her chest infection? She is a great loss to our little society – and of course we don't see much of you these days.'

It was the excuse her father had given people he knew for his wife's sudden withdrawal from the activities she'd once taken such an interest in, but it was only a matter of time before people discovered the truth about her excessive drinking.

'I work for a charity in London and I can't get down often.'

'Of course, I understand. Mrs Hendry told us. She is proud of you, you know – but you should not neglect your family, my dear. Your dear father has not looked well for a while now.'

Angela nodded and turned back to the flowers as he moved on. His words made her feel guilty, as if she hadn't already wondered enough times if her mother's breakdown had been caused by her deciding to leave home. Yet she was entitled to a life of her own, surely? And Daddy hadn't blamed her. He wouldn't want her to give up the work she loved and move back home.

Leaving the church, she was aware of a heavy sadness. She'd be devastated if anything happened to her father.

Of course she loved her mother, but there wasn't the same closeness between them – though perhaps she was fretting for nothing and her father was just tired and worried. It was only natural that he would be when her mother had taken to drinking – and the shop-lifting too . . . Angela still found it difficult to believe that the woman who had always been so proper and so proud could do something of the sort. Who could ever know what was in another person's heart and mind – even when they were your family?

Angela loved the walk from the church to her father's house, because of the fields stretching away to a rise in the distance where an ancient oak tree stood. The hedges and trees were a bit bare at this time of year, but the symmetry of the oak was always there, majestic and timeless.

Her thoughts turned to Mark. He was a good friend to Angela, more than that, and to her family – but he seemed to have placed a distance between himself and her. She knew that he'd taken Carole out again, because the nurse had told her before she left for the country, a sly look in her eyes that made Angela want to box her ears! She couldn't like Carole however much she tried and she couldn't understand why Mark would want to be involved with a girl like that . . . there was something she didn't trust about her. Angela couldn't say for certain what it was but she didn't think Carole was a very nice person.

Sighing, she brought her thoughts back to a happier place: the children of St Saviour's and the concert she was planning.

THIRTY-FOUR

Mark finally managed to catch up with Sister Beatrice – after he'd taken Carole out for that regrettable evening earlier in the week. God, what a fool he'd been! He still couldn't believe that he'd made such a stupid mistake. When he'd woken in that hotel bedroom next to Carole and remembered a little hazily the events of the previous evening, he'd felt sick and annoyed with himself. He could remember Carole suggesting they get a room because he'd had too much alcohol to drive, and he vaguely remembered her draping herself all over him in the lift; and he'd responded by kissing her with some passion. He seemed to remember that he'd wanted her badly then, but once they got inside the bedroom it was a complete blank. Yet Carole's hints and looks the next morning seemed to indicate that he'd made love to her even if he'd passed out afterwards.

Now Mark felt thoroughly ashamed of himself. To get drunk and take a woman he fancied to bed in a hotel was bad enough, because it seemed rather sleazy in retrospect – but when he scarcely remembered it that was worse. He wasn't that kind of a man and he felt ashamed of his behaviour – and devastated that he'd let himself down. If Angela discovered the truth she would be disgusted.

He regretted the impulse to drown his sorrows in goodness knows how many glasses of champagne. What had he been thinking of? It was a stupid thing to do and he wished he'd never asked the girl out. He wasn't in love with Carole. Yes, he'd fancied her – what red-bloodied man wouldn't in that sexy black dress of hers? Yet surely he should have had more sense. It was extremely embarrassing. How could he apologise and explain that he wasn't free to marry her . . . wasn't free because he was in love with someone else? He felt a bitter taste in his mouth as he realised that he'd probably scuppered any chance he'd had of winning Angela. If she knew what he'd done . . . it didn't bear thinking of. He'd been a damned fool!

Dismissing his own problems for now, Mark knocked at Sister Beatrice's door. He'd just spent half an hour talking to Terry and Nancy. Nancy was embroidering a square of linen with the initials *AM* in one corner. The design in blue silk was attractive and Mark asked her who the handkerchief was for, even though he had a good idea.

'It's for Miss Angela,' Nancy said, smiling contentedly. 'She likes blue, you see, and she wears it often. She has a lovely blue twinset just this colour.'

'It is very kind of you to do that for her, Nancy.'

'Sister Beatrice asked me what kind of schoolwork I was best at. I told her cookery and needlework, so she arranged for me to have some materials to embroider and make things – and I'm to have cookery lessons in the kitchens here three days a week. She asked if I could add up, write my letters and read, and when I said I could, she said it was all I really needed. I can probably do some exercises for the school as homework.'

'Yes, I dare say she is right,' Mark said. 'Did someone tell me you wanted to be a waitress and work at Lyons?'

'Sister Beatrice says I can't do that until I'm eighteen, because they wouldn't take me – but she said if I learned to cook there might be a job for me here until I'm old enough to leave St Saviour's . . . and she says we can keep our room for the time being.'

'Well, that was kind of her,' Mark said, glancing at Terry, who hardly ever spoke when his sister was in the room. The boy was staring moodily at the ground, taking little notice of anything. 'You seem to have settled down, Nancy – but what about Terry? What is he going to do?'

'He's all right with me,' Nancy said. 'He doesn't go to school, sir. Even when we lived at home, the school wouldn't have him. Pa went after them once, but they said . . .' She lowered her voice. 'They called him a dunce, sir, and told Pa to keep him at home out of harm's way.'

'That was very wrong of whoever told your father that.' Mark frowned, his dark eyes intent on the lad's face. He gave no sign of having heard his sister's remarks or Mark's answer, but Mark wasn't fooled. Terry was angry and rightly so. He deserved an education even if he was slow. His suppressed anger was seething inside him, and one of these days it was going to come out. 'A friend of mine has special books that help people to learn. I'll ask him for a couple of them for Terry – and a puzzle. It would give him something to do.'

'Terry likes doing things with his hands. He wouldn't mind helping the caretaker – or working in the garden. He isn't stupid, sir. He used to go down to the Docks sometimes and earn a few shillings carrying things; he's strong for his age. People are often surprised how strong he is.'

'I can chop wood for the boiler,' Terry said suddenly, confirming Mark's suspicion that he was listening to every word. 'I like chopping wood.'

The idea of Terry being let loose with a chopper made Mark go cold all over, but he merely nodded and gave the lad a serious look. 'Yes, I'm sure you do, Terry. We shall have to see if there are any jobs you can do to help here. It would be better than sitting alone while Nancy has her cooking lessons.'

He left them soon after, more than ever convinced that Terry needed watching. Anger had been building inside that lad for a long time and Mark was certain now that it only needed a small spark to set it alight. He must see if he could speed up the move for Terry. Somehow, he would have to get Nancy alone so that he could explain that there was a chance her brother could improve if he was given the right treatment, but he would always need to live in a secure environment. Left to himself, he was just going to build on his hatred of everyone and everything until something caused that simmering cauldron to explode.

When the time came, Nancy had to go along with it, to accompany her brother to the clinic and see him settled. If he fought the doctors there they would be able to deal with his tantrums safely, and under the right care he might retain his sanity. Despite his anxiety over the lad's mental state, Mark liked him. He could only guess at the years of abuse that had shaped him . . .

Because Nancy had been so nervous when she first came to St Saviour's, and was so obviously hiding something, Mark had sometimes wondered if she'd killed her father because of what he'd done to her. He'd had to probe deeper to be sure which of the two was the instigator of what had happened. Now he was pretty certain that she'd been protecting her brother, afraid of what he might say or do . . . and that meant Nancy either knew or believed that Terry was responsible for the fire.

Could he really have done such a terrible thing? Mark found himself shying away from what he was beginning to think must be the solution to the mystery, because it meant that Terry was really dangerous and might never be able to live a normal life. A part of his mind was still wrestling with the ugly truth when he reached Sister Beatrice's room and knocked at her door.

'Come in.'

Mark entered and saw that Sister Beatrice was standing by her filing cabinet with a sheaf of papers in her hand looking bothered. 'Am I disturbing you?'

'No, of course not. I was just looking for some figures for the repairs. You know we need some work done on the kitchens, and I've had a quote for the roof. That storm last month dislodged several tiles and the builders tell me it will have to be re-felted in places, because it has cracked and will start to let in water.'

'When were you thinking of having the work done?'

'Well, I've been told they can start on the 11th March and get everything finished in one day, but there will be workmen everywhere. We shall need to keep the children out of the way, so I'm going to ask Angela to arrange some trips to keep the young ones happy. The older children will be at school during the day so that's all right . . .' Sister frowned. 'You didn't come to discuss the repairs – is something wrong?'

'Well, yes, I think it may be,' Mark said. 'I've found a place for Terry, but they can't take him for another month – but I'm a bit worried about him. I fear his condition is worsening.'

'I'm not sure what to think,' Sister said as she sat down and placed the folder on her desk. 'Please sit down, Mark. Angela took the brother and sister to the pictures and tea the other week. She thought he was a bit sulky but he does what his sister says. The carers at night tell me he sleeps and doesn't scream out now so it appears he's getting better. I understand that Terry needs special care, which we cannot provide here – but could we find a school or something here? It is going to upset them both when we split them up.'

'I thought you wanted him moved as soon as possible?'

'Well, yes, I did, but he seems settled now. I thought Billy Baggins was a troublemaker at first, but now he's getting on well at school and most of the time he behaves . . . of course he never stops running everywhere, but boys will be boys, after all. You know best, of course, but I hate the thought of separating them,'

'I should have to talk to Nancy before we move Terry,' Mark said. 'But I have booked a place for him in the clinic and I think it will be necessary to move him in the future.'

'Oh, please give him a little more time,' Sister said.

'I think we misjudged him at the start. He's just an unhappy little boy who needs his sister.'

'I am reluctant to place him in a mental institution, because he has not shown himself as violent, merely surly and unbalanced. I do not feel that is sufficient reason to place an order of restraint. I shall not insist until the clinic can take him, but I really think we must make the arrangements soon for Terry's own sake, as much as anything else.'

Mark was thoughtful as he left her office. He understood Sister Beatrice's natural concerns about separating the brother and sister but was she right to think he was settling down or was it simply that Terry was getting better at concealing his frustrations? Mentally disturbed patients could be devious at times.

'Mark! Were you coming to see me?'

Mark's thoughts of Terry were suspended as Carole emerged from the sick room and walked to meet him, smiling. Her perfume, which she always wore despite it being an unwritten law that nurses didn't at work, reminded him of the evening they'd spent together. Her eyes held an intimate, inviting look and he was immediately wary. Going to bed with her had been a mistake. He didn't wish to hurt her or make her angry, but he had no intention of becoming more deeply involved with her.

'I'm going to stay in the country with my mother and her sister next weekend,' Carole said. 'There's a lovely old-fashioned inn where you could stay in the next village – if you wanted we could spend some time together . . .'

Warning bells rang in Mark's head. He was undoubtedly in the wrong, because he should never have allowed himself to be drawn into that kind of affair – and out of consideration he must let Carole down lightly.

'I'm afraid I'm just too busy,' he said. 'Perhaps another time.'

'Oh.' Something like anger flashed in her eyes, but in a moment it had gone. 'Yes, of course. Another time . . .'

Mark walked away. He had the feeling that Carole was watching him and he knew she was angry with him for turning her down, but there was nothing he could do. He would send her flowers, apologise for what had happened. After that, he would just have to find excuses for not seeing her again. He felt pretty rotten for his behaviour but there was no way he could pretend that he felt otherwise; she certainly didn't deserve it after what he'd done . . . but the last thing he wanted was to become even more involved so that he felt obliged to marry her.

Carole's eyes narrowed as she watched Mark walk away. Outwardly, she'd managed to remain calm, but inwardly she was fuming. No man did that to her! She'd thought he was well and truly caught, and he'd certainly been no trouble to coax into bed once they were at the hotel. He'd snuggled up to her naked body and murmured a name, but it was too indistinct for Carole to hear.

Unfortunately, Mark had been far too drunk to make love to her. He'd kissed her a few times and stroked her thigh and the small of her back, but then he'd turned on his back and fallen into a deep sleep. She'd hoped for better results in the morning, but she'd gone to the bathroom and when she returned he was already dressing, apologising for having to leave hurriedly. He had appointments he couldn't break but he'd talk to her later, so he'd promised in his haste to get away.

So the evening hadn't worked out as she'd hoped . . . but she didn't think Mark knew that; in fact she was certain he wouldn't have looked so uncomfortable if he'd remembered. Mark believed they'd made love and that meant she still had a hold on him . . . in fact she could have him in the palm of her hand. In a few weeks she would cry and tell him that she was having his baby. A man like Mark Adderbury wasn't the sort to turn his back on a woman he believed was carrying his child . . .

A smile touched her lips as she began to plan. She would go over the record book and wherever it had been initialled by Sister Beatrice she would change figures: just one here and there, but important drugs, drugs that could be dangerous. And then there was the rota . . . she could double-book one of the girls and that would cause chaos. Her smile broadened. She knew just who she was going to double-book.

Yes, she would have Sister's job before she'd finished – and with a bit of luck she would have Mark Adderbury on the end of her string too.

THIRTY-FIVE

'Tiddles has gone,' Betsy said, tears trickling down her cheeks as she leaned against Sally's legs and sniffed. 'We all loves him and now he's gone . . .'

Sally stroked her hair, smiling tenderly down at the tearful child, because she knew how much the little girl loved the stray cat the children had adopted. Pets were not supposed to be tolerated at St Saviour's, but the tiny kitten had turned up in the garden one day looking thin and vulnerable and the children had saved scraps from their meals to feed it. It had grown plumper and sleek and was a general favourite with the children and staff alike, and even Muriel had been known to save a few fish skins for their pet.

'Perhaps he's just hiding somewhere,' Sally said. She'd been off duty for a couple of days and wasn't sure what had been going on in her absence. 'Shall we all go in the garden and look for him? Everyone put your coat on and then we'll look. He might have got shut in the shed.'

'The shed is locked, miss,' one of the boys said. 'The caretaker keeps the key in the cellar.'

'Well, we can look through the window and if we see him, we'll fetch the key – but he might just be hiding. He could be somewhere in the house in one of the dorms.'

'We've all looked for him,' another of the girls said. 'He's been missin' a week – I think someone has stolen him.'

'No, that's just silly,' Sally said. 'Why would anyone want to steal Tiddles?'

Sally marshalled the children and took them out into the garden. They all ran round looking under things, calling to each other, and then everyone peered in through the shed window, but no one could find him. After she judged they had looked everywhere, Sally took the children inside again. Since several of them were obviously upset over the disappearance of the cat, she took them to the kitchens and asked Muriel if they could look in there and the scullery.

'I was wondering where the poor creature was myself,' Muriel said. 'Look as much as you like, my dears – but don't touch them sharp knives on the table there.'

The children promised they wouldn't and conducted a thorough search of the pantry, scullery, kitchen and the toilet area, returning with glum faces when no trace of the cat was discovered. Sally apologised for the intrusion and the search party moved off. Cloakrooms, the dorms, and every cupboard they saw were investigated, but still no sign of the pet was found.

'He must have wandered off,' Sally told the disappointed children as the bell sounded for their lunch. 'I expect he will come back again. Now off you go and wash your hands.'

Sally was shepherding them towards the bathrooms when Angela came to meet her. 'You're back then,' she said. 'I haven't seen you lately because you were away and I had a couple of days off work, too. My mother wasn't feeling well and Sister let me take my holiday to look after her. Did you have a nice visit?'

'Yes, lovely,' Angela said. 'What have you been up to this morning? I heard a lot of voices just now.'

'We were searching for Tiddles,' Sally told her. 'Apparently, he's been missing for about a week and the children are worried. You haven't seen him, I suppose?'

'No . . . now you mention it I haven't seen him for some days – since before I went home, when I think about it. He often comes to visit me in my office, likes sitting on my lap as I work . . . Do you think he's been knocked over in the street?'

'I hope not. The children adore him. I can't understand him running off, because he was so thin when he came to us and now he is well-fed.'

'Surely he wouldn't?' Angela frowned. 'Cats often get shut in places, don't they? I'll speak to the caretaker and ask him if he'll look in the cellar for us. It isn't safe for the children to look down there, but I'll speak to him now.'

'Some of the children do sneak down there,' Sally said. 'Billy Baggins used to and . . . I saw Terry coming from there a few days ago . . .'

'Terry . . .' Angela frowned. 'I wonder . . . No, I'm sure he wouldn't . . .'

'What is it?'

'Oh, I saw him with the cat a few days ago, and then I found the salt pots had been tampered with. He was

272

teasing it and it scratched him. He kicked out at it and I told him not to. He said he was sorry and the cat walked off, wagging its tail the way they do when they're angry. It didn't like Terry.'

'Animals always know.' Sally frowned. 'I don't trust that boy. There's something wrong with him if you ask me.'

'I think he's just moody, and he can be sullen, but he's all right unless you upset him.'

'You said the cat scratched him,' Sally reminded her. 'You don't think he would harm it?'

'No, I'm sure he wouldn't,' Angela said, 'but I'll go and find the caretaker now. I'll ask him to have a good look in the cellar – and in the cupboards under the stairs. Anywhere the cat might have got shut in.'

'Yes.' Sally gave a little shiver. 'You're still on for next week?'

'Of course I am. It's your birthday. I wouldn't miss it for the world.'

'Andrew will be seeing Mark Adderbury this afternoon. He'll ask him – it's booked for Friday next week. Don't forget.'

Angela promised she wouldn't and went off to look for the caretaker. Sally rounded up the children and then took them to the dining room. She settled them with their choice of meal and then Nan came up to her.

'Could you take some sandwiches and a pot of tea up for Staff Nurse Carole, Sally? She says she is too busy to come down for it this morning, because she has some new patients to admit to the wards.'

'Yes, of course,' Sally said, and went into the kitchen to fetch a plate of nicely cut tomato and paste sandwiches

273

and a fresh pot of tea. She wouldn't have chosen the duty for pleasure, but Sally never refused when Nan asked her to do something.

She took the lift upstairs, knocked at the door of the sick room and then went in. There was no sign of Carole, so she placed the tray on the desk and was about to leave when she saw that the record of medicines had been left open on the desk. Sally was puzzled, because it was normally kept in the cupboard with the medicines themselves. Glancing down at the entries, she saw that one column looked slightly odd and she brushed her hand over it, realising that an eraser had been used on a couple of figures. Someone must have made a mistake and wanted to correct it before Sister saw the book. She looked again and saw that the entry had been signed off by Sister herself – so why was someone erasing some of the figures?

Sally was puzzled but turned away from the book as she heard a child crying. It was coming from the bed at the far end of the ward and she saw it was a little boy, whose name she didn't know.

'Hello, I think you're new here,' Sally said, sitting on the edge of the bed. 'What is the matter? Do you feel ill?'

He shook his head, knuckling his eyes. 'I'm thirsty. I asked the lady for a drink but she wouldn't give me one . . . she said I must wait until she came back.'

'Is this your first day here?' Sally asked. 'Have you been ill?'

'I was sick,' the child said. 'I'm always sick when I go somewhere new – but I'm not ill and I taste bad.'

'Your mouth is dry, I expect,' Sally said. She looked

above the bed but there wasn't anything to say he couldn't have a drink. 'Would you like a glass of orange?'

'Yes, please,' he said, staring at her hopefully.

'All right, I'll get you one,' Sally said. 'What is your name?'

'I'm Alfie, miss. Alfie Jones.'

'Well, stop crying and I'll fetch your drink.'

Sally smiled at him, got up and went into the nurses' rest room. She made up a glass of the concentrated juice with water and took it back into the ward. As she started towards Alfie's bed, the door opened and Carole entered.

'What do you think you're doing with that orange juice?' she asked sharply.

'Alfie wanted a drink.'

'Please do not interfere. I've told you before, I am in charge here. Alfie is on a very strict regime. He has a tummy bug – something you wouldn't understand – and he can only have sips of water.'

'Oh . . . I'm sorry. There was nothing above his bed to say he couldn't have a drink.'

'I don't have to tell you. The night nurses will have the sense to check Alfie's notes. You should not even be here without a nurse to supervise.'

'I brought your lunch up because Nan said you were busy.'

'That does not give you the right to interfere with my patients. If you do so again I shall report you to Sister Beatrice.'

Sally bit her lip. Carole was being particularly nasty to her and she didn't know why. Perhaps she had been wrong not to check Alfie's notes, but Michelle and the other nurses always placed a nil by mouth notice above restricted patients' beds so that it was clear to everyone. Obviously Carole had her own routine and as a lowly carer, Sally couldn't argue. She apologised and left, feeling that she would like to tell the nurse what she thought of her, but if she did that she might find herself out of a job.

She was just leaving when she saw Carole snatch the book up and place it back in the medicine cupboard. It looked as if it was Carole who had been altering the figures – and she was annoyed because she thought Sally might have seen what she'd done.

Going back down to the ground floor, Sally was lost in thought until she saw a group of children gathered about Angela. They were talking noisily and some of them were weeping. Sally saw that Angela had something in her arms. She gave a little cry of distress as she realised that it was the children's pet, Tiddles, its body completely limp.

'Where did you find him?' she asked. 'The poor little thing looks just about dead.'

'He had been shut in a cupboard in the cellar,' Angela said, clearly distressed. 'When I asked Blake if he'd seen it he said he hadn't but he had a look and then thought he heard something and opened this cupboard. He can't understand how it happened, because he says he hardly ever uses that cupboard. It should be locked, because he keeps axes and sharp instruments for the garden in there.'

Sally lifted her brows but Angela gave a little shake of her head. 'I'm going to have to take Tiddles to the vet's,' she said, and looked at the upset children. 'We shall do what we can to help him, but he is very ill.'

'Do you know where the nearest vet is?' Sally said.

'I've rung for a taxi. I'm sure he will be able to take me. I'd better go – do what you can to help the little ones . . .'

Sally nodded and then gathered up the children, putting her arms around Betsy as the girl wept. 'You mustn't get too upset, children. Angela will do what she can for Tiddles. He was a naughty cat to run away and hide in the cupboard.'

Even as she tried to comfort the grieving boys and girls, Sally was conscious of someone staring at them. She turned her head and saw Terry watching. He saw her look at him and grinned, a horrible leer on his face that chilled Sally. She didn't have proof; it was impossible to know for certain, but she was sure in her own mind that he'd deliberately shut the cat in that cupboard and left it to starve to death out of spite.

She took the smaller children away to the schoolroom, noticing that Terry stood apart from them just watching them until his sister called him and he ran off. If Sally was sure her suspicions were right she would tell Sister Beatrice, but she would be asked for proof and all she had was a gut feeling that Terry knew more than he should about the cat's suffering . . .

THIRTY-SIX

'Where have you been?' Sister Beatrice asked when Angela returned to her own office nearly two hours later. 'I've been looking for you. I wanted to ask you about the staff rota.'

'I'm sorry but I couldn't let you know,' Angela said. 'Tiddles was found shut in a cupboard and close to death from dehydration and starvation. I took the poor creature to the vet immediately, but he told me it was too late to do anything and the kindest thing was just to put it to sleep.'

'Oh, how vexing,' Sister said. 'I suppose the children will be upset over the wretched thing. It's the reason I do not normally encourage pets, because when they become ill or die the children start crying over it. Cats are reasonably clean creatures once they're housetrained so I turned a blind eye to the adoption of that kitten. Blake should be more careful.'

'I'm not sure it was his fault . . .' Angela hesitated. 'It may have been shut in there deliberately.'

'Not one of the children?'

'I have no proof. It's just a suspicion.'

'Please tell me, Angela. I need to know everything that happens here.'

'Well, just over a week ago I saw the cat scratch a boy and he kicked it but I shouted and stopped him . . .' Angela paused. 'And some days later, I found all the sugar and salt pots in the dining room had been tampered with. I took them into the kitchen and washed them and filled them again. When I returned them to the dining room, I saw a boy run from the door. I believe he'd been watching me refill the pots.'

'You did not think fit to tell me?' Sister glared at her.

'I'm sorry, I realise I should have done,' Angela said. 'At the time I did not connect the two, nor did I think it more than a silly prank. I was going to tell you but you weren't here and then something came up and it went out of my mind. I believed there was some sort of quarrel between this boy and one or two of the children, and imagined he thought it funny to trick them into putting salt in their tea or sugar on their chips . . .'

'It appears that there is a great deal going on that I have not been informed of,' Sister said, annoyed. 'Are you going to tell me who this boy is that you suspect of shutting that poor animal in the cupboard?'

'I don't know he did it,' Angela reminded her. 'But I did see him run from the dining room that day – and I did see the cat scratch him. Terry is someone who doesn't make friends easily, and perhaps he just wanted to upset the other children . . . he might not have real-ised what would happen to the cat.'

'Terry . . .' Sister looked thoughtful. 'I see. That

279

makes a difference. You are certain that you saw him run away after you'd changed the salt pots?'

'Yes. He glanced back for an instant . . .' Angela felt awful, because she suddenly realised that she was very much at fault for not having told Sister sooner. 'I thought Terry was getting better, making friends – but since the day that he threw the porridge over Mary Ellen he has stopped going down for his meals. I don't think he talks to any of the other children except his sister. I'm sorry, I should have told you immediately.'

'Well, we all make mistakes. None of what you've just told me is conclusive and it doesn't add up to much, even when you put it all together – but because we know that Terry is such a fragile and disturbed child you ought to have kept me informed.'

'Yes, I've realised that and I do apologise. It won't happen again.'

'Well, as long as you understand why these small things must be reported, even if they seem insignificant, we shall say no more of it. Mark Adderbury feels that Terry needs special treatment, which he cannot receive here, and he is going to be moved soon – but that is confidential, Angela. I had hoped the boy was improving but there is a possibility that he could prove dangerous. These small pranks are merely those of a young lad taking a silly revenge. In the case of the cat it is unfortunate, very unfortunate, but like you I think perhaps he did not understand what would happen, and maybe we should give him the benefit of the doubt.'

'Of course.'

Sister nodded. 'Now, to the reason I wished to see

you, Angela. Firstly, I was going through the staff rota – have you made changes?'

'No, certainly not,' Angela said, puzzled. 'I never interfere with the rota.'

'Well, someone has,' Sister said. 'Fortunately, Jean asked me if she could change her duty, because she needs to visit the dentist, so I went over it to see what could be done – and I discovered that Sally had been booked in to work all day and then the late shift at night. I would never have made such a mistake. I was able to change Jean's duty and give her that shift so it worked out very well – but we might have been left with no cover, because Sally couldn't possibly have worked so many hours all at once.'

Angela was studying the rota Sister Beatrice had referred to. 'I can't understand it,' she said. 'That rota was on my desk waiting to be typed up – but I can see that an eraser has been used. You have crossed out Sally's name and inserted Jean's – but an eraser was used just here . . .'

'Well, it is a mystery,' Sister said. 'I cannot think I made the mistake – but thankfully, it was found in time.'

'Yes, that was fortunate,' Angela said.

'There was something more – ah, yes. I have arranged for the builders to come in next week on Thursday 11th. I prefer that the children are out so that they will not get in the way or come to harm. I know it is short notice, but can you arrange for yourself and some of the carers to take all the young children out on a trip that lasts all day? The older children will be at school until after the workmen have finished, and when they return they can congregate in the new wing until teatime, which will be later than usual.'

'Yes, of course,' Angela agreed. 'I'll take them to a museum in the morning or the waxworks, then have some lunch and perhaps we'll all go to see a children's film and then have tea before we come back – if that would be all right?'

'Do you have enough money in the treats box?'

'Yes, I think so,' Angela said. She would have no hesitation in paying for the cinema and tea herself, but she kept this to herself. 'The museum is free of course – and the waxworks doesn't charge us very much, because we have a special rate.'

'Very well, I shall leave it to you. Take as many of the staff with you as you wish. It will be a treat for them as well, and the more adults the easier it will be to keep control of the children.'

Angela stared at the office door as Sister Beatrice closed it behind her. Fortunately, there were not many patients in the sick room, although of course they and the nurse on duty would have to remain at St Saviour's, but Sister obviously thought that the emptier the place was the better for the builders. She smiled as she started to review her plans for the big day out. She would look and see what films were showing at the moment – a Walt Disney cartoon would be best, because all the children would love that.

She would have to take both Terry and Nancy, of course, but he should be all right, as long as Nancy was there. Angela had hoped she was wrong about him, almost sure he was simply recovering from a terrible experience, but now she wasn't so convinced. If Mark had told Angela he was thinking of having Terry moved to a secure unit where he could have special treatment she would have known what to expect . . . but they'd only spoken briefly since the night they'd cooked at her apartment. She suspected he'd been going out with Carole quite a bit, but it wasn't really her business what Mark chose to do with his spare time . . .

Angela would have liked to tell Mark her suspicions about what Terry had done to the cat, but didn't feel she could just telephone him and ask him over as she had previously. He was still her friend, but he'd seemed a little remote the last time they'd spoken . . . which, of course, he would be if he were falling in love with another woman. The thought was surprisingly hurtful to Angela but she told herself not to be foolish.

If Mark was arranging for the boy to be moved there was no problem, though she would be sorry to see Nancy leave. The girl was beginning to be happy here and to fit in, and she would hate to move to another home, but if her brother was sent away, she would no doubt wish to go with him.

Because her mind was busy with other things Angela simply didn't have time to worry about the mistake in the rota. Perhaps Sister had made the tiny slip herself.

Nancy looked at Terry. He'd been sitting staring out of the window for ages, a grin on his face that made her want to shake him. Why was he looking so pleased when every other child at St Saviour's was in tears over that cat?

A chill ran down Nancy's spine as she recalled an incident that had happened in the lanes where they lived a year or so earlier. Several cats had been found dead, poisoned people said, but one had been mutilated, its front paws cut off. No one ever discovered who had killed the cats, but Pa had complained that someone had stolen the arsenic he'd used for killing rats in the garden. Pa had accused Terry of taking it, and he'd given him a good hiding. Nancy had comforted him afterwards, but something Terry said when he was crying had worried her.

'I hate cats, Nance. I'm glad they're all dead.'

'But you didn't take that poison, Terry? You wouldn't do such a wicked thing as to kill people's cats, would you?'

'No, Nance. I never took it – Pa's rotten. He's always blamin' me.'

Nancy had believed him then. She would never have thought her brother capable of hurting anything . . . well, perhaps he might pull the wings from a butterfly trying to catch it, but putting poison down for people's pets . . . no, her little brother would never do that. But that was before the fire, before she'd seen Terry standing there staring at the flames shooting up the door of their parents' bedroom and seen the terrible look in his eyes.

'You didn't shut that cat in the cupboard, did you, Terry?'

Terry turned his head to look at her and for a moment the gleeful expression in his eyes made her go cold all over, and then in an instant it was gone and they filled with childish tears.

'Don't be horrid to me, Nance. You know I never done it . . . I hate things to be imprisoned, you know I do.'

'I know. I'm sorry, love, but it's just . . . well, I know you go down into the cellar sometimes. I thought you might have done it, by accident.'

'You don't love me no more,' Terry sobbed. 'Everyone hates me. I wish I were dead. I want to go home and be with Ma . . .' Tears streamed down his face, mixing with snot from his nose. 'I never meant Ma to die, Nance. I want her . . . I want her . . .'

'Oh, Terry, don't,' Nancy said, and put her arms about him, kissing the top of his head. She felt a wave of protective love overwhelm her. Terry hadn't set fire to the door of her parents' bedroom on purpose; he couldn't have done. She was wrong to think it, wrong to think that he might have shut that cat away because it had scratched his hand . . . because his hand still bore red marks from where it had lashed out at him. Cats and dogs never liked Terry; they hissed and barked and he'd been bitten twice as a very small boy. It was no wonder he didn't like them, but he wasn't really a bad boy and he wouldn't do the things her mind kept telling her he might have done. 'I'm sorry. I do love you, Terry. I love you more than anyone in the world and I'll always look after you.'

'Promise me, Nance,' he said, looking up at her with the eyes of a frightened little boy. 'You won't let him send me away? Pa was going to have me shut up for ever, somewhere they would beat me and starve me. You won't let him do that, will you?'

Tears were trickling down Nancy's face as she held her beloved brother in her arms. It was all Pa's fault. He'd said such things to Terry, threatened to send him to an asylum, and he'd abused them both. Even if Terry

285

had thrown his oil lamp at the door, he hadn't known what he was doing; he couldn't have done! She tried to push away the suspicions that haunted her. Terry wasn't evil; but he did have a temper, just like Pa and it was possible that he'd done something foolish without realising what would happen. And if that door hadn't been locked their parents might have got out . . . but Nancy couldn't bear to think about that. It wasn't Terry's fault if he wasn't quite right in the head. He couldn't help being the way he was. His true nature was sweet and loving and Nancy was going to protect him for as long as she could.

Mary Ellen knew who had shut poor Tiddles in the cupboard and she was going to do something about it. She'd wondered if she should tell either Miss Angela or Sally, though she wasn't a snitch – but it wasn't right that he should get away with this. She would tell him what she knew in front of his sister and Nancy would know what to do.

Her mind made up, Mary Ellen marched up to their room and thrust the door open. Terry was alone and standing at the window staring out at the garden, but he swung round as she entered and then he grinned at her. He knew why she'd come and he was laughing because of what he'd done to poor Tiddles.

'Why did you do it?' Mary Ellen demanded, too angry for caution. 'You're a rotten devil, Terry Johnson, and I'm going to tell your sister. You deserve to get the cane for this. If it were up to me you'd go to prison and they'd never let you out again . . .'

At this, Terry's mood turned and she saw the blaze

of fury in his eyes. He looked so strange and she was suddenly frightened of him. She wanted to run away, but she couldn't move, couldn't do anything but stare at him, mesmerised by the wild look on his face.

'I hate you,' he muttered, and she saw spittle on his mouth, the gleam of hatred in his eyes. 'I wanted to punish all of them for turning up their noses at me – but you more than all the others. It's your fault Billy doesn't like me any more. If you weren't here he would be my friend again . . .'

Mary Ellen swallowed hard and took a step backwards just as he sprang at her. His body knocked her off balance and she felt herself slam into the side of the bed and then she was lying on it and Terry had his hands around her throat. She struggled as hard as she could, pushing at his fingers as she tried to force them apart, but she was finding it difficult to breathe and Terry seemed so strong. He was wild and strange and the look on his face terrified her. She tried to cry out but no sound came and Mary Ellen was terrified. Terry wanted to kill her . . .

'What are you doing?' Nancy's voice stopped Terry. The pressure on Mary Ellen's throat was released and she could breathe again. He jerked away and then moved back, leaving her lying on the bed, and she saw a dazed, frightened expression in his eyes.

'He attacked me . . .' she whispered.

'Terry, how could you?' Nancy asked, and came up to them, pushing him out of the way and helping her up. 'You mustn't hurt Mary Ellen like that . . . are you all right?' Nancy looked so upset as she asked that Mary Ellen nodded, even though her throat felt sore.

'Yes,' she croaked. 'He killed Tiddles, Nancy. I know he did it – and he admitted it. He hates me – it's because I told Billy that he kicked Betsy and Billy told him not to. Billy wouldn't have fallen out with him over it if he'd said sorry . . .'

'It's a lie, Nance,' Terry said, and for a moment he stared at Mary Ellen as if he hated her, and then turned and ran from the room.

'I'm so sorry,' Nancy said. 'Please forgive him, Mary Ellen. He's not been himself since Ma died in the fire . . .' Her voice died as if she couldn't speak and tears trickled down her cheeks. 'Please, you won't tell – will you? I know Terry is silly sometimes, but he's all I've got and I love him. I'll make him say sorry – and I promise he won't do it again'

Mary Ellen hesitated, because Terry might not have killed her but he would certainly have hurt her badly if his sister hadn't come that instant. She knew he'd killed their pet cat and she thought someone ought to know about his wild moods, because surely Terry wasn't right in the head. Yet she wasn't a snitch – and she liked Nancy.

'I won't tell,' she said at last as she found her voice again. 'But you have to do something, Nancy. He's not right – he's ill in his mind, isn't he?'

Nancy nodded, her face pale and her eyes filled with tears. 'Yes, he's ill. I can't tell Sister Beatrice – but I shall tell Miss Angela. She will know what to do . . .'

'Where has Terry gone?'

'He'll be hiding somewhere,' Nancy told her. 'He used to run off down the Docks when Pa got mad at him – it's all Pa's fault. I don't understand why Terry went for you like that.'

'It was when I told him he should be locked up,' Mary Ellen said. 'His eyes went all funny and then he lunged at me . . . I didn't know he would be like that, Nancy. You should tell Miss Angela as soon as you can. Now, I've got to go to school and I'm already late.'

'Yes,' Nancy said. 'I shall . . . but first I'd better go and see if I can find him.'

THIRTY-SEVEN

Billy was whistling as he entered the boy's lavatories. He'd scored another goal for the school team that morning and he was feeling pleased with his skill and life in general. He noticed that one of the doors had the locked sign on the front but didn't take much notice, though most of the boys never bothered to lock themselves in. He went into an empty stall and emerged, remembering to stop and wash his hands the way Sally was always telling them to. About to leave the cloakroom, he heard a sound like a sob coming from behind the locked door and hesitated. Another muffled cry made him go to the door and knock.

'Are yer all right in there, mate?' he asked, though he had no idea who it was, but kids didn't cry unless they were in big trouble. 'Can I help?'

'Go away,' a voice he recognised answered. 'No one cares – they all hate me.'

'I don't hate you, Terry,' Billy said. 'Are yer sick or somethin'? Why don't yer come out and talk about it? We're havin' plum tart and custard tonight for tea.'

There was a pause, then, 'You don't like me 'cos I

was rude to that girl . . .' Terry sounded sulky and yet hesitant.

''Course I like yer, mate,' Billy said. 'We all have a barney now and then – but I like Mary Ellen too. Why don't yer come out and tell me what this is about?'

Terry made a snuffling sound and then opened the door. His face was red and Billy was shocked to see that he had cuts on his arms where his crumpled shirt was rolled up. In his hand he was holding a piece of broken glass and his fingers were bleeding.

'Were you tryin' ter kill yerself?' Billy asked. 'Nothin' ain't ever that bad, mate. Come on, let's wash yer hand under the cold tap and then I'll wrap me hanky round it for yer.'

Terry looked a bit dazed, but he held his hand out docilely and let Billy wash away the blood and then wrap his none-too-clean hanky round it. The marks on his arms were not as deep as those on his hands and they'd stopped bleeding.

'What made you do that?' Billy asked when he'd finished. 'Did Sister cane yer – or tell yer she would send yer away?'

Terry looked at him in alarm. 'She won't send me away – will she?'

'She threatened to send me orf once when I played her up,' Billy said, and grinned. 'She didn't do it, though – I reckon she's a big softie under all them frowns. She ain't too bad if yer don't get the wrong side of her. Come on, let's go and have some tea.'

Terry shook his head. 'I ain't hungry. I'll get Nance to bring me a bit of cake when she comes back.'

'What upset yer?' Billy persisted. 'If I can help yer I

will – yer still a mate, Terry. We all 'ave to stick together here, you know.'

'I can't remember,' Terry said, and now there was a scared look in his eyes. 'I think I did something bad . . . but I can't remember what it was.'

'Well, it's your loss,' Billy said. 'I'm off for my tea – I'm starvin'.'

Terry stared at the door of the cloakroom as Billy barged through it and left it swinging. He wrinkled his forehead as he struggled to remember why he'd run to the toilets and locked himself in. He looked at the bloody piece of glass on the basin and felt puzzled. Where had that come from and why had he cut himself with it?

He tried hard to remember, but it was like a black hole in his head. He knew he'd been in their room waiting for Nance to come back, but he couldn't remember anything after that until he'd become aware of the blood and the pain in his hand – and then Billy had banged on the door and made him come out.

Billy had been kind to him. He was his friend. Terry wasn't sure that he wanted to be friends with the other children . . . he vaguely remembered that there was a girl he didn't like, but he wasn't sure why.

Leaving the cloakroom, Terry went up to the room he shared with Nancy and discovered she was sitting on the bed, her hands up to her face.

'Nance . . . are you crying?' he asked. 'Why are you crying? Is it me? Have I done something bad?'

She jumped up and ran to him, putting her arms about him and hugging him. Then she saw the handkerchief round his hand.

'What happened?' she cried. 'Terry, what have you done now?'

'I don't know, Nance,' he said, and looked at her in distress and bewilderment. 'I was in the toilet crying and my hand hurt – and then Billy came and washed it for me. I cut myself on a bit of glass but I don't know how.'

'Oh, Terry . . . Terry,' Nancy whispered, half to herself. 'What am I going to do with you, love?'

'Don't cry, Nance. Please don't cry. I love you and I don't know what I've done – did I do something bad?'

Nancy looked down at him, studying his face as if she were trying to read what was in his mind. 'You don't remember anything – what happened before you ran off and hid?'

'It's all muddled up in here.' He touched the side of his head. 'Sometimes things go funny, Nance. It's like a fog behind my eyes and . . . then it's like a big black hole and I can't remember where I am or what I've done.'

'Oh, Terry, my poor little brother,' Nancy said, and kissed his cheek. He could feel her tears and it made him sad so he put his arms about her and hugged her. 'I love you so. I've got to look after you and protect you, but I don't know what I should do for the best . . .'

'You won't let that woman send me away, will you? Billy said she was going to send him away once – you won't let us be parted, will you?'

'No,' Nancy said, and her arms tightened about him. 'I'll never do that, Terry. I promise you.'

Beatrice sat staring at the papers before her on her desk. She was worried, because Mark had come to see her and told her that he had serious doubts about Terry and she'd dismissed them. If anything unpleasant happened to Terry it would be her fault. She hadn't wanted to be unfair to another child, because of the incident with Billy Baggins. She'd accused Billy of running off when all the time he'd been forced to help his rogue of a brother – and so she'd wanted to give Terry plenty of rope before she took her decision. However, if Angela was right about him . . . they could no longer wait and the boy ought to be moved as soon as possible.

She'd seen Terry outside in the garden with the caretaker a few moments ago. If Nancy were in their room, this was possibly a good chance to speak to her alone. The girl must understand that her brother needed more intense care than he could receive at St Saviour's.

Feeling reluctant but sure that she was right, Beatrice rose and walked from her office, her heart heavy. Never in all the time she'd been dealing with children had she faced such an unpleasant task. Most disturbed children were difficult, a few could be violent at times, but they usually responded to kindness, and Mark was very good at helping them – as was Mr Markham with his books about the big hairy spider.

They'd never had a child that was seriously mentally ill before. Had the brother and sister been taken to hospital and assessed it was possible that Terry would never have been sent to St Saviour's. When the police found them hiding down the Docks, they'd seen them as needing a home but virtually unscathed by the fire. However, they were not experts – Mark Adderbury was and his instincts had told him from the beginning that something was very wrong with Terry. Yet even he'd initially been reluctant to use his powers to remove the boy to a secure unit, which meant that if he'd decided to do so now he must be seriously concerned. Beatrice had begged him to wait. In such cases it was so difficult to be certain and it would be terrible to make a mistake . . . and yet for the good of the other children, Beatrice had to be firm.

Arriving outside the room the brother and sister shared, she hesitated, knocked and then walked in. Nancy was sitting by the window, some sewing in her hands, watching something in the garden. She looked round guiltily and then jumped up, dropping her needlework as she saw Beatrice.

'I'm sorry, Sister. I was watching Terry. He's following the caretaker outside, more of a hindrance than a help, but Mr Blake doesn't mind.'

'Yes, I know. I saw him. He enjoys doing things with his hands, doesn't he?'

'Terry isn't good with schooling, but he's strong – and he likes helping with the garden and the firewood.'

'You are very fond of him, aren't you?'

'Yes, Sister. I've always looked after him.'

'I realise that, and I know it would upset you to part with him.'

Nancy looked anxious, nervous. 'But you said we could keep this room . . . you said it was all right for me to have cooking lessons and Terry to help the caretaker . . .'

'Yes, and I hoped that might work for you both, but . . . things have reached me, Nancy. Things that worry me. I'm not sure that Terry has been behaving himself as he ought. I'm not accusing him of anything, but I am worried. Do you understand me?'

Nancy was silent, her eyes large and round, accusing.

Yet she was obviously listening, waiting in some trepidation for more – as if she were keeping a secret that no one else knew.

'Mr Adderbury thinks Terry is ill . . . mentally ill. Because of the fire, you see.' Beatrice tried to explain as gently as she could. 'It isn't his fault, and no one is angry with him, or with you, Nancy, but we feel that your brother needs special care – care we cannot give him at St Saviour's. It is Mr Adderbury's opinion, and mine, that he should be moved to a place where he will have a chance to be made well again. Given the right treatment Terry could recover and live a normal life – but he will have to go away for a while . . .'

'What happens to me?' Nancy was very pale, very still.

'There is a special clinic in the country, where Terry will be looked after by people who will give him the care he needs. You are to accompany him to the clinic so that he is not too alarmed, and there is a children's home where you could stay if you wish to be near him. You would go to school in the village and visit Terry now and then – unless you wished to return here and go down on the train when you want to see your brother, perhaps every other week or so. St Saviour's stands in place of a family to you, and the cost of your fares and expenses will be provided if that should be your choice.'

'For how long must he stay there?' Nancy demanded. 'Where is this place – is it a mental home? You're not goin' to shut our Terry in a place like that . . .' She was white-faced, tense, her nails turned into the palms of her hands. 'I won't let you. Pa said he would have him shut in the loony bin but I wouldn't have let him . . .'

'No, no, of course it isn't an asylum,' Beatrice said.

296

'I promise you, Nancy. Mr Adderbury doesn't want to do anything like that. He cares about children like Terry and he would not send him to this clinic if he didn't believe it was for his own good. If he remains here his condition may get worse and Terry might do something bad . . . something that would mean he was forcibly shut away. It might be too late to help him then.'

Nancy was biting her lip in distress. 'Why should I believe you? You promised we could stay here – and I can look after Terry. I can stop him doin' bad things. I can . . . I will; I promise I won't let him . . .' Nancy broke off, tears welling in her eyes. 'If you separate us and shut him away from me it will break his heart. I've always looked after him – please don't do this. Please . . . he doesn't mean to be bad . . . truly he doesn't. He doesn't understand what will happen . . .' Nancy stopped as if she realised that whatever she said it wouldn't change the decision. She was silent for a moment, then, 'When – when are you going to take him away?'

'Perhaps a few weeks, but quite soon,' Beatrice said. 'Try not to see it as a bad thing, Nancy. If Terry isn't treated he will get worse but if he is given the attention he needs in time he may be able to live normally. You might be able to have him home one day, when you've got a job and can look after him.'

'And if he doesn't get better? He'll be shut up there for ever in that place . . . he would rather die.' She looked desperate. 'Let me take him away. I'll find some-where for us to live – please, just give me a little money to start and you'll never have to see us again . . .'

'Oh, Nancy.' Beatrice felt her heart break with the pity of it. 'Do you think I want to do this, my dear? I wish you could both stay here, but I can't keep Terry – and I can't let you take him away. You don't understand, Nancy – your brother could be dangerous, to himself and others . . .'

'No, Terry didn't do it, he didn't hurt Mary Ellen,' Nancy cried out in such distress that she was speaking without thinking. 'He didn't mean to let the cat die . . . you mustn't let them shut him away, please. Please don't let them hurt him; he didn't understand what would happen . . .'

Beatrice felt as if she'd been douched with cold water. 'I wasn't accusing him of hurting another child . . . is that what he did, Nancy? Did you see him . . . did he attack Mary Ellen? I've heard nothing of it. This is a serious matter. You must tell me. If Terry has been violent things must be brought forward . . .'

Suddenly, the door, which had not been quite shut, was thrust openly violently, catching Beatrice sharply in the back and knocking her off balance. Terry rushed into the room, his face flushed with anger, his eyes wild as he stared at her.

'I didn't do nothin', you old witch,' he screamed at Beatrice. 'I hate yer. I hate all of yer and I ain't goin' away from Nance.' He ran at Beatrice, going for her with his hands and feet, biting at her hands as she tried to fend him off. 'I hate yer all . . . I ain't goin' ter that place . . .'

'Terry, stop it!' Nancy rushed at him, pulling him off as he continued to kick out and scream abuse at Beatrice. 'Stop it now, or I shall give you a good smack and I won't look after you.'

Terry went limp, his eyes blank. He was breathing

298

hard but he'd stopped fighting. Nancy threw a look of appeal at Beatrice, tears in her eyes.

'It's not her fault,' she said to him, and there was an air of resignation about her now, of defeat. 'Terry, you're not well, my love. You're going to a special place where they will help you. I shall come with you and I'll visit all the time – and when you're better we'll find a place to live together . . .'

Terry backed away from her, his eyes going desperately from one to the other like a terrified animal. 'You don't love me no more, Nance. You're like all the others, want ter lock me up. I hate yer all – and I'll get even. See if I don't.'

With that he whirled round, rushed through the open door and disappeared down the hall, running as fast as he could. Nancy was pale, anxious, as she stared at Beatrice.

'I'm sorry for what he did to you. He's upset because Pa told him he was an idiot and said he would have him put in the loony bin. He thinks that's where you're going to put him.'

'I'm sorry he heard what we were saying. I thought he was in the garden – I'm not sure how much he heard . . .'

'I have to look for him,' Nancy said. 'I must find him before he does something silly.' She fled from the room before Beatrice could stop her.

Beatrice stood for a while as Nancy went off in search of her brother. While his attack on her had been no more than an act of childish revenge, Nancy's blurted admission that her brother had attacked another child was more serious. Mark would have to bring the admission forward, or perhaps make other arrangements until the clinic could take him, if that was still the appropriate treatment. Beatrice felt so distressed that she hardly knew what to think. To her Terry seemed just a frightened, wilful boy but was there a very different personality hiding inside the child?

Finally, she left their room and walked slowly back to her office. The life of a child was in the balance. Beatrice felt no animosity or resentment towards the child that had attacked her so viciously, only pity and deep sorrow. To think that Terry might never be able to walk freely again in the sunlight was a terrible thing and it hurt – it hurt Beatrice to think that she had played even a small part in his descent into the darkness of a disturbed mind. Yet what else could she have done? Nancy had to understand why her brother needed hospitalisation, and she'd tried to keep it from the boy. How could she have guessed that he would return in time to hear what they were saying?

What was he thinking in his confused mind? He'd run off in a show of distress and temper, but there was nowhere he could go – unless he roamed the streets. Beatrice didn't want to contact the police yet, but she must telephone Mark Adderbury and ask his advice.

It was so very sad and she felt like crying, but would not allow herself to give in to tears. Nothing like this had ever happened at St Saviour's before and it made her feel guilty, as though she had caused the destruction of a child – it reminded her of another time; another child; a child who had died . . .

THIRTY-EIGHT

'I've searched everywhere, miss,' Nancy said. 'Sally and Alice helped me look but we couldn't find him anywhere. I think he has run away.'

'Where could he go?' Angela asked her. 'You told me you have no friends or relations. Surely, he wouldn't leave St Saviour's? Would he not be frightened on his own?'

'Terry always used to wander off when we were at home,' Nancy said. 'He mostly used to go down to the Docks. Someone gave him work for a few pennies and he was proud of himself for doing a proper man's work . . .' There was a sob in her throat. Her brother had run off for the second time and this time could not be found. He'd never been away a whole night and she was so frightened; she'd been going over and over everything in her mind and she knew she had to tell someone about her decision. 'Oh, Miss Angela, he's not right in his mind. I've known it since the fire . . . even before then I knew he was backward, but he's much worse now, and I'm frightened.'

'If he has a friend who gives him work and money he will look after him.' Angela saw her distress and took her hand. 'He will come back when he's over his temper, Nancy – but if you would like to tell me something, please do.'

'Terry is strange once he gets something in his head, stubborn and angry,' Nancy said, and looked fearful. 'Pa said such terrible things to him – you don't know . . .' Her eyes were full of unshed tears and sadness. 'He thinks if they put him in that place Sister Beatrice told us about he'll be beaten and shut up in a little room with no windows.'

'I'm quite sure Mr Adderbury would not condemn your brother to a life of misery, Nancy. I know that the clinic he speaks of is a nice clean place with large gardens and kind staff who look after their patients. They want to help Terry to get over his fear and his anger. Whatever happened on the night of the fire he is suffering because of it and from what you've told me, your father was cruel to him – and to you, I suspect?'

'I must tell you it all. I'm afraid Terry might do something terrible after what he did yesterday . . .'

'What was that?'

'I found him attacking Mary Ellen. I think he tried to strangle her but wasn't strong enough. I shouted at him and he stopped and then ran away. Mary Ellen promised not to tell anyone – and then Terry locked himself in the toilets and cut himself. He said Billy washed away the blood and put a hanky round his hand – but Terry couldn't remember what he'd done . . . hurting Mary Ellen or cutting himself.'

'That is very serious,' Angela said. 'He could be a danger both to himself and others. We must find him before it's too late.'

'I know. I promised him I wouldn't let them take him away, but I know he's getting worse since the fire . . .' Nancy gasped and smothered a sob; her cheeks went white, her gaze dropping as if she couldn't bear to look at Angela. 'Terry saw what Pa was doing to me and he heard me crying and screaming. He went for Pa something awful and fought him but Pa was too strong and he thrashed him. Then he threw him in his room, locked the door and took the key. They went out drinking, Ma and him, and I could hear Terry crying but I couldn't give him his supper. When they came home they were both drunk. Pa left his coat on the floor in the kitchen and when he'd gone to bed, I unlocked Terry's door and gave him some bread and dripping and a glass of milk . . . then I left him to rest and went down to clean the kitchen . . .' Nancy drew a sobbing breath. 'I was scrubbing the floor when I heard something odd . . . a roaring sound . . . and then I could smell smoke and I ran upstairs . . .'

Tears were trickling down her cheeks and she looked at Angela in near despair. 'Terry was just standing there . . . staring, not moving, but his eyes . . . the look in his eyes was so strange, miss. It was wild . . . and glad, as if he had done something clever, but then he saw me and suddenly he was shaking and he screamed for Ma and tried to get to the door. I knew we couldn't get in there because the fire was too fierce and the door was locked, so I pulled him away and he was screaming for Ma to come – but it was too late to help her . . .'

Angela put her arms about her and held her as she shuddered and trembled. 'Don't give up hope, Nancy. You don't know he did it, my love. You can't be sure . . .

perhaps your father did it in a drunken rage. Terry was so upset that he probably doesn't know the truth.'

'Terry cried out in his sleep, and when he woke he kept telling me he hadn't meant to kill Ma, but he believes he did when he remembers . . . but sometimes he just forgets the things he does.' Nancy paused, then, 'He – he may have shut the cat in the cupboard because it scratched him, but I'm sure he didn't mean it to die like that . . . he just forgot what he'd done. He told me that it's like a fog in his head and then it all goes blank.'

'People sometimes imagine things when they are upset and the fire was a terrible experience for you both,' Angela said, ignoring the mention of the cat in her desire to comfort the girl. 'It is because Terry is so distressed that he needs this treatment, Nancy. Sister Beatrice meant no harm.'

'I know.' Nancy blinked. 'She looked as if she wanted to cry when Terry attacked her and then went off like that . . . and I know he ought to be somewhere safe and secure, because he might . . . he might do something really bad.'

'When he is found Mr Adderbury will look after him, Nancy. He will visit Terry at the clinic and make sure he is being properly cared for – it's not like a mental institution, I promise you. We can only pray that your brother will recover with kindness and the right treatment.'

'You're so kind to us, miss,' Nancy said. 'I hope you're right. When Terry gets cold and hungry he'll come looking for me , , ,'

'Yes, I'm sure he will,' Angela said, but after she left Nancy and went up to her office before leaving for the evening she was anxious. Whatever Terry might have done he was still a child and the streets of London were dangerous for a young boy alone.

'No, we still haven't seen or heard of him,' Angela said when Mark telephoned her at her office later that morning. 'Sister Beatrice has decided that she must tell Constable Sallis what happened and ask the police to keep an eye out for him.'

'Yes, she must, because he was placed in her care. You are as sure as you can be that he isn't hiding at St Saviour's?'

'The stairs to the attics are securely locked now,' Angela told him. 'Everywhere has been searched more than once, including the cupboards under the stairs and the cellar. Billy Baggins and Mary Ellen organised a search and if the children can't find him, I'm pretty certain he isn't here.'

'Well, I dare say he will turn up. If his sister says he often went down to the Docks the police will make enquiries there. I'm afraid we can't do much until he is found – I blame myself, I should have taken him into protective care sooner.'

'You were waiting for the right place, Mark. He is terrified of being locked up in a mental institution. His father told him he was going to have him put in a loony bin, and if you'd had him sectioned it might have sent him over the edge.'

'Of course that was my fear. You always understand me, Angela – but it is possible that it is already too late. I blame myself for not acting sooner – and I must speak to Nancy myself. I need to understand her and her brother. For a while I did suspect she might have started the fire'

'Yes, I think it might be a good thing if you came here and talked to Nancy, Mark.'

'I shall cancel my next appointment and come immediately.'

Angela stared at the phone as it went down. They were at last getting to the bottom of the mystery surrounding Nancy and Terry, and she was fairly certain there was still something Nancy hadn't told her.

'The police are looking for Terry,' Mark said to Nancy half an hour later. Angela had joined them and they were in the girl's own room in order to make her feel as comfortable as possible. 'However, if you have any idea of where he is I should like to be present when he is found. Terry doesn't need people threatening him; he needs kindness and understanding. He isn't evil, Nancy, and I want you to believe that I shall do everything possible to make him well again.'

Nancy's cheeks were wet with tears. She scrubbed them away, and then, a sob in her voice, she said, 'It's all my fault, sir. Terry has got worse since the fire. He keeps saying it's his fault they died, but . . . it was me that locked the door . . .' She stopped abruptly, staring at him in fear, waiting for his reaction to the shocking announcement.

'You locked your parents in their room that night?' Mark looked at her incredulously.

'Yes,' Nancy met his eyes, her mouth trembling. 'Pa did things to me . . . terrible things. I think Miss Angela has guessed what . . .' She glanced at her and then away.

306

'But I didn't start the fire, sir. Honest, I never meant anything bad. Terry was frightened Pa would beat him again if he knew I'd given him some food and he begged me to stop him – so I locked the door and put the key in my pocket to prevent Pa coming out unexpectedly. I was going to unlock it but I went downstairs to clean up and forgot . . . and then I smelled the smoke.'

'So what happened next?'

'It was all so confusing that night,' Nancy admitted. 'When I got upstairs I saw Terry standing in his pyjamas just staring at the bedroom door, which was blazing. There was so much smoke that I just grabbed him and made him come away. He pulled back and wanted to get Ma out, but we couldn't get near that door: it was too late, so we just got our coats and ran away . . .' Nancy broke down with a sob. 'I couldn't save them and it was my fault. If I hadn't locked that door . . .'

'What makes you think it might have been your brother who started the fire?' Mark asked gently. 'It could have been your father – an accident or a drunken rage when he discovered the door was locked.'

Nancy hesitated, uncertain and still frightened. 'It was hard to see anything for the flames and the smoke, because even the mat on the floor was burning – but I might have seen a bit of pink glass on the floor. Terry had an oil lamp with a pink shade . . . and then he kept saying it was his fault and I've been so worried, but he's all I've got and I didn't want them to take him away . . . and now he's done other things and you're going to put him in one of those places . . .' Nancy covered her face with her hands.

'It is a private clinic and I am going to make it possible

for Terry to stay there for as long as he needs,' Mark said. 'I promise they will be kind to him and he won't be harmed. In time he may be able to live a near-normal life.'

'Not if the police think he killed our parents – and they will put me in prison for locking that door . . .'

'No, that isn't going to happen,' Mark said, kindly. 'What you did was to protect your brother from a violent father. It was unfortunate that the fire started and he and your mother died – but you don't know for sure if Terry started the fire and the police think it was probably your father in a drunken fit.'

'Mark.' Angela looked at him. 'Supposing it all comes out?'

'Whatever patients tell me is confidential,' Mark said. 'Even if I knew for certain I might not think it necessary to tell the police. Nancy is not to blame for what happened and she has suffered enough. At the moment Terry may be a danger to others and he must be found and taken to the clinic – but for now that is all we need to tell anyone else.'

'You won't have me locked up?' Nancy stared at him. 'It *was* my fault . . .'

'You haven't committed a crime,' Mark said. 'In some circumstances you might need to give evidence but for the moment I think we shall keep these revelations to ourselves, Nancy. Once Terry is more stable he may be able to tell us the truth of what happened that night; until then we do not want to make accusations, do we?'

'No, sir . . .' She caught back another sob. 'I've been so worried . . . thinking it was my fault.'

'Only if you intended to kill your father would it be

your fault – and I do not imagine you would have included your mother in that wish, would you?'

'No, I loved her. I hated Pa but I didn't want him to die like that . . .'

Mark smiled and looked at Angela. 'I think we know all we need to for the moment, Nancy. I hope you can stop blaming yourself now. Your brother's condition is probably the result of your father's cruelty, and I believe we may be able to help him – but it will take time, and we must find him before he does any more harm.'

'Yes, I know. Billy and Mary Ellen say they've looked everywhere here,' Nancy said. 'He must have gone down the Docks.'

'Then we shall tell the police to concentrate their efforts in that direction.'

He stood up to leave and Nancy looked at Angela. 'You don't think I'm bad, Miss Angela?'

'No, Nancy. I think your father was a bad man – and if anyone is to blame for what happened it was him. Had you not been terrified of what he might do to you and Terry, you would never have locked the door.'

THIRTY-NINE

'Let's talk about something more cheerful, if you can?' Mark smiled at Angela as they finished the cups of strong coffee they'd both felt in need of after that heart-rending interview with Nancy. 'Now, I understand it's Sally's birthday and we've both been invited to dinner to celebrate it. I must buy her a small gift – do you have any ideas of what might be suitable that she would like?'

'I should think a silk scarf might be acceptable,' Angela said. 'I'm very fond of Sally and I'm giving her a small pair of ruby earrings that were left to me by my godmother.'

'Yes, a good scarf is just right,' Mark said. 'I rather like Markham, you know. If he is thinking of settling down it would be an excellent thing for him . . . a man needs a reason to come home at night when he gets older. We all start to find life a bit empty unless we have someone special waiting . . .'

'Is marriage on the cards for you, Mark?' Angela felt a sense of sadness, almost of loss, because she knew she would lose him if he married Carole. The staff nurse would never tolerate the level of friendship between them that had been theirs for the past few years.

'Not just yet; I was speaking figuratively of the future,' Mark said. 'Anyway, try not to worry too much over the boy . . . and I shall see you next week if not before. I'm going down to the country to visit friends this weekend. And now I must leave you for I have appointments I cannot cancel.'

Angela watched him go. She had thought there was something odd in Mark's tone as he spoke of wanting to settle down in the future. Did that mean his relationship with Carole was more serious than she'd imagined?

A little sigh left her lips as she faced the prospect of losing a friend she had relied on for so much, though deep down she knew he was more than a friend to her. Of course Nick was ready to step into the breach, to be friend, lover and husband – but she could never see herself as his wife. She liked Nick as a friend, but she trusted Mark; he was almost as close to her as her father and they worked so well together. She thought he'd handled Nancy beautifully, and was glad she'd gone to Mark rather than Sister Beatrice. He was quite right to insist that the police should not be brought in at this stage. Until someone could unlock the hazy secrets in Terry's mind no one could know for sure if Terry was the culprit. It might have been an accident or the father's fault – and perhaps it might be better if the truth never was known. Mark had impressed on Angela that what she'd witnessed was confidential – and she must respect his decision. Terry was dangerous whether he'd set the fire or not, and once he was found . . .

A knock at the door broke into her thoughts, and she looked up with a smile of welcome as Nan poked her head round the door.

'Hello, have you got a minute?'

'Yes, of course,' Angela said. 'Shall I make a cup of tea for you?'

'No, thank you. I just came in to say that I'm leaving early today. I'm having a few days off. Eddie and I are taking the train to Cornwall this afternoon and I want to catch up on a few jobs at home before we go. We shall stay here for a couple of days – and I'm hoping to see Maisie.'

'Yes, I remember you told me you were going this weekend. Have a lovely holiday.'

'Well, I shall enjoy Eddie's company, but I'm not sure yet if Maisie will see me.'

'I hope she will for your sake, Nan. You deserve it because I know that none of what happened was your fault.'

'Well, I shall have a friend with me,' Nan said. 'You've got some trips planned this weekend, I know. You won't let this business of Terry stop you taking the children out?'

'No, of course I shan't; it wouldn't be fair to them. Sally, Jean and Alice have volunteered to come with me so don't feel that you ought to be here. You deserve your time off.'

'I'd best be off then. I only popped in to tell you I was going away. I've seen Sister Beatrice . . .'

Angela nodded and repeated her good wishes for the weekend. Nan always came over as cheerful, and she knew the young carers thought the world of her. The kind, motherly woman had made a new life for herself here, filling her world with the troubles of others and suppressing her own worries.

Angela too had made a new life for herself at St Saviour's, but she could not help regretting the loss of an important friendship. Mark was starting to drift away from her and she did not know how to stop the rift; perhaps she had no right, because he needed, wanted a close relationship and Angela didn't know if she would ever be what he needed; if she could ever truly love again. She thought she could have been happy for Mark if the girl had been anyone else – but she could not like Carole and she knew the feeling was mutual.

'She isn't right for him,' Angela said softly to herself. That must be what was at the root of her feelings. 'She isn't good enough for you, Mark . . .'

Her thoughts were suspended as her telephone rang again and she picked up the receiver. 'Angela Morton here.'

'Angela, it's Nick. I was thinking . . . dinner this evening if you're free? I've booked a table at the Savoy.'

Angela sighed because it was so typical of Nick to just go ahead and book. If he'd asked she would have preferred a quiet pub, similar to the one she'd visited with Mark – but he always took it for granted that he knew best, and Angela found she resented it. She almost turned him down, but she needed a bit of cheering up and since Mark wasn't available, it seemed she hadn't much choice.

Mark was frowning as he left his apartment and went out into the lift that took him down from the penthouse floor to the garages below. His work with the rich and sometimes famous had brought him all the trappings of wealth, including this fabulous Mayfair apartment in a prestigious block, which was perfect for spending several days a week in town – but if he married he would have to think of selling and buying a house instead, probably in the suburbs. A decent garden was the thing, because Mark wanted children. He hadn't truly thought about it for years. His first wife, Edine, had given birth to their son and it was the boy's loss that had caused the rift between them and led to her death. Since then he had not thought of a personal life beyond pleasant but casual relationships . . . until he began to fall in love with Angela.

Mark frowned as he admitted to himself that he had been, was still, in love with the beautiful young widow, who had turned to him in such distress after her husband was killed. Somewhere along the line, she'd become more than a friend. Carole was a very sexy and amusing young woman, but he wasn't in love with her.

He'd tried to stay out of her way since the night he'd had rather too much to drink and stayed overnight with her at that hotel, but he was forced to meet her in the course of his work and was far too polite and decent to hurt her more than he had already. He supposed he ought to tell her that it had been pleasant but was over – that would be the best thing he could do, but it would make things awkward at work.

Unfortunately, Mark couldn't remember what had happened between them that evening. If he'd made love to Carole he'd been too far gone to know about it, but the little smiles she gave him now and then made him think something must have happened – which was a nuisance. Mark had no illusions and he knew Angela was aware he'd taken the girl out a couple of times, something he very much regretted. He didn't feel that it would be appropriate to declare his love for Angela in the circumstances – he ought to leave a decent interval between that wretched night and any proposal he might make to the woman he truly cared for.

It was embarrassing, if nothing more, and he decided that on his return from the country and a visit to a friend from the war and his wife, he would tell Carole of his regret and break it off – perhaps over a coffee somewhere.

His mind settled on that issue, Mark got into his car and drove off. He'd phoned someone he knew at the police station and advised them to make a thorough search of the dock area. If Nancy was right her brother should be found quite soon – but the police had been warned that he might be violent and had agreed to keep watch and not move in until they called Mark. He would try to talk Terry out, to make him trust him, show him that no one wanted to hurt him; it was all he could do for now, and he must hope that it was enough.

FORTY

Nan looked round the hotel room she'd been given, pleasure taking over from the surprise she'd felt on arriving at the rather lovely old hotel. She'd expected more of a bed and breakfast place, but this was an old-fashioned hotel with an impeccable past. Its décor was a little faded, because nothing had been updated since some years before the war, but the furnishings were once good and the standard of cleanliness was excellent. Her room had a big window with a nice view of the cathedral and town, and it also had an armchair, desk and single chair, as well as the bed, wardrobe and dressing table; the biggest luxury of all was its own tiny bathroom.

She had just started to unpack when she heard the door knock and went to open it. Eddie stood there, looking a little uncertain. He'd taken off his overcoat and was wearing his old tweed jacket with the patches on the elbows and a pair of fawn slacks.

'I just wanted to know if you were happy with your room?'

'Yes, it's really nice,' Nan said, and wondered if she

ought to mention the cost of such a special room, but he'd said it was his treat and she didn't want to make a fuss. 'I've never stayed at such a nice place; even when I married Sam we went to a B and B.'

His face lit up with pleasure and Nan was glad she hadn't mentioned the money. She didn't think he had very much, but he'd planned to make things easy and nice for her this weekend and she wasn't going to spoil it for him.

'I'm glad you like it, my dear,' he said. 'Shall we go down for tea? You could order it in your room, but we can't really have it together like that . . . people might assume and we can't have that, can we?' His words and smile teased her and she felt at home with him. She would never feel threatened with Eddie and his kindness had gone a long way to healing the hurt inside her.

'Yes, lovely.' Nan had been looking forward to a nice bath and a rest on the bed, but she could do that later. 'I'd like that,' she said. 'The unpacking can wait until after tea. I suppose we can find out the times of the buses to the convent in the morning . . .'

'Oh, no need,' Eddie said. 'I've borrowed a car for tomorrow. I use buses in London but they taught me to drive in the Army. It will be much easier. We can telephone in the morning, enquire when Maisie will see you – and then we can have a drive round later and enjoy a meal somewhere before we come back here for the evening. It will make a little treat for us both.'

'Supposing she won't see me?'

'We'll face that when the time comes. Now let's go and have our tea. I've been told they used to have wonderful scones and honey . . . I hope they still do, though their scones won't be as good as yours, Nan.'

'Flatterer,' Nan said, and shook her head at him, but suddenly she didn't feel tired any more. She was here with a friend and she could face whatever the next day brought, even if her daughter still would not see her.

'Did you sleep well, my dear?' Eddie asked as they went down to breakfast the next morning. 'My bed was quite comfortable – a feather mattress, I do believe.'

'I slept very well,' Nan assured him. 'When do you think I should telephone – before breakfast or after?'

'I've already done it for you,' he said with his gentle smile. 'I explained about your busy life, how you help the children and staff at St Saviour's and how much it would mean to you if Maisie would see you just for a few minutes. Mother Superior told me that Sister Mary was still reluctant but she'd managed to persuade her that she ought to at least speak to you. We have to be there at eleven o'clock this morning – which gives us plenty of time to eat our breakfast and drive the ten miles or so to the convent.'

'She will see me?' Nan drew her breath in sharply, feeling a crushing pain in her chest. Tears stung her eyes but she held them back. 'Oh . . . I don't know what to say. I can hardly believe it. I've tried so many times and she would not even accept my letters . . . this is a miracle.'

'Well, perhaps it is divine intervention, my dear,' he said, his eyes twinkling at her. 'I usually find a little gentle persuasion works wonders.'

Nan stared at him in sudden comprehension. 'Persuasion . . . what did you do, Eddie?'

'Well, a friend of mine at the college where I do odd jobs happens to know the Bishop in charge of the convent,' he said, with a warm look. 'I suppose I did a little gentle arm-twisting – favours done in the past, you see. Mother Superior was asked in the nicest manner if she could see her way clear to having a talk with the youngest member of her house . . . and it seems a word from the Bishop has done the trick. I hope you didn't mind my having a word with my old friend?'

'I can't thank you enough,' Nan said, her throat tight with emotion. 'Oh, how kind you are. I'm so glad we met, Eddie. I didn't think I would ever like or trust a man again – but you are the kindest person I've met in a long time.'

'Now you will have me blushing. Come along, Nan; our breakfast awaits and I do believe I can smell good Cornish bacon.'

Nan shivered as she was shown into what seemed to her a small dark room and asked to wait. A fire of sorts was burning in the stone fireplace but it was nowhere near enough to keep the chill off the ancient and very thick stone walls. How could Maisie bear to live in a place like this? Nan was horrified that her once bright and loving daughter could have chosen such a life. What had that monster done to her? Such violent thoughts of what she would have liked to do to him assailed her that she was ashamed for having them in what was after all a House of God.

She went to the fire, trying to warm her hands, but she was shivering and perhaps not all of it came from the chill of the room. Hearing the door open behind her,

Nan went rigid, almost too afraid to turn and look, but she forced herself to do so and found that she was looking at a tall, thin woman dressed in grey with a white band around her face and a grey headdress covering over her hair – what did they call that? Was it a wimple? She must ask Eddie; he seemed to know such a lot, perhaps because he'd travelled when he was in the Army. The woman's face was gentle, but Nan did not know her. Could this be the same girl that had once looked at her with wild eyes and screamed that she, Nan, was to blame for what had happened to her?

'Maisie?' she whispered, her throat tight with emotion. 'Is it you?'

'I am called Sister Mary now,' the soft voice answered. 'But you named me Maisie. You wanted to see me . . . Mother?'

Mother, she had called her Mother! The word seemed drawn from her reluctantly but she had spoken it. Nan's eyes stung with tears and for a moment the words would not come. Everything she had wanted to say had flown, leaving her staring like a fool.

'I wanted your forgiveness,' she managed at last. 'I loved you so much, Maisie, but I'd just lost your father and my son, and I had to work so hard to keep a roof over our heads. I took that monster into my home, but had I ever guessed what he was doing to you – I would have killed him. I swear I would have hanged before I let him touch you. Please, you must believe me . . .' The tears would not hold back; she had no power to stop them, letting them run heedlessly down her cheeks. 'Please, can you understand and forgive me?'

'I forgave you when I gave myself to God.' Maisie's

voice took Nan's breath and as she looked at her daughter she saw a look of serenity and peace wash over the girl's face. 'It was required of me and I spent many hours praying for the grace of God so that I might let go of all worldly things.' She made a move towards Nan, her hands outstretched. 'I was not sure that I was strong enough yet to face you, Mother, but now I know that God has blessed me truly. I must ask you to forgive me so that we may part in peace.'

'I forgive you?' Nan asked in wonder.

'Yes, for I sinned against you. I was bitter and I said cruel things. I know now that you loved me and would not have allowed . . . but all that is past and in God I have no anger or hate. I am His and He has made me whole again.'

'So you are happy here . . . in this place?' Nan shivered and Maisie laughed. It was a laugh of childish delight, familiar and dear.

'You find it cold and cheerless? We grow accustomed to the cold, and we do not feel it. The body is nothing and the spirit is all. Here, we are one with Our Maker and ask for nothing but the food He gives us and the comfort of His love.'

'You will stay here all your life? It is what you truly want?'

Maisie took her hands, looking into Nan's eyes as she replied, 'Please accept my decision, Mother. I am at peace here. I could not live in the world you would have me return to for then I should hate and I should be in torment.'

'Shall I never see you?'

'Perhaps there will be a reason. If you were ill I might

321

ask permission to come to you, but I would ask you not to come here unless I am permitted to invite you – there are times when we ask guests to join us for special festivals.'

'Will you allow me to write to you?'

Again, Maisie's smile was so gentle and loving that Nan's heart caught.

'Yes, write to me once a month if you wish, and I will answer you when I feel that God wishes me to help you. My order does not forbid all contact with family but we are in the main a reflective order and do not encourage visits or other communication.'

'I see . . .' Nan looked deep into her eyes and saw that Maisie had given her all she had to give and she must accept it. 'Thank you for seeing me and explaining . . . for forgiving me.'

'It was God's wish,' Maisie said simply. 'Go from here in peace and do not mourn the loss of a daughter. If you love me be glad that I have found my salvation in His love.'

'Yes, I shall try,' Nan promised. 'Goodbye, Sister Mary.'

Maisie inclined her head and left the room by the door through which she'd entered. A moment later Mother Superior came to show Nan out, her smile one of consolation but also triumph, because she knew that she and her sisters had won. Nan understood now that Maisie belonged to them, to her God and the order who had taught her to find peace.

'Try to understand,' the nun told Nan as she opened the gate for her to leave. 'This is Sister Mary's home and her refuge. She could not survive in your world.'

Nan inclined her head but could not answer. Her emotions were in turmoil, swirling this way and that as she fought to understand them. There was anger and bitterness because her daughter had been stolen from her, but there was also the memory of that look in Maisie's eyes, of the peace that came from inside.

A part of Nan wanted to scream in rejection of this order of holy women who had taken her loving, rebellious daughter and turned her into a pale shadow, and yet another part of her was already coming to terms with what she knew was the end of her hopes. Maisie was lost to her. She could write to Sister Mary and she might be answered but there would be no reunion, no return to the old mother and daughter relationship – yet that had been lost the moment she'd let a monster into her home.

The pain was still there inside her, like a nagging toothache that goes on relentlessly until the surgeon pulls the tooth, but perhaps the terrible guilt had begun to ease, and in time she too might find peace.

'You are not sorry you went?' Eddie asked that evening after they had dined and sat in the hotel parlour by a roaring fire. 'I wondered if perhaps it was too difficult for you.'

'No, I am glad I saw her. She seems to be at peace, and she forgave me – asked for my forgiveness, though she need not . . .'

'You must let go of your guilt and accept that what happened was beyond your control. Maisie is at peace and you must try to forgive yourself now, my dear.'

'Sister Mary is at peace. Maisie . . . my daughter . . . no longer exists. It is as if she died . . .'

323

'Perhaps that had to happen.' He took her hand. 'I think that whenever you lose a child, whether it be through death, through a breach or simply marriage, it leaves an empty space behind. You've filled it with your love for the children of St Saviour's, Nan. Move on and let Sister Mary live her life and forgive her.'

'Forgive her?'

'Forgive her for not needing you, for becoming someone else . . . for growing up into a woman who knows her own mind.'

Nan blinked hard and held on to his hand. 'I couldn't have faced this without you,' she choked. 'Yes, I must learn to forgive, as she has.' A smile wavered, failed and then settled on her face. 'It will be easier tomorrow and in time I dare say I shall be happy for her.'

'Of course you will, because you're you – and I do like you very much, my dear Nan . . .'

FORTY-ONE

'You have no idea where Terry might be?' Constable Sallis narrowed his gaze as he looked at Nancy. 'There are no friends of your family who might take him in? It's very cold at night. Surely, he wouldn't sleep on the streets for all this time'

'I am so worried about him,' Nancy said, her mouth trembling. 'He's never been away from me at night. He must be so cold and hungry . . .'

'It's my experience that children usually return home if they are cold and hungry,' the constable said. 'I would wager he's found a friend who has taken him in and is feeding him.'

'There was a man on the Docks, as I told you,' Nancy said. 'I don't know his name . . . Terry might have called him Nobbler or Cobbler, something like that, but I'm not sure. He had a job moving wood, stacking it and helping out generally about the yard. That's all I can tell you, sir.'

'Well, it's something. I'll bet that he's either been working with this man or he's taken him home. He might have found a place to sleep on the Docks, in a warehouse or a shed of some sort – but if he earns a few bob he'll buy food. I'll report this again, miss, and I'll send someone to look, more thoroughly this time. There can't be so many places dealing with a lot of wood. Now, don't you worry, we'll find him.'

'Thank you, Constable,' Sister Beatrice said. 'Run along to the kitchens now and have your cooking lessons, Nancy. I'm sure Terry will turn up soon.'

'Bound to.' Constable Sallis added his mite with a kindly smile at Nancy, but looked concerned as the door closed behind her. 'He sounds just the sort of lad to land in trouble, Sister. We've been asking if anyone's seen him but we'll do another full search. There are a hundred places a boy like that could hide on the Docks, and you never know what sort of tale he's spun this mate of his.'

'Well, you can only do your best,' Beatrice said, and sighed as he took his leave. She had a busy week coming up. That afternoon a wealthy couple were coming to see some children who had been selected with a view to fostering one of them and then perhaps, if they all liked each other, adopting that fortunate child. It didn't happen often and Beatrice had thought long and hard about who she ought to choose. Mary Ellen had been set aside at once, because her sister, Rose, had made it clear that she was not for adoption. Sarah Morgan was perhaps a little older than the couple had asked for, though she was an intelligent girl who would have benefited from a family of her own. Marion was one of her choices, along with a little girl name Julie, who was just six, very pretty and had been here for two years after her parents were killed during the war – and Betsy.

Betsy was not a pretty child. Her hair almost always wanted washing and she was always snivelling, her nose running and her eyes red. If any of the children at St Saviour's needed a mother, it was surely Betsy. Yes, Betsy definitely deserved this chance, but the potential parents would probably choose Julie, such was the law of probability and luck.

The builders were due in a few days. They'd promised to do all the work in a day and were bringing in a team of carpenters, plumbers, electricians and roofers to tidy up a lot of small jobs that had needed doing for some months.

The phone rang and she reached for it, hearing Carole's voice as she answered. 'Sister, could you come down to the isolation ward please? I've got two sick children here this morning and I'm worried it might be measles. Will you have a look at them and tell me if we should have the doctor, please.'

'Measles? I'll come immediately.'

Beatrice frowned as she left her office. She wanted as few children as possible in St Saviour's on Thursday, because of the builders. It looked as if both the sick wards would have occupants, but they would be safe enough up there; the main thing was to get the little ones out of the way and she could leave that to Angela.

Constable Sallis decided that he wouldn't bother going back to the station to report what he'd learned. Sister Beatrice had asked him to come to her office and speak to young Nancy when he'd called on a routine matter. The girl had seemed certain that her brother would've gone down the dockyard, and he might as well go and have a look. He was due off duty in ten minutes, but when a child was in trouble he didn't mind putting in a bit of extra effort.

He whistled as he walked, pleased with life. He'd decided he would ask his girlfriend Sadie to wed him and settle down in a nice little house he'd been lucky enough to rent. He thought she might say yes and he was feeling good about things in general. His superior thought a lot of him at work and he was hoping for promotion next year if he took his sergeant's exams . . .

It wasn't a bad day down the dockyard. Still cool in the wind, but the hint of spring in the air at last – mind you, it would still get damned cold at night. He began asking questions of men he met. Had they seen a young lad hanging around, were they aware of a boy sleeping rough?

'Sorry, mate, I ain't seen anyone.' The same answer came back at him time and again, and then he saw the wood stack and walked towards the man standing close by.

'Have you seen a young lad anywhere about?' he asked the man, who stared at him as if he hadn't heard the question. 'I'm searching for a boy of about ten – hanging about in the yard or the sheds.'

'You want the boy?' The man's voice was guttural, foreign-sounding.

'Yes – his name is Terry. Have you seen him?'

The man didn't answer but jerked his head in the direction of some stacks of wood. The planks were arranged in piles with narrow walkways between them. Constable Sallis walked in the direction indicated, a smile of satisfaction in his eyes. It had been easier than he'd hoped. Not only would he have the satisfaction of

328

taking the runaway lad back to Sister Beatrice, it would look good on his record.

He saw the boy sitting on an upturned orange crate halfway down one of the aisles and moved purposely towards him. Terry looked up, startled and poised to run, obviously in fear.

'It's all right, Terry lad,' Constable Sallis said, holding out his hand. 'I've not come to arrest you. I'm just going to take you home where you belong.'

'No,' Terry muttered, backing away down the aisle. 'I'm not going nowhere with you. I ain't going ter let them shut me in that place . . .'

'I promise you I'm not going to shut you anywhere,' Constable Sallis said, smiling to show he meant no harm, but Terry suddenly reached up and tugged at a plank, and with a loud crashing sound the pile seemed to tumble into the aisle, cutting off his approach and knocking him flying into the bargain. One of the planks hit him on the head, pushing his helmet over his eyes so he couldn't see where the boy had gone and making him feel dizzy for a moment. He was stumbling out of the chaos Terry had caused when another constable came up to him.

'What the bloody hell do you think you're doing?' he demanded. 'Why did you go blundering in there after the lad when we'd had our orders to keep an eye on him and do nothing until Mr Adderbury came? My chief is going to be furious, because he owes Adderbury a favour and he isn't going to like this one little bit.'

Constable Sallis groaned. Why had he tried to do a good deed? He would get a rollicking over this and it wouldn't help his promotion chances for next year.

*   *   *

Mark listened to the news and frowned. There was no point in making a fuss and Sister Beatrice had every right to speak to the constable. It was a pity he hadn't checked in first, but it had been a lack of communication – and in part that was down to Mark.

'Well, nothing we can do now,' he said into the mouthpiece. 'If your chaps will keep their eyes open, we might find he goes back there when he's calmed down.'

Replacing the receiver, Mark felt annoyed with himself. He'd impressed on Angela that they should keep Nancy's confession private for the time being, but he ought to have let Sister Beatrice know that he had things going on in the background. She wasn't going to be pleased when she learned that the police constable had frightened Terry off and they were back to square one.

He had better go and have a word with her before anyone else did, because otherwise Angela might have to bear the brunt of her displeasure.

'I do not take kindly to being kept in the dark,' Sister said when Mark told her the outcome. 'Had I been informed that Terry was being searched for discreetly on the Docks I should not have asked Constable Sallis to search for him.'

'No, of course you wouldn't and it was entirely my fault,' Mark admitted. 'I'm afraid I rang a friend just before I went away for a couple of days and I didn't think of letting anyone know. I just assumed you would realise that he was being searched for . . .'

'Yes, of course I knew,' Beatrice said. 'I merely asked the constable if he had thought of the dockyard after Nancy said her brother often went there in the past.

330

Had I realised what you intended . . . I really do think I should have been told.'

'Yes, of course you should,' he admitted. 'I had intended to tell you this morning – but it was too late. I'd hoped I might coax Terry to come with me, but unfortunately he was frightened and ran off.'

'I do not think he would have come for you either,' she said, clearly still annoyed. 'However, it might have worked if I had not asked Constable Sallis to look himself. I was just so worried about him.'

'We all are,' Mark said, and sighed. 'He must be suffering and – you know that he attacked Mary Ellen?'

'Yes, Angela told me that, and I knew the police would look for him – but . . .' She shook her head. 'This will get us nowhere. We can only hope he is found again before he causes more damage.'

Mark inclined his head and left her, feeling like a scolded schoolboy, though of course she had every right to be annoyed, and he ought to have taken the time to let her know what he'd hoped for. He took a deep breath and turned towards the sick room. Carole was on duty today and he might as well get it over in one go.

FORTY-TWO

'Have coffee, in my lunch break!' Carole darted a look of indignation at him as they spoke in the hallway outside the sick ward, where they'd met as Carole was leaving for her break. 'Is that all you have to offer? It's ages since you've asked me out. I thought you cared about me and after . . . what happened between us? What is so important? You've been avoiding me.'

'I'm sorry; it's work,' Mark said. He rubbed his hand across his eyes. 'No, actually that isn't being honest. Look, we might as well talk about this now . . . I'm sorry for what happened that night, but I can't change things. I'm afraid it was just one of those things for me and I don't want to hurt you more – so I suggest we call a halt.'

Carole looked stunned. 'You intend to drop me just like that? I thought you were a decent sort of man, Mark Adderbury. I don't go to bed with just anyone . . .'

'I never thought you did,' he said. 'I'm really sorry, Carole, but it's best to be honest. I'm not in love with you. I've told you now so that you can find yourself someone who does love you in the way you want. I hope we shall still be friends.'

'Go away,' she said in a quiet, furious voice.

'I am sorry, Carole. It wasn't the right thing to do – but I was at a low ebb. I'm really sorry for what happened but . . .'

'I said get out!' She turned, eyes blazing. 'I have to work with you so I shan't tell you what I think of you – but don't imagine you're going to get away with this . . .'

'I am sorry.'

'Just get lost will you?'

'Very well. Perhaps we can speak again another day – forgive me.'

She didn't answer and Mark walked out of the ward, feeling very embarrassed and uncomfortable. He'd let Sister Beatrice down; he'd let Angela down; he'd let Carole down; and most importantly, he'd let Terry down, because he should have moved him sooner and not let the revelation come from Sister Beatrice. Mark would have spoken to the brother and sister together – and he shouldn't have left it so long. He wasn't sure what he could do to repair the mistakes made, but he would try.

Carole took a moment to recover before she carried on with her work. She'd seen this job as an opportunity to rise to the top of her profession and take over from Sister Beatrice. Not yet but in a year or so when the Warden retired – with a little help from Carole to speed her on her way. That was for the future and if she were Mark's wife the way would be cleared for her – although if she married perhaps it would be enough to be the wife of a rich man. Either way, Mark was the key to her plans. She knew he was important here, respected by everyone and a founder member of the Board. It had seemed as if everything was going her way, but now it seemed she'd miscalculated. Angela might still have a hold over him after all.

Furious, her mind toying with various forms of revenge, she vowed she was going to get even and not just with Mark Adderbury. Carole's pride had been hurt and she was going to make someone else suffer. As yet she wasn't sure what she could do, but if Mark Adderbury dismissed her as a little fool he could use and then discard, he'd discover his mistake. And if she could find the way, she would punish both Sister Beatrice and Angela Morton.

She took the problem home with her, thinking about it as she soaked for a long time in a hot bath and then sat drinking sherry until she was sleepy and finally retired to bed. A plan was beginning to form in her mind and she already knew how to punish at least one of the three.

Carole was still considering Mark's punishment when she went to work the next morning. The place seemed quiet when she arrived and Michelle reminded her that Angela and some of the carers had taken all the children who weren't at school, or who were too ill out for the day.

'It's only those in the sick bay and the isolation ward that have had to stop here, and some of them are pretty miserable over it.'

'So I'm here with only Julia for the day then.' Carole pouted at her. 'Just my luck to get stuck with her – she's as much good as nothing.'

'I find Julia is pretty good at helping with the poorly children,' Michelle said, standing up for her. 'The only carer I think better is Sally Rush – and she will probably leave in the summer to train to be a nurse.'

'God help the patients then,' Carole said sourly. 'I do hope she won't be coming back here when she's trained.'

'Sally is a lovely person and she'll make an excellent nurse. She can already change bandages and take temperatures, as well as dress a wound – picked it all up at night school and I lent her some textbooks. I can't see what you have against her.'

'Perhaps your standards aren't as high as mine,' Carole said, then walked off and left her to get on. She glanced impatiently at the little watch pinned to her starched white apron and then at the clock on the wall. Julia was already five minutes late.

Michelle didn't bother saying goodbye. Carole shrugged mentally. It didn't worry her that she wasn't popular with the other nurses or the carers. If she saw resentment in their eyes she ignored it, water off a duck's back to her. She was in charge unless Sister Beatrice took over, and that seldom happened. Carole wouldn't expect to make a friend of the woman she hoped to succeed one day, but she tried not to give her any reason to find fault with her work.

Julia arrived half an hour late, her dark hair untidy, her shoes needing a polish, and babbling feeble excuses about her little sister being ill and then missing her bus.

'Whatever is wrong at home, you should either be on time or find another job more suited to your capabilities. If I'd had an emergency I might not have been able to manage – and everyone else is out today.'

'Yes, I know. The builders are carting things into the kitchens and bathrooms and there's a lot of shouting going on down there.'

'Thankfully, we cannot hear a word of it up here.

Most of the children are not feeling too bad. We shan't get any food brought up today, because the kitchens are closed. We have biscuits in the tin and drinks, but you can take just half an hour for lunch at one o'clock – to make up for being late. We may have to fetch some sandwiches for the children later . . .'

'Yes, Staff Nurse,' Julia said, looking suitably chastened. 'I did telephone St Saviour's earlier from the call box on the corner of our lane. I spoke to Sally and she said she would let you know that I might be late . . .'

'Did she?' Carole frowned at her. 'That is typical of her carelessness. I was not given your message.'

It was late morning when Sister Beatrice visited. She brought a tray of sandwiches and some pastries, explaining that she had purchased them from a café in the next street.

'I'm sorry the kitchen is closed today. I know it is awkward for you,' Sister Beatrice said. She saw that Julia was giving a bed bath and indicated the time to Carole. 'Surely this should have been finished by now?'

'One of our patients wet the bed and we had to change sheets. We had to fetch clean from the laundry cupboard. It is awkward with it being just us – and Julia was half an hour late this morning. Apparently, she phoned and told Sally she would be late, but *she* did not see fit to leave a message before she went off. I could have done with some help earlier, and the measles cases have been running temperatures . . .'

'Yes, I do see that it has made things difficult for you with everyone being out for the day, but two of you should be able to cope.' Sister looked annoyed. 'Sally should have told you, though.'

'She is always careless and thoughtless. I do not trust her at all.'

'Really? I would have said she was an excellent worker, quite the best we've had here.'

Carole did not know why she went on, because it was stupid, but her irritation made her lie. 'Sally is rude and does not listen when I tell her to do something. I've had to reprimand her for shabby work more than once: beds not properly made and trolleys not thoroughly cleaned.'

'If her work has become slipshod I shall have a word with her,' Sister said. 'I shall leave you now to get on, but I'll be here all day, mostly in my office – or downstairs keeping an eye on things. If you need help, telephone me – or send Julia to find me.'

'Yes, Sister.'

Carole wished she hadn't been so quick to lie about Sally. Not that she cared if Sally was dismissed, but if Sister discovered that she hadn't told the truth it would go down as a black mark against her – but there was no going back on it now. She wasn't sure why she disliked Sally so much, but sometimes she looked at Carole oddly – as if she could see inside her head. Besides, she was as thick as thieves with Angela and that was reason enough to dislike the girl.

'I'm going to speak to Sister,' she told Julia half an hour or so later. 'I shan't be long – perhaps you can manage to keep an eye on things until I get back?'

Julia looked resentful but inclined her head and Carole left her making drinks for the children. Instead of going to Sister's office, she went immediately to Angela's and knocked but of course no one answered.

Entering, she closed the door softly behind her and went straight to Angela's desk. Opening the drawers one by one, she searched for something she could use to discredit the Administrator, but apart from a copy of the monthly report she found nothing of any use.

Carole thought for a moment and then extracted two pages, the second and the second from last. She looked for somewhere to hide them and then decided it would be best just to destroy them. At the very least Angela would have extra work to do; with luck she would just send the report in and get told off because it was incomplete.

Smiling at having struck a first blow against her enemy, Carole thought about her campaign against Sister Beatrice. She'd doctored the rota but that had been discovered before it caused trouble; also she'd altered the medicine record in a couple of places where Sister had signed it, but that wasn't enough in itself – perhaps if she took something and hid it . . . A smile touched her lips. She'd found it easy enough to get into Angela's office. She would put the stolen items in one of Sister's drawers, or hide them behind the filing cabinet . . . though the desk might be better, because she wanted the items found when a search was made. If Sister could be made to look as if she were getting forgetful, the Board would soon give her the push and that would leave Carole as the most senior nurse and with a good chance of getting what she wanted. Especially if Mark believed he owed her something . . .

It wasn't until later that afternoon that Carole found the message from Sally explaining that Julia would be late. It was on the desk, but someone had placed a stack of files on it. Carole read it with annoyance. Had she seen it, she wouldn't have reported Sally's carelessness to Sister, and she knew she ought to explain, but that would make her look a fool and she didn't feel like back-tracking on what she'd said earlier. She slipped the message into her pocket; she would tear it up later and say nothing about it. Why should she care if Sally was in trouble over it? The girl was going to leave soon anyway.

Mark could still feel the guilt churning over in his stomach regarding Carole. The knowledge that he'd been very much in the wrong wouldn't go away. He should have found an easier way of letting her down – of telling her that he wasn't in love with her. He'd never been very good at this sort of thing.

Something in Carole's eyes when he'd told her it was over was bothering Mark. He was normally a good judge of character but he wasn't sure whether she'd simply been angry – or if there was hurt beneath the natural reaction of angry rejection. He would have to apologise again, perhaps send her some flowers. He chided himself again, as if flowers could ever make up for what he'd done, but it was better than hoping the problem would go away.

Yes, at least he could do that, he thought, and picked up the telephone. He rang the florist he trusted and gave them a short message apologising for hurting her and asking them to deliver the flowers to Carole as soon as possible. It was never going to be enough, but he couldn't see what else he could do in the circumstances.

Having done what he could to put things right, though

of course if Carole was really hurt the flowers wouldn't help much, his thoughts turned inevitably to Angela. He'd known the last time they'd been together that he was fairly caught, the feelings he had too strong for him to find solace with anyone else. Angela's smile, the scent of her hair and her perfume, which seemed to tantalise him with her sensual sweetness, all of those things haunted his dreams.

He must speak to her. It was stupid to go on leaving things. His appointments finished for the day, Mark thought he might go down to the dockyard himself and take a look around, just in case Terry was still hanging around. After that he would drive to St Saviour's, invite Angela out for a nice quiet meal and then tell her what was on his mind.

FORTY-THREE

Beatrice watched as the builders carried out the last of their tools. They'd completed the work in excellent time and done a good job, which was a relief, because after knocking the price down she'd wondered if they would cut corners. The house was quiet, silent, as she walked through the ground floor, her footsteps seeming to echo eerily, noting all the improvements, like the new basins in the washrooms, some of which had been cracked and stained.

A little shiver went down Beatrice's spine, because she didn't like the feeling of emptiness, the sense of heavy sorrow that seemed to hang in the air . . . as if the spirits of the dead fever patients still lingered. What a thought! Those times were long gone and best forgotten. It was because the place was almost empty, echoing with her lonely footsteps. These rooms should be filled with laughing, happy children and she would be glad when they were back from their trip out, and the older ones returned from school. She'd purchased shop-made tomato sandwiches and fairy cakes, which were waiting under slightly dampened teacloths for the school children in the dining room for their tea. Not quite what they were used to, because Muriel and her staff provided a delicious treat of some kind most afternoons, but everything would be back to normal tomorrow.

Hearing a noise behind her as she prepared to leave the kitchens, Beatrice turned and saw the boy staring at her. For a moment she was stunned. Where had he come from? Surely he hadn't been hiding here at St Saviour's all this time?

'Terry . . .' she said at last, recovering her powers of speech. 'Where have you been? We've all been worried about you. Nancy has been desperate, afraid that you had come to some harm.' She paused and saw that he looked dirty, his hair limp as if he'd been in mud or slime or something. He'd certainly been living rough. 'You look as if you need a good bath, my lad. Let me take you upstairs. You don't want Nancy to see you like that.'

'Stay away from me, yer old bag,' Terry snarled. She noticed then that his eyes looked wild and as he brought his arm up from his side she saw a long thin knife. 'Yer turned Nance against me, yer and that posh bitch, givin' 'er things. I'm goin' ter pay yer back – yer first, and then the rest of them.' A high-pitched giggle left his lips. 'Once Nance comes back I'm goin' ter pour paraffin all over this place and set light to it.'

Beatrice shuddered because fire was the worst thing, the fear that had haunted her for years, but perhaps he was lying. The caretaker had been warned to keep the paraffin locked up. Surely he hadn't been careless with the key to the garden shed? No, no, she was certain it was just an idle boast, because if Terry had access to

342

the fuel he would already have used it. He was just trying to frighten her. All she had to do was to keep calm and regain control. Despite the weapon in his hand he was just a child and she had no need to fear him. Children always responded to firmness.

'Now do not be silly, Terry,' she said in a strong voice that belied the way she felt inside. 'You are not going to do anything silly. Nancy would be cross. She would tell you to put the knife down. Give it to me like a good boy and we shall not say any more about this.'

'No, I ain't goin' ter give it to yer.' Terry stared at her defiantly, his eyes moving wildly from side to side. His body was shaking and he was clearly in turmoil. 'I ain't goin' ter that place yer want ter send me. Me and Nance are goin' away. I found us a place ter live where they won't find us . . .'

'You cannot manage alone,' Beatrice said quietly. 'Please, Terry, listen to me. We can find a way to help you. Perhaps you need not leave St Saviour's . . .'

She knew she was lying, because the boy was a danger to himself and all of them, but she had to gain time, to think of something to calm him down. How long would it be before Nancy came back from the trip to the pictures? She'd gone with them to help with the little ones, because there was nothing for her to do here, and Beatrice had wanted the place as empty as possible in case of accidents with all the builders' materials lying around. She knew there was no one to help her. Even if Staff Nurse Carole could do something she would not call, because she would not risk the nurse's safety.

Could she take the knife from Terry? A struggle could be dangerous for both of them, because either one could be hurt accidentally. No, she had to try to talk it from him, to steady him so that he gave it up of his own free will.

'You mustn't do anything silly, Terry,' she said. 'Please, my dear, put the knife down. Nancy will be back soon – and she would be cross if she saw this, now wouldn't she? Let me get you something to eat. I'm sure you are hungry.'

'I hate yer! Yer tell lies . . . if I put the knife down, you'll send me away to the loony bin . . .'

'Oh, my dear,' Beatrice said, and the pity rose in her throat, choking her. How could she lie to this poor damaged boy? She wanted to weep with him, to take him in her arms and comfort him, to promise him that everything would be all right, but it would be such a wicked lie to deceive him. 'I am so sorry . . . so very sorry, my dear . . .'

As she moved towards him compulsively, Terry sprang at her and she felt a stab of pain in her arm as the knife blade pierced her flesh and she screamed. Terry was yelling abuse as he struck at her, the language of the gutter, as if all control had gone. Beatrice put her hands out to try to protect herself, catching at his hands, but somehow he thrust her off, and, as she stumbled and fell back against the table, he sprang at her again, a snarl of rage on his lips.

'No! Stop that now, my lad.' Father Joe's voice spoke from somewhere behind her. Beatrice was aware of blood seeping through the sleeve of her habit. Her gaze had become a little hazy and she was feeling faint, but as if from a distance she watched as Father Joe approached the maddened child.

'Don't come near me,' Terry warned. 'I don't want ter hurt yer but I'm goin' ter kill the old witch.'

'I can't let you do that,' Father Joe said, with authority. 'Give me the knife, Terry, now. I do not want to harm you, my child – but I shall not let you hurt Sister any more than you have already.'

Beatrice was swaying with faintness. She clasped her arm as the blood seeped through her fingers, vaguely aware that someone else had entered the room and was shouting at the boy to drop the knife. A struggle ensued as Father Joe tackled the lad and within a few minutes had grappled the knife from his hands. What happened then was very hazy, though Beatrice thought she heard Mark Adderbury's voice and a little later Angela's and then Nancy's, but they came she thought from far away.

'What happened? What did he do?'

'He stabbed Sister Beatrice. Get her upstairs to the ward and ask Carole to bind up that wound before she loses more blood.'

'What's wrong with Terry? Is he dead?'

'No. He's gone into shock and fallen down that's all.' Mark answered Nancy's question, because all she could see was his body slumped on the ground. 'I'm going to give him an injection to help him, Nancy, and then I'm going to take him away in an ambulance. You can't come with me, I'm afraid, but very soon we'll take him to the clinic and you can come then and see him settled in his room.'

'I'll help you upstairs,' Angela said to Beatrice. 'Help me with Sister, Nancy. There's nothing you can do for Terry now, just leave him to Mr Adderbury. He will do all he can. Believe me, you can trust him.'

It must have been about then that Beatrice passed out, because the next thing she knew she was lying on the bed in the nurses' rest room and Angela was standing by the bed, looking down at her.

'Terry . . .' she said faintly. 'What happened to that poor boy?'

'He collapsed. Mark had to sedate him just in case he came round and was frightened. He's been taken to a private room at the hospital, where he will be kept under observation until Mark can take him down to the clinic. He said something about tomorrow . . .'

Tears trickled down Beatrice's cheeks. 'I should have cared for him better,' she said. 'He was just a frightened little boy and I let him down – and now . . . .' She choked on her emotion and could not continue.

'No, Sister,' Angela said, and took Beatrice's hand in her own slender one. 'You must never think like that. We did all we could for him here but it was too late after the fire. He had been driven to the edge by that brute of a father and from what I understand it was Terry who most likely started that fire to punish his father for what he'd done to Nancy.'

'He was frightened of being shut away for ever, that's all . . .'

'Yes, and perhaps he will be. After Father Joe stopped him killing you, which I believe was his intention, he went into what Mark described to me later as a catatonic state. Mark says he may stay that way for good, but in the right place with good people about him, he may recover. We can only pray for him – but whatever happens you are not to blame.'

Beatrice inclined her head, aware now of the pain in

her arm. 'It was brave of Father Joe to tackle the boy. Is he all right?'

'He has some small wounds to his hands where he wrestled the knife from Terry, but Carole bound them for him after she'd seen to your injury, which was much the worst.'

Beatrice pushed her way up against the pillows. 'Carole should be off duty now. I must see to things . . .'

'You must lie there until you feel better,' Angela told her. 'Carole went off after she'd tended your arm and bound up Father Joe – and Staff Nurse Michelle is now on duty. Sally has volunteered to stay with her until Jean comes on at eight so everything is under control. Nan wants to come up and see you, and if you're ready I shall make you a nice cup of tea – if you feel up to it?'

'Thank you, perhaps I shall stay here for a bit longer,' Beatrice said because she'd realised that her head was spinning. 'I must thank you all for coming to my rescue. I did try talking to him, you know – but he was too frightened to listen.'

'Father Joe told us you were so brave. He was there for a while listening but dare not interfere. He acted only when Terry attacked you.'

'I wanted so much to save him from the abyss . . .' Beatrice blinked back her tears. 'I never thought he would really try to kill me. I only wanted to help him but he thought I meant to grab him and shut him away.'

'Father Joe says you're a ministering angel. He waxed lyrical about how you cared only for Terry and not one whit for yourself. I'm just sorry he hurt you so badly, Sister. I wished you hadn't had to face him alone.'

'Thank you – and Father Joe for his compliments. It

347

sounds as if he'd had a few tots of good Irish whiskey.' Beatrice discovered that she could laugh.

'It might have been the tot of brandy we gave him, but he certainly thinks the world of you, I can tell you that,' Angela said, her eyes bright with affection for the priest. 'He told me that we are all angels here, but that you were a saint – but perhaps I'm giving secrets away,' she teased. 'I can only say that you amazed me, Sister Beatrice. Even when you could hardly stand up and were clearly losing your senses, all you kept telling us was not to hurt Terry. Most people would think he deserved his punishment.'

'Oh no,' Beatrice said, tears trickling. 'No child deserves the life he will have now. I think I shall weep for him inside all my days.'

'It is very sad,' Angela agreed. 'I am going to fetch that tea – and perhaps a sip of brandy for medicinal purposes. Just lie there and rest and Nan will come up to see you. We were all very upset when we saw you were hurt.'

Beatrice sighed as she lay back against the pillows. She felt no resentment against the boy who had attacked her, merely pity. She knew that Nancy was going to be distraught, though perhaps in a way for her it was the best thing. Nancy had made herself responsible for her brother all her life, but now she would be free to grow and learn to live for herself. She was an intelligent girl, brave and able to fight off the hurts of the past and make a good future – and if ever the boy became calm enough to live outside the walls of a clinic perhaps she could look after him. Yet in her heart Beatrice feared that Terry would never be allowed to walk freely again. It was his desperation, because he too knew that he was ill and becoming worse, that had made her want to comfort him,

348

but in his confusion he had not recognised her true concern for him, and he had fallen into the darkness from where she doubted he would return. Mark might talk of improvements, but in all probability Terry would be little more than an empty shell, sedated and controlled by drugs, because otherwise the violence could return.

Tears wetted her cheeks once more before she brushed them away. Even the angels of St Saviour's could not save every damaged child that came into their care. Beatrice had many more needing love and understanding. She might never forget Terry, but she must push the grief to a dark corner in her mind, because there were so many others who needed the love that filled her heart for them. Hidden behind the calm, sometimes stern face she showed to the world, it was her reason for living.

'Well, then, Bea.' Nan's voice greeted her cheerfully as she entered the room bearing the tray of tea Angela had promised. 'What happens when I go out?'

'It's as well you weren't here,' Beatrice said dryly. 'There would probably be two of us lying here then, because you might not have been able to overpower him as Father Joe did, but I know you would have tried. I hope you haven't brought me any brandy as Angela threatened? A hot strong and sweet cup of tea is all I need and then I shall get up and see just what has been happening since I passed out.'

Nan smiled indulgently at her friend. 'When Angela told me you were looking fragile I said it wouldn't last. Here's your tea, my dear friend. I'm glad you are feeling a little better. You gave us all the fright of our lives – and poor Father Joe was in tears at the sight of you being helped off. Blamed himself for letting things go too far, but Angela says he was a real hero.'

FORTY-FOUR

Alice was just getting ready to go to work that evening when the door of her room was opened and her land-lady walked in. She had a look of outrage on her face and Alice's stomach clenched, because she guessed what was coming.

'Did you want something?' she asked, facing her proudly.

'You know very well why I've come,' the woman said. 'You're pregnant, aren't you? Oh, don't try to kid me, I know the signs – besides, I saw the baby clothes lying around.'

'You went through my drawers,' Alice accused her, angry herself now because she'd carefully put the things away as she bought them and they were still wrapped up. 'You had no right to do that. I pay my rent on time and . . .'

'Yes, I'll give you that, but for how long? You'll be out of a job soon – and, besides, I don't want a baby here. This is a respectable house and I don't let my rooms to girls like you. I'm not a hard woman. You can have two days to find somewhere else – but after that, out you go . . . and I shall want another week's rent in lieu of notice.'

'Two days?' Alice was horrified. It had taken her weeks to find this house and she knew what most of the others were like – the idea of living in somewhere that stank of stale cooking and worse made her feel wretched. Besides, if she had to pay another week's rent she wouldn't have enough money to pay in advance for a new place. 'Please, couldn't I stay – just until . . .' She saw the gleam in the older woman's eyes and knew she'd given herself away. 'All right, I'll go – but now I'm going to work.'

She pushed past the woman and ran down the stairs. Alice felt the fear rising again as she walked to St Saviour's for the evening shift. She knew Michelle's mother wouldn't have her back, because she would guess about the baby – and she was nearly as strict as her landlady.

What was she going to do? Sister Beatrice had told her only a couple of days ago that she'd found a place at the mother and baby home – and she'd said that she would consider taking Alice back if she was sensible and let the child go to a good family. It was the most sensible thing to do, Alice knew that – but she couldn't bear the idea of giving up her baby.

Jack might be no good; he'd gone off and left her to face this alone after she'd told him she was pregnant – but she still loved him, whether he was alive or dead, and she loved her child. Tears stung her eyes as she went into St Saviour's. Alice had no idea what she was going to do, but she wouldn't let them take her baby away – she wouldn't!

Nan was thoughtful as she went downstairs to the kitchen. She'd tried to be cheerful to raise Sister Beatrice's spirits, but the thought of what might have happened to her friend had cast a shadow over her. She'd thought she could accept that her daughter wanted to devote her life to God, but since then she'd begun to realise how much she would miss – her daughter's marriage, grand-children: it meant Nan had little to look forward to but a lonely old age. Had she lost Beatrice too . . .

Passing the staff room she heard an odd sound inside; it sounded like crying and Nan was immediately alert. Someone was in trouble and after what had happened you couldn't be too careful. She went to investigate and saw Alice slumped in one of the old armchairs, crying her heart out.

'What is it, Alice?' she asked, immediately con-cerned. 'What has happened to upset you? Is it because of Sister being attacked?'

'No, though I'm sorry for what happened to her. Is she all right?'

'She's resting, but it upset her a lot. That poor child . . .' Nan pulled up a hard chair to sit next to Alice and reached for her hand. 'Won't you tell me what's wrong?'

'My landlady is throwing me out; I've got two days to find another room,' Alice said, her eyes drenched in tears. 'Sister says it's my duty to give up the baby . . . and I've got no one to turn to. My sister can't help me and nor can Michelle. I don't know what to do . . .'

Nan was silent for a moment, and then she made up her mind. 'Then I'll tell you what we're going to do,' she said and squeezed the girl's hand. 'I'm going to take you to your lodgings tomorrow morning after you finish here and we'll fetch your things and you can stay with me.'

'But you can't want me to stay with you,' Alice faltered. 'I'm not married and people will talk – and there's the baby . . . you can't look after me . . .'

'Angela told me she can arrange for you to have the baby in somewhere private. We'll book you in as Mrs Cobb and say you're a widow. We can get you a ring and afterwards . . . well, we'll think about that when the time comes. Now, dry your eyes. We've got the children to see to, Alice, love, and they're all a bit upset over what has happened. Coming home to find Sister being almost stabbed to death and then Terry taken off – well, I dare say some of them are frightened. So pick yourself up and do your job and leave the future to sort itself out. You're not alone, Alice. I promise you that – and you never will be.'

'Oh, Nan,' Alice said, and took the hanky the older woman offered, wiping her eyes and blowing her nose. 'I'll wash this and give it back – I don't know how to thank you.'

'I shall be glad of the company for a bit,' Nan said. 'Now I've got to collect all these dirty cups and take them to the kitchen. You go and look after the little ones, Alice – and in the morning we'll sort that landlady of yours out.'

'Happy birthday, Sally,' Angela said, and presented her with a parcel wrapped in pink tissue and a card. It was the morning after the incident with Terry and outwardly everything was normal. 'Have you seen Sister this morning? I'm hoping she had the sense to stop in bed today, but, knowing her, I keep thinking she will pop up at any moment and ask us why we're wasting time.'

Sally laughed. 'We managed to persuade her to stay in the rest room overnight so that Michelle could keep an eye on her, but she was up early this morning and went home. Michelle begged her to take it easy and she promised she would, but I think she was in a lot of pain from her arm.'

'I imagine she would be,' Angela said. 'If we hadn't had a nurse on hand I should have insisted she went to hospital, but Carole said she could manage the wound easily, so it seemed best to get her tended quickly rather than her sitting in an ambulance and then waiting to be admitted.'

'I'm sure it is what she would want,' Sally said, exclaiming in delight as she opened her gift and saw the pretty earrings. 'These are so beautiful; thank you, Angela. I love them . . .'

'I'm glad,' Angela said. 'I'm afraid Mark will not be able to come this evening. He telephoned earlier to say he will call to collect Nancy later this morning and will leave a little something for you then – but he's taking Terry down to the clinic today.'

'I didn't expect a present from him . . . it's a pity he won't be able to come; the table is for four.'

'I've been thinking about it and I wondered if you would accept Nan as a substitute? I'm sure she would enjoy a meal out at a nice restaurant.'

'Would you mind? Mark was supposed to be your escort – what about that other friend of yours?'

'I don't think Nick would care to be a substitute, besides, I'd rather not ask him. I enjoy Nan's company and I think she might come – but it must be your decision . . .'

'Yes, of course. I like her too,' Sally said, but looked

a little disappointed. 'I just thought it would be nice if – it doesn't matter . . .'

The door opened at that moment and Nan entered, bearing an empty tray. She beamed as she saw Sally. 'Ah, there you both are. How is the birthday girl? I've got a gift for you in my bag, Sally. I'll give it to you before you leave this evening.'

'Nan, Mr Adderbury cannot be Angela's partner at dinner with Andrew and me tonight, because he has to take Terry to the clinic – I don't suppose you would help us out?'

Nan hesitated and then smiled. 'I wouldn't say no to a nice meal out. I'm being spoiled recently. What time do you want me?'

'Can we meet here at seven?'

'I'll be here,' Nan said, and then collected a load of dirty cups and mugs. 'As you see, I'm doing the kitchen girl's work again. I think it's a sore throat this time . . .' She picked up a full tray with a pleased look on her face, but at the door she stopped and turned back to Angela. 'I ought to tell you that Alice Cobb has come to stay with me for a while. I shall need to talk to you about things – but that will keep for another time.'

'I feel awful,' Sally said when the door closed. 'That invitation didn't sound right, did it?'

'Nan understood perfectly,' Angela reassured her. 'She's such a lovely person, Sally. She wouldn't take offence, and of course she understands it should have been two couples . . . except that I don't really have someone special.'

'What about you and Mark Adderbury?'

'I rather think he may have someone special now. At

355

the moment there isn't a romance in sight for me, Sally, nor do I wish for one just yet.'

'That's a shame. I think it would be good for you. Is Mr Adderbury really going out with Staff Nurse Carole, then?' Sally wrinkled her brow. 'He's too good for her. I think he's mad to prefer . . .' She broke off, red-faced. 'Sorry, not my business, is it?'

'Don't worry, I'm not offended, but it isn't our business of course,' Angela agreed. 'However, as a friend I feel he is making a mistake, though it isn't up to me to say. I hope for his sake she truly loves him. I think he had a bad experience in the past. I don't want him to be unhappy.'

'Well, if he ends up with her, I think he may regret it,' Sally said. 'And that's horrid of me, isn't it? Oh, well, I must get on. If Sister catches me gossiping she will have my guts for garters – whoops! Not very ladylike, but you know what I mean. Sister was asking me all sorts of odd questions this morning, about whether I liked my job here.'

'Strange. What did you say?'

'I told her I've always been happy at St Saviour's and that I'd like to come back when I've done my training as a nurse.'

'What did she say to that?'

'Just looked at me a bit funny and then said she was glad to hear it. Perhaps it's all this rotten business with Terry that's behind it in some way.' Sally put down her empty cup. 'That's another one for Nan to fetch. I'd better get back to the children, I left Nancy reading a story to them, but she will want to get ready for Mr Adderbury.'

Angela was thoughtful. 'Nancy has settled well here. I

don't know what she's decided about the future. I think I'll pop down and have a word with her now. I'll walk with you, Sally.' Sally slipped her earrings into her apron pocket. 'What did your mother buy you for your birthday?'

'Mum was lucky and got some new pink wool. She knitted me a twinset in two-ply and I didn't know a thing about it. Really pretty colour it is, lacy pattern with big puffed shoulders.'

'That sounds just perfect for you. Pink will set off your chestnut-brown hair,' Angela said. 'Gosh, it's nice to have a few things in the shops again, isn't it? Nan was telling me that most of her ladies at the widow's club buy old knits from the market, unpick them and wash the wool to straighten it and then knit it up again. The trouble is that very often there isn't enough of one colour so you have to do stripes of white or something.'

Sally giggled and nodded. 'Mum did that all the time during the war, and me and Brenda ended up with stripes everywhere. That war has a lot to answer for.' She linked her arm through Angela's and squeezed it. 'The best thing of all that happened is that you came to St Saviour's. I really like us being friends.'

Sally was thoughtful as Angela took Nancy away, and she began reading to the little ones. They'd seemed very absorbed, and Nancy had looked content enough reading to them, even though she must be so worried over her brother. Angela was right when she said the girl had settled in here.

Her thoughts turned to her own life. At home, her parents were happier now that Dad had a better job. Brenda had whispered last night in their room that she was thinking of getting engaged to a man who was the office manager of an import/export firm on the Docks.

'You haven't known Derek five minutes,' Sally had objected, and Brenda just looked at her with a soppy smile on her face.

'When you meet the right one you know five seconds later, or at least the first time he kisses you,' Brenda said dreamily. 'Derek is that bit older. He was in the Army for five years – but worked in logistics most of that time. His old manager recommended him when he retired so now he's earning a really good wage.'

'So will you have a nice house and be able to give up work?'

'Yes, but I'm not going to until the babies come,' Brenda said. 'Whatever I earn will be saved for extras. Derek wants to buy a car soon, just a nice little family saloon, but think of it, Sally – no more queuing for buses . . .'

'You're not just marrying him for the car and the house?'

''Course not!' Brenda looked affronted. 'Derek might not look like Errol Flynn but he's very romantic.'

Sally smiled at the memory. Brenda was a bit of a giddy goose but there was no doubting that her sister was in love – the look on her face reflected her happiness and she walked about in a dream most of the time. Why didn't Sally feel that way?

A few doubts had begun to work themselves into Sally's mind. She cared about Andrew, admired him and respected him, and he was wonderful company, so generous and so different from all the other men, boys really, that she'd met before – but was that enough? Sally had been swept off her feet at Christmas when Andrew first kissed her under the mistletoe, but she wasn't sure that her feelings for him were strong enough to last a lifetime.

Marriage to a man who was far above her in the class structure would mean that they would both have to adjust to the differences. Sally's parents were not happy about the idea of their daughter moving up in the world.

'You'll grow away from us, love,' Mum had said as they sat in the kitchen together over a cup of cocoa one night. 'I've got nothing against Mr Markham – I'm sure he is a lovely gentleman, but that's just it. He is a gentleman and he would not think much of us or where you live . . .'

'Andrew isn't like that, Mum. You're wrong about him.'

'Oh, Sally, love. I don't want to spoil things for you, but be very careful. Why don't you take your nursing course and then see how you feel? If he loves you, he'll wait – and if your love survives that time apart, well, I'll be the first to congratulate you.'

Sally had promised her mother she would give the idea some thought. In some ways, Mum was right. Sally's dream had always been to take that nursing course and she could now that her father was doing so much better. Andrew had hinted that they might think of getting married in a few months, and was talking of buying a house with a garden far away from Spitalfields. Obviously, he was thinking of children – and it was natural that he should, being that much older.

Sally was a little afraid that he would buy her a ring for her birthday. If he did that she would have to make up her mind and she wanted a little time yet. He was a special man and she thought she loved him . . . but did she love him enough?

FORTY-FIVE

Beatrice's arm was sore, but otherwise she felt quite well. It wasn't Terry's attack on her that was worrying her now, nor even the distress it had caused her to be told by Angela that Mark thought he might never come out of the catatonic state he'd fallen into – no, it was the fact that Staff Nurse Carole had lied to her about another member of staff.

Beatrice had had ample time to study Sally while she was a patient. Everything the girl did was meticulous, but done in a caring way that spoke of her love for the children and her work. Beatrice had stood that morning in the doorway of the classroom knowing that Sally was unaware of her as she read and talked to the little ones – and she'd asked Nan for her opinion of the young carer.

'Sally is the best I've had under me,' Nan told her without hesitation. 'What makes you ask, Beatrice? I would trust her with my life and that's a fact.'

'Yes, that has always been my own opinion,' Beatrice said, and sighed. It seemed clear that Carole had lied about the carer, trying to get her into trouble – but why should she? Was it just personal dislike? If so, it was wrong of Carole to bring personalities into the workplace. Had Sally taken a dislike to the nurse and rubbed her up the wrong way?

Carole should be able to handle something of that nature without complaining to her superior – but it was more serious than that, because Carole had deliberately tried to get Sally into trouble . . . perhaps even to have her sacked.

Beatrice's instinct told her that Carole wasn't the pleasant and caring nurse she'd hoped for when she took her on. Efficient she certainly was, her work could not be faulted – but there was something about her that Beatrice couldn't like.

What ought she to do about it? Did she want to retain the services of a nurse who could lie maliciously about a colleague? The answer must be no, but it was a problem not easily solved.

Carole was a good nurse and they couldn't afford to lose her. Beatrice would have to find a way to reprimand her without causing a breach that made working with her impossible. She must take her time and decide before speaking to Carole, because she needed to be quite sure that Carole's complaints were unfounded. She took the accounts book from her desk and opened it.

Her door opened and Angela entered.

'Oh, Sister,' she exclaimed. 'What are you doing? I'm sure there is no need for you to be working this morning.'

'We need to get this expenses sheet sorted out,' Beatrice said. 'It will be the Board meeting again next week and I'm sure I've made a mistake somewhere. If you look carefully, you will see that some figures have been erased and others inserted.' She sighed. 'I don't know how that could have happened . . .'

'Let me take it and go through it for you,' Angela said. 'I'll check it and type it up and then I'll let you go through it again. You're pushing yourself too hard and ought to take another few days off, at least.'

Beatrice sighed and handed her the sheet. 'To be honest I don't feel up to this at the moment. I think I will go down to the sick ward and have a word with Staff Nurse Carole, and then perhaps I'll go back to my room and have a bit of a lie-down for an hour or two. I do have a bit of a headache.'

'It is hardly surprising,' Angela said. 'After what you went through yesterday . . . most people would still be in hospital. Mark wanted to send you to the Royal London but I persuaded him to let our nurses look after you. If you refuse to rest I shall think I was wrong.'

Beatrice smiled. 'Has anyone told you that you are a very caring person, Angela?' To her surprise Angela blushed and shook her head. 'I want to thank you and Mark, Father Joe – and Nurse Carole too, I suppose. You were all good to me. I think I shall arrange a nice fruit cake and a glass of sherry in my office one evening – if you would come, Angela? I shall ask Mark Adderbury, Father Joe and Nan – and Carole perhaps next week . . .'

'Of course, I'd love to.' Angela's eyes lit with laughter. 'Sally and Mr Markham are taking me out this evening for Sally's birthday – and Nan is standing in for Mark. Has she told you?'

'Nan hasn't been to see me this morning. She did give me strict instructions not to leave my bed for three days.'

'Well, I'll take this list and get on with it . . . I'll see you later perhaps. Do please try to get a little rest.'

Beatrice pulled a wry face as the door closed behind her. People were so well-meaning, but she would rather be here doing something than sitting alone. Idle hands made work for the devil – that's what she'd been brought up to believe.

'I'm sorry, Carole,' Sister Beatrice said when she spoke to her senior nurse half an hour later. 'I appreciate that you are a good nurse, and I'm grateful for what you did for me last evening – but I cannot agree with your remarks about Sally Rush. I've spoken to various people about her, and everyone agrees that she is a dedicated and caring girl.'

Carole couldn't meet Beatrice's eyes. 'Well, perhaps it's just me she doesn't like, but I find her hostile and rude. I'm not sure I can work with her.'

'Then perhaps you should consider your future here,' Beatrice said. 'I intend to ask Sally if she would consider returning here to St Saviour's when she has finished her nursing training.'

The furious expression that Beatrice saw in Carole's eyes was only there for a very brief moment and had vanished in seconds, and the girl gave her what she could only term as a look of contempt mixed with triumph.

'I do not imagine I shall be here very much longer,' she said, and tossed her head. 'I may be getting married soon – although that is confidential at the moment, but I thought you should know.'

'I see . . . well, in that case I'm sure it will work out

well for everyone. May I offer you my congratulations? I hope you will both be very happy.'

Beatrice was thoughtful as she left the ward and walked back to her office. If Carole left to get married that would solve her problem. Staff Nurse Carole hadn't really fitted in at St Saviour's.

She glanced at the neatly typed accounts on her desk and saw that Angela had balanced the final figures perfectly. So where had she gone wrong? It hardly mattered now and she could only feel glad that her colleague was better at figures than she was.

Angela sat thinking about the accounts Sister Beatrice had given her. She'd checked the columns against the receipts they always obtained for goods and services and found the correct amounts. At the end of a time-consuming exercise, she'd discovered what had happened – someone had rubbed out the figures Sister Beatrice had entered and replaced them with inaccurate ones.

The writer had tried to copy Sister's hand but he – or more likely she – had been too quick and not as clever as she thought. Angela knew Sister Beatrice's hand very well and she was certain the nun had neither erased nor falsified the figures. Indeed, she had a pretty good idea who had done it, because she'd seen the distinctive handwriting before. She remembered the mix-up with the staff rota. Angela had thought little of it then, but now she wondered just what was going on – especially when she'd discovered the pages missing in the monthly report. Fortunately, she'd kept a carbon copy and was able to type the pages again quite quickly.

Someone was trying to make trouble at St Saviour's.

Angela was fairly sure it was Carole, but she could not for the life of her think why the staff nurse should do such a thing. However, she would lock her desk drawers in future – and she would watch out for any more tricks the girl came up with.

FORTY-SIX

The Dorchester Hotel took Sally's breath away when the taxi pulled up outside that evening. Of course she'd heard of it, of its reputation during the war of being the safest building in London. The Mayfair Hotel had moved its precious collection of Chinese porcelain here during the bombing, and its splendid dining rooms had played host to all kinds of famous people over the years. Ushered inside to bright lights, polished wood and soft carpets, Sally was glad that she was wearing the beautiful blue dress Angela had given her with some nearly new black suede court shoes she'd managed to find in Petticoat Lane. Her earrings sparkled and she'd brushed back her hair to show them off, feeling proud to be wearing something really good for once in her life – and yet this opulence, this taste of the high life was almost too scary for her to enjoy.

Andrew put his arm about her waist and gave her a little squeeze, as if he sensed her nervousness. 'This is what you deserve for your special day, my darling Sally,' he whispered and she felt pleasing warmth spread through her. Andrew's touch made her tingle all over. It would be foolish to let her nerves spoil the evening, but she was glad she hadn't known where she was going. Mum would tell her this was way out of her league. Perhaps it was, but she meant to enjoy her birthday!

'You're spoiling me, Andrew,' she said in a soft voice. 'It's like a palace . . .'

Andrew laughed down at her. 'Sally, you're so special,' he said huskily. 'It's no wonder you hit me for six and sent me spinning. I love you so much – don't ever change, will you?'

''Course not.' Sally grinned at him. 'Where do you think Angela and Nan are?'

'In the coffee lounge or the bar, I should imagine. We'll just hand our coats in and then have a look for them.'

Sally nodded, watching as a man and woman swept in with a small entourage and loads and loads of expensive cases. They looked American, wealthy, and as soon as they arrived at the reception counter the woman started throwing her weight around and demanding to know whether they had the best suite.

Sally had a fit of the giggles, but only shook her head at Andrew. He took her into the bar and they saw Angela and Nan sitting at one of the small tables. Andrew guided her towards their guests, who had been drinking what looked like fruit juices.

'I've ordered champagne,' Andrew said, and smiled at Nan. 'I'm honoured to have you as my guest. Sister Beatrice says she couldn't run St Saviour's without you – and I know my Sally thinks the world of you. Now, if you don't like champagne you must tell me. I want this to be a treat for everyone.'

'To be honest, I've never tasted it,' Nan said. She was looking smart in a blue tweed suit with a cream silk blouse, her hair brushed smartly into a D.A. at the back. 'However, I'm always willing to try – this is a night of firsts, Mr Markham. You could have knocked me down with a feather when Angela said we were coming here.'

'That's the spirit,' he said, 'and do call me Andrew please, Nan. We're all friends here.'

'You look lovely,' Angela told Sally, patting the seat next to her. 'Isn't it nice here? Do you know I've never been to the Dorchester before – John liked the Savoy and the Mayfair, and Nick likes trendy places.'

Sally sat next to her, feeling much more comfortable now that she was with her friends. Nan certainly wasn't used to places like this, but she was taking it in her stride, looking about her with interest, a smile on her face. It was meant to be an evening of celebration and she knew that Andrew had gone to a lot of trouble to order a special meal for them. Food was still not plentiful in the shops, but the best hotels always managed to find something decent from somewhere, often game or different kinds of fish, because it wasn't possible to ration them, and Sally knew that he was very partial to pheasant and venison; she would rather have something more ordinary but she wasn't going to let on if the meal didn't quite suit her.

Andrew's birthday present had been a gold cross set with tiny pearls on a thin gold chain, which had been a relief to Sally. She loved being with him, loved his gentle smile, his humour and his kindness to the children, but marriage was a big step and she needed more time to be certain of what she wanted. Sister Beatrice had asked to see her in her office the next day to discuss her future, and Sally knew that the time to make up her mind was fast approaching, but for this evening she was just going to enjoy herself with her friends.

'I hope you enjoyed your evening, my darling?' Andrew drew her close as they sat in the front seat of his luxurious car, his breath soft on her face as he kissed her lingeringly. He tasted a little of wine and peppermint and Sally smiled inwardly as she realised he'd sucked a mint so that his breath would be fresh when he kissed her goodnight. He was such a thoughtful man, such a darling, and she did truly love him.

His kiss deepened and Sally felt her body respond to a new and totally pleasurable feeling that she understood was desire. She melted against him, giving in to the fire racing through her body, making it clamour with the need to be one with him. Little shivers of pleasure went down her spine as his lips trailed her throat and she knew that if he'd asked she would have given herself to him in that moment, but Andrew was too much a gentleman and too thoughtful.

He drew back, smiling into her eyes as his thumb traced the fullness of her lips. 'I want to make love to you so much, my darling,' he said, 'but I won't risk your future to gratify my needs. I want to speak to your father and then we'll discuss getting married. I'd like it to be quite soon, but if you're not sure I'll wait for a few months until you're ready.'

Sally smiled up at him. A part of her wanted to tell him that she would like to be married as soon as possible, yet another part of her held back. She loved him, wanted to make love with him, but she was still too conscious of the divide between them to say yes just yet.

'I should like to wait for a little while,' she told him breathlessly. 'Give me a few weeks to think about it and then I'll give you my answer.'

'Of course, my darling. I didn't mean to rush you,' he said, and drew back. He was still smiling and yet she was aware of a slight withdrawal, as if she'd hurt him by asking him to wait.

'You didn't,' she assured him swiftly. 'It's just that it's a little soon for me . . . I need more time to be sure.'

Sally didn't know if she'd made things worse, but Andrew merely nodded, got out of the car and went round to open the door for her. Regret swathed her as she gave him a quick hug and then ran to her front door. She had no doubt that he loved her and she knew he was special, very special – so why hadn't she said yes immediately?

Walking down the busy Commercial Street, Sally's thoughts were mixed. Dinner yesterday had been excellent and she couldn't remember ever having enjoyed an evening more, but Andrew's passion in the car had made her very aware that he wanted more than just a few evenings out with her. He had gone away to a conference for a week and in a way, Sally was glad. It gave her a bit of space to think.

Sally passed an empty space where a large store had once stood, shivering as she remembered the Blitz and then the V1 and V2 rockets, which had been even more terrifying, and caused so much damage in Poplar and Bethnal Green. She'd come shopping because she'd been given the morning off. Mum wanted some special soap and she thought she'd seen an advertisement saying that one of the big shops had had some in.

'I'm buying bits for your sister's wedding,' Mrs Rush had told Sally as she gave her three pounds. 'If you see anything you think Brenda would like, buy it, please. She loves scented soap when we can get it – but a bit of lace to trim a petticoat or anything nice . . .'

Sally had taken the money and promised to use it wisely, but she thought the market would be the best place to spend it. There was a large market in Spitalfields but she thought she might go down the Lane on Sunday. All the spivs would be there with their suitcases, and the stalls would be busy with shoppers looking for bargains. New lace was almost impossible to find, but Petticoat Lane often had some good cast-offs from rich women who had lots of good clothes. It was fun to watch the stallholders auctioning things, their patter bright and cheeky as they tried to convince people they were getting a bargain. You had to watch out for the pickpockets, but as long as you kept a sharp eye you were all right.

Sally reached the shop that was supposed to have some stocks of soap in, but saw the queue was right down the road. By the time she got to the end of it anything good would have gone. It was always the same: if a shop had a consignment of something nice in it was gone in a day.

She sighed and decided to walk as far as Whitechapel High Street, and then make her way back to St Saviour's. If she couldn't find anything worth having she would save Mum's money and see what was going in the Lane on Sunday . . .

*   *   *

'Thank you for coming to see me,' Sister Beatrice said. 'Please sit down, Sally. I wanted to talk to you about the future and to discuss the possibility of you coming back here to work once you've completed your nursing training. If you still intend to take it up?'

'Yes . . . yes, I do,' Sally said, and suddenly she saw the way clearly. She had a future here at St Saviour's and that was what she wanted. Sally's feelings for Andrew were warm and might even prove to be lasting love, but she wasn't ready to leave her world behind for his just yet. Perhaps in a few years, when she'd become a nurse and grown more assured, more certain of herself. 'I shall apply for my training tomorrow in writing – and yes, I would like to return here one day. Even if I marry, I would like to work here until I have a family, and perhaps come back when my children grow up.' She raised her gaze to Sister Beatrice's. 'Am I asking too much of life . . . wanting it all?'

She saw that Sister looked pleased. 'You have ambition, Sally, and that is always good. When you marry it will be up to you and your husband whether you carry on working, but we need dedicated people here and I hope that you will continue to want to work with us. However, it is enough for now that you have stated your wish to return – and remains only for me to wish you well.'

'Thank you, Sister.' She was going to have to tell Andrew of her decision and hope that he was prepared to be patient. Sally would hate to hurt him, and yet she knew that she had to do this for herself, because she wasn't ready to be the wife of a man like Andrew Markham just yet. It would overwhelm her, rob her of the certainty of who and what she was. Sally had to grow in confidence, to become a nurse who could help to save lives. Only then would she feel she was his equal, and then perhaps they would stand a chance.

She just hoped that Andrew could accept her decision, because she wanted to go on seeing him, but her feelings towards him were like the good wine he'd been telling her about last night . . . they needed to mature and become fuller and more rounded.

She hoped he would understand. His conference would last a week before they'd see each other again. In the meantime she was going to get her application in to the nursing college.

FORTY-SEVEN

Mark drove Nancy back to St Saviour's and saw her inside. This was the second time they'd been to the clinic in the weeks since her brother's collapse and they'd had a long and helpful talk about her future and Terry's, and he believed she was feeling a little easier in her mind now.

'Terry is still very ill at the moment, as you know,' he'd told her. 'But he is in a safe secure place now and they will take good care of him . . .'

'Yes, I know he has to be there,' Nancy said, her eyes filled with tears. 'But he will be so unhappy and he will think I've deserted him.'

'Terry has been violent on more than once occasion and we simply had to remove him to a secure environment. I believe with the right kind of treatment we may bring him back from wherever he has gone, Nancy – but you must understand it will be a long and slow process . . .'

'But will he ever be well again? Shall I ever be able to bring him home with me?'

'That remains to be seen. The treatment may make him more docile – and quite often patients become accustomed to their home and wish to stay. That is not for me to decide. If various doctors believe him cured, it will be up to you and Terry to make up you your minds – but not until both of you are older and Terry is at least stable.'

'Yes, I understand. You've been kind, sir. Letting me see the room where he'll be – and the gardens are lovely, so peaceful.'

'You could stay nearby if you wished? I believe the home there is quite nice.'

Nancy shook her head. 'I want to stay at St Saviour's – at least until I'm eighteen. Then I shall see how Terry is and decide what to do for the best.'

'You're a sensible girl, Nancy. I'm only sorry this had to happen.'

'It wasn't your fault, it was Pa's,' Nancy said simply. 'What happened was terrible and I shall always wish I hadn't locked that door – but it was Pa's fault. If he hadn't been such a brute . . . none of it would have happened.'

'No, possibly not,' Mark said, and pressed her hand. As yet he wasn't sure whether Terry had known what he was doing when he threw that lamp at the door of his father's room. Perhaps he would never know for certain, because that secret was locked inside the boy's brain. Indeed, they none of them actually knew that the boy had thrown the lamp, though Nancy thought she'd seen glass from his lamp. However, in the smoke and confusion she might have been mistaken. Only Terry knew for certain and he might never be able to tell.

And now he really had to speak to Carole . . .

* * *

'Carole – can you spare a moment?' Mark's voice made her turn and for a moment her heart raced as she saw him standing there. He really was attractive up close and she'd found herself wishing she hadn't been so rude the last time they spoke. Perhaps if she handled things right, she might win him back even yet.

'What is it?' she asked in the soft tone she'd previously used to charm him. 'I have a break coming up soon, if you can wait ten minutes.'

'I'm not sure I have time,' he said, and glanced at his watch.

The action infuriated Carole, even though she was determined to keep her annoyance inside. If he imagined he could just sweet-talk her for a couple of minutes and then sail off into the blue, leaving her behind, he had another thought coming.

'I do think you should make time to talk to me,' Carole said, still in that deceptively pleasant tone. 'I was going to telephone you, but there has been so much going on . . .'

'Yes, I know – and I've got to leave shortly, I'm afraid. If you can't talk now it will have to be another day. I really just wanted to apologise again.'

'Perhaps you should take a few minutes,' she said. 'If you're at all interested in your child . . . your child and mine . . .'

She felt a thrill of gratification when she saw the colour leave his face. She had really taken the wind out of his sails now. His face was a picture as he struggled to take in the news, unable to process it properly. He looked so devastated that for a moment she almost felt sorry for him – but no one dumped Carole the way he had and got away with it.

'Are you certain? I mean it's not very long since . . . hardly a month . . .'

'Sure I'm pregnant or sure it's yours?' Carole glared at him. 'The answer is yes to both questions, because I've missed a period and I never do.'

'I was only asking one of them,' Mark said quietly. There was a strained silence before he spoke again. For a moment she thought he was going to deny her, to demand that she have an abortion or protest that it must be someone else's child, as he would if he had any memory of that night at the hotel. He really had been too drunk to know that he'd just gone to sleep, but Carole had let him think they'd been lovers the next morning. At last he seemed to take a grip on himself, lifting his head in a determined effort, though the words came out as a strangled whisper, 'Carole, I'm pleased – if you are? A child . . . well, that's something I've wanted for a long time. We'll marry, of course – if it's what you want?'

'Are you saying you don't?'

'No, of course I'm not. Look, Carole, this isn't the place or the time to discuss something so personal – but be assured that I'm happy about the child and I do want to do the right thing for all of us.'

'Mark, you do care about me?'

He hesitated and then gave her what she thought of as a forced smile. 'You know I find you attractive – and I'm sure we can work something out.'

'All right,' she smiled back, feeling a glow of pleasure at her own cleverness. He'd thought he was going to dump her but she'd make sure he was fairly caught, even though he was clearly reluctant. She would soon have him eating out her hand once she got him into bed properly, and she needed to as soon as possible. 'We'll talk when you get back to London, Mark. Have a good trip.'

'It will be anything but that,' he said grimly. 'It's something I have to do – and now I have to leave for my appointments in the country.'

Carole nodded and he left her. She went back to her work, checking the medicines after the ward round and locking the cupboard. Beds were made, the patients were washed and settled, medicines swallowed. Now she had little to do for the next hour or so but sit and write her notes and think . . . think about the lie she'd just told.

Mark had looked shocked when she'd told him she was pregnant. She'd seen him struggling with the news and she sensed that he'd spoken out of concern for the child he believed she was carrying. He wouldn't marry her if he remembered the truth; realised that he'd done little more than kiss and touch her before falling asleep. He'd been tired and the wine had done its work too well. Yet there was no doubt that he wanted a child . . . somehow she had to convince him to take her to bed and hope that by the time they got married she had managed to conceive one.

She wasn't quite sure what she'd do if it didn't happen. Could she get away with telling him she'd made a mistake or would she have to invent a miscarriage? She'd worry about that later; for now, her plan was working.

Angela was walking down the stairs a few days later when she saw Mark enter St Saviour's. It was now the beginning of April and for the first time it felt a little warmer. He smiled and waited in the hall for her to reach him. She thought he looked uncertain and awkward, and her heart went out to him because she sensed something was wrong.

'I was hoping to see you. I wanted you to be one of the first to know – I'm engaged to Carole.'

The news came as a shock, and sent her senses reeling, but she tried to keep a check on her feelings. She felt as if he'd slapped her and the pain seared her like a hot knife. For a moment she found it difficult and struggled to respond, and in the end all she could say was, 'I can only wish you happy, Mark. I'm sure you will be. Carole is a very pretty girl.'

Angela wasn't sure how she managed to keep her smile in place, because even though she'd known Mark had taken Carole out a few times, she hadn't expected this and it hurt – far more than she would ever have imagined.

Mark's smile was clearly forced as he replied, 'Yes, she is. I have no idea why she wants to marry me – but it seems she does.'

'She is a lucky girl,' Angela said warmly. 'When do you intend to marry?'

'Quite soon I think – no sense in waiting about. She might change her mind.'

'I'm sure she won't.'

'No . . . Carole has informed me she's having my child.' He looked rueful, uncertain, making Angela catch her breath as regret smote her. 'I have no choice . . . forgive me.'

The further revelation that Mark and Carole were

sleeping together was another blow, but she forced the words out. 'A child? That's what you've always wanted, isn't it?' Angela asked. 'I'm sure you will be very happy . . .'

'I shall welcome the child . . .' He sounded a little desperate, as if willing her to understand, but she was too hurt to respond and awkwardly, trying to put on a bright smile, tried to force the conversation on to other things instead.

'You will be coming to Sister Beatrice's little party in her office this Thursday? She wants to thank us for helping her when Terry . . .' Angela avoided looking at him. 'How did you get on yesterday? I suppose there is no better news?'

'Angela, please try to understand about Carole . . .' It was a cry from his heart.

She swallowed her desire to demand why he seemed so desperate for her understanding when he'd obviously been in the throes of a passionate love affair with the nurse. But there was no point. 'I'm happy for you – but you didn't tell me if there is news of Terry . . .'

'Yes, of course.' Mark made an effort to rein his emotions in, to keep things on a professional level, but the strain still showed on his face. 'Not yet. I doubt there will be unless they try some shock therapy – and I'm not sure he isn't better off as he is, but that isn't for me to decide, thank goodness. He is in his specialist's hands now.'

'It is a private clinic, isn't it? Who is paying for Terry's treatment?'

'I requested he be admitted.' Their eyes met and Angela's heart lurched. 'Please don't worry about it,

Angela. I'm on the Board and we'll find the money, somehow.'

For a moment Angela was struck by what a good man he was – why he'd become so important to her – and felt a need to let him know in some small way. 'Mark, that is so like you,' she said, touching his hand. 'Now, really, I must fly. I have a lot of work to get through and I'm busy this evening . . .'

'Who is the lucky man – Nick?'

'No, I have a charity meeting to attend,' Angela said. 'It's a housing committee.'

Mark frowned, then, 'I thought you were serious about Nick?'

'No, we'll only ever be friends – but I'm afraid that may not be enough for Nick. Goodbye, Mark.' Angela walked past him and through the door. She didn't look back but could sense he had turned to watch her. She'd had to walk off or she might have given herself away . . . revealed how much the news had really hurt her.

'Have you been avoiding me?' Nick asked when Angela answered her door to him that Saturday morning. He was carrying a bunch of roses, which he presented with a flourish. She held them to her nose but they were out of a hothouse and had no smell. 'May I come in?'

'Yes, of course,' Angela said, and smiled. 'I was just making coffee – and I've baked a seed cake. You've called at the right moment, but I warn you the cake is an experiment. I've never made it before.'

'Then I shall be the sacrificial lamb,' Nick teased, and followed her in. 'I've called several times recently but you're never here.'

'On Thursday I stayed late to have a sherry with Sister Beatrice and there have been a couple of charity meetings – oh, and I went out to dinner with friends the other week,' Angela said, indicating that he should sit down as she went to bring a tray through from her kitchen. 'Then I have rehearsals for our concert every evening. We planned it for Easter, but with all that's been happening I had to put it back for a while, so it will be later this month.'

'The fundraising been going well?'

'Yes, pretty well, though we shall always need more.'

'How long are you going to carry on working there?' Nick asked, watching as she poured coffee exactly the way he liked it and then cut the cake. He took a tiny bite and discovered that it was crisp on the edges and soft inside, the taste rather delicious. 'You're a better cook than you think – but of course you wouldn't need to do your own cooking if we were married . . .'

'Nick!' Angela gave him a warning look. 'I love the flowers and you're always welcome to call as a friend – but, please, no more talk of marriage.' She couldn't even think about this when she was hurting so much inside.

He stood up, tall, handsome and imposing, taking her hands to pull her to her feet and gaze into her eyes. She felt a tingle of something like desire deep inside, but resisted it. 'You are a beautiful woman, Angela, and too young to live alone for the rest of your life. I know you loved John – but you're not indifferent to me. You liked it when we kissed, please do not deny it.'

'I shan't deny it,' Angela said, and gazed up at him frankly. 'You are a special man, Nick, and some woman will be very lucky to be your wife – but that woman isn't me. I'm sorry. I won't deny that I've been tempted to go to get closer to you. I'm not frigid and I do get lonely . . . very lonely at times, but I'm not ready to marry – and if I were it would not be to you, Nick. You see, I've known real love and I want that again.'

'I care for you deeply. You could learn to love me . . .'

'No, Nick. Love isn't like that, you know it isn't. When it comes it hits you for six and you can't think of anything but the person you love – I don't feel that way about you. I'm sorry and I don't want to hurt you . . .'

'So you *have* been avoiding me! It was your way of giving me the brush-off . . . did you think I would just get fed up and fade away?'

'You're angry. I'm so sorry. I didn't want to make you angry, but I can only give you the truth. If you were interested in friendship . . . but you aren't, are you? It's a full-on love affair or nothing, and I'm afraid it has to be nothing. Nick . . . please, forgive me?'

'Why the hell should I?' he said, and the look he sent her gave Angela the shivers. 'Stay in your safe little world and may you rot there.' He almost spat the words at her. 'You're a damned fool and one day you will wake up and regret what you've thrown away.'

Angela did not answer, stunned into silence by the ferocity of his words. He looked at her angrily for a few moments and then walked to the door and went out, slamming it after him so furiously that a vase toppled from a small table and fell to the floor, breaking in two.

She stood staring at the door and the broken vase,

her throat tight and her eyes stinging with tears. Nick sounded as if he hated her, and she felt the pain of it ripple through her. Of course she wasn't indifferent to him; he was attractive and masculine and she'd been very tempted to go for the life he'd offered, but it wasn't what she wanted now. Once she might have settled for being the wife of a rich man, but now she wanted so much more . . . she wanted Mark Adderbury. It was clear to her now, but he was promised to someone else.

Angela walked across the room feeling numbed. She bent down to retrieve the pieces of the vase she'd really liked and took them into the kitchen. Staring at the roses Nick had brought, which she'd put in a bowl of water ready to arrange later, she was inclined to put them in the waste-bin together with the broken vase, but she couldn't do it. The roses were beautiful and they couldn't help it that Nick had upset her.

She took a vase and began to cut the stems and place them in water. It wasn't the end of the world because Nick had walked out on her, but Mark Adderbury was engaged to Carole and that left a peculiarly empty feeling inside her. Mark had been such a staunch friend that she felt his desertion more than Nick's – even though it was dog-in-the-mangerish of her.

Nick had every right to be annoyed. It probably seemed to him that she'd used him, but she'd thought it was enough to be friends.

And now she'd lost her best friend . . . a man she'd loved without really knowing it all this time.

FORTY-EIGHT

Michelle looked at the pattern for a baby's dress and the white wool she'd managed to buy on the market that morning. Knitting it would give her something to do when she was at home on her afternoons off or in the evenings, because now that Alice didn't have the money to go out dancing or to the flicks, and Sally was courting, Michelle found herself staying home more. Besides, her friend was going to need all the extras she could get and she wasn't even sure that Alice could knit, though she knew she'd been putting little things by for a while.

'What are you making that for?' Michelle's mother asked, frowning as she came in and saw her settled by the fire with the pattern and white wool. 'Michelle, you're not in trouble, are you?'

'No, Mum, I'm not,' Michelle said, looking at her mother's anxious face. Sometimes, she seemed so thin and pale it worried Michelle. 'It's for a friend of mine – one of the girl's at St Saviour's.'

'Good.' Her mother smiled wearily. 'You know we rely on you, love. Your father's scarcely ever in work since his chest got so bad. I'm not sure how we could cope with another mouth to feed and you'd be out of work.'

'Well, it isn't going to happen,' Michelle said. 'When I want babies I'll find a husband first – and at the moment that isn't on my horizon.'

'You're a good girl. I shouldn't doubt you. It's just that I can hardly manage as it is and your brothers seem to grow out of their clothes as soon as I buy them – Freddie ought to have new things if he's going to senior school, but I don't see how we can afford them . . .'

'No point in buying him new, Mum,' Michelle said. 'If you get him a pair of long trousers he'll put his knee through them the first time he gets into a fight. I bought this wool cheap on the market – and next week I'll see what I can find for Freddie. Trust me, I won't buy rubbish.'

'You should be saving to get married, not having to look after us.'

'I don't want to marry anyone, not for years anyway.'

Michelle's mother sighed and took some clothes that had been airing before the fire, leaving the kitchen with her arms filled. She was looking weary again and Michelle worried about her; she worried about all her family. Her father was on the verge of consumption, though he hadn't admitted it to her or any of his family and would hide it for as long as he could. Even though he never kissed anyone or coughed over them, Michelle knew he ought to go away and be treated, but until he gave in and conceded he needed to see a doctor there was nothing she could do.

Feeling worried, Michelle glanced at her knitting. She ought not to be fed up, when her friend was in far worse trouble. Michelle had loving parents and a good home, even if it was damp and unhealthy. She was fond of Alice and wondered what was going to happen to her when she finally had to leave St Saviour's, which she must soon. Alice had no chance of getting married if she continued to think of that rogue who had got her into trouble. All Michelle could hope was that her friend would come to her senses and think about marrying the one man who cared about her.

Alice left St Saviour's late on that Friday night. It was still chilly, even though everyone kept saying spring would soon be here, and she pulled up her coat collar, shivering. She was feeling so much better since Nan had taken her in. The bedroom was small but comfortable, warm and smelled of lovely polish. Nan was being so kind to her and Alice tried to repay her by doing little jobs – but in her heart she knew that it was only a temporary refuge. Once the baby was born she would have to try to find a new place to live. She'd talked to Nan about it once or twice and Angela had assured her that she would arrange for her to go to a private clinic to have the baby. Alice was going to get herself a wedding ring and in future she would be known as Mrs Cobb.

Although she still had a few savings, Alice was reluctant to use them just yet. Once she was forced to leave work she would soon find that her small store of money was dwindling.

Jack had sworn he loved her, but he'd driven off and

left her and everyone thought he was dead – except she couldn't quite believe it in her heart.

Somehow Alice was going to have to make a new life for herself. She wished she was clever so that she could be a nurse like Michelle. Sally Rush had told her that she was going to train to become a nurse one day. Sally would have a chance to make something of herself. If only Alice could do the same, but she'd left it too late, because no one would give her the chance now. All she could hope for was that she might be able to continue to work at St Saviour's after the child was born, but that depended on Sister Beatrice.

FORTY-NINE

'I'm glad you've come to your senses,' Sally's mother said as they sat in the kitchen eating Spam fritters, mashed potatoes and tinned peas for their supper that Sunday evening. 'It would never have worked, love. I know he swept you off your feet – and he's a really nice man – but he's from a different world.'

'Mum, please don't,' Sally said. 'I haven't even told Andrew about taking up the course yet – and it doesn't mean I don't love him, because I do. Sometimes I think I shall be miserable if he won't wait for me . . . but I know I have to do this for me. Once I have my training I shall be better able to understand the kind of world he comes from . . .'

'I don't see that at all,' her mother said. 'You'll be older and wiser perhaps – but the divide will always be there. It's been a lovely experience for you, Sally, but best if it finishes now.'

'No, Mum!' Sally jumped to her feet. 'I won't listen to this. I'm just slowing things down because I'm not ready – but I may still marry him one day, if he'll wait.'

'Where are you going? You can't leave good food.'

'Sorry, I couldn't force another mouthful down . . .'

'Not good enough for you now, I suppose. You want the fancy food they do at the Dorchester.'

'That's not fair, Mum. I'm going to the church hall to help Angela with rehearsals for the concert she's putting on at the end of the month. Brenda says she'll come down when she gets home after work. Tell her I've already gone.'

'Sally, eat your supper. Oh, I don't know. Since you started mixing with that Angela and Mr Markham you haven't been the same. Don't get ideas above your head, lass.'

'I'll eat the Spam fritters later with some bubble and squeak,' Sally said. 'Sorry, Mum, I can't stop.'

Sally almost ran out of the house, because she couldn't bear to listen to her mother going on about Andrew any more. She'd hoped Mum would leave her alone now she was going to do her training but it seemed she couldn't stop herself. Sally really wanted to be a nurse, but that didn't mean she no longer cared for Andrew because she did. If she were to lose him . . . but surely she wouldn't. He was patient and understanding and he would wait for her, she knew he would. As soon as he got in touch, she would speak to him, tell him how she felt – and then perhaps she wouldn't feel so guilty. It almost seemed disloyal to have come to her decision while he was away, but it had been far longer than the week he'd promised and the doubts had crowded in on her. It was very strange that Andrew hadn't contacted her when he returned from his course and it seemed ages since she'd seen him, though it was only three weeks or so.

She jumped on the tram and paid her sixpence fare. Sally was looking forward to helping with the concert, and she hoped Brenda would too. Sitting at home listening to the wireless and watching Mum knit wasn't much fun for either of them, and Brenda's fiancé was on nights at the moment . . .

'I reckon that Angela is all right,' Brenda said as the sisters walked home together after the rehearsal. 'The way Mum goes on about her you would think she was Lady Muck, but she isn't like that at all. She's fun and she makes me laugh.'

'Why do you think I like her? It isn't for the presents and the clothes she's given me. Angela has been my friend ever since she arrived at St Saviour's and I really care about her – she's almost like my own sister.'

'You don't like her better than me?' Brenda sounded a bit jealous.

'Of course I don't, love. We'll always be mates. I wish Mum understood me half as well as you do, Bren.'

'I'm lookin' forward to me weddin',' Brenda said, and squeezed her arm. 'That lace you got me is the best I've ever seen.'

'That was Sister Beatrice; her mother used to make lace and she'd got some in her drawer. Honest, Bren, you'd think she was an old dragon sometimes to hear some of the girls go on behind her back, but she has to be strict – yet I've always liked her and I'm going back there to work when I've trained.'

'You'll always have a job, like me,' Brenda said. 'Poor Mum couldn't do anything but scrub toilets when Dad was out of work and he wouldn't let her do that. We'll never be as hard up as they were when Dad was out of a job.'

'We're lucky, though, as a family,' Sally said. 'It didn't break us up, did it?'

'Nah, nothing could do that.' Brenda stopped and looked at their house. 'That's funny, all the lights are on . . . and there's a car outside the door.' She looked at Sally in sudden fright. 'Do you think one of 'em's ill?'

'I don't know,' Sally said, and started to run, Brenda pounding after her. She pushed open the door and rushed into the kitchen, her heart in her mouth. Both her parents were sitting there, looking serious. 'What's wrong? Mum . . . Dad . . . what's the matter . . .?' The breath died in her throat as she suddenly saw Mr Adderbury sitting with a cup of strong tea in his hand. 'Mr Adderbury . . . what . . .?'

'I'm sorry, Sally,' he said, put his cup down, stood up and came towards her, his expression grave. 'When I heard I drove straight here, because you're needed at the hospital immediately. I was coming to the church hall but your mother thought you would be back soon and so I waited . . .'

'What is it?' she asked, and yet the sick feeling inside told her that it could only be one thing. 'It's Andrew, isn't it?' she asked dully. 'Something's happened?'

'Yes, it's Andrew, he isn't dead, but he *is* critically ill,' Mark Adderbury replied. 'It was an accident to his car – a head-on collision with a drunk driver. I have to tell you, Sally – he may not survive the night . . .'

'No . . .' Sally moaned. 'Please no . . .'

'Sally, I'm so sorry,' her mother said, but she wasn't

392

listening, because if she did she might say something she would regret.

'Please, will you take me there?'

'Me too,' Brenda said. 'I'm coming with you, Sally. You can't go through this alone. I'm not leaving you until . . . we know, that's all.'

'Yes, go with her,' Mum said. 'Sally, I wish . . .'

Sally turned away and followed Mark out. She could feel Brenda's arm about her waist and moved closer, seeking comfort from the sister who loved her, because without it she might not have made it to the car. All Sally could think about was that Andrew was lying in hospital, perhaps dying, and she – she had been on the verge of telling him that she couldn't marry him because her training was more important to her.

'Oh, Andrew,' she wept inside. 'Andrew, please forgive me . . . and live for me, because I do love you. I love you so very much . . .'

His bed was the same as all the others in the ward, iron rails at each end, narrow and covered in a white cotton cover, though he was right at the end by the window and the curtains were pulled about it. He lay with his head on one single pillow, the case starched and stiff, just like the sheet folded neatly down at the top. The smell of disinfectant barely covered an underlying stench of sickness, and the coughs, moans and snoring from the other patients made Sally sharply aware of what her world would be like quite soon.

Andrew's head was bound by thick bandages that obscured most of one side of his face. His injuries were clearly severe, more so than Sally had realised even when Mark told her he was gravely ill. He didn't move so much as an eyebrow when she bent over to gently kiss the only piece of his face she could see.

'I love you,' she whispered, a sob in her throat. 'I love you so much . . . forgive me. I'm sorry . . .'

Sally wasn't sure why she was apologising; she only knew she felt guilty. Perhaps it was because she'd been planning her future without consulting him. Mum obviously thought her decision would end their relationship, but Sally couldn't believe that. Andrew loved her and she loved him; he would surely understand that she needed a little time to learn and grow, so that she could be a better wife for him . . . and yet she could hear him in her head, begging her never to change but stay just as she was.

'It's you and your funny little ways that I love, Sally,' he'd told her more than once. 'I don't care about class, but if I did I still would want you, because you're lovely through and through.'

'Oh, Andrew, my darling,' Sally whispered, tears slowly trickling down her cheeks. 'Please don't leave me. Come back to me. I want us to be together always.'

She wanted to do her training and become a nurse, yes, she did, but she also wanted to be Andrew's wife one day . . . but she'd hoped to be good enough for him so that when he met some of his posh friends he wouldn't need to be ashamed of her. No, Andrew would never have felt that way. It was Mum who had drawn the lines between the classes; she was the snob, not Andrew.

Sally wasn't sure how long they allowed her to stand by his side before she was told that the nurse needed to make him comfortable and asked her to wait in the visitors' room. In some ways it was like a few seconds and in others an eternity. She felt so alone, because Andrew was there and yet he wasn't . . . because the still form with all those wires attached wasn't the warm, loving man she knew. She wanted him to be there. She wanted so desperately to see him smile and hear his voice speaking her name, to tell him she loved him more than anything in the whole world.

'Please, Miss Rush, we need to look after him. Go and sit with your sister and the doctor will come and see you shortly.'

Sally walked numbly from the ward. Brenda was sitting in the small room set aside for patients' families and she got up and came to her, reaching out to draw Sally into her arms. She let Brenda hold her, but couldn't respond. It was as if all feeling had left her and she was aware only of emptiness, of an ache inside her that she was afraid might never go away.

'You ought to go home,' Sally said when she could focus her mind. 'It's morning . . . .'

'I told you I wouldn't leave you and I shan't . . .'

'He's leaving me, Bren,' Sally said, and looked at her sister in dread. The coldness had been creeping down her spine since she left the ward and somehow she knew . . . she knew even before the doctor in the long white coat came to speak to them. Afterwards, Brenda told her that he was good-looking and that his name was Dr Harrison, but all Sally would ever remember was the sadness in his blue eyes as he met her tearful gaze.

'I am so very sorry, Miss Rush,' he said. 'Andrew left us a few minutes ago. It was a severe haemorrhage brought on by the head wound. We did all we could to save him – but it wasn't enough. Mr Markham was a respected colleague and he will be much missed . . .'

Sally let out a moan of despair and then, for the first time in her life, she fainted. Brenda told her later that Dr Harrison moved like lightning to catch her and prevent her fall.

'He was great, Sally,' Brenda said enthusiastically. 'He carried you into a little rest room and placed you on the bed, and then he told me to sit with you and went off to call a nurse to look at you. It was only a few minutes before you came round, and then they gave us tea, and I called a taxi to take us home.'

But it was many days before Brenda said anything about the kind doctor or what had happened at the hospital, because when they left there together, Sally didn't know what was going on. She was in a daze, her mind so confused that she could hardly put one foot in front of the other. Without Brenda's arm to support her, she couldn't have moved. The grief and despair that had descended on Sally was like an enveloping fog that she couldn't penetrate. People spoke to her and sometimes she answered, but she didn't know what they said or how she responded.

Somehow Brenda had got her home and up to bed. She'd kept their mother at bay, though in the recesses of her mind Sally heard her mother crying and apologising, saying how sorry she was over and over again. Sally didn't even try to answer her. A barrier had arisen between them; it was all a part of the guilt and the grief and the simmering anger deep down inside her. Sally was at times aware of resentment, as if she wanted to blame her mother for having driven a wall between Andrew and her family, as if she'd been forced to choose, which of course she hadn't. She'd only meant to postpone things, but now somehow that had changed in her mind and there was a mountain of pain and guilt and grief and she couldn't see a way through it.

Perhaps the only way was to just lie down and die . . . to let go of all the hurt and the regret and the longing for things to be as they were and just let the clouds take her . . . drift away into the blue beyond and never return.

FIFTY

'That's terrible,' Angela said when Brenda came to see her in her office in the middle of the next day. 'I'm still trying to recover from the shock of hearing that Mr Markham had been killed in a car crash. It's such a waste of life. Sally must be devastated . . . I completely understand why she can't come into work. She shouldn't even think of it for a while. Sister will understand when I tell her.'

Angela felt a wave of grief sweep through her, because no one understood what Sally was going through better than she did. At least she'd had a short period of marriage. Sally had only known Andrew a few months, but he'd adored her and she'd loved him. It had been obvious that they were made for each other and would marry one day, even if Sally wanted to wait a couple of years. Once she'd passed most of her exams she could have spent more time with the man she loved. Angela was quite sure it would have worked out well.

'She won't even look at Mum,' Brenda said worriedly, 'Mum says she blames her for saying the things she did . . . about it being better if they broke up now, because it would never work between them.'

'Why did your mother think it wouldn't work?' Angela was bewildered. 'I know he was a few years older, but I don't think age is a barrier if you are truly in love – and they were . . . still are, as far is Sally is concerned.'

'Mum thought he was too far above us.' Brenda twisted a strand of fine hair nervously. 'She was afraid he would take Sally away from the family, that she would be ashamed of us.'

'That is ridiculous,' Angela said. 'Mr Markham was one of the least proud or class-conscious people I know. He only cared about helping people and he certainly didn't mind if they were a king or a caretaker.'

'Mum's like that.' Brenda sighed. 'Now she's feeling guilty and she wants to heal the breach between them but Sally just turns her head aside and refuses to look at her.'

'I expect she's just too unhappy to think of her mother for now,' Angela said. 'When it happened to me I almost hated my mother . . . she didn't understand but she kept saying things that made me angry. Well-meaning, kind but so wrong. Even Daddy did everything wrong, though he wanted to help. The only person I could speak to was Mark Adderbury . . .'

'Mr Adderbury?' Angela nodded. 'He came to fetch Sally and took us to the hospital. He gave me a number we could ring if there was anything more he could do, but . . . I don't think Sally would listen to him. She might listen to you, because she thinks the world of you.'

'I'm very fond of Sally and I shall certainly come to see her. I'll find out all I can – about the arrangements . . .'

'You mean the funeral? Will his family be there?' Brenda looked awkward. 'I mean, they weren't officially engaged. I know he'd spoken about marriage. Sally said he'd told her he wanted to live outside London and commute . . . that's one of the reasons she was worried about her training. I think she has to live in. They wouldn't bother taking her if she was married so she wanted to wait. Now she's regretting it . . .'

'I'll ask Mark about Andrew's family. I'm sure he'll know.' Angela sent Brenda a sympathetic look. 'I shall come to visit this evening . . . but you mustn't expect too much too soon. Sally will grieve for a long time.'

'I feel really bad, especially as I'm planning my wedding for May. I don't want to put it off, but I don't want to hurt Sally either.'

'Yes, I can see that is awkward for you,' Angela said. 'I'm sure Sally will understand, Brenda. You just have to be patient with her.'

Angela was thoughtful after her visitor had left. The news of the popular doctor's death had stunned all the staff when Sister Beatrice told them, and Jean had told her that the children were still crying. Many of the little ones had looked up to him as being between a father figure and Santa Claus, and they seemed to understand that he was sweet on their own Sally. He'd brought them copies of his wonderful books and puzzles, which he'd written and designed himself, and he'd read to them, teasing them and bringing joy to children who often had so little in their lives.

'It isn't fair!' Angela said aloud. 'He was such a kind, generous man.'

The door opened after a brief knock and Nan walked

in. She looked serious and Angela knew she'd come for a chat, because she'd brought a tray of coffee with two cups and some of her own jam tarts.

'What can we do to help her?' Nan asked, setting the tray down. 'I know she was planning to leave as soon as they had a place at the nursing college, but Sally is one of ours. I thought we might send flowers from all the staff – but is there anything more practical we can do for her?'

'Her sister has just left me,' Angela said. 'I'm going to ask Mark to find out the details of the funeral. He knew him better than we did . . . I think Brenda was concerned his family might look down their noses at her.'

'Well, she won't have to face them alone, because I shall be with her,' Nan said. 'I think Sister Beatrice intends to go as well, and I imagine you will?'

'Yes, I shall,' Angela agreed. 'I'll go for Sally's sake. I didn't know Mr Markham well, but I respected him. I think all the children will miss him and his stories about the big hairy spider.'

'The children loved his stories. I'm not sure what the idea was behind them, but the little ones just adored listening to him read – and all of them like the puzzles.' Nan shook her head. 'Why is it always the good ones that die young? Can you make sense of this world of ours, Angela? Sometimes I think God is laughing at us from up there, showing us that we are no more than pawns on the chessboard of life.'

'Gosh, that is very profound,' Angela said.

'Blame Eddie. He comes out with such things!'

'Wherever it came from it's right,' Angela said. 'I agree

that we should send some flowers for Sally and a card signed by everyone at St Saviour's – would you like me to organise that?'

'Yes, but you mustn't pay for it all. We must all put a few pennies in, Angela – so that it is really from us all. I think everyone here likes Sally and would want to wish her well.'

'Yes,' Angela said. 'We'll have a collection.'

'I've already started it; the tin is in the rest room,' Nan said. 'But I thought you might know what was suitable.'

'Sally likes spring flowers rather than hothouse blooms.' Angela frowned. 'Who has taken over Sally's duties for the moment?'

'I asked Nancy to look after the little ones this morning. She has them in the schoolroom and is reading to them, I think.'

Angela nodded and gave her an appreciative look. 'Yes, she will do that well. It's what she needed to stop her brooding over her brother.'

'She told me she thinks she would like to stay on here when she's older, either as assistant cook or a carer. I suggested that she talk to Sister Beatrice – and I think they've come to some sort of arrangement.'

'She would do well here, because she likes looking after people,' Angela said.

'I'll go and get on with my work and leave you to yours. You won't forget the card and flowers?'

'I'll buy a card and flowers in my lunch break,' Angela promised. 'I'm off to a meeting this evening after I've seen Sally.' Angela placed her empty cup on the tray. 'I'm speaking to a clothing manufacturer. He must get some waste . . . spoiled articles. I think someone told me it's called cabbage in the trade. I understand they knock the seconds out cheap to market traders, cut the labels out first of course. With a little persuasion he might give me a few bundles – just to clear them out of his way, naturally. I'll be doing him a good turn really.'

'Don't you ever stop?' Nan said, and went off, shaking her head with a wry smile.

Angela opened her drawer, took out some sheets of typing paper and inserted one into the machine. She'd hardly done a thing since she'd arrived that morning – but it was a day for talking, for offering comfort and receiving it. She'd just begun to type the first line of the monthly report when someone knocked at the door; it opened and Mark entered.

'Am I disturbing you?'

'No, of course not,' Angela said, but her heart caught with pain. 'I was hoping to speak to you later – please come in and tell me what you've heard. When is the funeral to be held?'

'I'm arranging it,' Mark said. 'I don't know if you were aware, but Markham had only one relative, his elderly aunt. She recently moved into a home for widows in Cheshire, and Andrew was going to sell her house for her to pay the fees. I think he visited regularly and he was on his way back from settling her in the home when the crash happened. His parents died in the 1920s, both of typhoid fever. His aunt saw him through college; I believe she more or less brought him up, though I understand his father left him a house and a little money – Mr Markham senior was a missionary and he and his wife were in Africa when they took ill and died.'

'So he had hardly any family. I wonder if Sally knows . . .'

'He didn't speak of it much; I only learned about his aunt when he asked me if I would be his executor a few months back. He said that his aunt might not live much longer and he wanted to be certain that his wishes were carried out in the event of his death – and that he knew I would do it.'

'Of course. He had complete faith in you, Mark.'

'Yes, it seems that way. It isn't a task I fancy, but I shall do what he asks, whatever it is. He had so many friends. I shall invite as many as I can trace to the funeral so it won't be quick – perhaps in a week or so, so that we can do things decently.'

'Yes, that may be better for Sally. She may be able to face it by then . . .'

'Poor girl. It was a rotten experience for her. I'm not sure how serious she was . . . Carole told me she was leaving to train as a nurse.'

'She is devastated, Mark. Yes, she wants to be a nurse, but she loved him very much. They would have married one day, I'm certain.'

'That makes it worse for her.' Mark sighed, and he seemed to hesitate, his look almost beseeching her – asking for what? Understanding? 'Let me know if there is anything I can do, please.'

'Of course; we must all do what we can.' She was managing to keep her manner friendly and calm – just. Inside, she was rebellious and finding it hard not to ask him why the hell he continued to look at her that way when he was going to marry someone else – the woman who was having his child.

'I must go now . . .'

'To see Carole? Naturally, you must.' Angela spoke through gritted teeth. If she was right about that woman he was making the biggest mistake of his life! 'I am sure she is looking forward to the wedding and all the excitement.'

'Carole is like me, she doesn't have much family – so it will just be a quiet wedding.'

'Oh, I see. I hope you will invite me?' Angela couldn't resist asking, wondering if Carole would want her there.

Mark looked at her sadly. 'If you would like to come, of course.' He inclined his head. 'Excuse me, I must leave you now.'

Angela sat looking at the door as it closed behind him. Mark didn't seem as happy as he ought and she couldn't help wondering if he had already begun to regret his decision.

FIFTY-ONE

Mark was conscious of deep regret as he left Angela's office and made his way to the sick ward. Carole would be waiting for him and he knew she was looking forward to making more plans for the wedding and their honeymoon; so far they'd only agreed on a church ceremony. She'd already told him she would like to go to Paris, and seemed set on talking it all over that evening at his flat. Why that held no particular appeal for him, Mark couldn't say: he only knew that when he'd been with Angela he'd been aware of a sense of loss.

Markham's death had shocked him. The man was a colleague and a good friend, one of the best, and a similar age. It had made Mark very aware of the fragility of humanity. If Markham had been snuffed out in the prime of his life, it could happen to them all – to him.

Was he really content to settle with a woman he didn't love? Mark knew he'd made a mistake by tumbling into bed with a girl just because she was sexy and pretty and made him laugh. He'd been a fool, but she was having his child – and that meant he was caught.

He would never desert his own child, because he'd seen too much of that kind of careless behaviour.

At least he would have that, a child of his own to love and care for, he thought. Sometimes he'd given up hope of a family. Edine had only conceived the one child and although Mark had known other women since his wife died, there had never been any hint of another; of course the ladies were older and more experienced so perhaps they'd made sure they were safe. He'd been shocked that Carole was pregnant, because it was only that one night – but of course they'd both had a few drinks too many. It was odd that he didn't remember anything . . . surely he ought to remember making love to her? A part of him wanted to reject her claim; it seemed so sudden and quick but if she was having a child it must be his, mustn't it? Carole was adamant that her period was regular and if she'd missed it . . . Mark didn't think she'd been out with anyone else since she'd been at St Saviour's so it had to be his.

He couldn't regret that he was to have a child, even if he wasn't certain of his feelings for the mother. In the circumstances he could only try his best to make a good marriage; he stuck a smile on his face as he walked into the sick ward. There were quite a few marriages that existed for the sake of the children, and he supposed he would manage to do as well as most. He'd been hoping there was a way out, but he'd better bite the bullet and start acting like a prospective husband. After all, he'd found her highly attractive at the start and he must surely have lost the respect of the woman he really wanted . . .

* * *

407

Carole frowned as she checked the medicine cupboard. Mark's visit had been brief and she had felt that he'd come more out of duty than pleasure. It annoyed her that he wasn't more demonstrative towards her. She'd imagined that the idea of having a child would please him, but he seemed withdrawn. He'd made an excuse about feeling upset over that colleague of his . . . Mr Markham.

Sally Rush had been going around with Markham. She was a fool; a man like that would never have married her, a girl from the slums. He'd just been having fun; she'd probably had a lucky escape. Not that Carole cared either way. She hadn't really known the popular surgeon, though she'd seen him and exchanged greetings, and she'd observed the children reading his books. Besides, she didn't like Sally. If she was vindictive she would think it served her right for trying to be something she wasn't, wearing Angela's cast-offs and thinking she could mix in the circles Markham came from. It would never have worked.

Mind you, it *was* rotten luck to lose someone you cared about. Carole had been through that herself too often, what with her fiancé, then her father and brothers – and that's why she was determined never to let herself really love a man again. Mark was decent, not bad-looking and not too old. He could provide her with the lifestyle she required – and she wasn't sure she wanted to go on nursing for much longer: certainly she didn't want to continue here, at St Saviour's. Unless she could take over the old dragon's job . . .

So far her meddling hadn't produced results. Perhaps she should have one last stab at getting rid of Sister

Beatrice, but it would have to be something bold. A smile touched Carole's lips as she looked at her list of tasks. She was about to give a boy his injection of insulin and there were only two bottles left in the little fridge where such medicines were stored. If she removed one and placed it in Sister's desk but left the records showing two it meant there would be no fresh insulin the day after tomorrow, because it had to be kept cool – and Michelle would be on duty then: it was Carole's day off.

Normally Carole would order more insulin immediately they got down to the last two, but this time she would wait. If the missing insulin was found in Sister's drawer everyone would think she was becoming forgetful . . . and even if it only succeeded in making Sister look a fool it would be worth it.

After all, what did it matter now she was going to marry Mark? Except that she wished Mark would look a bit happier. She'd thought he would be putty in her hands after she told him about the non-existent baby. Carole's monthlies had started that morning and she was feeling off-colour, but she had to keep that to herself. Mark mustn't know she'd lied to him – because if he did he might break it off . . .

Carole touched the wonderful diamond ring he'd given her when he'd taken her out on Sunday for lunch so they could talk about the future. She'd thought he might take her back to his place afterwards and they would end up in bed, but it hadn't happened. He'd seemed remote, serious, even when he gave her the ring. She couldn't wear it for work, but it was hanging on a chain with a gold cross her father had once given her, under her uniform. Everything she'd wanted was within her grasp: money, position as an eminent man's wife, and a life of ease and luxury. After her father lost everything just before the war and then went off to get himself killed playing the hero, Carole had vowed she would get back everything she'd once had She had to keep Mark sweet long enough to get his wedding ring on her finger – which meant she couldn't let him guess she wasn't pregnant just yet.

The trouble was he'd invited her to dinner that evening and might want to make love. A surge of panic went through Carole. She would have to invent a headache after dinner – find a reason for Mark to take her home rather than staying over at his place. He'd taken her back to his apartment on Sunday after they'd walked off their lunch but it had all gone sour when he'd had to rush off because his colleague was involved in an accident. He'd gone to fetch Sally Rush to the hospital, after dropping Carole off to sit at home and twiddle her thumbs. She felt a surge of annoyance. He ought to be thinking about her rather than Sally Rush – and why did Mark have to arrange the funeral and see to the will and things?

Carole wanted a man whose life centred on her and his home. Once they were married, she would make it clear that she wanted him to be at home when his day's work was finished.

Suddenly, the doubts had set in. She wondered if marriage to an older man who seemed to be more interested in his work and colleagues than her was really what she wanted – and yet what else was there for her?

She shook her head as she made a figure in the

right-hand column. No, she must go through with her plan. She gave a wince of pain as her stomach started to ache. She hated having the curse, especially when she was at work. Deciding to take an aspirin, Carole opened the large bag that contained all the things she carted with her every day and took out a strip of tablets, leaving it on the desk as she went to fetch a glass of water from the rest room.

Feeling sorry for herself, Carole didn't immediately register that someone had entered the sick room. It was only as she returned carrying the glass and saw Angela standing by the desk that she realised she'd left her bag open and right at the top was the packet of sanitary towels that she'd bought that morning. Had Angela seen them and the strip of aspirin – would she understand the significance of the two?

Carole went hot and cold all over, but then she realised it didn't matter. Angela couldn't know about the supposed baby. Mark wouldn't have told her . . .

'Did you want something?' she asked and zipped the top of her bag. 'I'm rather busy.'

'Sister asked me to fetch the medicine record book,' Angela said. 'She wanted to check that there is enough insulin. She thought there were two doses in the refrigerator – and I've checked to make sure: she is right. So we shall order those today? Is there anything else that you know is short?'

Carole cursed the interfering bitch. Was she a damned mind reader?

Well, her little ruse wouldn't work this time, but she would think of something else to pay them back . . . both of them.

'Feeling a bit under the weather?' Angela asked as she took the book Sister had requested.

'Just a headache,' Carole lied and scowled as Angela lifted her brows and then turned and walked from the room.

Damn the bitch! If she ran to Mark telling tales he might realise that she'd been lying.

FIFTY-TWO

Angela went carefully through the record book three times. As she'd thought, several figures had been erased and others inserted. According to the records they were completely out of some drugs and that just wasn't normal. Sister Beatrice had impressed on her right at the beginning that they must check these records each week and if anything was getting low they must reorder it at once.

'We do not want to be out of something we need urgently – particularly the insulin for our diabetic child,' she'd told Angela just that morning.

Every one of the alterations was next to Sister Beatrice's signature and that meant she would be the one to blame if anyone discovered these discrepancies. Angela considered whether she should take the book straight to the Warden or check the cupboard for herself that evening after Carole went home. Perhaps she ought to just tell Sister, because she would be very angry if she discovered that Angela had known and not told her.

Picking up the book, she went next door and knocked. Sister was holding something in her hand and staring at it in obvious bewilderment.

413

'Something wrong?'

'Yes, I have a packet of new dressings in my drawer and I have no idea how they got here.'

'Are they the new sterile dressings we bought last week?'

'Yes – how did you know?'

'They were marked as being used.' Angela handed her the record book. 'You will notice your signature next to the column showing we have none in stock . . .'

'Yes, but I put a one in the stock column when they were delivered. I know I did.' Sister looked at her, shock in her eyes. 'Why would I have taken them?'

'I do not believe for one moment that you did, Sister.'

'What are you saying?' Sister still seemed stunned, as though she doubted herself.

'If you care to look through these figures carefully and then check the stock cupboard I think you may find several errors. There are in all ten erasures. I think they are the ones to concentrate on.'

'But they all have my signature . . . I don't understand . . .'

'Someone is trying to make it look as if you are either careless or forgetful,' Angela said. 'You remember the accounts? You were puzzled because you never use an eraser. And the rota where Sally was double booked . . .'

'Yes, I do recall.' Sister frowned. 'Someone is making trouble for me – is that what you are telling me?'

'Yes, I'm afraid it looks that way.'

'Have you any idea who that might be?'

'I don't have proof,' Angela said. 'I have my suspicions, but I should like to check the medicines myself – with your help, perhaps this evening.'

'You mean after Carole has gone home?' Sister gave her a straight look. 'Why her, may I ask? She is a good, efficient nurse and I can see no reason why she would wish to harm me.' She paused. 'Are you sure this isn't personal, Angela?'

'I am quite sure,' Angela said. 'I think Carole has been lying about quite a few things and once I'm certain I shall confront her.'

'Then I shall check the cupboard with you and we'll see just what has been going on.'

Alice left St Saviour's after a long day on her feet. Her back ached more these days and she found the work tiring, because the children needed so much looking after and there was always another job waiting to be done. She'd changed Betsy's bed three times this week, because the little girl kept wetting it. Alice didn't know why the child was prone to bed-wetting; she supposed she ought to have spoken to a nurse about it, but Staff Nurse Carole had made it clear she didn't want to deal with girls like Alice, whom she considered beneath her.

Alice thought the little girl was unhappy, missing her mother. Because she cried a lot some of the other kids wouldn't bother with her. Mary Ellen tried to be kind and so did Marion, but Billy Baggins ignored her and most of the other kids made fun of her. Perhaps she ought to speak to Nan or Sister Beatrice about the child . . .

'Alice – how are you?'

'Bob!' Alice jumped as he came up to her out of the gloom. 'I was lost in thought and didn't see you. Are you on leave or another course?'

'I've got a week's leave,' Bob said and smiled at her. 'I thought you might like to go out one night – to the flicks or for something to eat?'

'Oh, Bob, it's so kind of you,' Alice said, regretful because she would love to be taken somewhere nice. 'But I can't let you spend your money on me.'

'Why not? It's mine and if that's what I want . . .'

'Bob, you don't understand,' Alice said, her throat catching. 'It wouldn't be fair to you . . .'

'Because you're havin' that bastard's kid?' Bob asked, and his face was grim in the yellowish light of the street lamps. 'No, Eric didn't tell me, even though I knew somethin' was wrong. I went round your house and your mother told me to clear off. Mavis ran after me and told me where you were living – and I got it out of her.'

'She shouldn't have told you. I don't want you to feel responsible for me . . .'

'I don't feel responsible. We know who's to blame, Alice – but I do care what happens to you. I care about you and I'd like to look after you, love. When I'm here I shall visit and take you out if you'll let me – and I'll find you a decent place to live after the baby's born, and help with money if you need it.'

'Why should you?' Alice demanded. 'None of this is your fault.'

Bob caught her by the arms, forcing her to look at him. 'Don't be so bloody daft, girl! I care about you whatever you've done. I'm not going away, Alice, so you might as well get used to me coming round. I know you don't love me – but I'm not askin' you to. I just want to look after you. Is that so wrong?'

'No . . .' Alice felt the tears sting her eyes. 'I'd like to go to the flicks tomorrow – if you're sure?'

'I wouldn't say if I wasn't, would I?' He grinned at her. 'I'll walk you home. Eric says you want to keep the baby and I'm glad – but if I were you I should buy a wedding ring before the baby comes. Tell people you're Mrs Robert Manning. I'll back you up and we'll get a place. I shall be away most of the time, as you know. Why not let people think I'm your husband? Lots of women have husbands away in the Army. It would make it easier for you.'

'Oh, Bob.' Alice sniffed hard. 'I wish it had been you.'

'So do I,' he said, and smiled gently. 'No use cryin' over spilled milk, Alice. We'll work something out for the future, you'll see.'

Alice swallowed hard but didn't answer. Bob hadn't asked her to marry him, and she was glad, because she would have had to turn him down, but he was willing to help her and she thought she might let him, at least until she could find a job that would allow her to look after herself and the child.

Bob was whistling cheerfully as he walked away from Nan's house, after waiting to see Alice safely inside. It looked as if she might let him help her find a home for herself and the unborn child. He was pleased that she wanted to keep the child, because it confirmed what he'd thought of her from the very beginning: she was a nice girl and cared about others.

Bob had known about the child for a couple of weeks now. It had taken him that long to come to terms with the fact that the girl he thought he was halfway to being

417

in love with was having that rotten bastard's baby. He hadn't been sure he could live with that and he'd taken time to think it through, the way he did everything. Some people thought Bob was slow, a bit colourless; he knew that Alice had thought that the first time they met, though he believed she liked him better now. Only when he was certain that he could accept the child, perhaps come to love it as though it were his own, did he decide to meet Alice.

Bob was hoping to show her that she could rely on him. Once the child was born Alice might wake up to the fact that Jack was a rotter and discover she liked him better. He chuckled to himself. It was a good thing he was a patient man, because he might have to wait for a while before she came to her senses and married him, but . . .

Bob never finished that thought, because as he started to cross the road a car came speeding out of the darkness, no lights showing in the dimly lit street. It caught Bob sideways as he turned, belatedly aware of its menace, tossing him and throwing him across the road as it disappeared into the distance and turned a corner.

FIFTY-THREE

Angela picked up the record of medicines and her note-book. She'd spent two hours checking the cupboard the previous evening, and made accurate notes of what was actually there, comparing it with the records of what had been bought and when. Two boxes of dressings and one of syringes were missing, also some sterilised needles and a box of tablets used for sedative drinks for sick children.

She and Sister had returned to their offices and made a thorough search. All the missing items had been found in Sister Beatrice's desk, hidden behind a pile of papers. She had been so shocked that she'd just sat and stared at them, unable to take in that someone had wanted to hurt her.

'I do not understand it,' she'd said, shaking her head. 'Why should she try to harm me . . . what have I done to her?'

'Of course you have done nothing,' Angela reassured her. 'Perhaps she wants your job here?'

'Ridiculous! She does not have the experience; the Board would never appoint her – they would look for a senior hospital matron.'

'Unless she happened to be the wife of one of the Board, perhaps?'

The colour left Sister's face and she sat down abruptly. 'No, really, I cannot believe it.'

'Well, I'm going to ask her for the truth,' Angela said. 'It is definitely her handwriting where your figures have been erased. That seven is nothing like yours.'

'You wish to speak to her yourself?'

'She is going to deny it, of course,' Angela said, 'but I know another of Carole's nasty secrets and I think I may just get her to make a little mistake of her own.'

Carole was searching the nurses' desk when Angela entered. The nurse looked harassed when she turned to see Angela watching her, and not a little annoyed. Fortunately, none of the beds were occupied by children this morning, which made it the perfect moment to confront her.

'What do you want?' Carole asked rudely. 'Have you had the medicine records?'

'Yes, I have the book here, Carole. I checked the cupboard last night – and discovered some surprising things.'

'What do you mean?' Carole demanded. 'I'm always careful about keeping it right . . .'

'Yes, I'm certain you are,' Angela said, sure now that she'd found her culprit. 'I've seen your little alterations and additions.'

'I've no idea what you mean. Those erasures are Sister Beatrice's, not mine – and I'm always finding mistakes in her work. She ticks things as being there but they aren't, as you must know if you checked the cupboard yourself.'

420

'Yes, I noticed certain items were missing,' Angela said. 'However, they have been found, and if you cared to look you will see that the record book is now accurate.'

'How dare you meddle with things that do not concern you? I shall tell Sister that you have been interfering. I dare say it was you that took the things. Now you're just trying to get me into trouble.'

'Oh, I think you can do that quite easily yourself,' Angela said. 'Sister knows all about it. She helped me check the cupboard and she and I found the missing items where you put them.'

'I didn't go near Sister's desk,' Carole exclaimed in fury. 'It could have been you that put them there . . .'

'Yes, but I didn't tell you where we found them,' Angela said, hiding her elation. 'You betrayed yourself, Carole. I knew it was you, but I might not have been able to prove my suspicions, but now I am certain, because you just told me.'

'You bitch!' Carole flew at her, trying to scratch her face, but Angela pushed her away and moved out of reach behind the desk. 'It's just because you're jealous – because I'm having Mark's baby and you can't stand that, can you? You wanted him yourself.'

'If I did want Mark I wouldn't try to catch him out with a dirty little trick like that,' Angela said. 'He may have gone to bed with you, Carole – but you're not pregnant. You have a period at the moment. I saw the evidence in your bag and you were in pain yesterday, and I'm afraid you were careless enough to leave a used towel in the bin in the nurses' rest room.'

'You checked?' Carole cried in disbelief, because she'd

remembered too late that she'd disposed of the towel as they usually did, wrapped in toilet paper. 'It could have belonged to Jean – she was here yesterday too. Michelle was on last night . . .'

'Neither of them have their periods at the moment, because I asked,' Angela said calmly. 'You're a liar and a cheat, Carole. You're not pregnant and you tried to falsify the accounts to hurt Sister Beatrice and you've made malicious attempts to alter this book for the same reason.'

'You can't prove any of this . . .'

'If I speak to Mark he will insist you see a doctor and I think at least one of my accusations will be proved – and you will no longer be working here. Sister Beatrice has requested that I give you a week's notice . . .'

'Damn you to hell!' Carole screamed. 'I don't need her rotten job – and as for you, if you tell Mark I'm not pregnant I'll . . .'

'Just what will you do, Carole?' Mark asked, walking into the ward at that moment. 'I think we both know that I asked you to marry me because you told me we were having a child . . .'

'I am – I was,' Carole screamed in frustration. 'It's that bitch, she's gone mad, accusing me of changing accounts and records . . .'

'I've just spoken to Sister Beatrice and she has told me everything,' Mark said. 'I knew Angela intended to confront you and I wanted to hear the truth. I think we both know nothing happened that night, Carole. It puzzled me, because I couldn't remember, and I thought it was unlikely that you would conceive the first time, even though you seemed so certain, but I do remember

422

now. I was drunk and I kissed you but that was all. It was my guilt that clouded my judgement and made me believe you.'

'Bloody marvellous lover you were,' Carole yelled, losing her head as the realisation that it was all over came to her. 'Well, you can have your darling Angela if you want her – and your ring.' She tore it from her finger and threw it at him. 'And Sister can keep her job. I've had enough of all of you.' She snatched up her bag and stormed out of the room.

'Angela, we have to talk,' Mark said as she put the record book in the cupboard and locked it.

'Yes, Mark. I'm going to be busy today – but perhaps you could ring me and we'll have a drink somewhere – soon?'

'Yes, of course,' he said. 'I'm sorry . . .'

Angela put the keys to the cupboard back in the desk and then left the room. Sister Beatrice would want to know what had happened – and she might be a bit displeased that Carole had left without serving notice. She'd left the unmasking to Angela but instead of the dignified reprimand Sister might have given, it had turned into a blazing row.

Angela could only hope that Sister would be more relieved than annoyed that her staff nurse had left in haste. As for Mark, things were not so straightforward. She wasn't ready to talk to him about Carole just yet. She needed to think . . .

FIFTY-FOUR

Alice looked up as one of the kitchen girls came into the staff room. At first she thought the girl had come to fetch the dirty mugs but she looked over her shoulder furtively, as though afraid of being heard.

'You're wanted urgently outside. He's waiting in the garden and says he has to speak to you – and he's in a hurry because he has a train to catch.'

'Who is?' Alice said, a cold shiver at her nape.

'He says he's your cousin – Eric, I think he said.'

'Why didn't you say so?' Alice ran out of the rest room. It must be something really urgent for Eric to come here. Was it her sister or one of her brothers? As she saw Eric standing uncomfortably near the side gate, she rushed up to him. 'What's wrong? Is it Mave?'

'No, it's Bob,' Eric said. 'He was knocked down by a speeding car after he left you last night . . .' He shook his head as Alice gasped. 'No, it's all right, love. He was lucky – just has a few bruises, that's all, but I thought you'd want to know he's in the London.'

'Oh no,' Alice said, tears pricking. 'He met me from work last night, Eric – I bet it's that Lee gang . . .'

'Why should they be interested in Bob?' Eric asked. 'I should think there could be others who might want to put a scare into him – he's a tough customer and he don't scare easily.'

'I wish I could go to the hospital straight away, but we're so short-staffed at the moment. It will have to wait until this evening.'

'Bob won't expect you to visit immediately, but I thought you should know.' He smiled at her. 'I'm sorry I have to leave in a hurry, but I have to get back to camp or they'll think I've gone AWOL.'

'You don't want to miss your train,' Alice said, and forced a smile. 'Thanks for coming to tell me.'

'It's the least I could do.' Eric hesitated, then, 'I think a lot of you, our Alice – and I know Bob cares about you. You could do a lot worse than him, you know.'

'Yes, I know,' Alice said, and sighed. 'I've been a fool, Eric. I've been lucky to have friends to help me – and I'll try to do better in future.'

Alice was thoughtful as she went back to work. If Bob really wanted to stand by her she would be daft to reject his offer – she only hoped Eric hadn't tried to soften the blow, because if Bob was really hurt she'd never forgive herself. Bob had once told one of Butcher Lee's men to leave her alone, and she was convinced that was the reason he'd been attacked. The Lee gang had once employed Jack and it was while escaping from them that he'd dumped Alice and sped off into the night in his car. If it hadn't been for them, he might have stayed out of trouble and still be alive. They were dangerous men and didn't like to be crossed.

Alice knew it was going to be a long day at work.

Usually she enjoyed caring for the children and didn't mind if she stayed late, but today she would be watching the clock, because she would worry about Bob until she'd been to see him in the hospital . . .

Alice could hardly believe it when she saw Bob waiting for her as she left St Saviour's that evening. She ran towards him, relieved that he hadn't been badly hurt.

'Oh, Bob,' she cried. 'I was going to visit you in the hospital; I thought you might be badly injured?'

'Just a few bruises. The doctor told me that I ought to have a broken leg at least, but I was lucky.'

'Eric said you were knocked down by a car? How can you be all right?'

'It's my martial arts training; I know how to fall,' Bob quipped, laughed and then winced as she grabbed at his arm. 'Just a bit sore still . . .'

'I'm so sorry, Bob. It's my fault for involving you in this mess.'

'How do you make that out?' Bob asked, and shook his head as she tried to explain. 'It had nothing to do with you, Alice. I told the military cops where to find that deserter who attacked you last year and they arrested him – he was badly beaten up for trying to resist arrest and I imagine he'll go down for a long time. I reckon it was one of his cronies that tried to do me down.'

'Bob . . . you must have known the Lee gang would come after you for causing them trouble. If that deserter informs on them . . .'

'He might get his sentence reduced if he does that,' Bob told her. 'I don't want to talk about them or him, Alice. I'm going to find a place for you to live and . . .'

'Bob, I can't let you after what happened,' Alice said brokenly. 'If you hang around me they will come after you again. They think I know something about Jack and they want him – but I don't know anything. Everyone says he's dead so why do they bother with me?'

'If they're following you, they must have a good reason; perhaps they don't believe what the papers said about his body being found in the fire, or they think you could tell them something they want to know – and that means you need looking after even more. I'm not goin' to desert you, Alice. I wasn't aware of the car coming up behind me with no lights until it was too late, but I'll keep a sharper eye out in future. It was a cowardly attack because they know I can take care of myself. Anyway, I care about you, Alice, and if you think I'm going to desert you, you can think again.'

'It's not right,' Alice said as he took her arm. 'I can manage, Nan and Michelle will help me.'

Bob looked at her hard. 'You're crying . . .'

'No, I'm not. It's just that you're so good and I don't deserve it . . .'

'You've got a soft heart, love,' Bob said, and tucked his arm in hers. 'I've got something nice to show you before we go to the flicks – but perhaps you'd rather wait for another day?'

'What is it?'

'It's your new home,' Bob told her, and grinned. 'It's one of the flats the council put up a few years back. The block escaped most of the bomb damage, which was a miracle, and there's a ground-floor flat empty. It needs a coat of paint in all the rooms but I can soon do that . . . and there's a bit of a yard and a shed where you can put things out the back.'

'One of those newish ones in Bethnal Green?' Alice asked, excited.

'Yes.' He smiled. 'We'll get the tram and take a look and then have a bite of supper before I get you back to Nan's house. I've put my name down for the flat and it will be my name on the rent book, so I'll be paying the rent, Alice.'

'Bob, I can't let you . . .' she protested, but he hushed her with a finger to her lips.

'In my pocket I've got something for you . . .' He took out a small box and opened it to show her a gold wedding band and a gypsy-style gold ring with three garnets and two small diamonds. 'You can wear these and pretend you're my wife, Alice – but if you want, we can get married and make it for real.'

Alice's heart jolted, her eyes wide and anxious as she looked at him. 'You can't want to marry me . . . knowing I'm carryin' Jack's child . . .'

'I can accept it if you can,' he said, 'but the choice is yours. They belong to you anyway. Put them on, because we have to get the key from someone and I don't want them to look down on you for a start.'

He took her hand and Alice allowed him to slide the rings onto her third finger; they fitted snugly and looked right for her. She gave him a tremulous smile but couldn't find the words to answer him. Alice wasn't in love with Bob, but the man she'd loved had let her down – and Sally's tragedy had brought the truth home to her. Life could be very short.

'It wouldn't be fair to you, Bob,' she said but she was wavering and his expression told her he knew it.

'I care about you, Alice. I think we could be happy together. Come and see the place I've found for us.'

Alice let him pull her towards the tram stop. Once on board, she looked at the rings on her finger and all of a sudden she knew she was going to do it. Jack was out of her life. She would never see him again. Bob knew she wasn't in love with him. If he was satisfied with just friendship and sharing a home, why should she turn him down?

She turned to smile at him, her hand reaching for his. Words were not necessary. Alice knew she was going to marry Bob, but once she was his wife she would be good to him.

She was lucky to get the chance. Poor Sally had lost everything. Alice wasn't going to risk that happening to her.

FIFTY-FIVE

'I miss Sally,' Mary Ellen said to Billy as they sat on the back stairs sharing a bag of Tom Thumb drops that Rose had brought for her. She sucked on the last of the tiny fruit drops, enjoying the mixture of flavours that you got from the sweets if you put a small handful in your mouth. 'When do you think she will come back?'

'Dunno.' Billy shrugged. 'It's rotten luck for her, ain't it? I reckon they were gonna get married one day – just like us.'

'It's "going to", Billy,' she said. 'Remember what Sally told you. You have to learn to talk proper if you want to get to grammar school and pass all them exams so you can be a train driver.'

'I forget sometimes,' he said, and grinned at her. 'Nancy's all right though, ain't she? I know she ain't really one of the carers, but she's standin' in for Sally in the mornings.'

'I'm goin' to ask Miss Angela when Sally's coming back,' Mary Ellen said. 'I heard she went to see her the other night and took some flowers and a card from the staff. I reckon we ought to send a card too . . . signed by all of us, all the kids at St Saviour's.'

'Now you're talkin',' Billy said, tipping his head to one side. 'Ask Miss Angela if she'll get us one. I've got three pennies in my pocket.'

'I've got the same. I think Marion will give us a penny or two and so will Sarah and some of the others. We want a really big posh one with satin on the front and then we can all sign it.'

'Go and ask her now before they ring the bell for tea,' Billy said. 'I'll have a whip round and see what we can raise. We might get some jelly sweets too.'

'No, I think it should just be a lovely card from all of us,' Mary Ellen said, jumping to her feet. 'I'll tell Miss Angela now – but first I'll go and see Nancy. I'm sure she will want to know what we're doing.'

'That's lovely, miss,' Mary Ellen said the next day when Angela showed her the card she'd bought with their one shilling and sixpence. It had a pretty picture of roses on the front and a big bow of satin ribbon. 'We're all going to sign it, every one of us – and then if you could take it to her for us, please?'

'Yes, of course I will, Mary Ellen. It is a lovely idea and I'm sure it will cheer her up a little.'

'When is she coming back? We all miss her. Betsy was crying for her last night after supper.'

'Yes, I miss her too,' Angela said. 'Sally is very unhappy, Mary Ellen. I know she will come when she can – but she's going to train to be a nurse one day soon.'

'And then she's coming back to us, she told us so,'

Mary Ellen said. 'Thank you for getting the card for us, miss. I'm going to make sure everyone signs it.'

'Yes, that will be nice for Sally.'

'Nancy is with the little ones now. I'll start there.' Mary Ellen went off, clutching the expensive card.

Angela sat looking at the door of her office, frowning as she thought about her first visit to Sally. She'd been in bed and Mrs Rush had been doubtful about sending her up to her daughter's room, but Brenda had intervened.

'If anyone can bring Sally out of herself it's Angela,' she said. 'They are friends, real friends, Mum – and that's what our Sally needs now. Friends she can rely on.'

'Well, she certainly won't listen to me.' Mrs Rush looked as if she wanted to burst into tears. 'I've tried telling her I'm sorry for what happened – and don't look at me like that, Brenda. I could cut out my tongue when I think of what I said to her that night. I couldn't know he was going to die . . .'

'I'm sure Sally will understand that when she starts to heal,' Angela said. 'What she needs is time. If I could just take her the flowers and card: they're from all of us.'

Mrs Rush had given in and Brenda had shown her up, knocking at her sister's door to announce a visitor. Angela had expected Sally to be in bed, but instead she was fully clothed, sitting on the counterpane and surrounded by pamphlets about nursing, half of which she appeared to have torn in half.

'These are from all the staff,' Angela said, sitting next to her on the edge of the bed. 'We all signed the card. Everyone is thinking of you, Sally. We wanted you to know that we understand . . .'

'How can they?' Sally asked and raised her head to look at her. Angela was shocked at how dull her eyes were. She wouldn't have been surprised had they been red from crying but instead they just looked empty, hopeless.

Impulsively, she sat forward and touched her friend's hand. 'I think I can understand a little. It isn't very long since I lost the man I loved . . .'

Sally made a negative movement of her head. 'I know you loved John, but it isn't the same. You were married . . .'

'Yes, for a very short time. I regretted we hadn't had longer – but do you know what I regretted most?'

Sally's attention was caught; for a moment interest flickered in her eyes. 'What? I thought you loved him and he loved you?'

'But we quarrelled on his last leave. It was just a silly quarrel but it hurt John and I couldn't forgive myself.'

Sally's hand clenched, as if she wanted to hit out at something or someone.

'I was going to tell Andrew I couldn't see him so often until my nursing exams were over. My mother was pleased. She thought it would split us up – and it might have. I was willing to risk that – but I didn't know what it would feel like being without him . . . knowing I could never see his face or touch his hand . . .'

A sob burst from Sally and she sat quivering as Angela put her arms about her. For a moment or two she tolerated Angela's hold but then she moved away, and her expression was hard. 'I'm not going to be a nurse now. There's no point . . .'

Angela saw that she'd torn up the details of the

nursing course. 'You mustn't just give up, Sally. Your nursing is important to you.'

'I don't know what I want,' Sally admitted. She looked at the flowers. 'Thank you for these – and the card.'

'It wasn't just me. Everyone cares about you – and the children miss you, Sally.'

'I can't come back yet. I should keep looking for him.' A little sobbing breath left Sally's lips. 'I just want the chance to tell him how much I love him . . .'

'Yes, I know.' Angela ached to comfort her, but Sally wasn't ready to be comforted. She had a mountain of grief, guilt and regret squashing her and it would take time to fight her way out from under it. Angela had known it was too soon to reach her.

Sighing now as she headed home, she turned her mind to her own problems. She'd been almost off-hand with Mark when he'd suggested they had to talk and she wondered if he'd taken offence, because he hadn't rung her or come to see her.

Perhaps he was upset because Carole had turned out to be a spiteful little cat who had lied to trick him into marrying her; perhaps Angela had been wrong to think he didn't really care for the girl.

FIFTY-SIX

Beatrice was sitting at her desk, staring at the words she'd written. Carole had been a disaster and she wanted to draw a line under the whole affair. The girl had run off without serving notice and without her wages for the week. Her packet was made up and it would remain in the drawer until the girl sent for it – if she ever did.

What worried Beatrice was how wrong she'd been. Carole had been her choice and she'd believed she was reliable. Now they had to start all over again, and how could she be sure that she chose a good nurse with good character? Carole's references had been excellent.

A knock at the door heralded Angela's arrival with the neatly typed monthly report, which she placed on the desk. Instead of leaving, she lingered, clearly wanting to talk.

'Something on your mind?'

'It's about Sally,' Angela said, and frowned. 'I saw her last night briefly. She says she'll be returning to St Saviour's next week – and she isn't going to take up her nursing place . . .'

'Why ever not? If any of my carers is suited to a nursing career it is Sally.'

'Yes, I know. I have tried telling her that but I can't get through to her. She seems better, even smiled at me and loved the card from the children – but she says there's no point in becoming a nurse now, that she should not try to improve herself but stay in her class.'

'Now that is arrant nonsense!' Beatrice cried. 'Where does she think I began? Just because some of my nurses had a better start in life, I certainly didn't. I had to begin at the bottom, and it was harder then than it is now.' She shook her head. 'I'll go and see her myself this evening. I thought I ought to wait, give her time – but she needs some straight talking before this rubbish becomes implanted too deeply in her mind.'

Angela smiled and inclined her head. 'Just what I thought – but it would be much better coming from you than from me. I am her friend and I shall be there for her when she's ready – but Sally looks up to you, Sister. She will listen to what you have to say. I think it is to do with her mother and some quarrel they had about her not being of Mr Markham's class.'

'And that is utter rubbish too. Andrew Markham was a lovely man and he hadn't a snobbish bone in his body. It's Sally's mother who sounds as if she's been putting foolish ideas in the girl's head.'

'Yes, I'm sure you're right. Mothers have a lot to answer for sometimes.'

'Indeed.' Beatrice looked grim. 'I'll go and see Sally this evening. Much as we shall miss her, she owes it to herself to go on with her nursing.'

* * *

436

'Sally, you've got a visitor. Please come down.' Mrs Rush stood at the door of her daughter's bedroom. Sally was lying on the bed cover, just staring at the ceiling. 'I don't know why you're sulking up here alone . . .'

'No, you wouldn't understand.' Sally didn't look at her. 'Angela won't mind coming up to see me and I'd rather talk in private.'

'Oh, I know you blame me,' her mother said, a mixture of pain and anger in her tone. 'You have to snap out of this, Sally – and it isn't Angela. It's Sister Beatrice. I asked her to go into the parlour but she insisted on following me into the kitchen – and I've your father's tea to get . . .'

'Sister Beatrice? Here to see me?'

Sally got up from the bed sharply, her respect for the nun making her respond despite a strong desire to be alone. It wasn't exactly that she blamed her mother for anything; after all she'd made the decision herself, but she couldn't forgive herself for thinking it didn't matter if Andrew wouldn't wait . . . that she'd been prepared to hurt him because of her own desires and needs. It was if God was punishing her for her ambition.

'All right, I'll come down now.'

Sally looked at herself in the mirror. Her eyes were no longer red, because the tears had dried up, leaving an aching emptiness behind. Nothing seemed worth the effort any more. She knew she had to return to work soon, but she shrank from the pity she would see in the eyes of her friends and colleagues; she didn't deserve their sympathy. She'd been selfish and horrid and she wished she could go back to before Andrew had left for that conference, to the moment when he'd said he

437

might bring her something special back and she'd known he was talking about a ring. She'd smiled and shaken her head, not wanting him to push things so fast, and that made her feel guilty – as if she was to blame for the accident, as if she'd caused it by her selfish decision. Yet Andrew hadn't even known of her decision, because she'd made it while he was away.

Having tidied herself quickly, Sally went down the stairs. Pausing outside the kitchen door, she heard Sister Beatrice's voice.

'Really, Mrs Rush, I'm quite comfortable here. You have a very pleasant home, similar to my father's house when I was a small child. We lived in Wapping then and he only moved out to a better area after his father died and he inherited the house. I'm quite accustomed to sitting in the kitchen.'

'But you're the Warden of St Saviour's and a nun . . . it's not right . . .'

'I'm just the same as your daughter and yourself, Mrs Rush. I happen to have a different job, that's all.' Sister Beatrice looked up and smiled as Sally entered. 'Ah, there you are, my dear. I am glad to see you and I wanted to talk to you about the future. I think it would be a good idea if you put your coat on and we went for a little walk. I always think it is easier to talk in the open air – besides, you look peaky and it will do you good.'

'You could be private in the parlour,' Mrs Rush said, but was ignored.

'I'll get my coat.' Sally took it from the hook on the door, following Sister Beatrice outside into the chilly night air. 'There's a café just down the road. We could have a cup of tea there. I'm sorry Mum is such a snob.'

438

'Your mother does her best, Sally. My mother thought she was doing the right thing when she persuaded me into making the worst mistake of my life.'

'Mothers . . .' Sally smiled a little ruefully. 'I didn't think you ever made mistakes, Sister. You always seem to know exactly what to do . . .'

'I wish I did,' Sister said. 'You're very young, Sally. At the moment you feel that life is over and you will never be happy again, but you will. In time the pain will ease and disappear to a small corner of your heart. It may never go completely, because I believe you sincerely loved him.'

'Yes, I did.' Sally caught back a sob. 'I didn't know how much until it was too late.'

'I once loved someone and lost him.'

'I'm so sorry.'

'Don't be, Sally. Out of that despair sprang my need to do something worthwhile. It was a struggle for me to be accepted as a nurse. I could have been an auxiliary immediately, but that wasn't enough for me. Nursing is a calling, Sally, not just a job.'

'Yes – but I'm not sure I could ever be good enough. I thought I could – but I wanted to be better than I am – and Mum says I've brought my present misery on myself because I should never have tried to be more than I am. I just wanted to be good enough for him, because I loved him.'

'Your mother is no doubt well-meaning but wrongheaded,' Sister Beatrice said in a tone that brooked no opposition. 'She does have a point, though. You thought Andrew was a class above you, but you were wrong; there is no such thing as class when it comes to love.

439

He didn't give it a thought and nor should you. Where nursing is concerned that is a vocation and class doesn't come into it. If you excel as a nurse you can rise to the top, whatever your background. I think you will be an excellent nurse, Sally.'

'I'm not sure I can . . .'

'Nonsense! You've already applied and I insist that you take up the position and then return to us when you have the qualification of State Registered Nurse. Indeed, I shall be very cross if you let me down. None of us knows what the future will be, but whatever happens to you in life, Sally, your nursing training will give you independence and a career.'

Sally had stopped walking outside the small café; its windows were steamed up and the paintwork was dirty from the filth of the roads left by passing traffic, but she knew the inside was spotless. 'Here it is – shall we have a cup of tea?'

'Is it clean and decent?'

'Yes, quite nice for simple food and they make a good cup of tea.'

'Then we'll go in,' Sister Beatrice said. 'I dare say you're feeling guilty, blaming yourself over what happened, even though you played no part in the accident.'

'How did you know?'

Sister Beatrice laughed and tapped the side of her long nose with her gloved finger. 'Most women feel that way at some time in their lives. I think it's something to do with our genes. We bear the guilt from the day we're born until the day we die . . . in history women were often seen as sinful creatures for tempting mankind by the holy men of their time, so it's bred into us.'

'That's a bit unfair, isn't it?' Sally asked, totally bewildered by a side of Sister Beatrice that she hadn't known existed.

'Completely,' Sister agreed heartily as she sat down on the hard wooden chair. 'But have you noticed that men can't manage without us? We have broad shoulders, Sally, most of us, and we can bear more than our fair share of grief, pain and work. Of course there are a few weak sisters amongst us, but we aren't a part of their brigade, are we, Sally? I think you're like me and you'll come through this and go on to become the woman Andrew knew you would be one day. He saw something in you that perhaps your mother cannot see. It won't happen at once, and the pain goes slowly at first – but I promise you that in the end you'll be able to laugh again.'

'You've made me feel better tonight,' Sally said. 'Thank you for coming, Sister. Everyone is so sorry for me, so apologetic. I think I needed a kick up the backside.'

'Any time,' Sister said, and smiled at her in a way that could only be described as wicked. 'Now, do you know what I quite fancy?' Sally shook her head. 'Do you think there's a chance they might be able to serve us fried egg and chips?'

'Well, what did she have to say?' Sally's mother asked when she returned to the kitchen. Brenda and her father had finished eating and were drinking tea. 'I suppose it was good of her to come – but hardly her business.'

'It was very good of her to come,' Sally said. 'She wants me to return to work on Monday and then to go on with my nursing career as planned.'

'Are you going to?'

'Yes, I think I shall. Sister Beatrice made me see that I owe it to myself to make what I can of my life.'

'You can listen to her . . .' Mrs Rush sniffed and looked upset. 'Haven't I been saying the same thing – but you won't listen to me . . .'

'Leave Sally alone, Mum,' Brenda said. 'I'm glad you're going to be a nurse, Sally, love, but it must be your choice – not Mum's and not Sister Beatrice's.'

'It is my choice,' Sally said, and heard her mother sniff louder.

'Now, Mother.' Sally's father intervened before she could speak. 'You can just stop that nonsense. If Sally is upset about what you said before the accident you've only yourself to blame. Personally, I liked Andrew. I spoke to him just the once or twice, but he loved my girl – and as far as I'm concerned that's all that matters. I wouldn't have minded them getting married, if it was what Sally wanted.'

'I know and I'm sorry I said anything,' Mrs Rush mumbled, and then burst into tears. 'I wish I could take it all back, Sally . . . I wish I could turn the clock back . . .'

'It's all right, Mum.' Sally struggled to get the words out, because it hurt too much. She hadn't forgiven her mother for all the things she'd said against Andrew, but she knew she had to take the first step or the divide would become too wide and too bitter. 'I understand. You felt uncomfortable with the idea, but if you'd really known him . . . Sister Beatrice told me how his parents were doctors and missionaries, and how he was brought up by his aunt after they died in Africa. I didn't know

442

any of that . . . yes, he had some money left to him, and he went to university and was clever, but underneath he was very like Dad.' She turned her tear-filled eyes on her father. 'He liked you too, Dad. I think he hoped you would be friends when we married.'

'I should have enjoyed that. He was a clever chap and I respect people with brains. He didn't live his life for the sake of money or position, he gave his time for free often and he cared for others – you can't say fairer than that . . .'

'No.' Sally felt the tears of release trickle down her cheeks. The pain wasn't going to go away for a long time, but perhaps Sister was right – working for others, dedicating her life to easing pain, particularly in children, yes, that was worth trying for. She'd been foolish to think she had to give it up to punish herself, because that's what she'd been doing – punishing herself for being alive when Andrew was dead. It wasn't her fault he'd died, and in her heart she knew that although he might have been disappointed, he would have accepted her decision and gone on loving her, helping her – because that was how he was. 'You can't say fairer than that, Dad.'

FIFTY-SEVEN

Angela's phone rang and she answered it automatically. 'Angela Morton – can I help you?'

'Angela, I hope you're not busy for a minute? I need to talk to you, my love.'

'You know I always have time for you, Dad,' she said. 'I was thinking I might try to get down again soon.'

'No, not just for the moment.' He sounded hesitant. 'It's the reason I rang you. Mark has been down here for a few days and your mother has been seeing him as a patient. He's persuaded her to go to a special clinic in Switzerland – and we're both flying out this weekend.'

'You're going with Mum?' Angela asked anxiously. 'Are you feeling well enough? I could come if you wish?'

'Your mother doesn't want you to come. She can't face you, Angela . . .'

'That's foolish, I only want to help her – and you.'

'She feels ashamed, I think,' he said. 'She hardly speaks to me, but of course I must take her – don't worry, I'm feeling better since my doctor gave me some new pills.'

'You know I'll help with the expenses.'

'Of course, my love. I'll come up to town and we'll talk about the future when I get back.'

'Yes – how long has Mark been treating her?'

'The first time was a few weeks ago. He came to the house while I was out and she must have asked him to take her on then. She doesn't tell me much, and they kept it a secret even from me, but once she'd agreed to go away, Mark asked me if I would consent to her having treatment in the clinic and of course I agreed.'

'Well, we must hope it helps her,' Angela said. 'Take care of yourself and let me know when you're back.'

'Of course . . .' He hesitated, then, 'Are you all right, Angela? You sound a bit subdued.'

'I'm fine,' Angela lied. 'Thank you for letting me know. I love you – and give my love to Mum too.'

'Yes, I shall. I'll see you very soon, love.'

Replacing the receiver Angela frowned. Once again Mark had kept her in the dark and she felt shut out. Naturally, he couldn't tell her whatever his mother had confided in her, but he could have told her that he was seeing her as a patient. Did that mean he still felt she was fragile?

She'd been regretting her off-hand manner that day in the sick room, but now she wasn't sure of anything. If Mark cared for her, why hadn't he at least phoned her – and why couldn't he have told her that her mother had become his patient?

Shrugging off her annoyance, Angela checked the list she'd prepared for Sister. She would take it to her and then visit Nancy. So far the girl seemed to be taking her brother's removal to the clinic quite well, but underneath she must be grieving.

* * *

Angela returned to her office that evening after having a long talk with Nancy. The girl was returning to school for another year so that she could get her leaving certificate, but once she left she would take up a full-time position at St Saviour's.

'It's what I want to do for now, miss,' she'd told Angela. 'If I can have Terry back one day I'll make a home for him, but for now I want to work here as a carer. I think I understand how some of the children feel – and perhaps I can help them.'

'You wouldn't rather try to be a teacher or a nurse?'

'I don't think I'm clever enough for that,' Nancy said truthfully. 'I'd rather not go back to school at all, but Sister told me she would be in trouble if she let me stay off indefinitely so I've decided I'll go.'

'Yes, I do understand how you feel,' Angela said. 'This has become your home, hasn't it?'

'I feel safe here, miss. I never had a real home – not for years anyway. It was all right until Ma turned funny, but after Aunt Molly died . . . well, everything went bad. Perhaps one day I'll have a home of me own, but I shan't get married.'

'You might change your mind one day, Nancy. Men are not all like your father . . .'

'What he did to me, miss . . . it's there in my head and it won't ever go. I couldn't bear anyone to touch me the way he did.'

'It wouldn't be like that, Nancy. I know how you feel now, but one day things may look different.'

'Sister said I could talk to Mr Adderbury about what happened, but I can't, miss – I can't ever tell anyone what he did . . . it shames me. I should have killed him rather than put up with it for years, but Terry did that for me – and now he's paying the price.'

'Perhaps they will let him come to you one day, Nancy.'

'No, I don't think so. He was always a bit strange, but as a little boy he was loving – it was after Pa started to beat him and mock him that he became violent . . .' Tears trickled down Nancy's cheeks. 'Pa ruined all our lives, miss. I'm glad he's dead but I wish it hadn't been Terry that killed him . . . I think what happened that night drove him over the edge.'

'Yes, I know – but you can't be sure. Perhaps it really was an accident,' Angela said, but she knew that Nancy would always believe it had been her brother, and because of that her pain would remain locked inside her until something happened to make it go away.

Angela had just sat down that evening with a tray of coffee and some delicious biscuits Nancy had baked for her. The girl was getting very good at her cooking. Slipping off her shoes, Angela lifted her cup to her lips as the phone rang.

'Angela, you're in,' Mark said. 'I wanted to tell you first . . .'

'Where are you?' she asked. 'You sound pleased?'

'Yes, it's good news about Terry. I'm at the clinic. We gave him some radical new therapy in the hope of bringing him out of the catatonic state he was in; it's all a bit experimental at present, but it seems to have worked. Afterwards, he was subdued, but aware of us talking to him and he seems to be taking things calmly.'

'That's good, isn't it?'

'Yes, we think so. It is very early days, of course, but my colleagues think that after a course of treatments we may be able to reach the tortured side of him and perhaps help him to come to terms with whatever happened.'

'Does this mean he will be able to come home one day?'

'That is something I am unable to answer,' Mark said. 'I wanted you to know that there is an improvement – and perhaps you can tell Nancy?'

'Yes, of course,' Angela said. She hesitated, then, 'You didn't tell me that you'd been treating my mother and she'd agreed to go to a clinic in Switzerland.'

'She particularly asked me not to,' he said apologetically. 'I know you would have preferred to be told – but I could not break my trust as her consultant. Please don't be angry with me, Angela.'

'I was just a little hurt. I know I was fragile after John died, but I'm so much stronger now.'

'Of course I know that,' he said. 'I'm so proud of you, Angela. You're doing a wonderful job at St Saviour's. You must know how much I think of you?'

'I wasn't sure . . .'

'All this business with Carole . . .' He sounded strange. 'I know what you must think of me – but I can't explain. I suppose I was low and I fell for a very obvious temptation. It makes me look a fool, I know, but we all make mistakes.'

'Was it a mistake?'

'Yes, and I'm grateful to you for exposing her lies. She was quite a schemer, it seems.'

'Yes – but she's gone now.'

'Yes . . .' He hesitated. 'I should like to have dinner soon, but it can't be just yet. I've been asked to do a series of lectures and I'll be out of town for some weeks. It's to help with the effects of war on men damaged by their experiences. I accepted before . . .'

'It's all right, Mark. I think we should give ourselves a little more time.'

'Yes, perhaps you're right.' There was a charged pause, then, 'I do care for you a great deal, Angela. I'll be in touch when I get back.'

Angela sat staring into space after he hung up. She had a curious ache in her heart, because surely if Mark truly loved her he could have made time to take her out before he went off on this lecture tour. Perhaps he was too embarrassed to admit he'd fallen for a girl who had obviously used him. At any rate, he wasn't ready to commit to Angela.

She sighed and stood up. She would go to tell Nancy the news and then . . .

Her door opened and Nan entered with a bright smile on her face. 'I've got some wonderful news for you,' she said. 'Alice has just told me – she is going to marry a soldier. His name is Bob and he knows all about the child and that rotter Jack Shaw. I've told her I'll help with the reception and the other things she'll need, though he's giving her some money for clothes. He's got some time off now and they've arranged it for next week. She brought him in to see me last night and he seems a nice lad.'

'That's wonderful,' Angela said. 'Exactly what we all need after what's been happening here! I'd like to contribute to the wedding breakfast, Nan, but you needn't tell Alice – and you may know what can I get her for a present?'

'I know she likes modern stuff, but I imagine they will need everything: china, linen, pans – anything you can find, I should think.'

'Yes, of course.' Angela nodded.

'Sister is delighted,' Nan said. 'She'd been pressing me to persuade Alice to have her child adopted, but now of course it will all be respectable. I shan't have to sack her and she could come in to work here for a few hours when she's over the birth – if she wants . . .'

FIFTY-EIGHT

'You look really pretty, Alice,' Sally said as she twisted Alice's fine fair hair into a knot of fluffy curls at the back. Alice had washed it earlier and it had taken an age to dry, because they didn't have a blow dryer. While they waited for her hair to set, Sally had filed and polished her friend's nails with a natural pale gloss. Alice had sat patiently while Michelle had applied a tiny touch of rouge to her cheeks and a pale rose lipstick to her mouth. 'I had no idea you could look this beautiful.'

'I'm not beautiful,' Alice said and laughed, putting both her hands on her bump. 'I'm too fat and this isn't what I'd have chosen to look like for my wedding if I'd had a choice.'

'Well, you're several months pregnant,' Michelle told her in a no-nonsense tone. 'Bob would've married you weeks ago if you'd let him . . .'

Alice looked regretful. 'Bob isn't the father and I felt it was wrong to push another man's child on him – but he doesn't seem to mind. I'm so lucky and I don't deserve it.'

'Of course you do.' Sally gave her hair a final pat.

'Bob knows the truth and he still cares for you so you should just accept it and be happy.'

'Yes, I am happy,' Alice said, feeling slightly uncomfortable. Sally had lost the man she loved to a tragic car accident and it must have cost her a lot to come here and help Alice get ready for the wedding. 'You're all so good to me.'

'We all care about you, Alice. You're one of us and after that awful man left you in the lurch . . . well, marrying Bob is the best thing that could happen to you.'

'Yes, I know.' Alice wasn't certain in her own mind that she'd done the right thing, but in a few hours she would be Mrs Robert Manning instead of plain Alice Cobb. 'As I said, I'm very lucky.'

'Well, I reckon it's Bob that's lucky,' Mavis said, bringing the pale cream suit that Alice had chosen for her wedding. It had a loose wrap-over waist and a skirt that fell about her hips in fine pleats, ending just below her knees. The jacket was long and covered her bump, though nothing could quite hide the fact that she was around six months pregnant. 'You'll make him a good wife, Alice, and you're a real good cook.'

'At least Ma taught us both to cook,' Alice said, a wry smile on her lips.

'Is your mother coming to the wedding?' Michelle asked as Alice placed the tiny hat on her head; it was a confection of net and flowers in pink and red and went well with Alice's red shoes and gloves.

'No, she refused, told Dad she was ashamed of me and wasn't going to relent just because I'd trapped some idiot man into weddin' me.'

'She couldn't have said that?' Sally gasped in horror. 'Oh, Alice, that's so unfair of her. Bob wants to marry you – and you haven't done anything a lot of other girls in love haven't done before you.'

'It doesn't matter,' Alice said and glanced at Nan, who stood watching them all. 'Nan has been as good as any mother to me – she will be my baby's granny, won't you, Nan?'

'Of course.' Nan smiled at her. 'Me and Eddie are looking forward to the christening – and babysitting . . .'

Alice smiled back. 'Bob says I've got to stay home now and take care of myself until the baby is born – but he doesn't mind me doing a few hours at St Saviour's afterwards.'

'My mother might help with babysitting for a few hours sometimes,' Michelle said. 'It's a pity your mother won't – but at least your father is coming to the wedding.'

'He said he wouldn't miss my wedding for the world. He was angry over the child and the fact that it was Jack Shaw's.' Alice sighed. 'But he's forgiven me now that I'm marrying a decent bloke and he likes Bob. He'll visit me and he'll make sure that Mave and my brothers can come when they like too. I just hope he'll stay sober.'

'Of course he will,' Mavis said. 'He won't let you down today, Alice.'

'Are you ready, Alice?' Her father's voice came from outside the door. 'The cars are here. We've got to leave or we'll be late.'

'Yes, Dad, I'm ready now.' Alice picked up the small posy of pink roses that Bob had sent to her as her father opened the bedroom door. 'Will I do?'

'You look lovely,' he told her and offered his arm. 'I'm proud of my girl, Alice. You're a lovely lass, kind and decent, and don't you let anyone tell you different.'

Alice smiled, the cloud of doubt that had hung over her since she woke that morning beginning to disperse. She had been helplessly in love with the charmer, who had swept her off her feet, making her forget all she'd been taught, but he'd left her in the lurch and she'd promised to marry Bob – and she would be true to him.

Alice stood with her hand on her new husband's arm, a fluttering sensation inside as he thanked everyone for coming and for their lovely gifts.

'We are grateful for everything,' Bob said, 'but most of all it's good to know we've got such good friends. I hope you will all support Alice when I'm away – and I thank you all for coming today. We have to go now or we shall miss our train.'

The next minute they were leaving the pub and their guests, standing for a moment outside on the pavement as the car Bob had hired waited to take them to the railway station. Alice tossed her bouquet in the air and Angela caught it, laughing as the others teased her and asked who the lucky man was. Neither Sally nor Michelle had tried for it, though Jean, Mavis and Nan had reached up, but somehow it had fallen into Angela's hands. She laughed and smiled, waving at Alice as they got into the car, joining her good wishes to all the others.

Bob had spoken for both of them when he'd thanked them for being their friends just now. Alice felt blessed to know that so many people cared about her. She'd known Michelle and Sally would come, also Angela, but the others had been a bonus – and her father's support had meant everything. He'd bullied her brothers into cleaning themselves up for once, and they'd come along, looking uncomfortable in white school shirts, trousers and ties, but grinning all over their faces as they threw handfuls of confetti over her. She knew they'd come for the wedding tea more than anything else, but she was just glad they were here. Her mother's absence was hurtful but no more than she'd expected, because Mrs Cobb was a stubborn woman and it would take an earthquake to move her once she made up her mind.

'Everything all right, Alice, love?' Bob asked when they were in the car and speeding towards the station. 'It was a nice do even if it was in a pub and not a hotel – didn't you think?'

'Lovely,' Alice said, and smiled at him shyly. 'You've made everything lovely for me, Bob – thank you for all you've done . . .'

'You don't have to be grateful,' he said, looking serious as he reached out and took her hand in his. Alice's hand trembled because she was nervous, though determined not to be. 'And don't be worryin' your head over the future either, love. You married me because I asked and because it was better for you – but I know you're not in love with me. I don't mind, Alice, because I love you and I believe you will come to love me – but I'm patient. I can wait and that means for all of it. I don't expect you to hop in bed and make passionate love, but I hope you'll let me hold you and kiss you sometimes . . . and we can be more than friends in time.'

'Oh, Bob,' Alice said, and her eyes stung with tears. 'You're so good to me . . . I don't know why you care for me, but I'm so glad you do. I may not be ready for marital relations yet, but after the baby is born . . .'

'Let's wait and see,' Bob said, and leaned in to kiss her gently on the lips. 'I'll never force you. I promise you that, Alice. I'll just wait and hope until you're ready.'

Alice nodded and held onto his hand. She was too filled with emotion to answer, but she hung on as if she would never let him go. Bob was a decent man and one day . . . one day she would repay all he'd given her.

FIFTY-NINE

It had been a lovely wedding the previous day, Angela's one regret being that Mark hadn't been there with her. She was missing him more than she would have believed but he hadn't rung her once since he'd left on his lecture tour and she thought he was avoiding her.

Approaching the door of Sister's office, she heard the gentle laughter coming from inside. Father Joe was visiting, and by the sound of them they were enjoying a chat and a drink.

Another chuckle from inside Sister's office made Angela turn from the door with a smile on her face. Her business would wait until the morning. It was time she was on her way home if she was going to have a meal before the last rehearsal for the concert, but first she wanted to speak to Sally. Much to Angela's surprise, Sally had helped Alice get ready for her wedding, and although she hadn't smiled much during the reception, she'd made the effort to go and that must surely show she was improving.

She thought about Mark as she sat in the back of the taxi and let it take her to Sally's home. Later, she would be seeing Father Joe herself at the rehearsal at the church, but she wanted to change first and have a bite to eat. Perhaps she could persuade Sally to come to the rehearsal.

Pulling up her coat collar against the cold wind, she got out of the taxi and paid the driver off. She could catch a bus easily from here later on. Her heart lifted as she went to the door and it was opened by Sally herself.

'Angela,' she cried. 'I was just getting ready to come to the rehearsal . . .'

'That's great,' Angela said. 'I popped round to see if you would help . . .'

'Come in and join us for tea. It's only Spam and bubble and squeak but you're welcome to stay and have some.'

'I was going to have Welsh rarebit, because it makes the cheese go further. Muriel was complaining when I saw her earlier today, because the Government cut the cheese ration again last month and there's never enough,' Angela said and followed her in. 'I should love to stay if your mother will have me, though I ought to change . . .'

'Of course she will,' Sally said. 'Mum likes you now she knows you. Besides, she knows you're my friend, and you can borrow one of my jumpers for the evening if that will do. My pink twinset if you wish . . .'

'I'd be glad to borrow a jumper,' Angela said. 'What about that grey one with the pink stripes?'

She laughed, because it felt good to be sharing Sally's things, just as Sally had shared hers. It put them on a new footing, real friends willing to help each other, and Angela hoped it was a friendship that would last for

458

life. She slipped her arm through Sally's as she went into the warm kitchen that smelled of delicious frying and home baking.

Sally seemed to have weathered the worst days, and in the weeks since Andrew's death it seemed she'd managed to come to terms with her grief. It was a new start for her and they must all do what they could to help her.

'Are you feelin' a little better?' Father Joe asked Sister Beatrice. 'I promised Angela I'd be at the hall to help her this evening and I'd best get off, but not before I know you're all right.'

'Of course I am,' Beatrice said stoutly. 'Mark Adderbury told us Terry was making progress – but I do feel responsible for his breakdown.'

'None of it was your fault or Adderbury's. I'm thinking it was already too late before he came to St Saviour's. The damage was done long since and in the poor lad's mind was such terror that nothing could have saved him.'

'Perhaps,' Beatrice agreed. 'Well, you get off, Father Joe. I've got some sick children to visit – and then I shall make a tour of the dorms.'

'I shall call in again soon.' He finished his drink.

Beatrice sighed as the door closed behind him. Even after some weeks, she still felt the weight of Terry's confinement heavy on her conscience and knew that it would live with her for a long time, even though it wasn't her fault.

Shaking her head, she left her office and walked heavily along the corridor. Nancy had a future here, and that was good. Beatrice would do all she could to help her settle. As soon as she was fifteen, she would move her into a room of the Nurses' Home and give her a job.

Sometimes the staff were excellent and stayed for a long time, at others they came and went. Alice had married and that was a good thing; it meant she had not needed to dismiss the girl when she began to show signs of her pregnancy. It was ridiculous that a ring on the third finger of her left hand should make her respectable, but that was the way things worked for young women. Perhaps one day it would change but Beatrice doubted it would be just yet. She was so pleased that she hadn't sacked Alice when Nan first told her, glad she'd given her another chance, and she prayed that Alice's marriage would be a good one.

Sally was ready to work once more and Beatrice was glad that the young carer had decided to go ahead with her nursing training. She hoped she would return to them at the end and looked forward to seeing her become a nurse.

As for Mark Adderbury, well, she could only pray that he would find happiness in his personal life. He deserved someone warm and loving . . . and then there was Angela. She was always so efficient, but when she didn't know she was being observed sorrow was there in her eyes.

Beatrice had known enough personal suffering. She'd put it all behind her when she entered the convent and took her vows, but there were times when she remembered. She didn't always see eye to eye with Angela, but they rubbed along most of the time. Beatrice had come to terms with the woman's appointment at St Saviour's; it freed her to look after the children and the staff and she approved of much of what Angela had suggested.

Entering the isolation ward, she found the lights dimmed and Nurse Paula sitting on the edge of one of the beds, helping a child to drink his milky cocoa. Micky had come out in a rash but Beatrice thought it was just a non-infectious skin complaint. However, she wouldn't release him to the dorms until she was sure.

Nurse Paula looked up and smiled, taking the empty cup from the child and watching as he settled down.

'He was feeling a bit thirsty so I made him some cocoa.'

'Is he running a temperature?'

'No, he seems fine to me. Most of my patients are doing well and nearly ready to go back to the dorms . . .'

'Don't tempt the fates,' Beatrice warned. 'We'll have a rash of measles or something – and we can do without complications until Staff Nurse Wendy arrives.'

'I'm happy to do extra shifts until then,' Paula said. 'Michelle said she would too – and Anna says she is willing to put in a few extra hours if it will help.'

'Thank you, all of you,' Beatrice said, and smiled. 'I shall be here all evening so just call me if you need me.'

Deciding that she was worrying too much, she continued her round. All was peaceful and quiet, apart from a few snuffles and coughs, the children safe in their beds. Her carers were keeping an eye on things. Beatrice may as well go back to her office and start checking that schedule, but she would put the kettle on first and make a cup of tea.

It had been a hard few weeks one way and another,

but she had good people around her. Life must go on and she could only hope that they would have peace at St Saviour's for the foreseeable future. It was the children that mattered, and as long as she could go on providing a good home for those unfortunate children who needed her, she was content. She had known pain and despair in her own life and because of it she'd sought refuge in the convent. God had had a purpose for her even then, directing her where she could do His work.

Oh yes, she was certain that it had been God's purpose for her. The thought filled her with exhilaration and all the shadows seemed to lift as she looked forward to the years ahead that she would spend here caring for those in need.

Read on for a sneak peek of the compelling new story featuring the staff and children of St Saviour's Children's Home.

The Christmas Orphans **will publish in autumn 2016.**

'Wait until I catch you, you little bitch.' The man's voice struck terror into the hearts of the two small girls hiding under the stairs. 'I'll tan your hide, Sarah, you see if I don't.'

Samantha squeezed her twin sister's hand reassuringly but didn't say a word, because Pa had sharp ears and even the slightest sound might give their whereabouts away. She hardly dared breathe as she heard the sound of doors being opened and slammed shut as their father searched for them. Tears were trickling silently down Sarah's face when Samantha touched her cheek, knowing that her beloved twin sister was weeping, though not a sound came from her lips. Both of them knew that if Pa found them they would both be beaten, but Sarah would bear the brunt of it because Pa hated her. He blamed her for causing their mother's death, as she'd been born last and it had taken so long that Ma had been exhausted and died soon after.

Neither of the girls had known their mother, but Pa said she was a saint and, when drunk, accused Sarah of murdering her. Samantha had come quickly and the parents had been gazing fondly on their daughter when Ellie May was gripped with terrible pain once more and this time it had gone on for hours, ending with Sarah's birth and Ellie lying in an exhausted fever from which she never recovered.

When the girls were little, a woman had come in every day to take care of them and to cook Pa's meals. She was a pretty woman, sharp when addressing the twins, especially Sarah, and quick with her hand, but whenever their father was around she was all sweetness and light, and he was taken in by her every word. When she said Sarah was awkward, stubborn and rebellious, Pa agreed that she must be kept in check, but he left the chastising to Jeanie.

Although he had drinking bouts every so often, he'd been content enough whilst Jeanie looked after the house and everyone had expected they would marry one day, but just over a year previously, a few days before the twins' tenth birthday, there had been a quarrel and Jeanie had left them, vowing never to return and swearing that Ernie May was an impossible man. She said he'd taken advantage of her good nature and she wouldn't put up with it a minute longer – declaring that only she would have had the patience to take care of brats like his, and that she would have no more of it. After that, Pa's temper had grown worse and he'd taken against his daughters, particularly Sarah, who had caused all his troubles and killed her sainted mother. He wished she'd died at birth and wanted only to be free of his responsibility towards the twins.

Samantha knew all this, because Aunt Jane had told

her when she'd visited a week before. Their aunt was a tall thin woman with a sharp face and a hard mouth. Samantha had asked her why Pa hated them so, but Sarah double so, and her aunt told her everything in a voice that felt to Samantha like the lash of a whip. Sarah had merely stared at Aunt Jane, taking very little in as always. It wasn't that she didn't understand anything, as Pa and Aunt Jane thought, but she was slow at putting things together in her mind and she couldn't form the words properly unless Samantha told her how.

'You should have been an only child,' Aunt Jane had told Samantha plainly. 'The other one caused all the trouble by killing your mother. My brother adored his wife and they wanted a child, even though she was always a little fragile. The doctors told her she ought not to have children, because of her weak heart, but she wouldn't listen – and Ernie could refuse her nothing. All would have been well had that idiot not taken so long to come and killed poor Ellie.'

'But that wasn't Sarah's fault,' Samantha said feeling protective of her sister. 'I'm sure Ma wouldn't have blamed her, if she'd lived.' In Samantha's mind her mother was a beautiful angel, and sometimes when Sarah was silently weeping and Samantha was hurting with her twin's pain, she'd felt the presence of someone warm and loving and believed it was her ma. Sometimes, she felt that their mother was close by, caressing them, and she thought Sarah sensed it too.

'Ellie was as soft as butter over kids and I dare say she'd have loved her,' Aunt Jane said, a bitter twist to her mouth, 'but she's gone and Ernie has never been

465

the same since. He drinks because he can't bear it that she's gone and he hates Sarah.'

'It isn't fair,' Samantha said. 'Sarah doesn't mean to break things but she's clumsy and it just happens . . .'

'Well, I've told you why your pa drinks and I've made my offer,' Aunt Jane said, her manner blunt. 'Your pa doesn't want either of you and he's made up his mind to go away to work at sea – and that means you'll be on your own. I'll take you in, Samantha, and gladly – but I won't have her. She should be in a proper home where they take care of girls like that . . . I could ask at St Saviour's. I hear Sister Beatrice is a good woman, even though she's a nun and I can't abide them as a rule . . .'

Samantha had looked at her beautiful sister and wondered how her aunt could speak so coldly of a child who was so innocent and lovely. Her soft fair hair framed perfect features and her wide blue eyes were soft, a little vacant and dreamy, but her smile was like sunshine, the light coming from her sometimes so bright that it made her twin blink with its radiance. Samantha knew that, although twins, they weren't alike; her hair was a darker blonde, her eyes more grey than blue, and they could clash with storm clouds when she was angry – or that's what Jeanie had told her when Samantha flew into a temper to protect her sister.

Why did her aunt want to put Sarah in a children's home? It wrenched at Samantha's heart to think of being separated from the twin she loved and she vowed that she would do anything to keep them together, but she wouldn't tell her aunt that, because she'd just get angry and tell her she was a fool.

'There's nothing wrong with Sarah, she just needs a little patience and kindness, that's all,' Samantha said, facing up to her aunt. 'I'm nearly eleven now. I've been helping Sarah to wash and dress, and making supper and breakfast for us all since Jeanie left – and I can look after us both. I shan't go anywhere that Sarah isn't welcome.'

'Suit yourself then,' her aunt said, pulling on neat grey gloves. She was dressed all in grey without a touch of colour, and Samantha knew her house was dull and dark, just like her. If she'd gone there without Sarah there would be no sunshine left in her world. She loved Sarah with all her heart and she was never going to abandon her, no matter what anyone said. 'The offer is there, but I shan't run after you – and I won't take her. The best place for her is an asylum . . .'

Samantha hadn't answered her, because she was upset and angry. Why could no one see that her twin was the dearest, sweetest girl ever? Willing and obedient, she did everything Samantha told her and she never screamed defiance or did anything naughty – and it certainly wasn't her fault that she'd broken Pa's favourite pipe.

Despite his unkindness and careless brutality, Sarah adored her father and she often picked up his slippers or a discarded jacket, nursing the object in her arms and crooning a little song that no one else understood. Samantha had tried to listen to the words but although tuneful and pretty, the words were indistinct and came from somewhere inside her twin's hazy mind.

That evening, just before Pa was due to return for his tea, which Samantha had prepared for him, Sarah had assisted by laying out the table in the big kitchen, as she'd been shown. When Samantha came through from the back scullery with a pot of hot potatoes she'd been boiling, she'd seen her twin had taken down Pa's pipe rack from the shelf of the larger kitchen and was stroking one of the pipes. Samantha had immediately been anxious, because she knew the delicate long-handled clay pipe was one of Pa's favourites.

'Put that down, Sarah, and help me with the dishes,' she said and Sarah jerked out of the dream she'd been in, her fingers snapping the long thin stem of the pipe. 'Oh, Sarah,' she cried, distressed, because she knew what it would mean. 'What have you done?'

Sarah had dissolved into tears and before either of them realised it, Pa had come in and was staring at the broken pipe.

'You little devil!' he said and lunged at Sarah, swiping her across the face with his fist and sending her back-wards. He was a big man with a thick neck and strong, his blow knocking the fragile girl off her feet. Sarah had fallen against the oak dresser and the shock of her body hitting it made a china teapot tumble from its shelves and break into pieces. 'Now what have you done? Imp of Satan, that's what you are!' Pa roared at her. 'That belonged to your sainted mother. I'll kill you. I've had enough of your wickedness . . .'

Sarah stared at him in horror and then ran from the room before he could grab her and punish her.

'Pa, she didn't mean to do it!' Samantha said and threw herself between them. She was still holding the pot of hot potatoes and when Pa caught hold of her, he burned his hand on the pot. 'It was an accident . . . Oh, Pa, I'm sorry . . . I didn't mean to burn you.'

Pa thrust her away but instead of going after Sarah, he picked up his jacket and went out of the kitchen, pausing at the door to glance back at Samantha. 'If I find you still here when I get back, I'll kill the pair of you,' he threatened and went off in a fury, slamming the door behind him.

Samantha placed the cooking pot on the floor near the range to keep warm and then went in search of her sister. She'd found her under the bed in their room and it had taken several minutes to coax her out.

'Sarah didn't mean to . . .' she sobbed in Samantha's arms. 'Pa's cross with Sarah?'

'Yes, he is,' Samantha said and hugged her. 'But he'll go down the pub and have a few drinks and forget about it. Come down and have some supper. We'll put Pa's in the range to keep warm for him.'

It had taken Samantha ages to coax her sister downstairs and even then she ate only a few mouthfuls of the food. Sarah had left her sitting on the hard chair in the kitchen while she washed the pots in the scullery. After the kitchen was tidy she took her sister upstairs and put her to bed. Pa had threatened things before when he was angry but then he would get over it and perhaps bring them a packet of chips home for their tea the next day – but this time he hadn't got over his temper.

Samantha had woken to the sound of her twin's screams, something she'd heard so seldom that she knew Sarah was terrified. As her eyes accustomed themselves to the light, which came from a lamp in the hall, she saw Sarah lying on the floor and Pa standing over her kicking her as if she were a piece of filth he'd found in the gutter, his savagery beyond anything Samantha had ever seen.

Without truly thinking what she was doing, Samantha seized the chamber pot she had used earlier and flung the contents over her father. Some of the urine went into his face and must have stung his eyes for he was temporarily blinded and screamed out in a mixture of pain and frustration.

'You little hellcat, you've blinded me . . .' he cried and stumbled towards her.

Samantha pulled her twin to her feet and, taking her hand, propelled her along the landing and down the stairs, seeking refuge in the large cupboard under the stairs. She pushed Sarah right to the end and crawled after her, shoving some empty cardboard boxes in front of them in an effort to conceal their whereabouts if Pa looked inside.

'I know you're in here,' Pa's voice was suddenly very close and the stair cupboard door was jerked opened, the light from his torch waving about. It touched on Sarah's face but she must have been hidden from him, because he swore and slammed the door shut again. 'I'm not coming back – do you hear?' His tone was loud, penetrating the door and reaching Samantha. She trembled as he went on, 'You can starve before I come back, do you understand me? You're to go to your aunt, Samantha – and that Imp of Satan can go to the devil for all I care . . .'

Samantha held her breath as the minutes ticked by. The noise had died down now and the house was quiet. Pa must have gone to sleep by now surely. Yet she dared not risk coming out until he'd left for work. Putting her arms around Sarah, she held her close as they both shivered in their nightclothes, but now the house was silent and Samantha decided to venture into the hall and find a coat to keep them warm.

It was very dark and she had to feel her way along the walls, frightened of making a noise and bringing Pa down on them again, but the house seemed unnaturally silent. She took their coats from the old wooden hall-stand and carried them into the cupboard. At least they were safe here and perhaps when Pa came back tomorrow, he would be sorry for his show of temper. He was always worse when he'd been drinking and Samantha couldn't believe he'd really meant to kill either of them.

In the morning the girls were stiff, cold and hungry when they crept out. The black marble clock on the kitchen mantle said it was past six o'clock. Pa went to work at six every morning so unless he'd slept over he must have gone, though Samantha had been awake for ages and she'd heard nothing. The range hadn't been made up and it was cold in the kitchen, but the one in the scullery was still warm. Samantha stoked it up and added the coal and wood her father had bought in the previous day.

She was hungry and looked in the pantry, but discovered that the half loaf of bread left from their meal the previous day was missing, as were the cold sausages and the cheese that had been on the pantry shelves. Pa must have taken them for his dinner at work. All Samantha could find was some stale fruitcake she'd made earlier that week; there was just enough to cut each of them a slice and, she discovered, there was sufficient tea left to make a brew, though only a drop of milk and no sugar.

It would be weak tea and warm them through a little, she thought, as she carried what there was through to the kitchen. Sarah was staring at the kitchen shelf, a look of dismay on her face.

'Pa's pipes gone,' she said. Her gaze travelled around the kitchen, the look of fear and puzzlement growing. 'Tankard and coat gone . . . Pa gone . . .'

'No,' Samantha cried as the fear struck her too. 'He couldn't have gone . . . He's coming back, he must be . . .'

Looking around the room, she saw that the few treasures that had stood on the dresser shelves, like their mother's tea caddy and a pair of silver berry spoons, had gone. All that was left was an assortment of china that didn't match and a brass tin, where pins and bits were stored.

She put down the tray she'd been carrying and ran from the kitchen and up the stairs, flinging open the door of her father's room. He wouldn't have deserted them just like that . . . surely he wouldn't? Pa wasn't really a bad man; it was just that he missed their mother and got drunk sometimes.

As soon as she looked round the room, Samantha knew that it was true. Her father had few possessions he treasured and only a couple of extra shirts and his best suit, which he wore only for a funeral or a wedding. The cupboard was left open, as if he'd torn everything from its place in a hurry, and his brushes and shaving things had also gone from the washstand.

The truth hit Samantha like a drenching of cold water.

Their father had been planning to abandon them all the time, just as Aunt Jane had said. He might have told Samantha had Sarah not broken his favourite pipe, but instead he'd gone down the pub to get roaring drunk and then he'd tried to kill Sarah.

Yes, he really had meant to do it, perhaps because he knew Aunt Jane wouldn't take her. Perhaps he'd thought it better for everyone if Sarah were dead?

Samantha couldn't believe what her thoughts were telling her. No, Pa wouldn't do this . . . he wouldn't attack his daughter and then go off leaving them both to starve – but he had. She sat down on the bed, feeling empty, drained. What was she going to do now?

If she took Sarah to Aunt Jane, she would send her twin to a place where Samantha knew she would be unhappy. She would never see her – and that would break both their hearts. What people didn't understand was that they lived for each other and felt each other's pain and sorrow. Samantha's body still ached from the kicking that Pa had given her twin, and that realisation brought her out of her shock. She must look after Sarah. She must be hurting all over, because Samantha was, and Sarah bore the scars of more than one beating.

For now she would go down and see what she could do to help her twin. They must look after each other, because there was no one else they could trust – no one who would take them both in.

Samantha knew there was no money in the house. Her father never gave her a penny. He paid the rent and brought home the supplies they needed – and he'd taken all they had with him. She looked about the room, knowing that the contents wouldn't fetch more than a few pence from the rag and bone man; nothing of value had been left for them. Samantha was frightened of Alf, the man who ran the scrap yard, but she might have to go there and ask him what he would give her for the contents of the house.

There were still a few things in the scullery and kitchen, things that had belonged to their mother. Sarah had broken the best china pot, but there might be some copper pans and a few silver spoons in the drawer.

Yes, she would go to the scrapyard later, after she'd got Sarah washed and dressed. Samantha wasn't sure what she ought to do next, but she knew they wouldn't be able to stay here because the rent was due that Saturday and Pa wasn't here to pay.

She would not go to her aunt's house, she decided, as she went into the kitchen to discover Sarah nursing the clay pipe she'd broken the previous evening, which Pa hadn't bothered to pick up from the floor. Tears were trickling silently down her cheeks and Samantha knew that her twin understood Pa had gone. She didn't realise the implications for them, of course, but Samantha would look after her. She would find somewhere they could stay; there were still bombed-out houses waiting to be pulled down and rebuilt after the war. Samantha knew that tramps and homeless people slept in them and so could she and Sarah, just for a while – just until she decided what to do. First she had to sell everything of value she could and then she would take Sarah away . . .

'Put that in your pocket and come and eat your cake,' she said. 'We'll be all right, Sarah love. I'll take care of you now.'

Sarah's smile was loving and trusting as she looked at her. 'Samantha take care of me,' she repeated, and sat down at the table to eat her cake and drink the tea that was now cold.